GRIFFIN'S SHADOW

GRIFFIN'S SHADOW

LESLIE ANN MOORE

BOOK TWO OF THE
GRIFFIN'S DAUGHTER TRILOGY

 Avari Press

LANCASTER, PENNSYLVANIA

Published by Avari Press
Lancaster, Pennsylvania
www.avaripress.com

First edition: February 2009

Library of Congress Cataloging-in-Publication Data

Moore, Leslie Ann.
   Griffin's shadow / Leslie Ann Moore. — 1st ed.
   p. cm. — (The griffin's daughter trilogy ; bk. 2)
   ISBN-13: 978-1-933770-04-8 (pbk.)
   ISBN-10: 1-933770-04-X (pbk.)
   I. Title.

   PS3613.O5643G77 2009
   813'.6—dc22
                                          2008033926

Printed and bound in the United States of America

0 9 8 7 6 5 4 3 2 1

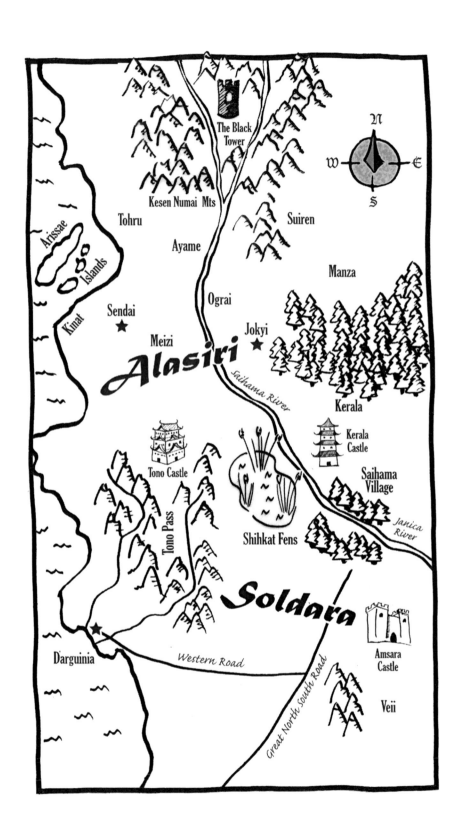

To my family and friends, both old and new.
You make it all worthwhile.

TABLE OF CONTENTS

Part I

Part II

Part III

Part IV

Prologue

Igh above the broken spires of a ruined fortress, an eagle soared. His wings, black against the cerulean of a cloudless sky, cast a swift-moving shadow on the glittering snowfield below.

A snowshoe hare instinctively flattened itself to the frigid ground as the shadow glided across its path. A little fox, robed in her fur coat of winter-white, trotted along from bush to boulder, stalking the hare, keenly aware of her rival floating overhead. She paused in the shadow of an outcrop, nose twitching, and licked her lips.

The eagle had spotted the fox but had already dismissed her as inconsequential. Long before she got within striking distance of the hare, he would swoop down, snatch the prey with his razor-sharp talons and take to the skies again, leaving the fox with nothing but frustration and an empty belly.

As he prepared to strike, the eagle felt a cold tendril of energy tickle the edge of his mind. Before he could process the meaning of this strange sensation, the tendril lashed out and seized his consciousness.

With brutal efficiency, the tendril ripped away the eagle's awareness, and as the magnificent bird plummeted, lifeless, to the ground, an ancient entity flooded the vacated skull with its own rapacious mind.

Freshly re-animated by the will of the Nameless One, the eagle broke its fall, pulling out of its death dive to rise steeply into the air once again.

The fox, sensing her rival had backed off, closed in on the prey, pounced, and with a snap of her jaws, broke the hare's neck. She lifted her head and yipped in triumph, then scooped up her prize and trotted off toward the safety and warmth of her den. She and her children would sleep with full bellies tonight.

With a flap of his wings, the eagle banked sharply and sped southwest. Three days later, his withered carcass dropped from the sky and a raven rose to take his place. Two days and nights of flying brought the raven to the walls of a great castle standing guard over a thriving city. It, too, died before reaching the goal, but many more ravens called the castle grounds home.

Another bird leapt into the air and circled the castle precincts, searching the ground with sharp eyes until it spotted the thing its master needed. The raven landed at the edge of a great expanse of gravel and scooped a small shiny black stone into its beak.

This should do, thought the Nameless One. He sent his small slave winging back to the rooftops to wait for the one it had been sent to find.

It did not have long to wait.

Part I

1

Daughter of the Griffin

y father is Keizo Onjara, King of Alasiri!
Jelena Sakehera stared at Lord Sen, her new father-in-law,
uncertain that she had heard him correctly.
Surely Father-in-law is mistaken! I can't possibly be the daughter of a king!
A tide of conflicting emotions surged through her—elation that she at
last knew her sire's name, dismay that her existence could prove trouble-
some for him, fear that he would reject her outright, and hope, yes even
hope, that he just might accept her, despite everything.

The Sakehera family had gathered together in their private sitting
room, to share the evening meal and discuss the day's events. Tomorrow,
the entire family would quit Kerala Castle, ancestral seat of the House
of Sakehera, to journey west to Sendai, capital of Alasiri. War with the
Soldaran Empire threatened the elven homeland, and the king needed
his great lords and generals in the capital so planning for the defense of
the country could begin. As Commanding General, Lord Sen's place on
the King's Council was second in importance only to the king's brother,
Prince Raidan.

The final days of the month of Kishan heralded the end of summer;
even as fall approached, the daytime heat remained oppressive. Only after the sun had set did the air cool down to something close to tolerable.
With the darkness came gentle breezes—full of the fragrances of honeysuckle and night-blooming jasmine—that ruffled wall hangings and caressed
sweat-damp skin.

Jelena and Lord Sen sat apart from the others, on padded stools near
one of the open windows. Briefly, she looked away from her father-in-
law to glance around the room at the rest of the family. Lady Amara, her
mother-in-law, lounged on her favorite couch, reading aloud from a book of
children's stories to her twin daughters Mariso and Jena. Lord Sen's Heir,
Sadaiyo, and his wife Misune, huddled together on a bench at the far end

of the room, completely absorbed with one another. Ashinji—Jelena's heart always skipped a beat whenever she looked at her husband—sat cross-legged on the floor mats, talking to his sister Lani.

Jelena sucked in a breath, struck once again by amazement at her turn of fortune. That she had been taken in by this family and accepted as a daughter, still felt too good to be true, and yet...

Here I am, a former kitchen drudge...whose father just might be the king of the elves!

"I don't know how my old friend's path crossed that of a human girl's, or how it all led to the making of you. The evidence is all circumstantial, and I could still be wrong," Lord Sen continued. Jelena refocused her attention back to her father-in-law. "But I don't think so. I know that ring. Only members of the Onjara family wear the White Griffin. *Onjara* means 'griffin' in ancient Siri-dar. Yours is actually a copy of the official Ring of State the king wears. All children of the sovereign are given non-magical copies to wear as signets. Keizo wore the ring you now possess before he ascended the throne. The fact that he gave it to your mother must mean that he had very strong feelings for her."

"The woman who raised me—Claudia—always said my mother and father loved each other, and that my father gave my mother his ring so, one day, I might use it to find him. I always took that story with a grain of salt," Jelena said.

"Grain of salt?" Sen repeated quizzically.

"An old Soldaran expression. It means to doubt a little. I'd always hoped to find him some day, but I kept telling myself to be prepared for him to reject me. I still cannot believe what you're telling me is true, though! Why would the king travel alone in the borderlands?"

"Keizo wasn't king yet back then. His eldest brother Okame ruled, so he had no expectations of ever sitting on the throne. Okame had a family, you see—three sons and two daughters.

"Keizo was restless as a younger man and often traveled far from home. He even journeyed to the human lands east of our borders...not to the Empire, of course, but there are still human countries not yet under the yolk of the Soldarans and who don't hate us. Ai, the stories he used to tell... I remember a time, 'bout eighteen years ago, when my old friend Zin—all his close friends called him that back before he became our king—showed up at my gate dirty, thin, and hobbling on a poorly set broken leg.

"He wouldn't tell me exactly what had happened to him, only that he'd had an accident, but that he'd received help from someone. This person kept him alive until he was strong enough to make it back home."

"My mother," Jelena whispered.

"Seems so. Keizo was tight as an oyster, though. Never said any more about it. He stayed near two weeks, then returned to Sendai. Shortly thereafter, word reached us that King Okame and his entire family had drowned in a sudden unseasonable storm off the coast of the Arrisae Islands. They'd been spending time at the royal retreat on the main island. The ship bringing them back to the mainland struck a reef during the gale and foundered. Everyone on board perished. When next I saw my childhood friend, he was my king and I was accepting the post as Commanding General of the Armies of Alasiri."

Sen fell silent, as if he knew Jelena needed a few moments to digest the astounding revelation he had just laid upon her.

My father is the elf king! How am I ever going to take this all in?

Jelena had lived with the shame of her mixed blood all her life, and even when she thought she had escaped racial bigotry, she had encountered it again, albeit in a less virulent form, among her father's people. Now, she had just learned the blood of elven royalty flowed in her veins.

Will this make any real difference? I am still hikui...a half-breed, she thought.

The twins squealed in delight as their mother finished reading.

"Please, Mother...," Jena begged, and Mariso breathlessly completed the sentence, "Read us one more!"

"No, girls," Amara replied as she closed the book. "It is time for you two to go to bed. We must get up very early. "

"Ooooooh!" the children cried.

"Girls! Do as your mother says," Sen commanded, his voice stern, but affectionate. "You don't want to get left behind tomorrow morning because no one can wake you, do you?" Mournfully, the two little blond heads shook in unison. "Very good. Now, come and kiss your old father good night."

After Amara had taken the twins off to bed, Jelena resumed her conversation with Sen.

"What will all of this mean, Father?" Jelena asked. "If I'm truly the king's daughter, does that mean I'm a...a *princess?* Even though I'm hikui? You said my existence will complicate my father's life. How so?"

"Keizo has a younger brother, Prince Raidan, who is officially his Heir, at least until he marries and produces a child...an okui child," Sen replied. "So far, the king has shown no inclination to marry, and his longtime companion has not born him any children as yet. The prince...well, let's just say he won't exactly welcome with open arms anyone who could become a potential rival to his claim."

Jelena frowned. "So you think Prince Raidan—my uncle—would view me as a threat?"

"Yes," Sen replied.

Jelena shook her head. "I've gone from bastard half-breed scullery maid to king's daughter in the blink of an eye.... This is all so unreal."

"What are you two talking about over here? You both look so serious." Ashinji had come up behind her and he now slipped his arms around her waist. "You've been huddled with my wife for too long, Father. I miss her and want her back." He planted a kiss on the side of her neck, then rested his chin on her shoulder.

Jelena's breath caught in her throat, the way it always did when Ashinji kissed her there. "Your father had some important news for me, Ashi, about my own father," Jelena explained. "I'll tell you everything later, when we're alone."

Ashinji looked first at his father and then at Jelena. "I gather from the looks on your faces that the situation isn't entirely good," he commented.

Sen said nothing and Jelena turned her head to kiss Ashinji's cheek. "Later, I promise," she repeated.

"Well, then! I think we'd all best get to bed," Sen said, loud enough to catch Lani, Sadaiyo, and Misune's attentions. "We've got an early start tomorrow morning."

"I'll meet you in the stables at dawn, Father," Sadaiyo said as he and Misune exited the sitting room, arm in arm.

"G'night, Father," Lani murmured sleepily, planting a quick kiss on Sen's cheek as she followed her oldest brother out. "'Night, Ashi, Jelena."

"I'm still surprised that Mother and the girls are coming to Sendai with us," Ashinji said after Lani had left.

Sen shrugged. "It's been years since your mother saw the capital. I think she's grown a bit restless out here in the country and wants to get a taste of the city for a change. I also know she's looking to show Lani off...

Not much in the way of useful young men this far east, you know. What better place to snag a rich young heir than at court, eh?"

Jelena remembered Ashinji mentioning his sister had taken a fancy to Misune's older brother Ibeji.

Perhaps Father-in-law believes one match between the Sakehera and the Dai families is enough, she thought.

"Come, husband. Let's get to bed," she said.

Ashinji nodded in agreement and as the two of them headed for the door, Sen called out, "First light, children! Don't oversleep!"

* * *

Later, as they lay snuggled together beneath the coverlets, Jelena told Ashinji everything his father had told her about her sire.

"If this is true and you really are the king's daughter...it could change everything, Jelena," Ashinji responded, his voice soft and pensive. Jelena could hear the worry behind his quiet words. She grabbed his chin and pulled until he looked into her eyes.

"It changes nothing, Ashi. None of us knows how the king will greet the news that he has a hikui daughter. He may reject me outright. Or he may acknowledge my existence but refuse to have any direct contact with me."

"Or he might accept you with open arms and proclaim you his Heir."

"You know as well as I do that I can't be his Heir. It's the law. Even if, by some miracle of the gods, he does accept me, I will still be your wife and a Sakehera first. My future is with you, no matter what."

"I still can't help but worry about where this all could lead," Ashinji murmured.

He slid downwards and rested his head between her breasts. Tenderly, Jelena ran her fingers through his hair. "You'll never lose me, Ashi, I promise," she whispered. He said nothing and instead replied with his body.

As they made love, his caresses were gentle as usual, but at the same time, a little desperate. Afterwards, he held her tight against him, as if he feared to let go; even as they both drifted off to sleep, his arms never loosened.

2

Departure Day

Jelena...wake up, love. We must get ready to go."

Jelena groaned and pulled the covers over her head. She'd had some difficulty falling asleep last night, so it seemed as if she had just drifted off. Now, Ashinji was pestering her to get up.

Ohhhh, I don't want to leave this bed. I'm too comfortable!

A little candle flame of memory sparked in her head. She sat up abruptly, and her forehead met Ashinji's nose with a painful smack.

"Owww!" they both yelled.

"Ashi, are you all right?" Jelena cried, rubbing her head with one hand and reaching out to her husband with the other.

"Mmmmph," he mumbled behind hands cupped over his nose and mouth. Jelena grabbed his wrists and pulled his hands away, then gasped with dismay.

"Goddess' *tits*, your head is hard, woman!" Ashinji growled. "That is the last time I try to wake you with my nose pressed to your face!" In the feeble glow of the night lamp beside the bed, Jelena saw the slow trickle of scarlet that ran down from one nostril and dripped off Ashinji's chin into his open palm. "Ai, this is going to really hurt later on," he sighed.

Jelena bit down on her lower lip, unsure if she wanted to laugh or cry. Ashinji must have noticed her stricken look, for he immediately sought to reassure her. "I don't think it's broken, just bloodied. I've had plenty of these before, every soldier has. Don't worry." He crawled out of bed and padded over to his floor chest where he proceeded to rummage through its contents. He pulled out a piece of cloth and pressed it to his nose.

Jelena got up and sidled over to wrap her arms around Ashinji from behind. She laid her cheek against his head; even after a day and a night, the aroma of sweet almond still clung to his hair.

"Careful, my love," Ashinji warned, his voice muffled by the cloth pressed to his nose. "If you keep touching me like that, we'll never get out of this room and my father will be forced to leave us behind." He twisted in her embrace to face her.

"I think we have a little time yet before we must go," Jelena whispered, her eyes smoldering with desire. The bloodied cloth slipped from Ashinji's fingers.

A soft knock at the door interrupted their kiss. "Oh, damn, damn..." Ashinji muttered. "That must be Akan." Jelena scrambled for the bed and dove beneath the coverlets while Ashinji threw on a robe and went to open the door.

"Good morning, my lord. I've brought you something to eat." Akan was a small, older man, lame in the left leg from a childhood accident. He had served as Ashinji's valet ever since Ashinji had been old enough to have private quarters. Whenever his young lord returned home on leave, Akan resumed his old duties.

The valet entered, carrying a large tray in his hands. He limped over to the low dining table and set his burden down.

"Thank you, Akan." Ashinji said, sniffing and wiping his nose on a sleeve.

The valet bowed. "I hope my lady likes blackberries," he said, glancing discreetly in Jelena's direction. "They were picked fresh just yesterday. My lord Sen instructed that the best should be sent up this morning especially for your enjoyment."

Jelena sat up, careful to keep herself covered. "I love blackberries! Tell my father-in-law I said 'thank you'." Akan smiled and bowed to Jelena then turned once more to Ashinji. "The bath is ready whenever you and my lady wish to use it. My lord Sen says not to dawdle." He smiled again in gentle amusement. "I'll send up Jawara to assist with your armor when you are finished. Uh, my lord Ashinji, do you need help with your nose?"

Ashinji grimaced and shook his head. "No, thanks. I think I have things under control." Akan nodded, bowed a final time, and departed.

Jelena bounded out of bed and threw on a robe, then sat down at the table and began attacking the blackberries with relish while Ashinji sipped a mug of tea. Besides the berries, Akan had brought smoked fish, fresh bread, soft cheese flavored with herbs, and the favorite breakfast food of all elves—or so it seemed to Jelena—sour yogurt.

"We'll be on the road at least seven days, possibly longer. The wagons and my mother's carriage will slow us considerably." Ashinji commented.

He grabbed the yogurt and took a mouthful directly from the pot. Jelena wrinkled her nose in distaste. Try as she might, she could not cultivate a taste for the thick, tangy, fermented milk.

"I'm still not exactly sure why my mother chose to come along," Ashinji continued. "She's never expressed any interest in attending court before."

"Your father says it's to find Lani a husband. Many more boys to choose from!" Jelena giggled.

Ashinji shrugged. "I guess that's a good reason. It's true my parents will have a much bigger selection in Sendai than they would all the way out here. I don't know how cooperative Lani will be, though. My sister has a mind of her own and a strong will to match. She's set her sights on Ibeji Dai and I'm not sure she can be dissuaded."

"Perhaps your parents will allow Lani to choose for herself who she wishes to marry, like they did you."

"Sadly, no. Lani is too important. She's the oldest girl and tradition dictates the match made for her must be as good as the one made for the Heir." Ashinji sighed. "Lani and I are a lot alike. I know how much she resents being treated as a commodity, but that's how things are. The twins, now, they are the truly fortunate ones. No one will much care who they marry, or even *if* they marry. Youngest children are the only ones allowed that kind of freedom."

Jelena hadn't had much opportunity to interact with Ashinji's favorite sibling, but she resolved to get to know Lani better while they traveled to the capital. "We'd better go down to the bath house," she said. "You heard what Akan said. No dawdling!"

The newlyweds found it hard not to linger in the bath house; the sheer sensual bliss of the hot water made it nigh impossible to hurry. They almost always ended up making love whenever they shared a bath, and it took a mighty effort not to give in to the urge to do so now.

Back in their chamber, Jelena busied herself with last minute packing while Ashinji checked his armor a final time. He had no plans to wear it on the journey, but he still needed to make sure it was in perfect condition before Jawara, the steward in charge of all the family armor and weaponry, came to fetch and stow it with the baggage.

Jelena sighed as she examined the piles of clothing laid out on the bed. Amara had given her several new sets of garments as a wedding present;

now that she could finally trade her plain cotton and wool for the fine silks and linens of a noble lady, Jelena wondered at her reluctance to wear any of the new outfits.

"Ashi, will your mother be upset if I do not wish to wear any of the new clothes she gave me?" she asked.

"What, do you not like them?" he responded, pausing in his task to look at her.

"I do. I love them, but..." She shook her head, exasperated at her own ambivalence. "I am the wife of a nobleman now! I am supposed to dress like one, not like a...a servant!" she huffed, holding up one of her well-worn cotton tunics. "Truth is, I feel more comfortable in simple things," she admitted.

"Wear whatever you like, love," Ashinji replied. "You'll look beautiful, regardless."

Jelena smiled gratefully at her husband.

"I will be in the saddle all day, and my new clothes are far too nice to ruin with dust and horse sweat. That's settled, then. The new things go with the baggage."

As she donned her old tunic, scruffy breeches and riding boots, she wondered if she would ever feel truly comfortable in anything else.

Jawara the steward came for the baggage and armor, and with a message. "My lord, you are needed in the lower yard right away," he said.

"I'll see you later." Ashinji gave her a quick kiss and left Jelena to finish her packing in solitude.

Not much remained for her to do, other than extinguish the lamps. Slinging her saddlebags over one shoulder, she glanced once more around the room, then departed, leaving the door ajar so Akan would know that he could enter at will. Taking the outer stairs two at a time, she descended to ground level and started toward the stables.

Sendai! I'm going to Sendai to meet my father, the king!

She gave in to excitement and laughed aloud.

* * *

"Jelena, really! You must learn to dress more appropriately now that you're a member of this family. It simply won't due for you to go around looking like one of the servants, even if it *is* what you're accustomed to."

Jelena felt a rush of irritation, but suppressed the sharp retort that sprang to her lips in favor of a more measured response. She regarded Sadaiyo's wife with a cool eye. "I'm sorry if my clothes don't measure up to your high standards, Sister, but for now, this is what I wish to wear," she replied in as even a tone of voice as she could manage under the circumstances.

Misune Sakehera cut an imposing figure mounted upon a tall, bay stallion. She was truly the most beautiful woman Jelena had ever seen. Her jet-black, waist-length hair, secured at the nape of her neck with a heavy silver clip, gleamed like satin in the morning sun. The horse, as beautiful and imperious as its mistress, flattened his ears and glared at Jelena out of one liquid brown eye. Jelena, still afoot and leading her trusty mare Willow, prudently kept her distance.

Misune's regal nostrils flared. "Don't use that tone with me, girl," she replied. "You should be grateful for instruction from your betters. Just because you've somehow managed to gain a place in this family doesn't mean you're anywhere near the equal of the least one of us." With a dismissive wave of her gloved hand, Misune turned the stallion's head and rode off, leaving Jelena shaking with anger.

Is it always going to be this way? she raged. *Will I have to take this abuse for the rest of my life, no matter where I go?* Jelena wrestled with the near overwhelming urge to run after Misune, to scream into that haughty face that she was the daughter of the King of Alasiri and that no one, not even the future Lady of Kerala could speak to her so rudely ever again.

She took a deep breath to steady herself.

I don't even know for sure that Keizo Onjara will even acknowledge me as his daughter. Besides, Misune would just laugh in my face and accuse me of lying. No, I can't be the one to announce my father's identity. It has to come from him.

"Ah, there's my beautiful wife!" Ashinji strode up, looking a little harried. He patted Willow's glossy neck, then asked, "What's wrong? You look upset."

"Nothing's wrong, Ashi. I'm just..." Jelena forced herself to smile. "I'm just anxious to be off," she lied.

"Hmm," Ashinji replied, cocking his head and skewering her with his brilliant, green gaze. "I know when you're not being honest with me, love. Tell me what's bothering you." Jelena sighed and told him about Misune's rude words. "I'll have to have a talk with my brother's wife," Ashinji responded through tight lips.

"No, Ashi, please don't! You'll only embarrass me more. If you inter-fere, it will only confirm her belief that I'm weak and helpless. I can handle Misune in my own way."

Ashinji gathered her into his arms. "Whatever you wish, love. I'll leave it to you. Ummm, c'mere," he murmured, leaning in for a kiss.

"You two really shouldn't engage in that kind of behavior in public. It's unseemly. I'm sure Father agrees."

"Sadaiyo, please. Not now!" Lord Sen growled.

Ashinji turned cold eyes toward his brother. Sadaiyo stood just behind their father's right shoulder, coolly resplendent in green and black brocade, despite the warmth of the morning. He wore upon his brow a circlet of gold. Heavy gold rings adorned his fingers, which today were sheathed in the finest black kidskin. He looked every inch the Heir, as gaudy as a pea-cock in contrast to Ashinji, who wore the plain, serviceable brown and green leathers of a common soldier.

Sadaiyo's expression blended equal parts mockery and amusement. "I'm only pointing out that they should demonstrate a little more restraint...a bit more decorum. Though perhaps it's too much to expect from a girl with no breeding and a man who would marry such a girl."

"*That's enough!!*" roared Sen. Jelena, shocked by his uncharacteristic outburst, took a step backward and fetched up against Ashinji, who stood as rigid and still as if he had been turned to stone. "You will apologize to your brother and to my daughter-in-law, and you will treat her with the respect she is due as a member of my House. *Is that understood?*" Sen's eyes blazed with fury.

An uncomfortable silence descended on the yard as everyone's atten-tion focused on the drama playing out in their midst.

Sadaiyo's face blanched, and his hands dropped to his sides. His eyes, normally sardonic, had gone blank, like a pair of blue-grey glass spheres. He turned to face Ashinji and bowed stiffly. "My apologies, Brother. Please forgive my rudeness. My behavior was inexcusable. My apologies to your wife as well." He refused to look at Jelena, which chilled her more than any threat that his eyes could make. Instinctively, she groped for Ashinji's hand, and a quick glance at his profile sent a sick wave of fear churning through her gut. At that moment, she had no doubt that Ashinji and Sadaiyo were inexorably headed for a mortal showdown if someone or something didn't intervene.

"I accept your apology, Brother," Ashinji replied. His grip on Jelena's hand tightened almost to the point of pain, then relaxed.

As quickly as Sen's anger had erupted, it subsided and then seemed to dissipate altogether. He slapped each of his sons on the back in turn. "Come, now, boys. Let's not ruin a perfectly good morning. Not very dignified, arguing in front of the staff, y'know. Sadaiyo, go collect that wife of yours. Then, mount up. You too, Youngest Son. The day's a'wasting and we've a fair piece to ride before we reach our evening camp. Jelena, my dear, I shall require your services as messenger today. I want you to ride ahead to announce our arrival to Lord Nadaka. You know the way, of course."

"Yes, Father," Jelena replied crisply. Sadaiyo spun on his heel and stalked off. Sen watched him go, then shook his head and sighed. He glanced at Ashinji, then walked away toward the main entrance of the castle, where Lady Amara and the three Sakehera daughters awaited the carriage that would transport them to Sendai.

Jelena looked into Ashinji's face, so cold and still that it seemed more like a carved mask than the face of a living man. "Ashinji," she whispered, and like a split wineskin, his whole body appeared to deflate as he relaxed into her arms.

They clung to each other in silence, needing no words to communicate their feelings to one another. After awhile, Ashinji pulled away and said, "You'd better mount up and get going. Nadaka's estate is a good four hour's ride from here and they'll want at least a couple of hours to prepare for us."

"Ashi, please promise me you won't argue with your brother. It worries me how much bad feeling there is between you. Promise!"

People and horses swirled around them like the waters of a river split by a boulder, but Jelena was deaf and blind to it all. At this moment, all that existed in her world were Ashinji and herself, and all that mattered to her was his safety.

Ashinji reached out and caressed her cheek, and a soft smile curved the corners of his mouth. He nodded. "I promise...for you, my love...that I will try. Now, you'd better go." He held her stirrup as she mounted Willow, then stood at the mare's head as she checked the security of her gear. When she finished her inspection, she gathered the reins. Ashinji stepped aside, out of the mare's way. Jelena looked down at him and her heart melted in a warm, sweet rush.

"Be careful!" Ashinji called out as Jelena clapped her heels to Willow's flanks and the mare started toward the main gate. "I'll see you tonight!" He waved and turned to walk back toward the stables.

"Jelena! Jelena, wait!" a voice cried out. Jelena pulled Willow to a stop as Kami came trotting up, huffing and puffing. The young guard drew in a huge breath and let her words spill out in a rush. "I'm so glad I caught you before you left! I didn't want you to leave before I had a chance to say goodbye."

"Kami, you should not be running like that in your condition!" Jelena chastised.

Kami made a face. "Oh, stop! I'm pregnant, not sick! You're as bad as Gendan. Besides, the doctor says that exercise is good for both me and the baby."

Jelena smiled. "This is not 'goodbye', Kami, only 'see you again soon'. When I return, we will share a bottle of wine and I will tell you all about Sendai."

Kami sniffed and wiped at eyes brimming with tears. "I'll miss you, Jelena," she said.

"I will miss you, too."

The last thing Jelena saw as she left Kerala that morning was Kami, standing in the middle of the lower gate, waving.

3

A Face In The Night

Lord Nadaka proved to be a gracious host, despite his tendency toward pomposity. He grandiosely referred to his home as Nadaka Castle, even though it was, in actuality, a large manor house and not a castle at all.

Jelena had delivered messages to Nadaka Castle before; when she rode through the gate, tired and dusty from the road, a stable boy took Willow while one of the house servants ushered her into the main room.

Lord Nadaka recognized her immediately and seemed quite taken with the fact that his liege lord had chosen to spend the night on his estate. Still unaware of her changed status, he nonetheless kindly offered to let her await the arrival of the rest of the family in the main room, and gratefully, Jelena accepted. A serving girl brought in bread, cheese, ripe red apples, and beer; munching contentedly, Jelena settled down on a bench to wait.

The warm, close air of the room, combined with a full stomach, worked its magic, and soon, Jelena found it impossible to keep her eyes open. Using her saddlebag as a pillow, she stretched out on the bench and fell quickly into sleep.

She awoke to the sound of voices. Sen and Nadaka came bustling through the front door, Ashinji and Sadaiyo close at their heels.

"Ai, there you are!" Ashinji came over and planted a firm kiss upon her lips. Jelena saw Lord Nadaka's eyes widen in surprise.

Apparently, so did Sen. "Nadaka, I see you've shown my new daughter-in-law your fine hospitality already...I thank you."

"My lord...I ...I thought the girl was just your messenger," Nadaka stammered, his round face flushing crimson. "Had I known...."

"Easy, my friend," Sen replied jovially. "I meant no reproach. Jelena and my son Ashinji here, were just married. She is an exceptionally modest girl, so I'm not surprised she didn't tell you." Nadaka looked as if a large stone had just been rolled off his chest.

"Poor Nadaka," Ashinji whispered. "Why didn't you say something to him?" He glowered at her in mock anger.

Jelena shrugged. "I don't know. I figured he'd find out in due time...Besides, the look on his face was worth the wait!"

"Modest, huh! You're wicked, that's what you are!" Ashinji smiled.

That evening, the two families dined on the best fare Nadaka Castle could provide, which Jelena found to be fine, indeed. She could see the intense curiosity about her in the faces of Lord Nadaka and his family, but they were all much too polite to ask any direct questions, other than those concerning the details of the wedding.

After the meal, Nadaka's six daughters staged a Bal Oku recital for the entertainment of their guests. Bal Oku—an ancient form of musical theater revered as high art among the elven people—employed highly stylized singing and dance to tell stories, usually tales from elven mythology. The slow, ponderous rhythms and droning quality of the music were not to Jelena's taste; when the last chord shivered into silence, she felt an intense sense of relief.

"That was absolutely dreadful," Ashinji whispered into her ear. She had to fight hard not to giggle as she clapped politely along with everyone else.

After the girls had collected their instruments and filed out of the room, Sen, stifling a yawn behind his hand, said, "Ai, Nadaka, it's been a long day. It's time my family and I were abed. We've got another long stretch of road ahead of us tomorrow."

"Of course, Lord Sen," Nadaka replied, rising quickly to his feet. His wife promptly followed suit. "Lady Nadaka and I are honored to give up our own sleeping quarters to you and your family. Your guards and servants are welcome to bunk down here in the main room, or out in the yard, if any would prefer to sleep under the stars."

"Most generous of you, Nadaka. My thanks." Sen inclined his head.

Jelena sighed inwardly.

I would much rather sleep outdoors on the hard ground than in the same room with Sadaiyo, she thought, *but I can't ask Ashi to give up the comfort of a soft bed, not after he's spent all day in the saddle.*

Lord and Lady Nadaka's bedroom proved to be quite large, with plenty of free space in which to spread out. Thick, well-cushioned mats covered the floor, and Nadaka had provided more than enough bedding to make reasonably comfortable arrangements. Sen and Amara took the large bed and everyone else, including the twins, staked out floor space. The two girls chattered like bright little birds in a special language known only to themselves as they happily made their pallets.

Just before he retired, Nadaka poked his head in and informed them that the family's bath house was at the disposal of anyone who wished to use it, either tonight or tomorrow morning. With a cheery good night, he left them to themselves.

Jelena assembled a cozy pile of blankets and pillows in the corner farthest from the bed, and after stripping down to her undertunic, she flopped onto the makeshift pallet with a grateful sigh.

Why am I so tired? It's not as if I haven't spent hours in the saddle before...I hope I'm not coming down with a fever.

Not even Sadaiyo's close proximity could keep sleep at bay. She drifted off to the soft murmur of conversation between Sen and his two sons.

Later, she awoke to find Ashinji settled beside her, sound asleep. She lay still and listened to the sounds of the night: Lord Sen snoring softly from the bed, crickets chirping outside the open window, and from the opposite corner, a lot of rustling.

At first, she didn't recognize what her ears heard until a sigh and a soft moan made it all too clear. The last thing Jelena wanted to be privy to was Sadaiyo and Misune's lovemaking.

Gods...must I listen to this?

Misune let out a little gasp and Jelena buried her head beneath the covers. Sen snored on, oblivious. Ashinji stirred but did not wake. The sound of the lovers' bodies moving together grew more frenzied.

Hurry up and finish, for the gods' sake!

The thought of Sadaiyo so close to her while in the throes of sexual passion filled her with disgust. She wondered how Misune would feel knowing that her husband had attempted to rape the woman his brother loved, purely out of spite.

She'd be really angry, but only because her husband would consider dirtying himself by having me, Jelena thought bitterly.

At last, the thrashing stopped. Jelena breathed a sigh of relief and emerged from her refuge. She tried to relax and clear her mind, but the peace of her night had been shattered, and now she feared that sleep would elude her.

She lay staring at the ceiling, wide awake and a little queasy. The light from the night lamp cast faint, dancing shadows on the wood beams above her head. As she watched, the shadows seemed to grow darker and then coalesce into the vague shape of a face.

At first, she thought her eyes were deceiving her. She blinked a few times, but the face remained; in fact, it seemed even more distinct. She could now identify a dark smudge of a mouth, the suggestion of a long, straight nose, and two black holes where the eyes would be.

I should be afraid, she thought, but for some reason, she felt more curious than fearful, perhaps because Ashinji lay beside her.

Or maybe because what I'm seeing is not really there.

The face began to fade almost as quickly as it had formed until nothing remained but the flickering shadows created by the night lamp. Jelena blinked again, already convinced she had imagined the whole thing. She closed her eyes and willed herself to relax, and soon, Ashinji's rhythmic breathing lulled her back to sleep.

* * *

Sen rousted them all just before sunrise. After everyone had a quick turn in Nadaka's bath house, they sat down to a light breakfast in the main room with the Kerala staff. Three of Nadaka's serving women circulated among the tables, pouring tea.

Ashinji indicated that Jelena should sit and he would bring them their food. While she waited, her mind recalled the strange vision of the night before. Had the face she'd seen been real, or merely a disturbing hallucination, fabricated out of night shadows and dreamstuff?

And if it was real, who or what is behind it, and more importantly, what did it want? Could this...this whatever it is... have been drawn to me by the blue fire?

Am I in danger?

Ashinji returned with two bowls of porridge and a plate loaded with thick slices of fresh-baked bread. A servant came by and filled their mugs with hot black tea. They ate quickly, for Sen wanted to get as early a start as possible. As she ate, Jelena considered whether she should tell Ashinji about the face or keep it to herself. She decided to say nothing for now; since she didn't know for sure if the whole thing were real or imagined, she didn't wish to unduly upset him. If it happened again, she would tell him.

After breakfast, Sen instructed Jelena to ride ahead again this day, and herald their arrival to their next host, Lady Shona. Shona was Amara's first cousin and childhood playmate, and it had been several years since they'd last seen each other.

"I'll pack my saddlebags and leave right away," Jelena declared.

"I'll come see you off," Ashinji said. The two of them excused themselves and headed for the stairs leading up to the second-level sleeping quarters. It took only a few moments to collect her things. Before donning a light coat against the early morning chill, she tugged on the chain holding her father's signet and drew the ring from beneath her tunic. Sliding the warm metal onto her thumb, she held her hand up before her eyes to stare at the stylized griffin inlaid into the onyx surface. Perhaps, if she stared hard enough, the ring would reveal some of what dwelled within the soul of the man for whom it had been made. Perhaps it would tell her if acceptance or rejection lay ahead.

If only it were that simple.

"You're worried about meeting the king, aren't you?" Ashinji asked.

Jelena slipped the ring off her thumb and dropped it back inside of her tunic where it came to rest between her breasts. She laid her head against Ashinji's shoulder. "Yes, I'm worried," she replied. "Maybe it would be best if he never knows about me."

"If Silverlock is your father, he has a right to know," Ashinji said, stroking her curls.

"Silverlock?" Jelena looked at Ashinji questioningly.

"The king's hair is silver, hence the nickname."

"Of course," Jelena whispered. "My birth mother told Claudia that my father called himself...*Zin*." She reverted to Soldaran, and said, "'Zin' means silver in Siri-dar!"

"Yes. Your cousin Magnes told me about Zin when we first met and I questioned him about you. I didn't make the connection at the time." He bent down and hoisted her saddlebag to his shoulder. "C'mon. It's getting late. You'd better get going."

He escorted her to the stables and waited with her while one of Nadaka's stable boys saddled Willow and brought her out. Jelena swung into the saddle with practiced ease and adjusted her stirrup leathers while Ashinji secured her bag. He grasped her hand and placed a kiss—light as a feather—on her palm. His eyes sparkled with desire. "I'll see you tonight," he murmured, "and by the Goddess, I'll not lie next to you all night again as if we were brother and sister!" Jelena drew in a deep breath of the cool morning air, trying to slow her racing heart. The merest thought of Ashinji's touch sent shivers of delight coursing down her spine, sparking that peculiarly sweet ache between her thighs that only he could soothe.

Ashinji turned and retreated toward the house. As he approached the open doorway, Sadaiyo stepped through. The two brothers paused and exchanged words. Jelena—too far away to hear—frowned with worry as Ashinji pushed past Sadaiyo and disappeared inside. Sadaiyo lingered on the front porch, and as his gaze swept the yard, he caught sight of her. An unpleasant smile twisted his handsome mouth. Jelena's chest tightened in disgust. Quickly, she gathered up her reins and turned Willow's head toward the path leading out to the main road.

Sadaiyo's sharp, sardonic laughter followed after her, stinging her ears as she rode away.

* * *

High above, in a sky aglow with the crimson and orange of sunrise, a raven traced lazy circles in the still air. Its bead-like eyes fixed on the road below, watching.

At last, a horse and rider appeared, cantering easily on the smooth, well-tended road. The raven spun on its wingtip and plunged downward, an inky streak against the brightening sky. It landed on the branch of a chestnut tree growing along the grassy verge some distance ahead. There, it waited.

A short time elapsed before the horse passed beneath the tree in a jingling, creaking rush. The bird's keen eyesight caught a glimpse of the rider's face—sun-bronzed skin, a melding of human and elven features—topped by a wild mane of dark, coiled hair.

The raven cawed—a harsh, brazen sound—and launched itself skyward. A compulsion to follow spurred it on, and it could not resist. Like a black arrow, it shot after the rider, maintaining a discreet distance so that it would not be noticed. The bird had no instinct left for self-preservation; for many days, it had gone without food, water, or rest. Relentlessly, inevitably, the force that drove it also drained its life energy in the process.

When at last it fell from the sky, another bird sprang aloft and took up the chase.

4

Sendai

There it is, my love. Sendai Castle." Ashinji pointed toward the west.

Jelena held her hand up to shade her eyes, but could see only what appeared to be a large, forested hill against the glare of the horizon.

"I can't see the castle...only trees." She squinted in a vain attempt to discern the outlines of the fortress.

"It sits at the top of the hill. You can just see the highest roofs from here. They're covered in blue tiles."

Jelena shook her head, frustrated that she seemed to lack her elven sire's sharper-than-human eyesight. "Where is the city?" she asked, abandoning the search for the castle.

"You'll see," Ashinji replied. He flashed a wicked grin, as if keeping some particularly astounding secret. "Sendai will amaze you, I promise."

They had been on the road for ten days and had another half-day of travel yet before them. The party had paused to rest at a crossroads. Some of the Kerala guards stood at relaxed, yet watchful, attention, while others took their ease on the soft grass. Amara and her daughters had abandoned their carriage and now rested in the shade of a horse chestnut tree. Just beyond the intersection, the road mounted a small hill. Ashinji and Jelena stood at the summit, gazing ahead toward their destination.

Ashinji slipped his arm around Jelena's waist, drawing her close in a companionable embrace. His eyes sparkled with anticipation, but she sensed that it had nothing to do with her.

"What are you thinking about, Ashi?" she asked.

"How good it will be to see the Peregrines again. I've never been away from my company for so long." Ashinji had spoken many times of his fondness and respect for the men and women of Peregrine Company. He derived strength from their camaraderie and professionalism, and they made his life as a captain in the king's army more bearable.

"Will your people be shocked when you return with a wife?" she asked, playfully tweaking his nose.

He grinned and tweaked hers in kind. "Perhaps, but they will be pleased for me as well."

"Yes, but how do you think they will react to me?" She couldn't stop the note of worry that crept, unbidden, into her voice.

Ashinji turned her by the shoulders to face him. "I know you are afraid of how you will be treated, and I can't promise that there won't be any problems, but Sendai does have a sizable hikui community. After we get settled, I'll take you to Jokimichi, the district where most of the hikui live. You can finally meet other people who look like you."

With a small shock, Jelena realized that Ashinji had pointed out to her a startling fact; in all her months of residing among the elves of Kerala, she had not once seen another hikui. Aneko hardly counted; the First Sergeant of the Kerala Guard lived as okui, despite her own admission. Jelena's heart beat a little faster with excitement. What would the hikui of Sendai be like? Her mind buzzed with questions that would have to wait until she reached the city.

"Ho there, children! Come to admire the view, eh?"

Ashinji and Jelena turned as one to the sound of Lord Sen's greeting.

"Father, have you got your spyglass with you?" Ashinji inquired. "I'm sure Jelena would like to get a closer look at Sendai Castle."

"I do, I do," Sen replied. He unhooked a small rectangular leather case from his belt and removed the spyglass. "This came all the way from Great Arrisae Island. The Islanders make the finest navigational tools in the known world. Your mother-in-law gave it to me." He extended the exquisite, brass and wood instrument and handed it to Jelena.

"I hear you, Father," she assured him. "You are asking me, in a roundabout way, to please be careful with it!"

Sen's whole body shook with laughter. "Clever *and* beautiful! 'Course I knew that already. Now, hold the narrow end up to your eye, that's it! D'you see the castle now?"

"Yes, yes, I can see it!" Jelena exclaimed.

Looking through the spyglass, it seemed as if she had traversed much of the distance to Sendai in the wink of an eye. "This is amazing," she sighed, fascinated by the power of the spyglass to draw such a distant object closer.

She could make out some of the larger details of the structure, such as its overall architecture and relative size to the hill upon which it stood, but they were still too far away to see much more than that. She lowered the glass and reluctantly gave it back to Sen, who carefully returned it to its case.

"Thank you, Father," she said, smiling.

"We should be at the city gates by sundown," Ashinji said, glancing into the sky to check the position of the sun, which hung just past zenith.

"We'll ride straight in and go directly to the castle," Sen instructed. "I'll send someone ahead to announce us, but it won't be you, Jelena. As of this moment, you are no longer employed as my messenger." He looked Jelena over with narrowed eyes. "Hmmm, I've not said anything because we've been traveling, but...my dear, it's time you put away those old clothes."

"Oh, Father. I...I'm sorry!" Jelena felt her cheeks burn as she realized how shabby she must look compared to the rest of the family. "I'm so used to dressing this way...All my new things are packed away in the baggage. I'm not sure if I can get to them."

Ashinji took her hand and squeezed. "Father, what Jelena's wearing right now doesn't really matter. We've been on the road for the last ten days. We can worry about it later."

"Yes...yes of course you're right," Sen agreed. "Come now, you two. It's time we were on our way."

* * *

The remainder of the day passed easily. The party rode alongside fields of ripe grain and orchards nearing the harvest. The farmland surrounding Sendai was second in productivity only to the disputed Tono Valley. The farmhouses they passed were of varying sizes, but every one, from the smallest cottage to the grandest manor exuded an air of peace and prosperity.

A war could destroy all of this, Jelena thought.

Late afternoon found them passing through the more heavily populated suburbs. The farmland had gradually given way to an open forest of oak and beech, within which the people had chosen to integrate their settlements, rather than clear the land. Here, the houses stood much closer together, each one set in its own garden. Small workshops, storefronts, and inns were interspersed among the dwellings. Signs now marked the lanes and byways branching off from the main road.

Along the way, many folk paused to watch as the large party clattered past. As Ashinji predicted, they reached the main gates of the city proper just as the sun came to rest on the horizon.

Jelena could only stare, speechless with astonishment.

"I told you Sendai would amaze you," Ashinji said. "Welcome to the City of Trees."

Never in her wildest imaginings had Jelena considered that an entire city could be built within the confines of a forest. A wide swath had been cleared outside the city's walls, but not within; from the base of the inner wall, trees marched in unbroken ranks into the city proper.

The walls themselves, though built of massive stone blocks, looked like a natural feature of the land; a dense overgrowth of flowering vines crept up to just below the parapets. A formidable, double-towered stone gatehouse guarded the main entrance, and the shadow cast by the artificial cliff face spread premature nightfall over a large section of the town below. As they drew closer, Jelena got a better look at the walls' luxuriant drapery of vegetation.

Each vine sported fragrant clusters of white flowers amid rows of brutal thorns, easily as long as her index finger. She shuddered at the thought of what that punishing curtain would do to anyone who tried to scale it.

They passed beneath the gatehouse and rode into the city itself, entering via a broad, gravel-bedded avenue lined with a bewildering assortment of shops, inns, and taverns. Many of the buildings were constructed around the boles of the trees, incorporating them into the design of the structure. Ladder-like staircases snaked up the trunks of many of the larger trees, leading to structures set on platforms among the spreading branches.

The street teemed with people, all intent on the business of life. In shop windows, above doorways, and along the streets, lanterns flared to life, banishing the dusk. Other lights, twinkling like stars overhead, hung from boughs, balconies, and the upcurved ends of roof gutters.

As in the rural district and suburbs, the city exuded an aura of prosperity, but despite the appearance of normalcy, Jelena could sense a subtle undercurrent of tension floating in the air, like the smell of far-off corruption. She studied individual faces among the throng and found on every one the unmistakable marks of worry.

The elves of Sendai were afraid.

She pointed out her observation to Ashinji.

"The people know that war with the Soldarans is coming," he replied, tight-lipped. "The population of the Empire is easily ten times that of Alasiri, with an Imperial Army at least triple in number to our fighting forces. The odds are very much against us. The people know it, the king and his council know it, yet we have no choice but to try to defend ourselves. If we don't stop the invasion, the humans will overrun all of Alasiri and take our land for their own in order to relieve the great pressure of their growing population. It would surely mean death or slavery for most of us."

Jelena shivered with dread. She knew from firsthand experience how humans, or more specifically, how Soldarans felt about elves, and she had no doubt of the truth of Ashinji's words. A conquered Alasiri would be dealt with harshly, its lands depopulated with brutal efficiency and quickly resettled by landless Soldarans eager for homesteads of their own.

Jelena tried to imagine such a catastrophe and couldn't. Her mind would not, *could* not form those images of horror and despair, simply because she had never experienced death and destruction on such a massive scale. She prayed that she never would.

Ashinji had fallen silent, and the set of his jaw told Jelena that he no longer felt like talking, so she turned her attention to the castle ahead.

The great fortress of Sendai Castle sat atop a hill rising from the heart of the city, dominating the view from all quarters. The broad road upon which they approached led to the edge of a vast, gravel-covered parade ground laid out beneath the castle walls.

The architecture of the castle closely resembled that of Kerala, except on a much grander scale, and rendered almost entirely of whitewashed stone instead of wood. The red light of the dying sun painted the walls a bloody crimson.

A mounted figure emerged from the shadows beneath the main gate and approached at a trot. Jelena grinned as the figure resolved itself into Aneko. As second in command of Kerala's guard, she had gone ahead to announce the arrival of the king's Commanding General.

Aneko pulled up and saluted briskly. "My lord, the Steward of Sendai Castle is pleased to send you his greetings and requests that you proceed to the outer ward where he awaits your arrival."

"Thank you, Sergeant. You may return to the line," Sen replied. "Sadaiyo! Ashinji! By me."

Ashinji flashed a quick smile toward Jelena as he moved his horse forward to position himself at his father's left hand. Sadaiyo took his place at the right. He looked every bit the nobleman in his brightly colored silks and conspicuous jewelry while Ashinji could have easily passed as his father's Captain of the Guard, were it not for the fact that he rode at Sen's left hand.

Jelena now found herself riding beside Misune, who studiously ignored her. She did not mind; she wouldn't have known what to say even if her sister-in-law had deigned to speak.

Lord Sen and his entourage passed through the castle gates into the outer ward. There, they were met by the most diminutive man, human or elf, that Jelena had ever seen. He stood no more than the height of a well-grown human child of six or seven years. The air of importance with which he carried himself, and the large gold chain of office that hung about his neck told her that this must be the Steward of Sendai Castle.

"Ah, ah, so good to see you again, Lord Sen!" the little man exclaimed in a high-pitched voice.

"And you, Karogi. It has been awhile," Sen replied warmly.

"The king sends his greetings and has charged me personally with seeing to the comfort of you and your family. Your guards will be shown to the barracks and the servants that you don't require right away can go directly to the staff hall.

"Lu! Attend!" A young boy, dressed in the livery of a page, sprang forward. "Take Lord Sen's civilian staff to the hall. Get moving, boy! Ajisai, show Lord Sen's guards to the barracks and see that the horses are taken care of." A lanky youth stepped forward and gestured to Gendan, indicating that he and the rest of the guards should follow him.

Jelena ferociously suppressed an urge to laugh. The sight of this tiny man snapping orders in his squeaky voice struck her as comical, but she had no doubts as to the enormous power he wielded within the hierarchy of Sendai's vast staff.

He deserves my respect, she chided herself, *not my derision.*

Sen dismounted, Sadaiyo and Ashinji following suit. Ashinji then came to steady Willow's head while Jelena slid from the saddle. Misune flung herself down from her cranky stallion and strode boldly up beside her husband to pose, hand resting on her sword hilt, like the haughty warrior princess she fancied herself to be. Jelena would have preferred to

remain in the background, but Ashinji led her forward with gentle insistence. Sen walked back to the carriage and escorted Amara and the Sakehera daughters forward.

"Lady Amara, this is a wonderful surprise! So good to see you! My,
my, your daughters have all blossomed into such lovely young ladies. My
lord, I remember your eldest son, Lord Sadaiyo," the Steward bobbed as
he spoke, "and of course Lord Ashinji, welcome back, my lord! Peregrine
Company will be overjoyed to have its captain returned to it, but I do not
know this beautiful and formidable lady." Karogi proffered a courtly bow
to Misune.

"This is my Heir's new wife, the Lady Misune Sakehera," Sen replied
with a touch of pride in his voice.

Karogi bowed again. "My congratulations to you both," he piped. He
then turned to Ashinji after flicking the barest glance at Jelena. "My lord,
will your servant be sharing your quarters, or will she need a cot in the
staff hall?"

Misune snickered. Jelena's cheeks ignited.

"Jelena is not my servant," Ashinji said. His eyes had gone hard and
cold.

Jelena laid a hand on his arm and squeezed. "Ashi, it is an honest mistake," she spoke very softly, so that only he could hear. She felt no anger, only
resignation and understanding. A hikui girl dressed in simple cotton and
leather—of course this little man had mistaken her for Ashinji's servant.

"Hmmm, uh, my youngest son has also married recently. This is my
other daughter-in-law, Jelena," Sen explained hastily. Jelena glanced over at
Sadaiyo and cringed at the smirk on his face. The sight of his enjoyment
of her humiliation made her burn with renewed hatred.

Karogi cast a dubious eye over Jelena, but he was a consummate courtier, and swiftly adjusted his attitude. "A thousand apologies to you, my lady,
and to you, Lord Ashinji. Please forgive my stupid blunder. It seems, then,
that congratulations are in order for you as well, my lord. Am I to assume
that you and your new bride will be needing accommodations within the
keep itself, rather than the barracks?"

"Yes," Ashinji replied curtly.

"Very good, my lords, my ladies, please come with me, then."

They followed the tiny steward—who walked far more quickly than
Jelena would have guessed possible—across the spacious outer ward and

through a second set of gates that pierced the inner walls of the castle. After traversing the smaller inner ward and a flight of wide, shallow stone stairs, they reached the massive double doors of the keep itself. A pair of guards snapped to attention as they approached.

The doors to the keep stood open. Karogi swept through, waving perfunctorily to the guards. As Jelena passed over the threshold, she looked about her with awe. Even the twins remained silent and wide-eyed.

This is the biggest building I've ever seen, she thought.

The steward led them across a wide entrance hall toward a broad staircase. The expansive space flickered with shadows cast by the flames of dozens of brass lamps—many fashioned in the shapes of fishes, roosters, lions, and other animals—hanging from chains attached to the ceiling. Stone columns spaced at regular intervals supported the roof overhead; finely woven, well-padded matting covered the stone floors.

There seemed to be no one else about, not even servants. Jelena realized that most of the people of the household would be involved in the evening meal, either eating it, or serving it.

"Lord Sen, the king has requested that when you have gotten your family settled, that you attend him in his private study. He has several matters of importance that he needs to discuss with you," Karogi said as he led the way up the stairs. They climbed two flights and passed down a long corridor into one of the castle's many towers. "Your lodgings," Karogi announced as he threw open a door.

The tower was, in fact, a multistory apartment, with a common room at the base and several bedchambers on the floors above. It had a private entrance from the yard below, and the biggest and most luxurious of the several bathhouses set aside for guests stood directly across the yard.

"Your baggage is on its way up, my lord," the steward assured Sen. "The lamps are lit, and there is wine, beer, and fruit juice for the children. I shall send servants to assist you straightaway."

"My thanks, Karogi," Sen replied. The steward bowed, and, quick as a cat, he departed.

The twins immediately clamored for permission to go find a bedchamber for themselves and Lani.

"Yes, yes, girls. Go ahead." Amara wearily waved towards the staircase leading to the upper floors.

"Come on, Mariso, Jena," Lani called. She shepherded the chattering girls upward, admonishing them to be careful and not to run.

"Where do they get all of that energy?" Sen muttered. Looking around, he spotted a sideboard upon which stood a couple of pitchers, a carafe, and an assortment of glasses and cups. He poured a glass of wine and handed it to Amara. Helping himself to a cup of beer, he then claimed the most comfortable chair in the room for himself and sat down with a grateful sigh. Amara settled on a couch set before the unlit fireplace.

"I'm sorry about what happened earlier, Jelena. Please forgive me." Sen said. "I should have introduced you properly, as you deserve. Rest assured that it won't happen again." He raised his cup to his lips and took a long, deep swallow.

"If she insists on dressing like a servant, no one should be surprised that she's treated like one," Sadaiyo commented. He had also helped himself to the wine; he and Misune now sat on a smaller couch near the window, sharing the cup between them.

"I dress this way because it is comfortable," Jelena replied, her voice low and hard. Sadaiyo sneered. She turned her back on him and went to pour a glass of wine for herself and a cup of beer for Ashinji. She briefly entertained the idea of throwing the pitcher at Sadaiyo's head.

No. Why waste good beer on such filth?

"Comfortable though it may be, it is not suitable garb in which to go before the royal court," Amara gently pointed out. "I think the new green outfit I gave you as a wedding gift should do nicely."

"Yes, Mother. I'll be sure to unpack it first thing," Jelena replied.

A knock at the door signaled the arrival of the baggage, along with several servants bearing trays. With the efficiency of experience, the servers soon had a hearty meal laid out—turtle soup, cold poached fish, a platter of steamed vegetables, wheat cakes fried to a crisp, golden brown, several loaves of bread, and a small wheel of hard yellow cheese. Apples and berry tarts made up dessert.

The delicious aromas of the food set Jelena's stomach to rumbling; however, decorum dictated that she, along with the rest of the family, must wait until Sen and Amara had taken what they wanted before serving themselves.

The food tasted as good as it looked. As they ate, Sen spoke. "I expect the king'll have a lot to discuss with me, so most likely, it'll be a late night," he said between mouthfuls. "Prince Raidan will probably be there, too. Sadaiyo and Ashinji, you'll accompany me, of course, though I doubt you'll need to stay the whole evening."

"The king will be calling the war council soon, don't you think, Father?" Ashinji asked.

"Yes, when all of the lords entitled to sit in council have arrived, he will, but I don't know who all is here yet. Jelena, I'll need your ring. I intend to show it to the king this very night."

"Yes, of course, thank you, Father!" With eagerness born of hope, Jelena pulled the ring out from its hiding place beneath her tunic and slipped the chain over her head. She presented the ring to Sen and returned to her seat on a floor cushion next to Ashinji.

Sen held the ring up before his face, where it swung gently, back and forth, like a fortune teller's pendulum. Pensively, he examined the gleaming white band of metal for a few heartbeats, then closed his fist around it and shifted his gaze to Jelena.

"Jelena," he began, "You know family means everything to us and—right or wrong—a person with no family can't expect to rise very far in elven society." He paused to look at Amara, who nodded in agreement. "When you married my son," he continued, "you became a member of the House of Sakehera which, though no small thing, is not the same as knowing the house from which you came."

As if sensing her anxiety, Sen smiled in reassurance. "It's an understatement to say that your life has changed since you first came to us," he said, "but it will be nothing compared to what could happen if your true father embraces you as his own. Are you ready to face that?"

"I'm ready for whatever happens, Father," Jelena replied, but her bold words rang hollow in her own ears. In truth, she didn't know which she dreaded most—acceptance or rejection.

"Are you implying, Father, that she could be the daughter of a noble house?" Sadaiyo asked, eyebrows raised. "That's impossible! What self-respecting elf of good family would mate with a human? Her mother could have stolen that ring, or found it in a field somewhere. A marchland farm boy's by-blow... Now that I could believe!" Misune laughed at her husband's cruel words, her golden, lioness eyes flashing with mean-spirited amusement.

"Shut up, Sadaiyo!" Ashinji growled, rising halfway from his seat, hands knotted into fists. Jelena reached out to restrain him.

"What's wrong, Little Brother? Can't stand to hear the truth about your precious little mongrel?" Sadaiyo retorted, rising to his feet in anticipation.

"That's enough!" Amara cried. Before anyone could react, she sprang from the couch and launched herself at her eldest son. Planting her hands against his chest, she shoved Sadaiyo hard. He fell backward into Misune's arms where he lay, staring up in shock at his mother's face. Amara stood over him, rigid with fury. "Sadaiyo, you have *no idea* who and what this girl is, none at all!" She spat her words like slingshot bullets.

Sadaiyo flinched as if struck, and all the color drained from his face. He swallowed hard and bowed his head. Misune wisely followed suit. Jelena had never seen Amara so angry nor Sadaiyo so cowed, and she found the vehemence of her mother-in-law's outburst disturbing.

What does she mean, who...and what...I am? Is she talking about my father...or something else?

"You will never again speak to Jelena in so disrespectful a manner. Need I remind you that you insult your father and me each time you insult her? She is our daughter-in-law now, and we were the ones who gave our consent to her joining our family."

"Please forgive me, Mother," Sadaiyo murmured, his proud head still bent in submission.

"Don't ask me for forgiveness. I'm not the one to give it to you!" Amara retorted. Sadaiyo opened his mouth as if to reply, then apparently thought better of it and remained silent.

"Your mother is right." Sen spoke up, his own voice razor sharp. "Like it or not, you are all family, *my* family, and by the One, you will behave like it! Things are going to be very different soon, you mark my words!"

No one moved or spoke for several heartbeats.

Sen finally broke the tense silence.

"We're all tired and filthy from the road, but that can't be helped. The king has commanded my presence, so I must go. You two, c'mon." He jabbed an index finger at Sadaiyo and Ashinji, then gestured toward the door.

With a soft "I love you" whispered into her ear, Ashinji kissed Jelena on the lips and followed his father and brother out of the apartment. Without saying a word, Misune fled up the stairs, leaving Jelena and Amara alone in the sitting room.

Jelena's mind whirled with unvoiced questions.

You have no idea who and what this girl is...

"Mother, what did you mean...what you said to Sadaiyo just now?" she asked.

Amara returned to the couch and settled down with a weary sigh. She patted the cushion next to her. "Come sit by me, child," she commanded. She held out her hands so Jelena could see the intricate designs tattooed on both palms. "These designs are not meant as mere ornamentation," she explained.

Jelena nodded in understanding. "I always thought they must have some higher meaning."

"For those with the knowledge to read them, they are sigils—magical symbols."

"Of what, Mother?"

Amara stared at her hands for a moment before folding them in her lap. "Jelena, I've a confession to make. It concerns your blue fire. When you first came to me for help, I told you I was unsure of its exact nature, but in truth, I've known all along what it is."

Jelena had always suspected Amara knew more about the mysterious and frightening blue energy than she admitted to, but to hear her mother-in-law confirm her suspicion still disturbed her. The look of firm resolve mingled with profound sadness on Amara's face disturbed her even more.

"I had to keep the full truth from you until now, Jelena, because I did not want to frighten you, but things are moving far too swiftly. I'm just so sorry that you will have this burden to carry along with everything else you'll have to deal with."

"Whatever burdens I have to carry, I'll have Ashinji to help me. As long as he's by my side, I won't be afraid," Jelena replied, trying to sound as brave as she could, but realizing that Amara saw through her false courage.

"There's no shame in being afraid, Jelena. You are young, but I have faith in you. I believe you possess great strength—far more than you know—and you are going to need every bit it of it in the end. Now, listen carefully...."

* * *

Later that night, Jelena lay awake in bed, awaiting Ashinji's return and trying to make sense of Amara's revelation. She turned it over and over in her mind, but from every angle, it seemed so unbelievable. Jelena had the utmost respect for Amara's powers as a mage, and she felt certain that every one of her mother-in-law's fellows in this mysterious Kirian Society were equally as Talented, but...

Surely they've made a mistake! How can I possibly be this Key they've been awaiting? Shouldn't the one chosen to carry such powerful magic be someone with the strength to control it?

Tomorrow, Amara had promised to present her to the other members of the Kirian Society who lived in the capital, and then her training would begin in earnest.

But what exactly am I being trained for?

That was the one question Amara had refused to answer, saying only that, in time, Jelena would understand everything.

5

A Secret From The Past

Raidan Onjara, Lord of Meizi, Crown Prince of Alasiri, was a troubled man.

The cause of his disquiet lay on the desk before him, scribbled in a thin, spidery hand on two sheets of rumpled brown paper.

Raidan re-read the report for the third time.

Your Highness, I send you greetings.

As an itinerant healer here in the borderlands, I have had the occasion to see many kinds of illnesses among our people, who, as you know, live in close proximity to human settlements. The folk here are largely of mixed blood, and they contract many of the same sicknesses that strike humans; however, their elven blood bestows upon them a certain resistance to diseases that would otherwise fell a human.

Recently, I paid a visit to the farm of an okui family by the name of Lwenda. There, I saw something most peculiar and troubling. At the time of my first visit, only the father had fallen ill. According to his wife, he had complained first of a headache and sore throat. Soon afterward, he became feverish, and so weak he could not stand. Three days later, he developed hard swellings in his neck, armpits, and groin.

When I examined him, I found the swellings to be firm, inflamed, and discolored. The patient's wife and children were, quite naturally, terrified that he might die. I questioned the wife closely about her husband's contacts with any humans that lived in the area. She readily admitted that both she and her husband had frequent dealings with the human folk of a certain village just across the border, as well as several human traders who traveled the area calling upon all of the farms thereabouts—human, hikui, and okui.

She then told me a troubling tale of a sickness spreading rapidly among the humans, killing many of them. They called it the 'black death', because it apparently turns a human victim's skin a mottled purple-black just before the unfortunate wretch meets a rather messy and painful end.

In my readings, I have come across many references to the 'black death', so I am familiar with the symptom. Heretofore, it has been commonly believed that we elves could not contract this disease. Yet, there I stood over the sickbed of an elf, looking at a man with the unmistakable signs of the 'black death'! I did what I could for the man, and tried to reassure his family, but I did not have much faith in my own mind that anything I did would make a difference. Sadly, I was correct.

Three days later, the youngest child, a girl, fetched me back out to the farm. Her father was dead, and now, her mother and all the rest of her siblings were ill. By the whim of the Goddess, this one child had been spared the sickness but not the agony of having to watch her entire family die, for die they did, despite everything I tried to do to prevent it.

Your Highness, as Court Physician and a learned colleague, I knew you would wish to be informed of this new and frightening ability of the human plague to attack our people. I fear for the health of the Tono garrison, as well as all of Lady Odata's people, for they are our first line of defense against any invasion mounted by the Soldarans. Goddess help us if our forces down here, small as they are, should be further reduced by the ravages of disease.

Your Obedient Servant and Colleague,
Kujaku Remei

Raidan sighed wearily and leaned back into his padded chair. He rested his chin upon steepled fingers and pondered the implications of the information contained within Remei's report. As a trained doctor, Raidan had studied most of the medical texts written by elven physicians, as well as a few written by human doctors. He knew of the 'black death'—an ancient scourge of humankind—but only as a medical curiosity, something an elven healer would study purely for the sake of knowledge. No elf had ever contracted the disease...until now.

Something has changed, the prince thought, *some fundamental aspect of the disease itself, to allow it to attack elves now, as well as humans.*

A controversial theory, put forth by the human physician Nazarius, sprang to Raidan's mind. The theory proposed that some diseases were caused by a particle or essence that entered the body of a healthy person and then somehow disrupted its natural function. This mysterious essence could pass—by as yet unknown means—from one person to another, causing illness in some while sparing others.

Prince Raidan believed in Nazarius' theory. The essence that caused the 'black death' in humans had somehow been altered, but how? *Could the Soldarans have done this deliberately as a first assault in order to weaken our troops guarding the Tono Pass?* The prince shook his head. *Impossible. The Soldarans have little real magic and this is certainly beyond their science. More importantly, though, is the question of how will we protect ourselves against it. Remei is quite right to be concerned about the health of the fighting forces stationed in and around Tono Castle.*

Sweeping the papers up into his hands, Raidan went to see his brother the king.

The prince's apartments lay at the opposite end of the main keep from those of the king's. He had a fair distance to walk, but walking had never bothered him. Most of the castle's inhabitants were still at their dinners; the few people Raidan encountered along the near silent corridors, servants all, bowed politely as he passed. His footfalls made little sound on the finely woven reed mats covering the stone floors.

His mind remained so preoccupied with the disturbing contents of the report crinkled in his hand that he arrived outside the king's quarters with no conscious memory of the journey.

The two soldiers of the King's Guard standing at either side of the painted double wooden doors snapped to attention. Ignoring them, Raidan pushed open the left door and strode through.

He crossed a large antechamber—dimly lit by a few small brass lamps—to stand before a smaller set of doors that opened into the inner sanctum of his brother's private apartments.

A second pair of soldiers, also elite King's Guard, stood watch over the finely carved wooden panels. They, too, came to attention at Raidan's arrival, but this time, he did not continue forward.

Not even the Crown Prince could enter the king's private quarters without permission.

"Tell the king I'm here," Raidan commanded.

"Yes, your Highness," the taller of the two guards responded. He disappeared through the portals while his partner assumed the traditional defensive stance—hand on sword hilt, spear extended over the doorway in a crosswise block.

Raidan understood their duty well; each member of the King's Guard would defend the king with his or her life against all attackers, even should those attackers be members of the royal family.

He waited, as he knew he must, albeit impatiently.

The first guard returned. "The king will see you now, your Highness," he announced. Then, in unison, he and his partner stepped to either side of the doors and inclined their spears away from the prince.

Raidan entered and made his way to his brother's study. He found the king seated at his writing table, flipping through a stack of papers. The king looked up, head canted slightly to one side; for an instant, Raidan saw, not his brother sitting there, but their father.

Keizo Onjara, also known as Silverlock, King of Alasiri, pursed his lips in a frown. "What's wrong?" he asked. "You look as though your wife just threw you out."

Raidan shook his head. "If only it was so simple," he replied in a heavy voice. He sank onto a low couch opposite the king's desk and brandished Remei's report. "I've just received this from a traveling doctor down in Tono. It's not good." He offered the papers to Keizo. The king took them and began to read.

When he'd finished, the king laid the papers down beside the others stacked on the desktop and looked at his brother. "What do you advise?"

"At present, I have no advice, other than to warn Lady Odata, though I'm sure she is well aware of the situation." Raidan ran a hand through his sable hair. "If this plague takes hold amongst the troops of her garrison, Tono will lie defenseless, leaving the way open for the Soldarans to sweep clear through to Sendai."

"Which is why we must move the bulk of our armies into the Tono Valley as soon as possible," Keizo said. He tapped the pile of reports before him with a well-manicured forefinger. "Intelligence has been coming in from as far south as Darguinia. Empress Constantia has begun a full-scale mobilization of her armies. It appears as if she intends to send at least two divisions north to retake Tono."

"We both know her ambitions are more far-reaching than just retaking Tono," Raidan replied. "The Soldaran homeland is bursting at the seams. The humans breed like field mice and they need more land. They look north to Alasiri and they see our fields and orchards, and all of the open land we have, and they covet it. The empress would happily slaughter us all in order to re-settle her excess population in our territory."

Keizo rose from his chair and paced about the small room, filling its confines with his nervous energy. Raidan followed his brother's movements with his eyes, holding his body still, betraying none of the tension he himself felt.

Abruptly, Keizo stopped pacing. He closed his eyes and pressed his hand to his forehead, then spoke. "I estimate that we have until the end of next spring to prepare. That gives us almost eleven months. Constantia won't risk coming out until then. She's not nearly ready yet, and besides, the Tono Pass will be blocked with snow until the end of Daira at least. Then, there's the late season rains. If she marches on us before Kishan's over, she risks her forces getting bogged down in mud." Keizo shook his head. "No. She won't march until early Nobe, I'm sure of it, and we must be ready to meet her. As you pointed out, if we don't stop her at the Tono Valley, all is lost."

Raidan opened his mouth to reply when a soft knock at the door interrupted him.

"Come!" the king called out.

One of the guards stepped into the room and offered a crisp salute. "Your Majesty, General Sakehera awaits your pleasure," he announced.

Keizo's face broke into a smile. "Send him in." The guard saluted and withdrew.

"Now that Sakehera is here, we can plan in earnest," Raidan said. The prince had a keen regard for the gruffly affable Lord of Kerala, stretching back many years to the time when he, Keizo, and Sakehera were just boys. Young Sen had spent several years fostering at the court of their father, Keizo the Elder, where he had gained a secure place for himself as Keizo the Younger's favorite companion. Even then, he had often demonstrated a cunning intelligence that seemed at odds with his placid exterior. Raidan considered him one of the best minds in the realm.

A good man to have on one's side, if the need should ever arise, Raidan thought.

The door swung open and Sen Sakehera strode briskly in, trailed by two younger men. All three bowed in unison. "Your Majesty," Sakehera said.

"My friend! It's been too long! Come, your king gives you permission to embrace him!" Keizo held out his arms and the two men embraced with unabashed pleasure. "You look exhausted," the king observed.

Sen flashed a rueful smile. "We've just arrived. Haven't even had time to knock the dust from our boots." He indicated the two young men behind him with a wave. "I've brought my sons."

"Yes, I see," Keizo nodded. "Captain Sakehera, you have been away from my service for quite some time now. Your company—the Peregrines, I believe—will be pleased to have you back."

"I sincerely hope so, Your Majesty," the younger of Sen's sons answered politely.

Raidan recognized Ashinji Sakehera and knew him to be a captain in the army, stationed in Sendai; his older brother Sadaiyo, Sen's Heir, he did not know.

"Sakehera, your son Ashinji has a fine reputation within the service," Raidan said. "He is a young man with a very bright future." Sen beamed and laid a hand on the shoulder of his second son, a simple, yet telling gesture.

Skilled at both the art of observation and the science of deduction, Raidan surreptitiously studied Sen and his two sons. A slight downturn of the mouth, the appearance of a tiny crease between the eyes; the details were so subtle that even Raidan might have missed them had he not been specifically alert. Sadaiyo Sakehera hid his emotions well, but Raidan could still read them.

Jealousy was a terrible, corrosive force and when it stood between two brothers, it would surely destroy one or both of them. Raidan could only guess at the reasons for Sadaiyo Sakehera's hatred of his younger brother, but one factor might be favoritism.

Sen had made it quite clear, with only a single gesture, which of his sons he loved best, and it was not his Heir.

Keizo sat at his desk and indicated with a wave of his hand that Sen should sit as well. The Lord of Kerala settled down on a cushioned stool with a grateful sigh. His sons moved to stand behind him.

The king regarded his old friend thoughtfully, then spoke. "I've tried to keep you as current as possible on the situation, but here is the latest," he began. "The Soldarans are preparing for an attack, but they won't be ready for nearly a year. That much you already know. We've just learned that there is an outbreak of a deadly disease known as 'black death' sweeping through the human population just over the Tono frontier."

"But this is good!" Sen exclaimed. "This 'black death' will pose a serious danger to the empress's troops. It could do half our work for us, if we're lucky."

"I would agree, except that it seems this plague can now attack elven-kind as well as humans. Raidan has received a report from a local doctor working in Tono. He personally tended an entire okui family that had fallen ill, and he fears that they were only the beginning."

Sen shook his head, clearly troubled by this disturbing new develop-ment. "I had problems with human bandits last spring, raiding farms on my southern border," he said. "There were reports about a strange sickness afflicting some of the folk who'd suffered raids. I figured the bandits had to be the source, though there'd never been any other times I could remem-ber where elves came down with a human sickness. I sent my son Ashinji to investigate. He did find and destroy a gang of raiders but whether any of them carried the illness..." Sen shrugged.

"Did any more folk fall ill after your son wiped out the bandit gang?" Raidan asked.

"Not to my knowledge," Sen replied. His grey-green eyes darted from side to side, then locked onto the king's face. "Great Goddess!" he exclaimed. "I've just had a thought, and it's not a pleasant one."

When Sen failed to elaborate, the king prompted him. "Yes, what is it?"

"If I was the empress, I'd first send a smaller, more mobile force early on, to the northeast, before the first thaw."

"That would mean..." Raidan began, but Keizo finished his sentence.

"Sending part of our army back to Kerala, further worsening the odds when the major offensive is launched against Tono. We are already out-numbered at least three to one. If we are forced to defend ourselves on two fronts..."

"I don't think Constantia wants to spend the resources to keep two separate armies in the field at the same time," Raidan interjected. "Her ultimate goal is the conquest of Alasiri. In order to accomplish this, she must take Sendai. She can't come straight at us from Darguinia because she won't be able to get an army through the Shikhat Fens. The surest way to open a road to the capital is by taking the Tono Valley."

"I agree with you, Brother," Keizo said, "but I also believe that she'll send a diversionary force into Kerala, regardless."

As the lengthy discussion progressed, Raidan continued his observa-tion of Sen's two sons. Sadaiyo, clearly annoyed at having to stand, strug-gled to hide his displeasure. His arrogant face and proud bearing spoke of one used to getting his way in all things. His garments, though dusty and rumpled from travel, were rich and fashionably cut.

In contrast, Ashinji wore the smooth, expressionless visage of a professional soldier, trained to stand for long stretches of time. Despite his high station, he had chosen to wear the plain, serviceable clothing of a cavalry officer. Only his eyes betrayed his interest in the tactical discussion; Raidan could sense a keen mind behind the blank face.

The prince felt a momentary pang of pity for Sen Sakehera. The general had always been shrewd, competent, and completely devoid of arrogance. Raidan understood now why Sen loved his younger son with such tender devotion and his Heir, perhaps, not at all.

No good can possibly come of it, Raidan decided.

"Ai, Goddess, I am tired," Sen grumbled. "I need a hot soak and a good night's sleep to clear the cobwebs from my head. I'll be of far more use to you tomorrow, Majesty."

"Please forgive me, old friend," Keizo apologized. "I am keeping you from your much needed rest." He glanced at Sen's sons. "I'm sure all of you will be happy to seek your beds."

"There is one last thing I want to discuss with you before we go," Sen said. The king nodded. "Last spring, I took a young girl into my employ...a *hikui* refugee, fled from her home in Amsara, the Soldaran duchy across my southern border."

Raidan sensed an immediate, profound change in the attitudes of both younger Sakeheras. They stood like two hounds, alert and quivering, one with hostility, the other with apprehension.

"From Amsara, you say?" Keizo leaned forward with interest. "What about this girl?"

"A few weeks ago, she saved my life during a hunting accident. If it hadn't been for her sharp-shooting, I would have been gutted on the tusks of a wild boar." Sen chuckled. "I'm still amazed by it. A single arrow, right through the eye! Anyway, as a reward for saving my sorry backside, I promised to present her to you." Abruptly, Sen's cheerful expression turned serious. "Majesty, she is seeking information on the identity of her sire."

"Who is an elf, I presume?" Keizo asked.

"Yes." Sen gazed intently at the king. "She has a signet ring which she claims the man who fathered her gave to her human mother, so she would know that she came from a noble elven house." Sen paused.

Raidan stared at his brother. Keizo now sat rigidly upright in his chair, his fingers clenched and bone-white upon the armrests. "Go on," the king said slowly.

"I have the ring with me. I promised Jelena that I'd show it to you. I believe that you may be able to shed some light on...on her possible identity."

"Show me the ring now," the king commanded, holding out his hand.

Without another word, Sen reached into a small pouch at his belt and withdrew an object, which he dropped onto Keizo's open palm.

The king stared at the ring in his hand for several heartbeats, then closed it up in his fist. He leaned back in his chair and gazed past Sen's head, his eyes unfocused, as if lost in a memory.

Raidan stared at the king in astonishment. He recognized the ring immediately as his brother's, made especially for Keizo and presented to him on the day he had achieved his majority. Supposedly, Keizo had lost it many years ago. Raidan wore a similar ring, in keeping with the tradition of all Onjara princes. Both rings were non-magical copies of the White Griffin Ring of State that now encircled the third finger of Keizo's right hand.

How, by the One Great Goddess, did my brother's ring fall into the hands of a half-human girl?

"You say the girl's name is Ja..."

"Jelena, Majesty. A popular Soldaran name for girls, apparently. She soon proved herself a good worker and became a valuable member of my household. We all became quite fond of her, especially my son Ashinji. So fond in fact, that he married her!"

Keizo focused on Ashinji, his expression unreadable. "Your son is married to this girl? You freely gave your permission?" he asked.

"Yes, Majesty, I did. She had no family to speak for her...so there was no one else I needed to consult." Sen's eyes narrowed; his voice remained meticulously neutral.

A disturbing suspicion nibbled at the edges of Raidan's thoughts. He cast his mind backward in time. A little over eighteen years ago, just before the tragic accident that had set him on the throne, Keizo had returned from a journey in the far eastern reaches of Alasiri, several weeks late and with a poorly mending broken leg. It had taken all of the skills of the court physician and the magical abilities of a well-known mage to restore his brother's leg to full function. Keizo had always insisted an elderly farmer and his wife had rescued him after he had taken a nasty tumble from his horse.

Raidan had always known his brother concealed important details about what had really happened; long ago, the prince had suppressed most of his Talent in favor of scientific training, but he still retained the ability to Truthread. Despite knowing of his brother's deliberate deception, Raidan had never pressed Keizo on it. He had decided to respect his brother's privacy.

Now, it seemed that the truth might, at long last, be revealed.

"Sen, my old friend, I want you to bring the girl to me tonight... now, in fact."

"Now, Majesty? I...I think she's probably sleeping...."

"That doesn't matter. Wake her if you have to." Keizo's voice held the unmistakable tone of a command.

"Yes...of course." Sen stood and bowed, his sons following suit. All three men then left the room.

Raidan sat and stared at the side of Keizo's face for several heartbeats. Finally, he summoned the voice to speak.

"This girl, Brother...who is she? I need to know the truth!"

"So do I, Brother," the king replied.

6
Questions And Answers

Keizo tightened his hand around the ring. "I've never told anyone the entire story of what happened to me during those weeks I went missing, just before I became king. There was a girl...a human girl. She saved my life. Let me show you her face."

Raidan opened his mind and allowed Keizo to share the image—a face, unmistakably human, smiling and dark-eyed. Even now, the prince felt the potent emotions the memory awakened in his brother.

"You *loved* this human, Zin?" Raidan asked.

"Yes. I would have died, if not for her."

"A *human* girl..."

"Is it so hard to believe?" Keizo snapped. "We elves and humans are not that different, not really! Yes, I loved her and she loved me, but in the end, I had to leave her. I gave her my prince's ring as a token of my love. I never considered the possibility..." The king paused, then whispered, "Brother...I think Sakehera's hikui stray might be mine."

With those words, the very foundations upon which Raidan had built and ordered his life crumbled and blew away like dust upon the wind. A cloud of anger threatened to overwhelm his mind, but he quickly suppressed it.

I can't let Keizo know how his confession has affected me. There's too much at stake!

Raidan rose to his feet. "If this hikui girl is yours, Brother, you must handle the matter with the utmost care. The last thing Alasiri needs right now is a scandal."

"Don't you think I know that?" Keizo glared at Raidan with challenging eyes. "But if she is my child, I'll not turn my back on her."

"I think it's time for me to leave you alone. When you've finished interviewing the girl, send for me." Raidan turned on his heel and stalked from the room.

Keizo has fathered a child!

The words buzzed through Raidan's brain like a swarm of angry hornets as he strode down the deserted, night-silent corridors of the castle. The implications were enormous and far-reaching.

What if my brother decides to acknowledge this girl? Will he attempt to set her above me and my sons?

That must never be allowed.

I'll kill her myself if it comes down to that. I'll not let some bastard hikui rob me and mine of what is rightfully ours!

Keizo the Younger had ascended the throne of Alasiri only after a freak accident had claimed the life of King Okame—Raidan and Keizo's eldest brother—and his entire family. Keizo had yet to marry; in fact, he had shown total disinterest in the idea, and his longtime companion, Lady Sonoe, had so far produced no children.

As long as his brother remained unmarried and childless, Raidan and his sons were Keizo's official Heirs.

It won't matter if this girl is Keizo's offspring. She's a half-blood, and illegitimate. By law, she can't be the Heir, unless...

Keizo could officially recognize and legitimize her, but in order to name her as Heir, he would have to change the law of the land. The King's Council would surely fight such an action, and in the end, Raidan doubted the elven people would accept a hikui as their future sovereign.

Let Keizo recognize this girl as his daughter, let him bestow upon her every rank and privilege of an Onjara princess. She can be no threat to me, unless she foolishly dares to set herself up as one. And if she does, she can be eliminated.

Raidan took a deep breath to steady himself.

I must remain calm. I've nothing to worry about.

His heart ceased its headlong gallop and his steps slowed as he approached the double doors that led to his family's private quarters. As he entered, the sound of his wife's voice, raised in anger, drifted from an inner chamber. He followed the trail of heated words into his wife's day room.

Princess Taya Onjara stood with her back to the door, hands clenched into fists by her side. Her head whipped around, green eyes flashing, as Raidan entered the room. "By the Goddess, your son has really done it this time!" she exclaimed.

Raidan's heart skipped a beat. Even after forty years of marriage, he still thought Taya the most beautiful of all women.

The object of his wife's fury—their eldest child, Raidu—stood before her, radiating defiance. She turned away from Raidan to face their son. "Go ahead... Tell your father, if you dare!" The young man's chin lifted in obstinate refusal.

Raidu had always been rebellious by nature—even more so, now that he had officially reached adulthood. Raidan knew he ought to deal with his son's perceived misdeed immediately, but he could not afford any distractions now.

"Not now, Wife," Raidan responded.

Taya's eyes widened in surprise. She opened her mouth to object but Raidan cut her off. "Whatever Raidu has done this time, we will deal with it later. I have serious news." He turned toward Raidu. "It's late, Son," he said quietly. "Go to bed." Raidu regarded his father speculatively for a few moments.

There's so much of his mother in him, the prince thought. *Same green eyes and auburn hair, same nose and chin.*

Raidu departed with a final backward glance, leaving Raidan alone with Taya. He reached out and grabbed her hands, and before she could speak, he opened his mind to her.

Taya entered easily through the mental link they had forged years ago, a link that had grown stronger and more secure with the intimacy of their long marriage. She soon knew everything he did about the girl claiming to be Keizo's daughter.

Taya withdrew, then lifted her right index finger and traced a glowing symbol in the air. As it flashed, then dissolved, Raidan felt the tingling caress of magical energy against the bare skin of his face and hands.

The two of them stood in silence for several heartbeats, then Taya said, "The room wards are up. We can speak freely." Raidan nodded in understanding. "This girl is undoubtedly an Onjara, and dangerous, Husband, but not in the way you think," Taya continued.

"What do you mean?" Raidan replied. "How do you know for sure?"

Taya drifted over to the room's single, large window, open to the cool evening breezes. "What I am going to tell you now must not leave this room, Husband. Only two others know the entire truth, and it is vital that it remain so, for now."

Raidan felt a chill finger stroke his backbone.

"I and my fellows in the Society have known about this girl for some time, and we believe..."

"What?" Raidan exclaimed, shock roughening his voice. "You've known about her... and you didn't tell me...or my brother? How can this be?"

"Please, Husband, just listen to me, now!"

"You knew about this girl all along...and, yet you said nothing," Raidan whispered. His nostrils flared, the only outward sign of his growing anger. For the first time in all the years he'd been married, he felt the bitter sting of ...

No. Betrayal is too strong a word. Never that, not from her.

Unconsciously stroking the gold wedding bracelet on his right wrist, he chose his next words with care. "There is nothing you do that has no sound reason behind it, Wife, so...because I trust you above all others...I will listen and...hold...my...temper!"

Taya sat down on the padded bench beneath the window and after an instant's hesitation, Raidan joined her.

"The Society believes that this girl is the vessel chosen by our predecessors to harbor that which they sought to safeguard from their...no, from *our* greatest enemy," Taya explained in a soft, steady voice. "The Key has returned."

"Is this...this key some kind of magic?" Raidan asked.

"Yes," Taya replied. "A very powerful and dangerous magic."

In addition to her high office as Crown Princess of Alasiri, Taya served as Mistress of the Kirian Society—the secretive collective of mages whose members were drawn from the most Talented of all of the land's trained practitioners. Most of the time, Raidan stayed out of Taya's way whenever she and her fellow mages met and conducted their business within the royal apartments, but occasionally, he couldn't help but overhear some of what they discussed. He had never once doubted that he'd heard only what they had deemed safe for outsiders to know, and he had no memory of hearing anything about a key.

"The accounts are clear," Taya continued. "The chronicles of the Society state that the Key will return to the material world harbored in the body of one born to the Onjara lineage. My colleague, Amara Sakehera, has lived closely with the girl for several weeks now. In fact, her son and this girl were recently married. It was Amara Sakehera who first discovered the Key within her new daughter-in-law, and she alerted the rest of us."

"But this girl is hikui, and I'm still not entirely convinced that she's an Onjara. How could a half-blood have the necessary strength to carry such a burden?" Raidan shook his head, his mind still unwilling to accept his wife's words, despite his gut's insistence that she spoke the truth.

"She is an Onjara, Husband. Sen Sakehera suspected the truth months ago, when the girl first came to Kerala, but he had to wait until he knew her character before he could act."

"Goddess' tits," Raidan cursed, not knowing whether to be angry with Sakehera, or grateful. "My brother's ring. Of course she would've shown it to Sen...That's how he knew. She came to Alasiri looking for her elven sire, after all!"

Taya nodded. "Her Onjara blood gives her strength enough. I and my colleagues here in Sendai are to examine the girl tomorrow. We'll know more then. But make no mistake. We all firmly believe she is the Key."

Taya was the only person he knew with a keener intelligence than his own. Raidan trusted her instincts completely. "If you say this girl is your long-awaited Key, then I know it's the truth," he said. "Keizo will surely claim her. He might even attempt to get the council to go along with changing the law so that she can be named Heir. What then?"

"It won't matter. Her fate is already sealed." Taya looked down at the intricately tattooed palms of her hands. "We of the Society are tasked with re-securing the Key. In order to do this, the magic must be separated from its present vessel." She paused, then added, "The vessel cannot survive the Sundering. The girl won't live long enough pose any threat to you or our son." Taya laid her head against Raidan's shoulder. "Rest easy, love," she soothed.

Raidan could feel her caressing his mind and using her magic to subtly influence his mood, but, because he trusted her implicitly, he allowed himself to be calmed.

"I know you are angry with me for not telling you the truth when first I learned of it, my love, but I was sworn to secrecy, as were we all. The danger was...is... just too great."

"So you keep saying, Wife." Raidan lifted Taya's chin and stared deep into her eyes. Her hair smelled of jasmine, a fragrance she knew he found irresistible. He slipped his arm around her waist. "You know I'd rather leave magical business to you and your fellow mages, but this...this seems too important." Raidan could feel his agitation returning. "Just how worried should I be?"

"This is the task of the Kirians," Taya stated firmly. "You need not concern yourself directly...Not yet, anyway. All you need to be sure of is that this girl poses no threat to you, Husband."

"If you say this is so..." He fell silent, but despite Taya's assurances, he still felt unsettled.

With an effort, he forced himself to turn his mind to the matter of their son. "Tell me about Raidu. What's he done now? I don't suppose it will go away on its own, whatever it is?"

"Not without help," Taya responded dryly. "It seems our son has been consorting with a certain hikui girl in the town... the daughter of his favorite boot maker."

"Oh, Goddess, no!" Raidan groaned and covered his eyes. "Please don't tell me..."

Taya sighed. "I'm afraid so. The girl is at least four months pregnant, Raidu tells me."

"Damn him! Well, royal by-blows are nothing new. Is he certain it's his?"

"Oh, yes. He admitted to taking certain...magical means to insure her fidelity, but not her infertility." She clicked her tongue in exasperation. "He is quite proud of himself!"

Raidan shook his head. "Perhaps the girl won't want the child."

"Of course she'll want it! It's a royal bastard!"

"First my brother and now my own son!" Raidan muttered with bitter amusement, unable to ignore the irony of the situation. "Raidu must learn to deal with his own messes," he stated flatly. "Since he's admitting it's his, he'll do the honorable thing and support the child and its mother, but with his own money, not ours."

They sat quietly for a time, each of them lost in thought.

I must not let events control me! As soon as they do, all is lost!

All of these things can and will be resolved, my love, but you needn't worry about them now... Let me soothe you, Husband...

Taya folded his hands in hers and leaned forward to gently press her lips to his. Raidan felt the familiar, welcome stirring in his loins that always happened whenever his wife touched him. The anger and frustration built up within him drained away, and desire took its place. He pulled Taya hard against him to deepen their kiss. The wards remained in place; no one could enter the room without Taya's leave. They were completely safe.

Raidan reached up and removed the ornate gold pins that held Taya's hair in place. With a shake of her head, she sent her auburn tresses tumbling down around her shoulders and back. Her jade-green eyes smoldered as she let her simple lounging robe slip to the floor. Languidly, she moved from the window seat to the couch and lay upon it, ready to receive him. Raidan took a moment to savor the sight of his wife's nakedness, then eagerly freed himself from the confines of his own clothing.

With a heartfelt sigh, he sank into Taya's embrace. After so many years together, they no longer needed words when it came to the mutual pleasuring of their bodies, and at the exact moment of climax, Raidan felt his consciousness merge with his wife's; for a time, they were as one, sailing together on successive waves of ecstasy.

It was this unity of consciousness that Raidan so craved, loved, and valued. Because he could only achieve it with Taya, he had no desire to make love to any other woman.

Afterwards, they lay together on the couch, sipping cool, sweet wine from silver goblets. As Raidan stroked his wife's smooth back, his thoughts were wistful.

Ai, when we were young, Wife, you could get me up again with just a smile... Ah, well. That time is past now. Age does take its toll.

This realization did not make him sad, though. The intensity of their lovemaking had only grown stronger as they had aged, even as the frequency had declined.

It's an equitable trade.

He breathed in the intermingled scents of jasmine and sex and allowed his mind to float. Taya shifted in his arms, then sat up and looked down at him, frowning "Husband..." she started, but he laid a finger on her lips.

"Hush, Wife. Not now," he whispered. "Tomorrow."

7

The Search Is Over

J elena... Wake up."
Jelena awoke with a start. She had no memory of having fallen
asleep. She opened her eyes and extended her arms to Ashinji, a drowsy
smile curving her lips. The bed in which she lay felt soft and comfortable,
and she would not have stirred for anyone except her husband.

Despite her weariness and the lateness of the hour, the sight of his face
sent a tingle of desire coursing through her loins. "What are you waiting
for? Come to bed," she whispered invitingly.

"Jelena, listen to me," Ashinji murmured. "You have to get up and get
dressed now. The king has commanded that you be brought to him."

Jelena sat up, all sleepiness evaporated. "The king has sent for me?
Now? But...but it's the middle of the night!" In the dim light cast by the
single lamp, Ashinji's eyes looked as dark as the sea during a tempest and
she saw fear in their depths.

Her heart leapt like a deer. "Ashi, what's wrong? What is happening?"
She reached out to him and the coverlets slipped off her bare torso. Ashinji
drew her to him and held her so tightly, she gasped. She could feel his
body shaking. He caressed her breasts and she responded with a sigh, her
nipples hardening under his gentle fingers. She buried her face against his
neck, drinking in his scent.

As she slipped her hands beneath his tunic, he groaned and pulled
away.

"We can't do this now. My father is waiting downstairs. Get up and
I'll help you dress." He twitched back the covers and scooped her up, setting her on her feet by the side of the bed.

"I...I haven't had time to unpack...I have only my old clothes.... What
am I supposed to wear?" She stood with arms wrapped around her body,
shivering, though the room was not cold.

"Your old clothes will have to do. I don't think the king will notice what you are wearing." He reached into the wooden chest at the foot of the bed and pulled out Jelena's tunic and trousers.

As she donned her garments, she watched Ashinji from the corner of her eye; she could see him struggling to remain calm. Jelena swallowed hard and took a deep breath. "We've spoken of this, Ashi. If the king is my real father, it changes nothing."

"You're wrong, love. It'll change everything," Ashinji said quietly.

Jelena sat down on the edge of the bed and pulled on her boots, then rose to check herself in the looking glass. She plucked at the coiled mass of her hair, fluffing it into a less unruly arrangement, then squared her shoulders. "I'm ready," she declared. Ashinji pulled her close and kissed her neck. "Don't be afraid, Ashi," she whispered. "I'm your wife now. No one, not even the king, can separate us!"

"The king can do whatever he likes with his own," Ashinji replied, then took her hand. Together, they descended the stairs to the sitting room.

Sen and Amara stood side by side in the center of the room. Both of them fixed their eyes upon Jelena as she entered. Without warning, a wave of dizziness overcame her and she staggered against Ashinji, who locked his arm around her waist to keep her from falling.

"What is it, love?" Ashinji's face looked stricken.

"Jelena! Are you feeling ill, my dear?" Sen must have noticed her momentary distress."

"I just felt a little dizzy...It's nearly passed," she said. Ashinji stared at her, frowning. "Ashi...really. It's passed, I promise," she added. "I'm just very nervous about meeting the king."

"Jelena...This is what you've been waiting for!" Sen laid a reassuring hand on her shoulder. "Tonight, your search ends."

"May Ashi come with me?" Jelena asked.

Sen nodded. "We will accompany you to the king's presence, but he will speak with you alone. Come now, let's not keep him waiting."

Amara kissed Jelena lightly on the forehead. "Don't be afraid..." then added in mindspeech, *Remember who you are!*

Jelena nodded in reply.

"I don't know when we'll be back. Don't wait up!" Sen called over his shoulder as they departed. "She will, of course," he muttered as he closed the doors behind them.

Sen led the way through the dim halls of the night-shrouded castle. Jelena gripped Ashinji's hand as if her very life depended on not letting go. After passing through a set of large doors guarded by a pair of stone-faced soldiers, the three of them walked through a final set of doors into a small room furnished with a writing table, a couch, and several stools. The man seated at the table looked up as they entered.

Jelena knew immediately that this must be Keizo Onjara.

The guard who had announced them withdrew, and the king stood. Jelena dropped to one knee and lowered her head in the Soldaran style as Sen and Ashinji bowed.

"Majesty, this is my son's wife, Jelena," Sen stated. Jelena sensed, rather than saw, the king move to stand in front of her. His presence felt like a glowing furnace, blasting her with energy. She felt something within her respond, tugging like a hound eager to slip its lead. She dared to look up.

Eyes grey as a winter storm met hers, yet she saw no coldness there.

"Thank you, old friend," the king replied, then addressed Ashinji. "Captain Sakehera, I need to speak to your wife in private, if I may." His level voice revealed nothing of what he might be thinking.

Jelena looked over her shoulder at her husband. The king didn't need his permission, of course, but Jelena saw that Ashi appreciated the gesture of respect. He nodded and replied, "Of course, Majesty." A single tear gathered at the corner of his left eye, but he reached up and dashed it away before it could fall. Sen looked at her and smiled, then he and Ashinji exited the room, leaving Jelena alone with the king.

"You may sit," Keizo said, indicating a cushioned stool to her right. Jelena got up off her knee and settled upon the stool. She folded her hands in her lap and kept her eyes downcast.

The king sat in the chair at his writing table. "How well do you speak Siri-dar?" he inquired.

"Well enough, your Majesty," Jelena answered. "I am getting better every day."

"Your accent is still quite heavy," he commented, but she heard no unkindness or criticism in his tone. "Your name is Jelena." He phrased it as a statement, not a question. "Tell me about yourself, Jelena."

Jelena raised her eyes.

Ashinji and Sen both, at times, had referred to the king as Silverlock, and Jelena now knew why. The hair from which he derived his nickname fell unbound to just below his shoulders. He looked to be about the same age as Sen, with a lean and ascetically handsome face. Fine lines creased the corners of his eyes.

He wore a deep blue tunic and trousers of raw silk, richly decorated with an embroidered pattern of sleek, calico carp. Padded socks and leather sandals covered his feet. He wore no jewelry save a large ruby in his left ear and a heavy signet ring of white gold upon his right hand. He held his left hand closed around something.

The king studied her closely, as if trying to memorize every detail of her face. Jelena had to struggle not to squirm under the intensity of his gaze. He tilted his head to one side, expectant.

Nervously, she cleared her throat.

"I was born at a place known as Amsara, in the castle of my uncle the duke. My mother was his only sister." Jelena told her story concisely, with little embellishment. She had no desire to inspire pity in this man, nor did she want any special favors from him. She only wanted to know if she had the right to call him 'Father'.

As she spoke, Silverlock continued to study her, but his manner remained reassuring, and she felt her apprehension slowly melt away.

"And so, my father-in-law brought me with him to Sendai, so that I might ask your help, Majesty." Jelena fell silent, her story concluded.

"Sen Sakehera is my oldest friend. We were boys together," Keizo said, a wistful note coloring his voice. He rolled the hidden object around in his left hand, then opened his fingers to reveal Jelena's ring. "But even Sen didn't know certain things about me...until tonight."

"That is my ring, Majesty, but...of course, you already know that. Did it tell you anything...about who my father might be?" Jelena asked. She almost dared not breathe.

"Let me tell you a story now," the king replied softly. "Many years ago, a young man set out on a journey to visit the home of an old friend who lived far to the east, a friend he hadn't seen in awhile. While on the road, he heard stories of increased trouble with humans in the border areas to the southeast. Because he held a high position in the land, he felt it was his duty to investigate, and so he made a detour for that purpose."

"While riding through the forest along the border, the man stumbled upon an armed human patrol. The humans immediately gave chase, and the man rode for his life, knowing that if the soldiers caught him, they would kill him. He managed to lose his pursuers, but his horse stumbled badly and threw the man down into a dry creek bed. He landed hard and broke his leg."

Jelena gasped in dismay, but said nothing, not wanting to disturb the king's train of thought.

"He lay for a very long time in that hot, dry streambed, tormented by pain and thirst. He nearly lost his life, but the Goddess at last granted him mercy and sent his deliverance in the form of a woman. This woman shielded him from his enemies and tended his body while his injuries healed."

"Ai," the king sighed, "those weeks were so long, pain-filled, and fraught with peril... not just for the man, but for his caregiver as well, for, you see, they were in constant danger of discovery. The man pleaded with the woman to leave him and return to her home. He knew that if she were found harboring him, she would share his fate. Her own people would kill her, just as they would kill him. She refused."

It's just as Claudia told me...as my mother told her, Jelena thought. She dared to look directly at the king as he spoke, and imagined what her mother's feelings must have been like while gazing at the same face.

"A strange thing began to happen between the two of them," the king continued, "although, if one thinks about it, it doesn't seem so strange after all. Like a rose through winter snow, love bloomed in their hearts. The strength of his feelings took the man completely by surprise, but the woman confessed to him that she had known, from the beginning, that this was meant to be."

"They spent three, joyous, heart-wrenching days as lovers. The man, despite his pain, made love to his dear one with intense, bittersweet passion. They both cried many tears of anguish, for they knew their love could never leave the shelter of their hiding place. It had to end when he became strong enough to make his escape."

"On the day he left, the man gave the woman the only possession of his that he had to give. A small remembrance, perhaps, but after all, it was enough." He leaned forward, his eyes locked to hers, then said, "I slipped my ring onto Drucilla's finger and left her behind. I never looked back, dared not, for if I had, I might not have had the strength to leave, and we would both be dead now. And you would have never been born."

Jelena felt a mantle of calm descend upon her. All of her anxiety melted before the power of the king's revelation.

Keizo slipped her ring onto the middle finger of his left hand, then extended both hands, palms down, towards her. Her ring was an exact match to the one he wore on his right hand. Both rings gleamed softly in the lamplight, but the king's seemed brighter, somehow. Jelena could only stare, first at Keizo's hands—so fine and beautiful—then at his face.

"One final test remains, a confirmation, really, of what I know in my heart to be true." The king removed the ring from his right hand and held it up before Jelena's eyes. "This is the White Griffin, the Ring of State that has passed down from one Onjara sovereign to the next. It has been over a thousand years since its making, and it contains powers that only one of true Onjara blood can awaken. Your ring is a copy of this one. " He held out his hand. "Put it on, Jelena."

Jelena looked at the ring on his palm, so like hers and yet.... "What if I put it on and nothing happens?" she whispered.

"Something will happen," the king declared. His tone left no room for doubt. Jelena picked the ring up off his palm and slipped it onto her right index finger.

The metal flared to life and glowed like a blue-white star, startling Jelena and dazzling her eyes. She felt the energy of the ring's magic pulling at her; deep within herself, her own magic—that which Amara called the Key— stirred in response. She looked at the king in astonishment. "It...I..." she stammered, unable to say anything more.

Keizo nodded in understanding. "Jelena, I could not have known that I left Drucilla with child, though I plead guilty to pushing the potential consequences of acting on our love from my mind. It was terribly selfish of me, and I realize that my excuses can only sound disgustingly weak to you...you who had to suffer from those very consequences. I never would have left you among your mother's people if I had known about you. Somehow, I would have found a way to rescue you."

Deep within her, Jelena felt a dam burst. She opened her mouth to cry out, but a mere trickle of sound escaped her lips, a barely breathed word.

"Father..."

The king opened his arms. "Come, Daughter," he whispered.

Jelena went to him, laid her head upon his chest, and lost herself in his embrace.

This can't be happening! I must be dreaming and I'm going to wake up any moment!

"What are you thinking, Jelena?"

Jelena sighed and opened her eyes. Keizo gazed earnestly at her, faint worry lines creasing his forehead. "I was just wondering when I was going to awaken from this beautiful dream," she answered.

"'Tis no dream, child. I'll gladly pinch you to prove it." He smiled, and Jelena's heart fluttered. That this man...*this* man, of all men, was her father seemed truly astounding.

"I...I do not know what to say, how to act. I'm just a...a..." She searched in vain for the correct word but the king spoke before she could.

"You are a daughter of the House of Onjara. In ancient high Siri-dar, *onjara* means 'griffin'. Our line has ruled unbroken in Alasiri for over a thousand years. Never doubt your blood, Jelena."

"You said that you loved my mother. How is that possible, that an elf could love a human?"

The sweet notes of a nightingale's song wafted in through the open window on a whisper of breeze. The glow cast by the brass lamps highlighted the planes of the king's face. His eyes were pensive. "Does not Ashinji Sakehera love you? It's easy, Daughter, when a man and a woman see each other as just that, and they refuse to allow petty distinctions to cloud their ability to give and receive love. Drucilla, to me, was my savior. I didn't see a human female when I looked at her, I saw the woman I loved."

Jelena looked down at her palms and saw the callused, work-roughened hands of a servant, not the fine smooth ones of a princess.

How will I ever find a place in my father's refined world, she thought.

A sudden wave of fear swept over her. "I...I cannot do this!" she gasped. "I haven't the slightest idea of how to be a...a princess! I was raised as a servant! I'm still amazed that Lord and Lady Sakehera have accepted me, but I don't for a moment believe that any of your other lords will. You don't have to pretend, Father. I know my very existence will cause trouble for you." Desperately, she looked up and dared to meet the king's eyes, searching for the slightest hint of anger or regret, but she saw only tenderness and understanding.

"I know that you're afraid, child. It's only natural. But you must trust me. I am your father and I will protect you."

Jelena closed her eyes and drew in a slow, deep breath. "I do trust you," she replied.

"Good," Keizo said. "And now, there is the question of your marriage."

Jelena's eyes flew open. "You can't make me give up Ashinji! I won't!" she cried, pushing herself out of the king's embrace. She took a step back from him and stood with hands clenched, her whole body trembling.

"And you think that it is proper for my only daughter to be wed to a mere second son with no lands or title, even if he is the child of my oldest friend, eh?" Jelena looked up sharply and caught the barest flicker of a smile tugging at the king's mouth. "Do you love lowly Captain Sakehera?" he asked.

"With all my heart!" Jelena whispered fiercely.

The king remained silent for several, agonizing heartbeats, arms folded across his chest, simply watching her. She forced herself to hold his gaze without wavering. At last, he spoke. "Then I, too, shall love him as a son." He held out his hand and Jelena went to him. After a moment, she relaxed in his arms and pushed aside her fears and uncertainties.

"You are so much like her," he murmured. "Same nose, same hair..." Gently, he stroked her curls.

"The only part of my mother I wish I could give up," Jelena responded ruefully.

Keizo laughed, but she heard a note of sadness in his voice. "Truly, I would have joined my life with Drucilla's if things had been different."

"The past can't be changed, Father. All we have is the present," Jelena said, looking up into his face.

"And the future is not yet written." He kissed her forehead and released her. "It's very late and I know you are tired. Go back to your husband now. I will send for the two of you tomorrow."

Part II

8

The Woman In Red

Ashi, you'll squeeze the life out of me!" Jelena gasped. Ashinji loosened his fierce hold and cradled her body more gently against his.

"I'm sorry, my love...it's just I still can't believe I'm not going to lose you," he whispered into her ear. Jelena caressed his cheek and entwined her fingers in his hair. She lay her head on his chest and felt the steady, slow pulse of his heart beneath his skin. A delicious lassitude weighted down her limbs. She wished never to move from this place.

It had been a long, emotionally exhausting night, and the two of them had only just crawled into their bed, after closing the shutters against the rosy glow of dawn. The king had provided her with an escort back to the Sakehera family quarters, and after thanking and leaving them at the door, she had entered to find Ashinji and both his parents awaiting her return.

Sen and Amara exchanged embraces with her, but neither one asked any questions; still, Jelena knew her in-laws would expect a full account after she had gotten some much needed rest. Sen had promised to allow her and Ashinji to sleep undisturbed for as long as they wished.

Now snug beneath the coverlets, Jelena's mind drifted for a while in the gray country between the waking world and the realm of dreams. At first, she remained aware of the comforting warmth of Ashinji's body next to hers, but gradually, she lost all sense of him as her consciousness slipped away and she found herself walking alone on a featureless, unending plain.

A leaden sky merged with the dull horizon. She felt no breath of wind, nor heard any sound. Off in the distance, she spied a peculiar splash of color and altered her course to move toward it.

The blot of color gradually came into focus as Jelena drew closer, resolving itself into the figure of a woman. She stood straight and regal as a queen. She wore a long gown of vivid flame-red, form-fitting and low cut, a perfect match to the fiery tresses that cascaded around her shoulders. A mask, porcelain-smooth and white as bone, concealed the woman's face. Only her eyes were visible, sea-green and glowing with chilly intensity. A round black stone, hung upon a gold chain, nestled in the cleft between her pale breasts.

Jelena's eyes were drawn to the stone almost against her will and as she stared into its depths—helpless to look away—she realized that the stone seemed *alive* somehow. She shuddered in horror as the malignant intelligence coiled within its crystalline structure extended a tendril to caress her mind. Jelena moaned in fear and tried to run, but her feet had merged with the gray dust, trapping her where she stood.

You cannot run, little one, the woman crooned in a voice as sweet as honey. *Nor can you escape your fate. He will have the Key, and his triumph will be assured.*

Without warning, the woman raised her hand and struck Jelena's face. A blood-red fingernail, sharp as a dagger, scored a burning trail across her cheek.

Jelena screamed...

...and awoke, fighting for breath.

"Jelena! I'm here...you're safe, love!" Ashinji pinned her flailing arms to her sides and held her tight as she struggled. "You were having a bad dream, that's all, but you're safe now!"

The surreal terror of the dream leaked from her body, leaving her weak and trembling. "I feel sick," she whispered, and pushing out of Ashinji's arms, she fumbled for the chamber pot.

Ashinji rubbed her back as she purged. Afterward, she lay against the pillows, drained and miserable as he stroked her hair and face with gentle fingers. "Can you handle a little wine, or perhaps tea would be better?" he asked.

"Tea, I think," Jelena answered.

"I'll just get rid of this," Ashinji said, gingerly picking up the chamber pot as he left the bed. Jelena heard him slip through the bedroom door and pad down the stairs. Her stomach did another roll and it took all of her concentration not to vomit once more. She wondered at the vividness of the strange dream and its unsettling effect on her. She had experienced nightmares before, but never had they resulted in physical illness.

She opened her eyes at the sound of Ashinji's return. He carried a tray with a teapot and two cups, along with a small round loaf of bread. He carefully placed the tray on the bed.

"The family's up and eating breakfast. Mother thought a little plain bread would help to settle your stomach," he said.

"Ugh, I don't know, Ashi. Maybe just the tea." Jelena sat up and leaned forward to allow Ashinji to mound the pillows behind her back. He filled both cups with the hot brew and placed one in her hands. Tentatively, she raised the cup to her lips and took a small sip.

The morning sun glowed through the shutters of their bedroom window. By the strength of the light, Jelena guessed it to be well past dawn. She had only been asleep a couple of hours, at most. Ashinji drank his tea in silence, studying her over the rim of his cup with worried eyes.

"I suppose we'd better get up and get dressed. I don't think either of us will sleep any more today." Jelena sighed and took another, larger sip of her tea.

"How do you feel?" Ashinji asked.

"Better. The tea is definitely helping." Her rebellious stomach did not feel in quite such an uproar any longer.

"Tell me about your dream."

Jelena sorted the images in her mind, trying to make sense of them, then recapped her vision as best she could recall. "I had the same dream once before, or one very much like it, except the woman in the red gown wasn't there that time," she added. "She frightened me, Ashi. I felt like I was in the presence of evil, but it didn't seem to come directly from her, which was odd. It came from the strange stone she wore around her neck. What can all this mean?"

"Dreams aren't literal. Their imagery is symbolic," Ashinji explained. "The woman could represent an actual enemy...or an ally, sent to warn you. One of the most common manifestations of Talent is lucid and prophetic dreaming. My own small Talent manifests that way. I dreamt of you long before I found you on that riverbank. This woman in the red gown...she spoke to you of a key.... A key to what, I wonder?"

"Oh!" Jelena exclaimed. ""With all the worry and excitement about my meeting with the king...I completely forgot to tell you!"

"Tell me what?"

"Yesterday evening, right after you and your father and brother went to meet with the king, your mother sat me down and told me she knew all about my blue fire." After she had repeated to Ashinji what Amara had told her, she shook her head and said, "I still have trouble believing any of it is true, but how can it not be? Your mother has said it is so."

Ashinji tugged hard on the rings in his ear, frowning. "Why didn't my mother tell me any of this?"

"Perhaps she did not wish to worry you. Ashi, your mother says that the Kirian Society can deal with...this key thing."

Ashinji shook his head and a stray lock of hair fell across his eyes. He brushed it away impatiently. He took her face between his hands and looked deep into her eyes. "Whatever this all means, if it bodes danger for you, I will protect you." He kissed her on the lips then, with visible effort, smiled and said, "A delivery came for you just now."

Jelena raised an eyebrow. "Who would want to send me anything?" she asked.

"I think it's from the king," Ashinji replied, pausing for dramatic effect.

"What? What is it?" Jelena cried, goaded by the look of sly amusement on her husband's face.

"I saw a most becoming tunic and trousers in green and blue with a matching pair of slippers. Quite suitable for a high-born lady, or, dare I say, a princess? Shall I go get them, or perhaps you'd rather keep your old clothes?"

Jelena growled and playfully punched Ashinji's shoulder. "I'll take the new things, thank you very much!" she exclaimed, then sighed and looked down at her hands. "I may be the king's daughter, but I don't know if I'll ever get used to the idea of being a princess," she remarked softly.

Ashinji did not reply, and when Jelena looked at him to gauge his thoughts, she could see the war he waged with his feelings—apprehension and happiness together made of his face a shifting landscape of emotion. She knew Ashinji found it just as hard to process the stunning change in her circumstances as she did, and Jelena believed she understood why.

All of her life, she had struggled with feelings of inferiority. Because she had believed herself unworthy of it, she had almost let the blessing of true love slip through her fingers. Now, the man who had freely given her this most precious of gifts suffered from the very feelings that had afflicted her for so long.

"I love you, Ashi," she murmured. "You'll never lose me, no matter what."

"I'm only a captain in the army, my love," Ashinji said. "I have nothing but what my father, and when he's gone, my brother, chooses to give me." He hung his head as he spoke. "You've said to me in the past that you felt you were not worthy of me, but in truth...it is I who is not worthy of you, Jelena." The pain in his voice tore at Jelena's heart.

"Stop talking nonsense, Ashinji Sakehera!" she chided. She grabbed his face and forced him to look at her. "You are stuck with me. Did you not promise to always protect me?"

"Yes, but..."

"But nothing! I am proud to be an army captain's wife.... Here, let me show you."

She pushed him down and straddled his hips. As their bodies joined in the timeless rite of lovemaking, Jelena strove to drive out all of Ashinji's doubts with the strength of her passion. Afterward, as they lay in each other's arms, the steady rise and fall of Ashinji's chest soon lulled Jelena back to sleep.

She awoke a short time later to find Ashinji propped on one elbow, watching her. She rubbed her eyes and yawned. "How long have I been asleep?"

"About an hour. Mother just knocked. She says it's time for you to get up and get dressed."

Jelena sat up and stretched. "She's presenting me to the other members of the Kirian Society today," she said.

"Oh, yes. My mother's mysterious society of mages. I had no idea she even still practiced magic until she started tutoring you. The idea that this 'blue fire' of yours must be removed from you because it's too dangerous for it to remain where it is...it scares me, love." He huffed in annoyance. "I just wish she'd told me about all of this herself."

"Please try not to worry, Ashi," Jelena said, stroking his cheek.

"Impossible," he replied. He rolled out of bed and crossed to the window to crack open the shutters. Jelena smiled with admiration. The sight of Ashi's bare backside made her want to drag him back to bed for another lovemaking session, but she knew Amara waited downstairs.

"How do you feel?" he asked, pulling a robe over his nakedness. "Nausea all gone?"

"Yes, thanks," Jelena replied. "The tea really helped. Truth be told, I haven't felt myself lately...I just hope I'm not coming down with the flux." She swung her legs over the side of the bed.

"What? You've been ill and you didn't tell me?" Ashinji came over and sat beside her, frowning. "How long has this been going on?"

Jelena sighed. "Since Nadaka Castle..."

"Nadaka Castle!" Ashinji cried. "That was over a week ago!"

"Yes, I know, but really...Ashi, it's nothing. I didn't want to worry you."

"You didn't want to..."

Jelena laid a finger on his lips to forestall any further outburst. "Hush, Husband. It's nothing. Truly."

"Everyone is keeping secrets from me," Ashinji muttered crossly.

Jelena kissed him. "I love you, Husband," she said, and her words seemed to mollify him. "Now, where are my new clothes?"

Ashinji stood and went to scoop up a bundle by the door. "Your new raiment, my princess," he announced in his best imitation of a court herald's pompous voice. He held out the garments with a flourish. "My mother brought them up." Jelena took the clothing from him and spent a moment admiring their color and cut.

"My father is a man with exquisite taste," she commented.

Having no time for a proper bath, they had to make do with a ewer and washbasin. Afterward, Jelena put on her new outfit, marveling at the luxurious feel of the fabric. It brought back the bittersweet memory of the gown she had worn on that fateful Sansa night at Amsara Castle, nearly a year ago.

Ashinji, as usual, donned his plain, soldier's leathers. When he had finished dressing, he sat down at the end of the bed. Jelena braided his hair in a single queue, a task she had taken to doing for him each morning, just as he had made it his job to comb the snarls from her mane each evening. These small, loving gestures served to strengthen the bond between them.

When she had secured the braid with a leather tie, she stepped back and he stood and turned to face her. He raised his hands as if to touch her, then lowered them to his sides. "You...you look beautiful," he whispered. "Your Highness."

"No, Ashi, never 'Highness' to you," she insisted, shaking her head. "Only 'Jelena' or 'my love'."

He nodded and offered her his arm. "Allow a simple soldier to escort his lady, then," he replied.

She smiled and slipped her arm through his.

9

The Veil Is Lifted

From atop its lofty perch on the blue tiled roof of the keep's north tower, the raven watched and waited. Or rather, the intelligence that had enslaved the bird and now used its eyes waited, knowing that soon, the woman would come to walk in the garden below.

The bird held a shiny black stone within its beak. It knew nothing of the purpose of the stone; in fact, it knew nothing at all. The mind that now controlled the bird's body had obliterated the tiny part of its brain that had contained its rudimentary self awareness. It served as a tool, nothing more.

The sun passed zenith, and still, the raven waited.

At last, the woman came, as she always did, alone except for a small, silky-haired dog capering by her side.

The raven spread its wings and sprang from the roof. It glided unsteadily downward and came to a rough landing on the gravel path at the woman's feet. The stone tumbled from its beak.

The woman let out a startled cry and the little dog jumped back in a frenzy of barking. The raven stretched out its neck and squawked.

The woman swiftly recovered her composure. She turned and scooped the dog into her arms. "Hush, Jewel!" she scolded, and clutching the struggling animal to her breast, she approached the bird where it crouched upon the path, unmoving. She stopped a few paces away and stood regarding the raven with cool sea-green eyes, her sensuous mouth twisted a little in puzzlement.

The aura of her Talent outlined her body in a fiery halo.

He knew she was the right choice.

From across the vast distance that separated them, through sheer force of will, the Nameless One summoned a wave of energy and sent it spinning through the aether. It tore through the frail body of the raven and blasted the woman between her eyes. She fell backward onto the ground, her brilliant red hair fanning out on the gravel beneath her head. The dog tumbled out of her arms and fled, yapping in terror.

He spoke to the woman, mind to mind.

When he finished, he withdrew, leaving behind a link with which he could join with her when needed.

The ultimate tool was prepared and ready to use. It would bring the Key to him so he could complete the Working.

Deep within the icy darkness of his prison, the Nameless One writhed in pleasured anticipation of his freedom.

Back in the garden, the woman awoke from her swoon. She moaned softly and massaged the back of her head, but despite the pain, her eyes sparkled with understanding. She rose to her knees and searched the path until she found the black stone. Clutching it tightly in her hand, she climbed to her feet.

As she turned to run back toward the keep, the hem of her gown scattered a pile of scorched, black feathers.

* * *

"Jelena, these two of my colleagues, plus myself, are the only fully active members of the Kirian Society," Amara stated. She inclined her head toward the two women who sat, side by side, on a silk-upholstered couch. "Princess Taya Onjara, wife of the king's Heir and Mistress of the Society," she indicated the older of the two with a nod, then acknowledged the younger, "...and Lady Sonoe Kazama, official Companion of the king."

Jelena bowed low, in the elven style.

"Her manners are good, at least," Princess Taya commented. "Come here, child, and sit. We have much to discuss." Jelena quickly obeyed, settling cross-legged on a floor cushion at the feet of the two women. Amara pulled up a chair and sat to the right of the couch.

No one spoke for a long while, or at least, not out loud. Jelena kept her eyes on her folded hands, but she did not need to see the faces of the three women to know that they conversed in mindspeech. A surge of irritation threatened her composure, but she quickly suppressed it. The Kirians would address her when they had need to.

At last, Princess Taya spoke. "Jelena, I can only imagine the immense emotional strain you've had to endure in so short a time. How do you feel about all of this?" Jelena looked up sharply, surprised by the question.

"How do I feel?" She studied each of their faces, worried that this was some sort of test, and if she gave the wrong answer, they would deem her unworthy. She ran her tongue over lips gone dry and cleared her throat before answering. "I feel...uncertain. I mean, I am overjoyed to have finally found my father, and relieved that he accepts me, but...but my presence may cause him a lot of trouble, and I don't want that. As for the other, I have to admit that I am still struggling to understand just what part I am to play in this upcoming battle with...with..."

"The Nameless One," Lady Sonoe said, finishing Jelena's sentence. Her green eyes shimmered hypnotically. Jelena bit her lip.

There's something about her...

Jelena felt as if she had met her father's Companion before, though she knew she had never laid eyes upon the striking red-haired sorceress until now.

Suddenly, she remembered.

My dream!

"Do you know why we do not speak the true name of our adversary?" Lady Sonoe asked.

Jelena nodded. "A thousand years ago, when the Kirians defeated the sorcerer king Onjara, they stripped him of his power and erased all references to his true name from the records," she answered.

Lady Sonoe could be the woman I saw in the dream, but...but then that must mean the vision showed me an ally...not an enemy. Why, then, did I feel so afraid?

Aloud, she continued, "The Kirians did this to prevent the power of his name from falling into the wrong hands...of those who might use it to awaken him and usurp his magic for their own purposes."

"Very good." Princess Taya inclined her head in approval. "Amara says you are clever and a quick study. There is much to do to prepare you, but I have no doubt that you'll be ready. Now, there is just one final ordeal you'll undergo today. Sonoe and I must scan you. We both need to see for ourselves just what it is that you harbor."

Jelena took a deep breath; she had been expecting this. "May I lie down?"

"Of course," Princess Taya replied. Jelena made herself comfortable, closed her eyes, and waited.

This scan didn't hurt nearly as much as the first one Amara had performed on her back at Kerala. Jelena found the discomfort far more bearable because of the special breathing technique her mother-in-law had taught her. Even so, she felt wrung out and a little sick afterward. She remained prone until Amara lifted her into a sitting position and pressed a cup to her lips.

"Drink this, Daughter. It will ease you," Amara urged. Jelena swallowed a mouthful of the pungent, bitter liquid, gagged, then forced herself to swallow again. Almost immediately, she felt better. Resting her head against Amara's shoulder, breathing in the faint scent of lavender that clung to her mother-in-law's skin and clothing, a profound sense of peace seeped into her bones. Briefly, Jelena wondered if this was an effect of the drug she had just ingested, but then she decided to enjoy the sensation and not question its origins.

She allowed Amara to ease her back onto the pillows. She could hear the three women murmuring above her but it sounded more like the sighing of the sea heard from afar. She fell into a light doze, and when she awoke, she found herself lying in her own bed, still fully dressed. Someone had thoughtfully removed her shoes.

The drug Amara had given her had the desired effect; Jelena's fatigue and nausea—aftereffects of the mind scan—had dissipated. She felt as refreshed as if she'd slept an entire night, though the quality of the light streaming in from the bedroom window told her that no more than a couple of hours had passed, at most.

Plenty of time to go down into the city, she thought. Ashinji had left the family quarters shortly after breakfast in order to reunite with his company and spend the day with them. Jelena did not expect to see him again until evening, so she would have to go on her own.

No matter, it'll be an adventure. I'd better change clothes, though. Don't want to risk getting my fancy new outfit dirty.

The Sakehera quarters were quiet and still as Jelena made her way downstairs. *The entire family must be out*, she thought as she departed and made her way to the front of the castle complex, where she paused just outside the main gates to scan the vast sweep of the parade ground. Thin wisps of cloud smeared the otherwise perfect cerulean of the sky. She glanced over at the impassive guards standing motionless at their posts. They all stared straight ahead, ignoring her. She pulled a wide-brimmed hat down on her head and set off across the empty expanse, gravel crunching beneath her boots.

As she walked, Jelena thought about all that had transpired over the last two days, and, not for the first time, a swooping feeling of unreality seized her. The ground beneath her feet had, metaphorically, shifted so drastically that she felt uncertain if she would have the ability to walk the new terrain. She reached up to touch the familiar, comforting shape of her father's ring, back in its accustomed place beneath her tunic. The king had returned it to her and had promised to have a smaller copy made to fit her finger.

He had made no other promises, but this did not surprise or upset her. Jelena wanted nothing from Keizo Onjara that he did not wish to freely give her.

It's enough that he's acknowledged and accepted me as his daughter.

As for the Kirian Society, she still didn't know what to make of them. Clearly, they believed they would soon be called upon to battle this so-called Nameless One, but Jelena had a hard time accepting that ancient, evil ghosts could rise up to menace the living world. Still, they had promised to train her to use what Talent she had, the prospect of which filled her with excitement.

As she made her way out of the castle precincts and down into the city, the sights and sounds of the streets captured and held her full attention. Never had Jelena seen so many people gathered into one place.

Her main objective was to find the hikui district, called Jokimichi. Ashinji had promised to escort her there himself, but she had released him from his obligation so that he might spend the entire day with his company. In lieu of his personal guidance, he had provided her with written directions, so that she could locate her destination on her own.

She paused outside of a shop selling all types of iron implements and glanced around, getting her bearings. *This must be the street of the ironmongers,* she thought, noting that all the shops in the vicinity stocked similar wares. Ashinji's directions indicated that she should walk to the end of the street and turn right at the first crossing.

As she made her way along the street, Jelena strained to take in every detail. As children, she and Magnes had loved to look at Duke Teodorus' big, leather-bound book about the Imperial city of Darguinia. The book contained drawings of all the architectural marvels of the ancient capital of the Soldaran Empire. Jelena could still remember the sense of wonder she had felt while thumbing through that book, imagining what it would be like to stroll Darguinia's elegant streets.

That childish wonder was as nothing compared to what she felt now, walking through the streets of Sendai. How the elves had managed to so thoroughly integrate their city within the confines of a mighty forest seemed nothing short of astounding. Most of the houses and shops were constructed of wood, topped with roofs of brightly glazed ceramic tiles. She saw buildings of stone as well, and even a few made of red brick, but these looked like meeting halls, rather than private homes or shops. The streets were paved in gravel with cunningly worked stone gutters and curbs.

The people of Sendai themselves appeared to be well-fed and prosperous; Jelena soon discovered that physically, there existed a bit more variation among them than she had previously believed. The folk of Kerala all tended toward fairness of skin and eye color. Now, she saw some elven people with skins the color of bronze lamps, and a very few had complexions so dark, she thought at first that they must be of an entirely different race, but they were, indeed, elves.

For a girl who had been raised in the insular world of a Soldaran castle, the city of Sendai seemed like the busiest, most exciting place in the known world.

The street of the ironmongers crossed a smaller road and as Jelena turned the corner, she nearly stumbled over a boy curled in a tight little ball against the side of a building. She gasped in dismay as her foot connected with the small body, then exclaimed in shock as the child scrambled to his feet and she got a look at his face.

He's hikui!

The boy stared at her for a heartbeat, then took off running.

"Wait! Come back! I want to talk to you!" Jelena cried out, but the child quickly disappeared, lost among the throng.

Jelena's heart fluttered as she looked around with more deliberation, searching for other faces with humanish features.

She spotted an old man in front of a tavern, sweeping out the doorway, his face weatherworn and deeply furrowed. The hands that clutched the broom handle were gnarled and thickened with the joint-ill.

Jelena stood in the shadow cast by the shop opposite the tavern and watched the old man for a time. The stoop of his shoulders, the stiffness of his movements, his shabby clothes, the way he looked downward whenever another person walked by him; all of these things Jelena took notice of and a nasty suspicion took root at the back of her mind.

The old man finished his task and retreated into the tavern. Jelena started walking again, her eyes only confirming what her heart didn't want to believe. She saw more hikui scattered amongst the crowds of elves, and always, they seemed to be engaged in the most menial of tasks: unloading wagons, carrying burdens behind elven masters, sweeping, washing, hauling refuse. Those that weren't laboring appeared to be beggars. Not once did she see any elf in similar circumstances.

It seems as though my kind aren't treated any better here than I was back in Amsara, she thought. *It's as if I've had a veil over my eyes, hiding the truth, but now, the veil's been pulled away. How naïve I've been! Ashi loves me and I know he only wants to protect me, but he should have been more honest about things!*

A cloud of melancholy settled over her, and the day that had started out so bright and full of excitement now seemed much more dim and sad. She contemplated returning to the castle, but quickly changed her mind when she sighted a well-dressed hikui woman at a street stall, purchasing pies.

Jelena's spirits lifted.

Perhaps not all of my kind live at the bottom of elven society after all!

The woman completed her purchases and moved along up the street. Jelena hurried after, determined not to lose sight of her.

If I could just talk to her...I know she'll tell me the truth.

The woman soon turned off the main street into a narrow lane. She walked quickly; Jelena followed as close as she dared, not wishing to be too obvious in her pursuit, yet not wanting to lose her unwitting guide in the maze of small streets and alleys. She realized she had no idea how to get back to the main thoroughfare leading to the castle. She would eventually need to ask for directions; for now, though, she was content to let this woman lead her onward to whatever encounter the gods had mandated for them.

The forest began to thin out and soon Jelena found herself in a clearing within the city. Well-kept, modest houses lined the hard-packed, dirt lanes. The people she saw were all of mixed blood.

This must be it! I've found Jokimichi! She felt a rush of excitement and quickened her pace in order to catch up with her guide.

"Excuse me please!" she called out.

The woman had paused in a doorway, a key in her hand. She looked up as Jelena approached.

"Yes, may I help you?" the woman said, a little smile on her lips. Her face still had much of its youthful beauty, despite the lines brought by middle age. Her dark brown hair, streaked with silver, hung down her back in a neat braid.

"I...I..." Jelena cursed herself for her awkwardness. Why did she feel this way—shy, yet exhilarated? She wanted to fling her arms around the woman but at the same time, she wanted to flee. She stared helplessly into the kind brown eyes, too tongue-tied to speak.

The woman set her basket down on the ground and took Jelena's hand. Her palm felt rough and warm. "Are you ill, child? Is there something I can do for you, someone I can fetch?" she asked.

"N...no, no," Jelena spluttered, finding her voice at last. "I'm not ill, just lost. Well, not lost, really. I wanted to find this place, wanted to find others..."

"Others?" The woman raised an eyebrow.

"Yes, others like me...like you, mistress. I am not from around here, you see."

"That is abundantly clear. Your accent gives you away. I haven't heard its like before."

"I'm from Soldara, mistress. My Siri-dar is not so good yet."

"Your Siri-dar is quite good," the woman responded. She leaned over to pluck the basket off the ground. "Well, I suppose you'd better come in, then." She fitted the key into a shiny brass lock, turned it, and gave the door a gentle shove with her foot. Jelena followed her into a small entry hall and waited while her hostess closed the door and set the basket down on a low table.

"Welcome to my home," the woman said. "I am Sateyuka."

10

The Weaver's Tale

*J*elena snatched off her hat and sketched a quick bow. "My name is Jelena, mistress," she replied.

"What a lovely name," Sateyuka said, "and so different. You are a long way from home, Jelena. How is it that you find yourself in Sendai?"

"It is a long story, mistress."

Sateyuka smiled wryly and shook her head. "Please, Jelena. Call me Sateyuka. There are no masters or mistresses in this house, only hard working common folk. Come into the sitting room. I'll make tea and we can talk."

Sateyuka led Jelena through a sliding door made of thin wood into a cozy little room just off the entry hall. Three low chairs, a table, and some floor cushions made up the room's simple furnishings. An unlit fireplace anchored the wall opposite the door. Sateyuka crossed the room to throw open the shutters of the single window, letting in some of the late afternoon sunshine and fresh air. A heavy mesh screen shielded the interior of the room from passers-by.

"Make yourself comfortable. I shouldn't be too long." Sateyuka smiled and whisked from the room, brown braid swinging.

Jelena settled into one of the chairs to wait.

I have so many questions, she thought. Would Sateyuka be willing to answer them all? Or would she soon tire of her overeager young guest and find some excuse to send Jelena on her way?

I suppose I'll find out.

Sateyuka returned quickly, bearing a teapot—whimsically shaped like a fat-bodied hen—and two cups on a wooden tray. In addition to the tea, two of the little pies that Jelena had observed her hostess purchasing just a short time ago were laid out on cloth napkins. Sateyuka set the tray down atop the table and poured each of them a cup of tea.

"Careful, it's hot," she warned as she passed a cup and a pie to Jelena. She then sank into the chair opposite her guest.

Jelena bit into the pastry with a sigh of delight, savoring the mix of honey-sweetened crushed nuts and berries. She had to stop herself from devouring the confection in a single bite.

"I'd heard rumors there were folk of mixed blood in Soldara," Sateyuka said. "We here in Sendai have a tightly knit community, and I know of no one who has ever had any contact with hikui from beyond the borders of Alasiri." She paused to take a sip of her tea, and to appraise her young visitor over the rim of her cup.

"I was born at a place called Amsara," Jelena said, setting her teacup down on the table. She finished the pie and brushed the last crumbs from her fingers. "The duke's only sister—my mother—died giving birth to me. My uncle could never really accept me as family because of my elven blood, but he couldn't turn his back on me, either. He sent me to be raised in the servant's hall. Luckily I had a foster mother and a cousin who loved me."

"We hear stories of how hikui are treated in the human lands, and some among us say that we should be thankful we live here in Alasiri." Sateyuka frowned and Jelena thought she could hear the faintest trace of bitterness in the older woman's voice.

"It's true that Soldarans have no places of honor or dignity in their world for mixed-bloods. The priests teach the people that elvenkind are the offspring of demons...and therefore, have no souls. They say that any child born of a mating between an elf and a human is soulless as well." Now, Jelena's voice trembled with bitterness. "The people of Amsara take their religion quite seriously."

"Is that why you fled your home? To escape ill treatment at the hands of humans?"

"Partly so, yes. I also wanted very much to find the man who fathered me. On her deathbed, my birth mother passed on to my foster mother a ring that she said belonged to my father. She also swore that she and my father had truly loved each other."

"A powerful force, love. It makes us do brave things...and foolhardy ones as well." Sateyuka's soft brown eyes grew hazy, as if she wandered in the country of her memories, reliving a moment in her past both painful and sweet. With a sigh, she refocused her attention on her visitor. "So, now I know part of the tale of how you came to be in Alasiri," she said, smiling. "What brings you to Sendai? Have you reason to believe your father may be here?"

Jelena paused, considered how much of the truth to tell Sateyuka, then decided that the facts of her elven parentage must remain close-kept until the king decided otherwise.

"I came here with the Lord of Kerala. I am married to his younger son."

Sateyuka's eyebrows shot up. "Your fortunes have risen, indeed. The House of Sakehera is old and powerful. Lord Sen is well respected among the people, okui and hikui alike. He is the only lord on the King's Council who has spoken up in support of equal rights for our folk." Jelena shifted uneasily in her chair, eager to ask the question that had been uppermost in her mind since she first entered Sateyuka's small, neat house, but yet afraid of the answer.

"I know Lord Sen and the people of Kerala are...more tolerant. This they told me themselves. Most of them accepted me, and treated me well." *With one notable exception*, she thought. "But I wish to hear the truth spoken of...the truth which I can see with my own eyes as I walk the streets."

Sateyuka sipped her tea in silence for several heartbeats, her expression thoughtful. When at last she spoke, her response seemed careful and measured.

"My husband Azareshu died several years ago," she said. "He was a master weaver—one of the very best in the city—but because of the laws that forbid a person of mixed blood from becoming a member in any of the craft guilds, he was denied access to the best markets. Still, we managed. With hard work and perseverance, we built our business into one of the biggest weaving and dye shops in Sendai. That was before the fire."

She paused, her mouth set in a thin, tight line, as if, at any moment, a wail of grief might break forth. Jelena waited in silence, recognizing the sight of old pain freshly recalled and felt anew.

After a moment, Sateyuka regained her composure and continued. "It was no accident—the fire—although we didn't find out until after the flames had been put out. We lost our entire inventory and most of our equipment as well. My husband suffered lung damage from the smoke. He kept running back into the burning shop to save whatever he could, which was precious little. When it was all over, we were left with two looms, one dye vat almost too warped by heat to use, and three bales of raw wool. Not much with which to rebuild a shop as big as ours had been.

"The next day, while searching the ruins for anything that might be salvageable, my eldest son came across a medallion half-buried in the ashes. It was one of the tokens worn by apprentices of the Weavers and Dyers Guild. Somehow, it had survived the flames. Engraved on the back was the insignia of Kai Kaiori, our biggest competitor."

"This Kai Kaiori sent apprentices to burn you out? But why?" Jelena immediately realized the naievite of the question.

Sateyuka laughed sharply. "Kai Kaiori is a high ranking member of the Guild. Our shop had been seriously cutting into her business, a situation that she couldn't tolerate!"

"Did you confront her?"

"My husband and sons went to her shop with the medallion as evidence, but it was useless. She denied she had anything to do with the fire, and she challenged us to prove otherwise. Azareshu tried to fight. He went to the authorities, but they refused to investigate. He even petitioned the king, but we never received a reply."

Sateyuka rubbed at her eyes, either to relieve an itch or wipe away tears— Jelena could not tell. "The stress of it all proved too much for my dear husband. His lungs became worse and soon, he was too weak to rise from our bed. He died, and my sons and I were left alone." Sateyuka fell silent, but only for a moment. Their eyes met and Jelena saw a woman who had survived unbearable grief and hardship, yet remained unbowed, with not a particle of self-pity anywhere within her to otherwise poison her recovery.

"After Azareshu died, I determined to rebuild. Thankfully, we had some money put aside, so I was able to rent a small space and purchase enough supplies to deliver some smaller orders. Ai, things were very hard that first year, but we survived. Our best customers were patient. They refused to abandon us, and because of them, we were able to stay afloat.

"Now, the business is almost back to where it had been before the fire. My eldest and his wife are the master weavers now. My other daughter-in-law oversees the dyeing and my youngest son attends to all of the daily business matters. I see to the accounts."

Sateyuka raised the teapot with an expectant lift of her chin. Jelena held out her cup for a refill. "I've told you all of this, Jelena, so that you can better understand what it's like for us. A few hikui families have managed to prosper, despite how things are, but most just get by, and too many still live in poverty, though Alasiri itself is rich. Still, we live our lives as best we can. We get married, raise our families, run businesses, pay taxes.... As long as we remain separate—apart from mainstream elven society—the burden of our situation is barely felt by many of us, and the okui folk can go on pretending that we are all content. It's only when the interests of a hikui collides with that of an okui that the ugly truth rears its head."

Jelena sighed and forced herself to relax back into her chair. Sateyuka hadn't revealed anything Jelena didn't already suspect. "What am I to do?" she mused. "How can I reconcile all of this with what my life has become?"

"You are very lucky, child," Sateyuka pointed out. "You are protected by virtue of your marriage into the House of Sakehera. Legally, you now have the same rights as an okui."

"Maybe so, but it does not change the fact that I am still hikui. How can I live with rights that are denied others of our kind?"

"I haven't the answer to that question, Jelena. Only you know what is truly in your heart. If your husband loves you and you love him...and I can see that you do by the look in your eyes...then perhaps that is all that should count for you right now. These are weighty matters, these questions of the rights of hikui people. Many women and men, both stronger and wiser than you and I, have spent their entire lives fighting for equality under elven law for our people. It has yet to happen." She pursed her lips thoughtfully, then added, "Perhaps it never will."

Jelena set her cup down with care and rose to look through the ornate window screen out into the street. The sunlight glowed orange and mellow; soon, dusk would fall. She hadn't realized how much time had gone by. Talking with Sateyuka, sharing tea and pies with her—it had felt so comfortable and safe, like how Jelena imagined visiting a favorite aunt would be.

She turned to face her host. "I must go," she murmured, then in a slightly stronger voice, added, "This has meant a lot to me. Thank you."

Sateyuka stood and held out her hands; Jelena clasped them warmly. "You must come back to see me again," the older hikui woman said, her soft brown eyes twinkling. "I have many friends here in Jokimichi, all of whom will welcome you and lend support, if you should feel the need." Jelena understood the implied message behind the other woman's words. "I wish you luck and pray that all will turn out for the best."

"Thank you," Jelena replied.

Sateyuka saw her to the door, and after giving Jelena directions back to the avenue that led up to the castle, stood at her threshold and watched as Jelena made her way up the street. At the first crossing, Jelena turned and waved before rounding the corner. Sateyuka lifted her hand in farewell.

As Jelena headed back toward the castle, she realized a seed had been planted within her this day. What form it would take as it grew, she could only guess at, but one thing she felt certain of: her relationship with Ashinji and his family—with all elves for that matter—would never be quite the same.

* * *

"It's wrong, Ashi! Wrong and unfair!" Jelena exclaimed as she paced around the sitting room, hands clenched into fists at her side.

"I agree, love, but it is the way it is." Ashinji sprawled on the couch beside the hearth, watching Jelena as she stalked, filling the room with her righteous indignation.

Abruptly, Jelena halted and rounded on her husband. "How can you be so...so unconcerned?" she demanded, glaring at him through narrowed eyes.

Ashinji sat up and held out his hands. "Please come and sit down," he beckoned gently. After a moment's hesitation, Jelena came and settled beside him, allowing herself to be held. At first, she remained rigid with anger, but the feel of Ashinji's body against hers worked its own special magic and her fury slowly cooled. She sighed and relaxed into his embrace.

"I'm not unconcerned, love, just practical," Ashinji said, brushing her cheek lightly with his fingers. "The weaver and her family deserved justice, and it sounds like they didn't receive any. It is unfair, but the majority of okui don't even acknowledge that there's a problem. They truly believe that all hikui are content to live as our servants and laborers, never stopping to consider that the hikui woman or man they employ might just have higher aspirations."

"Why are your parents different, Ashi?" Jelena asked. "Even though your father objected at first to our marriage, he did come around. Why?"

"I believe it's because they were both raised in the borderlands where matters of blood and race are not as important," Ashinji replied. "Many people out on the frontiers have a human or two hidden in their family trees."

And a few, like Aneko, pass as okui, Jelena mused silently.

Jelena thought about the crime done to Sateyuka's family and wondered how many other hikui had suffered unjustly—were still suffering—and her anger kindled anew. Ashinji must have sensed her hardening mood, for he pulled away and regarded her with cautious eyes. She looked into his face and, for the space of a heartbeat, she saw, not the man she loved, but the visage of an oppressor.

Gods, what am I thinking!

Jelena gasped with dismay. The anger fell away, to be replaced with intense sadness and regret. "Oh, Ashi," she whispered and her eyes filled with tears. That anything could make her look at Ashinji with something other than love felt like an unbearable agony to her spirit, yet the injustice inflicted upon hikui by pure bloods remained undeniable, and she could no longer ignore it. She remembered Sateyuka's words—*If you and your husband love each other, perhaps that will be enough*—and slowly shook her head.

"What are you thinking?" Ashinji asked.

"About..." Jelena paused, then drew herself up with new determination. "About how much I love you. And about how I can't ignore what's going on when I might have the power to help change things. I'm the king's daughter, Ashi! I'm the king's *hikui* daughter, and that obligates me to take action."

Ashinji reached out and pulled her close. "I'm proud of you," he said. "King Keizo is a fair man. I believe he'll listen to you."

"Halloo! Where is everyone?" Lord Sen's booming voice rolled into the room just ahead of the general himself, who strode in, trailed closely by Sadaiyo. Both father and son were dressed in heavy leathers, sweat-stained and dusty from the saddle. "Amara!" he called out, then noticing Ashinji and Jelena, he said in a somewhat quieter voice, "Hullo, children. Do you know where your mother is?"

"I think she and Misune took the girls out to tour the castle gardens, but they should be back very soon. It's nearly dark," Ashinji replied.

"Taking Lani out to dangle her in front of the eligible young bucks, is more like it," Sadaiyo commented. Sen frowned.

"Must you always be so crude, Sadaiyo?" Ashinji responded, tight-lipped. "At least try to control your natural savagery where our sister is concerned."

Sadaiyo shrugged at the insult, unfazed, and said, "While you've been lazing away the day on your backside, Father and I have been out working." He crossed the room to stand by the hearth. Jelena eased herself off the couch and went to sit on the floor near the window. She found it difficult enough being in the same room as Ashinji's brother. At the very least, she would put the length of the room between her and him.

"Your brother and I accompanied the king and Prince Raidan on a tour of the city's defenses," Sen explained. "Fortunately, most of the fortifications are sound, but I can't say that about the old fort out on the Meizi Road. That'll have to undergo major renovations before winter. Some enterprising local has turned it into an inn. Raidan was livid! I thought his head would burst!" Sen chuckled at the memory. He turned and addressed Jelena. "The king has invited us all to dine with him this evening. You'll get to meet your uncle Raidan and his family, Jelena."

"I've already met my uncle's wife this morning," Jelena said, remembering the strength of command that had radiated from Princess Taya.

My uncle must be a man of great strength himself, to have such a wife, she thought.

"Oh, yes. The Kirian Society. She is part of that, isn't she?" Sen sniffed loudly and rubbed his nose on the back of his hand. "Hmm, well. I need a bath and a drink. The rest of you'd better think about getting ready, 'cause we don't want to be late." He looked pointedly at Sadaiyo, then turned and stumped up the stairs.

With Sen's departure, an uncomfortable silence descended upon the sitting room. After enduring several moments of the tense atmosphere, Jelena spoke up.

"Ashi, let's go to the bath house now." She stood and held her hand out to him.

"Good idea," Ashinji replied. The two of them left Sadaiyo standing by the fireplace, his eyes hooded and inscrutable.

11

Two Blessings And A Curse

Things are happening so fast, Ashi...perhaps too fast." Jelena sighed and lay back on the bed beside Ashinji. "In two days time, I am to be presented to the King's Council as Keizo Onjara's daughter... and then..." She paused, momentarily overcome. Ashinji gently rubbed the back of her neck, offering silent support. "And then," she continued in a shaky voice, "my father will present me to the people of Sendai, legitimize me and invest me with the title of Princess."

The king had made his announcement that evening during dinner in his private quarters.

"My uncle Raidan and his sons...What must they think?" she mused.

Prince Raidan, Princess Taya, and their two sons—sullen Raidu and cheerful, curious young Kaisik—had greeted her politely enough; with the exception of Raidu, they had treated her as a welcome new family member. When Keizo had announced his plans, however, Jelena felt the change in her uncle's attitude like a breath of chill wind upon her face. Raidan had remained unfailingly polite, but his hazel eyes had gone flint-hard.

Ashinji stretched languidly and stifled a yawn behind his hand. "The prince is a good man, and well-respected...and he is loyal to the king," he said. "You have nothing to fear from him, I'm sure." He frowned. "I couldn't help but notice how your father's Companion kept staring at you all evening. It was a little disturbing...like watching a lioness licking her chops over a rabbit."

"Yes, she did make me feel a little uncomfortable, but she's a Kirian, after all...she knows about my blue fire. I think she must be able to sense it somehow."

"Perhaps," Ashinji replied.

"My cousin Raidu did a fair amount of chop-licking over your sister, Ashi," Jelena commented.

"Huh. Don't think I didn't notice. Lani's at that age now. She's beautiful, smart—and marriageable—and she knows it." Ashinji rolled over and pulled Jelena against him. His hand strayed down to rest on her thigh.

"Whatever changes are in store for us, we'll face them together, love," he whispered.

Jelena twined her fingers in his hair and kissed him.

* * *

"Mother, Father...Misune and I have an announcement to make," Sadaiyo said. The family had just sat down to breakfast. Jelena had awakened that morning to more nausea, and had no appetite. Ashinji, ever sensitive to her mood, kept throwing worried glances her way as she slowly sipped a cup of tea.

"Well, what's your news, Son...tell us," Sen urged around a mouthful of bread. Sadaiyo took Misune's hand and together, they faced Sen and Amara. "We waited to tell you because we wanted to be sure." He paused for effect, then crowed, "Misune is pregnant. You're to be grandparents!" Misune smiled triumphantly.

"Goddess be praised!" Sen whooped with joy. Amara rose from her seat, embraced Misune and kissed her on both cheeks. She then turned and put her arms around Sadaiyo, who seemed caught off-guard by his mother's affection. Awkwardly, he returned her embrace.

"Today is a very good day for this family," Sen said. He stood up, arms half-raised as if he, too, were about to embrace his son; instead, he reached out and squeezed Sadaiyo's shoulder, then his arms dropped to his sides.

For only a moment, Jelena saw something she'd never seen before—Sadaiyo's cold face transformed into that of a child desperately yearning for his father's love—then, just as quickly, the child faded and the man returned.

"I'm glad I've...at last...made you happy, Father," Sadaiyo said, a rough catch in his voice.

Sen sniffed and rubbed his eyes. "Yes...well...," he huffed and sat down.

"Jelena, how are you feeling this morning?" Jelena looked up, surprised by her mother-in-law's question.

"Not well, Mother, but it's nothing, really," she assured.

"It's not nothing," Ashinji countered. "Mother, Jelena has been unwell for nearly two weeks now."

Amara nodded, a knowing look in her eye. "Perhaps it's time to send for a doctor," she said.

"Oh, no, Mother, please. I really don't need a doctor."

"Yes...you do!" Ashinji glowered at her.

Amara exchanged a look with her husband. "I believe I'll send for one right now," she said.

Jelena nodded in acquiescence. She knew when to give in.

Later that morning, as she and Ashinji waited in the sitting room for the doctor to arrive, Jelena, who had sensed a mood change in her husband beyond worry for her, prodded him to talk.

They had the room to themselves; Sen and Sadaiyo had gone out on official business, Misune and Lani had retreated to the bathhouse for a long soak, and Amara was upstairs dressing the twins.

"What's gotten you so upset, Ashi?" Jelena laid her hand atop his and gazed at his profile. "I know you're worried about me, but..."

"Yes, of course I'm worried," he responded, then said, "That was the first time I've ever seen my mother embrace Sadaiyo like that. I don't think he quite knew how to react."

"Your parents are thrilled that their Heir is expecting his own Heir," Jelena replied. "It means the House of Sakehera will continue after your father is gone."

"Of course, you're right..." Ashinji paused, then exclaimed, "Ai, Goddess!" He shook his head slowly, eyes closed. "I know it's evil of me, but...I can't feel any joy for my brother. I'm ashamed, Jelena... ashamed to admit I would secretly enjoy any misfortune that might befall him."

"Oh, Ashi." Jelena rested her head on his shoulder. "There is nothing about you that is evil. If you feel this way about your brother, then it is his own doing. He has tormented and abused you your entire life. You aren't the one who should feel ashamed, it's him!"

"Have I told you lately how much I love you?" Ashinji brushed his lips against her neck.

"Yes, but I can never hear it enough." A knock at the door interrupted the moment. Amara had declined to accept full-time servants while they lived at Sendai, and so it was left to the younger family members to perform certain tasks like opening the door to visitors.

"I guess I'll have to answer that." Ashinji got up and exited the room, returning a moment later with a tall, gray-haired man in tow.

"Lady Sakehera summoned me to attend her daughter-in-law," the man said to Ashinji.

"Yes, Doctor. You are here to examine my wife. She has been ill for nearly two weeks now."

Jelena stood up and came forward. The doctor's eyebrows shot up, but he swiftly recovered. "Come, let's sit and you can tell me about your symptoms, my girl," he prompted gently.

After Jelena had described the nausea and dizziness that had plagued her, the doctor nodded and asked, "When did you last bleed?"

Jelena had to stop and think.

It has been awhile, she thought. *Gods! Could I be...?*

Aloud, she said, "I...I think it was...well, before we left Kerala. At least two months...but I've been late before. I thought...I didn't think anything of it."

"Hmmm, yes," the doctor replied. "Captain Sakehera, I need to examine your wife now. Perhaps you'd feel more comfortable waiting in another room?"

"Oh, no! Ashi can stay with me," Jelena insisted.

"Very well." The doctor indicated that she should lie down on the couch. After poking and probing Jelena with experienced hands, the doctor finished his exam by holding two fingers to the large vein in her neck for several heartbeats. He nodded once, apparently satisfied.

"Well?" Jelena asked. "Am I...?"

"Yes, my girl," the doctor replied. He smiled and the creases at the corners of his eyes deepened. "And since you appear to be in excellent health, your pregnancy should proceed smoothly."

"Ashi! Did you hear?" Jelena cried.

"I heard, my love...I heard!"

"Doctor, is it as I suspected?" Amara had appeared at the bottom of the stairs.

"Yes, my lady. Your daughter-in-law is indeed pregnant, and if she carries like most hikui women, she should deliver by next spring." The doctor opened his leather satchel and removed a glass vial full of fine, white powder from its depths. He then poured a small amount of wine into a glass and shook a few grains of the powder into the deep red liquid, swirling it around until the powder had dissolved. Holding the glass out to Jelena, he ordered, "Drink this now. If you feel sick later, mix a pinch of the powder into a little wine, just as you saw me do, then drink it down. Just a pinch, mind! I will make arrangements with your mother-in-law to see you regularly from now until you deliver."

"Thank you, doctor," Amara said. "I will see you out." After Amara and the doctor had left the room, Jelena wrapped Ashinji in a fierce embrace.

"Ashi, we've made a child!" she whispered and pressed his hand to her still-flat belly. "Our first child is in here!" She wanted to leap from the couch and fly out the window to soar high above the castle roofs. She longed to release the wild music in her soul and let the world know she carried a new life within her.

"My love...my beautiful wife." Ashinji's voice shook with the strength of his joy.

Slowly, Jelena ran her hands across her belly, savoring the wonder of it all.

Oh, dear Claudia...Heartmother! If only you could see me now! she thought. *Your baby, your little girl. Soon, I'll have a baby of my own.* Hot tears flooded her eyes.

"The One has blessed us doubly this day." Amara re-entered the sitting room and came over to kiss both Jelena and Ashinji.

"You knew, didn't you, Mother?"

Amara smiled and touched Jelena on the cheek. "I've suspected for several days, now, but I thought perhaps you'd figure it out for yourselves."

"I feel very dumb," Jelena mumbled.

"Nonsense, girl," Amara retorted. "You've never been pregnant before, so you've no cause to reproach yourself." She looked toward the stairs. "Where are the twins? They know I'm waiting on them...Girls! Girls, come now!"

In a flurry of shrieks and giggles, Mariso and Jena came hurtling down the stairs at the sound of their mother's voice.

"I'm taking the girls into the city to get them some new clothes," Amara explained. "They grow so fast..." She shook her head in mock despair. "It seems as if I'm replacing everything I have for them every few weeks!" The twins, as usual, were chattering bundles of energy, each girl mirroring with uncanny precision the movements and mannerisms of her sister.

"You'd better go or they're going to burst!" Jelena exclaimed, laughing.

"I've sent for some fresh food for you, since you barely touched breakfast. It should be here any moment.... Yes, yes, girls! We are going now!" Amara gave Jelena a quick peck on the cheek, then herded her little daughters out the door.

Jelena's hand crept up to her cheek to touch the spot where Amara had kissed it. The skin tingled a little, as if a residue of her mother-in-law's Talent had been deposited there. Until now, Amara had shown little inclination toward physical affection with Jelena other than the occasional pat on the hand. It felt deeply significant, this breakthrough, and for the first time in their brief history together, Jelena knew with certainty that Ashinji's mother accepted her completely.

"I hate to leave you, love, but I've got an officer's meeting I must attend," Ashinji said. "We'll tell Father about our baby tonight. He'll be beside himself. Two grandchildren in one day!"

"Of course, you must go. I understand," Jelena replied. "I'll just...um, maybe go to the stables and visit Willow. She must be very restless by now. She's not been ridden since we arrived."

"I'll see you tonight, then." Ashinji kissed her and departed, leaving Jelena alone in the stillness of the now deserted apartment.

A knock at the door broke her reverie. She opened it to find an elderly hikui man holding a tray. A young hikui woman stood behind and to the side of the man. Jelena pulled the door open a little wider to admit the pair.

"Your meal, my lady," the man murmured as he swept past her to place the tray on the dining table. He bowed once, then exited, leaving the woman standing alone by the open doorway.

Jelena regarded her with curiosity. "Is there something you need?" she asked.

The woman—a girl really—nodded, all the while looking past Jelena's shoulder into the room. "I was sent to serve Lady Sakehera. I am supposed to look after her daughters," she answered in a pleasant, contralto voice. "My name is Eikko." She bowed her head. Jelena guessed her to be about nineteen years old, plain of face and tending towards plumpness. She had wrapped her dark brown hair in a neat bun at the nape of her neck.

"Lady Sakehera and the twins just left. If you were supposed to accompany them into the city, you're too late," Jelena replied.

The girl gasped, her hazel eyes wide with distress. "I was told to be here promptly at the ninth hour! I know I'm not late! Oh, this will reflect badly upon me!"

Jelena couldn't help but feel a rush of sympathy for the girl. "It's going to be all right, Eikko," she said soothingly. "Lady Sakehera left early. She must have decided she didn't need help after all."

Jelena paused to study the other girl's face. She could see, beneath the distress, a frank curiosity in the young hikui's eyes— curiosity about her.

She made a quick decision. "Please come in, Eikko. I would very much like to talk to you."

"Oh, I really shouldn't..." the girl said.

"I won't keep you long, I promise," Jelena assured.

"Well...all right. But I really can't stay. I need to go tell my boss what happened."

"Are you hungry?" Jelena picked up a sweet bun from the breakfast tray and offered it to the young servant.

"Oh, no!... I'm not allowed," Eikko replied, shaking her head.

"Not allowed to eat breakfast?" Jelena responded quizzically.

"Not allowed to eat in front of *you*..." Eikko's voice trailed off and she lowered her eyes.

Suddenly, Jelena understood. "You know who I am, don't you?"

"Yes...Your Highness."

Jelena shook her head in astonishment. "How is it that you know? My father has made no public announcement...I certainly haven't gone about flaunting it...How can you know?"

Eikko seemed amused at Jelena's bewilderment. "Servants talk, my lady," she replied.

Of course! How could I possibly think my identity would remain a secret from the one group of people who know everything that goes on here? Jelena nearly laughed aloud at her own foolishness. "I should have known the answer to my own question," she said.

Eikko shrugged. "Perhaps, Highness."

Jelena frowned. "Please don't call me that. I'm really no better than you."

"You are the king's daughter, my lady. That makes you a princess," Eikko said, her tone indicating that she didn't understand why Jelena could not see the simple logic of the situation.

"If you knew more about me, I doubt you'd feel the way you do. I'm hikui, same as you...an ordinary person."

"Whose father just happens to be the king," Eikko pointed out. "No, my lady, you are far from ordinary."

Jelena sighed and picked up a sweet bun. Realizing the draught the doctor had given her had done its job, she hungrily bit into the bread. Noticing Eikko surreptitiously eyeing the food, she asked, "Have you eaten yet this morning?", and when the other girl shook her head, she added, "Please have something. I insist."

"No, my lady. I really am not allowed. If my boss were to find out, it would go badly for me." Eikko's eyes implored Jelena not to ask again.

Guilt poked Jelena like a sharp blade. "I can't sit here and enjoy my meal while you go hungry," she muttered, dropping the half-eaten bun back on the tray. She shook her head in dismay, remembering how Sateyuka's words had confirmed the painful truth of how her fellow hikui were treated.

"Are all the servants in the castle hikui?" Jelena asked as she settled into a chair by the window.

After a moment's hesitation, Eikko sat on a floor cushion. "All of the lower-downs, are," Eikko replied. "The bosses are mostly okui, of course, though a few of us have made it up to that level."

"The okui serving here don't mistreat you, do they?" Jelena asked carefully.

Eikko framed her answer just as carefully. "The king doesn't knowingly allow any of his servants to be mistreated, your Highness, but...things are as they are."

Jelena sighed. "Maybe now, when the okui see that the king has a hikui daughter and that he loves her, things will be different," she said quietly.

"Perhaps," Eikko replied. "I really should be going, my lady. If I don't report back soon..." The servant girl climbed to her feet.

"Thank you, Eikko, for staying and talking to me," Jelena said, rising to her feet as well, "even if it was only for a little while. I've had so few opportunities to talk to other hikui," she added. "I hope we'll have another chance."

Eikko's warm smile transformed her plain face into something resembling loveliness. "I hope so, too...Highness."

Jelena flinched. "I...I would rather you didn't call me that," she said. "I really don't deserve that title."

Eikko remained silent as Jelena escorted her to the door. Just before stepping across the threshold, the hikui girl turned to face Jelena. "Yes, you do," she whispered, her eyes alive with unspoken meaning, before she hurried off.

* * *

"The One bestows yet another blessing on my House." Sen folded Ashinji into his arms. "My son," he whispered. "You've made me so very happy." Sen held his son for many heartbeats, and never before had Jelena seen or felt their special bond more strongly. Finally, Sen released Ashinji and moved to embrace Jelena. "You, also, have made me very happy," he said, his gray-green eyes shining. He planted a firm kiss in the center of her forehead then released her.

The remains of the evening meal had yet to be cleared from the dining table; Jelena and Ashinji had delayed their announcement until after the family had finished eating.

"I need to tell my own father soon," Jelena stated. She shook her head, laughing. "He just found out he's a father, and now he's to be a grandfather as well!"

"He will be as happy as I am," Sen replied. "Though I foresee a potential problem between us." His face curdled into a scowl.

"What problem, Father?" Ashinji asked anxiously.

"Both of us will want to cuddle and spoil our grandchild, but we can't do it at the same time. I predict a great deal of arguing over exactly whose turn it is to hold the baby!" Sen's mock scowl melted into a mischievous grin.

"I wonder if I'll have any time with my own child!" Jelena exclaimed. She turned toward Ashinji in entreaty, but he just shrugged and smiled. Jelena smiled in response, full to bursting with love for her husband and his father.

Amara, who had been sipping tea on the sitting room couch, Lani by her side, entered the conversation. "Jelena, now that you are pregnant, we must be especially careful with your training," she said. "The energy within you can cause great harm to your unborn child. It must be meticulously controlled until the correct time."

"You're worrying me, Wife!" Sen rumbled. "Nothing...nothing at all must harm this grandchild!" He nervously plucked at his earlobe. "You know how talk of sorcery unsettles me. Whatever this business of the Kirians is, must it involve Jelena?"

Before Amara could answer, Sadaiyo, who had said nothing until now, spoke. "Goddess forbid that anything should happen to this *particular* Sakehera grandchild, for is this child not also an Onjara and thus far more valuable to you than my own, Father?" He made no attempt to soften the bitterness of his tone.

Jelena's happy mood evaporated. Ashinji stiffened and she felt him struggling to remain calm.

Sen's face fell; his eyes darkened with anger and sadness. "How can you say such a thing, Son?" he asked.

"Sadaiyo, not now..." Misune murmured, almost too low to be heard.

"I'm only speaking the truth, Wife," Sadaiyo shot back. "Father agrees, but he'd never admit it—has *never* admitted it—though it's always been plain to me and everyone else in Kerala! Ever since my little brother came mewling into the world, anything that is a part of *him* will be more precious to you, Father, than anything I can ever give you."

The air in the room grew heavy, as oppressive as the atmosphere right before a summer thunderstorm.

"I think I'll go up to bed," Lani murmured.

"Take your sisters," Amara directed softly, gesturing to the two little girls asleep before the hearth. Lani nodded, kissed her mother's cheek, then rose to gather the twins up, one under each arm. They complained drowsily, but went along without much more fuss.

"Sadaiyo," Sen said as soon as Lani and the twins had departed, "you are my firstborn...my Heir. When have I ever given you cause to doubt my regard for you?"

Sadaiyo shook his head in incredulity. "Every time you look at my brother," his eyes flicked to Ashinji's face then back to his father's, "I see in your eyes the love you have for him...love I never had, nor ever will. Oh, I understand it," he said, raising his hand to forestall Sen's response, "but understanding is a long way from acceptance."

"Brother, you need feel no jealousy toward me. I've never been a threat to you." The anguish in Ashinji's voice nearly broke Jelena's heart.

"Not so, Little Brother!" Sadaiyo replied. "The people of Kerala love you about as much as they hate me. How will I ever govern them without their support? As long as you are around, my position as Lord will be severely compromised."

"That is not true, Son! Our people don't hate you!" Sen objected. "Perhaps, if you showed them a little more compassion..."

"Like Ashinji, perhaps? Oh, yes... kind, compassionate Ashinji! I'm sick to death of you—you and this...this half-breed who pretends she's as good as a pureblood because she's the king's bastard whelp!"

"*Sadaiyo!*" Amara's voice cracked like a whip.

Sadaiyo rose to his feet, ignoring his mother's warning. "You've never said it, Father, but I know you wish it. You wish that your *precious* Ashinji could succeed you as Lord!"

Father and son stared at each other for several agonizing heartbeats.

"Go ahead," Sadaiyo bluntly challenged. "Admit it!"

Something in Sen seemed to snap. Jelena saw his control give way and she braced herself for the consequences.

"Goddess forgive me, but it's true!" Sen whispered hoarsely, then hung his head.

"Father!" Ashinji cried. He struggled to rise, but Jelena locked her arms around him and held him down with all her strength.

"I can't lie to you anymore, Sadaiyo." Sen raised his head and Jelena witnessed something she never thought to see—Sen weeping. The sight of his tears seemed to temporarily dampen Sadaiyo's anger. Father and son stood a handspan apart, each searching the other's face for something—*anything*—that would banish the terrible pain between them.

"I'm so very sorry, my son," Sen murmured.

For an eternity, no one moved or spoke.

"Damn and curse you, *Brother*," Sadaiyo whispered at last.

"Sadaiyo," Amara called softly this time, breaking the leaden silence. Sadaiyo turned to regard his mother with flat, pain-filled eyes. "Come here," she commanded.

Even in his current state, Sadaiyo did not dare disobey his mother. Like a sleepwalker, he went to her side and sat down. Gently, Amara slipped her arms around him and rested her forehead against his. She closed her eyes. "Leave us, all of you," she ordered.

"I'm going for a walk," Sen mumbled and headed for the outer doors. Misune, loathe to leave her husband but fearful of disobeying a direct order from her mother-in-law, reluctantly retreated up the stairs.

"Let's go to bed," Ashinji whispered. "I really need to be in your arms right now." Jelena nodded and took his hand. She glanced at the eerily still tableau of Sadaiyo and his mother, then looked away. The two were obviously joined in trance, and to Jelena, it felt like too intimate a thing for her to see.

When she and Ashinji finally fell into their bed, they held each other for awhile, taking comfort in simple closeness. Eventually, Ashinji moved to rest his head on Jelena's belly, as if by doing so, he could somehow cross the divide that, by nature and necessity, now separated him from his unborn child. Jelena stroked his hair with one hand and wiped away her tears with the other.

By mutual, unspoken agreement, they remained silent about Sadaiyo's outburst and Sen's agonized confession. Jelena understood that things were too raw now. There would be plenty of time later to sort things out.

After a time, they both drifted to sleep.

* * *

Emerging from a tangle of disturbing dreams, Jelena sat up in bed, a vague sense of alarm jangling her nerves. She glanced over at Ashinji, who lay on his side, face slack. Too unsettled to remain in bed, Jelena finally gave up and slipped from beneath the covers, moving carefully so as to not wake her husband. She threw on her robe and went to sit in the window seat, pushing open the shutters so she could look out.

Thousands of stars glittered overhead in a clear, black sky. The moon had not yet risen—the bulk of the castle lay in darkness below, like a slumbering dragon. She leaned out over the sill and inhaled deeply of the cool air.

A tiny whisper of sound, like the soft chime of a bell, caused her to start. She peered into the darkness below, trying to pierce the veil of shadow that obscured the source of the mysterious noise.

A ghostly, bluish light flickered to life and revealed the dim outlines of a figure standing in the yard directly below the window. As Jelena watched with growing unease, the light waxed stronger, resolving itself into a perfect sphere that floated just above the head of a woman with fiery red hair.

Sonoe stood looking upward, right into Jelena's eyes.

Jelena hissed in surprise and fell back from the window, nearly tripping over the hem of her robe. Trembling with reaction, she crouched on the floor beneath the sill, her thoughts racing.

What is my father's Companion doing here at this time of night?

The beautiful mage's eyes had looked like two black stones set in alabaster. Jelena felt a sudden wave of fear, like the cold exhalation from a freshly opened tomb.

This makes no sense! Sonoe is a Kirian, and if not a friend, then at least an ally!

Profoundly disturbed, Jelena scurried for the safety of the bed and Ashinji's comforting presence. She climbed in, pressed herself against him, then lay unmoving for the rest of the night.

12

Ascension Day

This hikui girl, your Majesty. You are certain she is yours?" Lady Odata of Tono asked, disbelief coloring her voice.

"Yes, quite certain, my lady," the king replied, clearly irritated by the implication. "The White Griffin confirmed it. You know as well as I that it only reacts when one of the true blood of Onjara touches it. I'd be happy to demonstrate to all of you!" He pounded his fist on the polished oak of the council table in frustration.

"Easy, Brother," Raidan soothed. "Your lords only want assurances that this isn't some sort of deception. You can't blame them for that."

"No...no, I can't. You are right," Keizo admitted. He sighed and unclenched his hands, laying them flat on the table. "My apologies, my lords and ladies."

Raidan observed his brother over steepled fingers. They had spent most of last night arguing over how best to handle this situation. Raidan had urged caution, recommending that Keizo present the girl to the Council, but hold off on any public proclamations to legitimize her. Keizo would have his hands full just dealing with the shock and dismay of his advisors. He didn't need a public outcry to add to his troubles.

In the end, though, Keizo remained resolute. The Council and the elven people would know about his daughter, and, in time, come to accept his decision—or so he believed.

Now, faced with the full wrath of his lords, Keizo remained in control, handling the situation well enough, considering.

Several of the lords shouted simultaneously, but one voice in particular—Morio of Ayame's—rang out above the others. "Your Majesty, where is this leading? You have no child of your blood, save this girl...this *hikui* girl. If you legitimize her, then you are as good as declaring that you plan to name her your Heir!"

"That I cannot do, my lord of Ayame. It is against our law," the king replied, tight-lipped.

"How do we know you won't suspend the law?" Lord Morio continued. "With respect, Majesty, if you try, there are many of us who will oppose you! The elven people will never accept a hikui as their ruler!" Many voices cried out in agreement, adding to the general cacophony.

Sen Sakehera, who had been silent until now, finally spoke up. "My lords and ladies, I pray you, *shut up!*" he roared. All shouting ceased and every eye fixed upon the King's Commanding General. "That's better," he said. "Now that I can hear myself, I'd like to get in my few humble words, with your permission, Majesty." The king waved his hand in consent.

"It was I who brought Jelena here to Sendai. My son Ashinji found her along our southern border, fleeing from bandits. If he hadn't come along, she'd be dead, and so would I, because some months later, Jelena saved my life. I owed it to her to try to help her find her elven kin." He glanced at the king, who sat very still, face impassive.

"I've come to care for this girl very much, and so has my son. I know her mind, far better than even her own father does," Keizo's mouth twitched at this, but he otherwise showed no reaction. "and I know that she has absolutely no desire to be anything other than my son's wife."

Lord Sen turned to regard Raidan. "Your Highness, Jelena is no threat to you, even if the king claims her publicly."

Raidan heard the unspoken message in Sen's softly spoken final words and saw the promise in his eyes. *You'd go to war against me to protect this girl!* he thought. *We'd both better pray to the One that it never comes to that, for then I'd have to destroy you, my friend!*

The Lord of Kerala sat down and glanced around the table at his fellow advisors. A heavy silence, full of consternation and confusion, blanketed the room. The air hummed with energy, the result of fourteen individual Talents amplified by proximity and stress.

The whole situation threatened to give Raidan a vicious headache. He rubbed at his temples. "Brother, why don't you send for Jelena now? I think it's time that your Council meet your daughter and see for themselves just what she's like."

"I'll go and get her myself," Keizo murmured.

The king stood and exited the room. He returned a moment later with Jelena on his arm. "My lords and ladies, I present to you my daughter...Jelena."

Raidan's eyebrows lifted in surprise at the transformation his niece had undergone. The girl wore a splendid, multi-layered court gown, an ornate silver headdress resting on her tamed locks.

By the One, she's really quite pretty, he thought, *and if she weren't a bastard Onjara, and already married, she'd have no trouble finding a place as a concubine to some minor lord or court official.*

Jelena held her head high, but Raidan sensed her nervousness; to her credit, she masked it well.

"My lords and ladies, I thank you for receiving me," the girl addressed the Council in excellent, though heavily accented, Siri-dar. "Please allow me to sit and answer any questions you may have for me."

Well said, girl, Raidan thought.

The king snapped his fingers and a servant came forward with a chair, which he placed next to the king's. Keizo waited while his daughter sat with admirable grace and adjusted her skirts, then folded her hands demurely on her lap.

Keizo resumed his seat and held up his hand before anyone could speak. "Before you question my daughter, I have an announcement to make. There will be an official ceremony of legitimization for her in two days time. I will then present her to the people." The king calmly gazed at his advisors, daring them to challenge him.

"Tell us about yourself, child," Lady Odata spoke up first, breaking the tense silence.

"I was raised in the house of my mother's brother, Duke Teodorus of Amsara," Jelena began, her voice quiet but steady. "My mother bore me in disgrace, disowned by her own family because she confessed to the crime of lying with an elven man. She died giving birth to me, so I never knew her, except through the stories told to me by my foster mother."

Jelena went on to tell her tale of growing up outcast among the humans of Amsara, ignored or openly despised by most of them; her foster mother and human cousin became her only sources of love and emotional support.

"I lived and worked as a kitchen servant for most of my life. I never dreamed anything else was possible for me, so I made the best of it.

It wasn't all bad, though. My cousin Magnes taught me to read and write, to ride a horse and shoot a bow. He even taught me a little about swordplay and how to defend myself with a knife."

"Why did you run away, then?" Lord Morio asked, his voice sharp.

"My uncle, the duke, was preparing to sell me as a concubine to another lord. I could live as a servant, but I would not be made a slave. So...I left."

Many of the lords stirred uneasily.

Struck a sensitive spot, has she, Raidan thought. *How many of you keep hikui concubines to warm your beds, eh?*

"My cousin came with me to protect me. We ran into a gang of bandits on the border between Amsara and Kerala. My husband...I mean, my future husband—Captain Ashinji Sakehera—rescued my cousin and me, but I got badly hurt. Captain Sakehera took us both back to Kerala where I received treatment for my wounds. Even before I had fully recovered, Lord Sen offered me a place in his service as a messenger. I accepted and worked to make a good life for myself in Kerala. I had friends, decent work, and most important of all, I had my freedom."

"What became of your human cousin?" old Lady Saizura asked in a thin, reedy voice. She wore an antique gown and an outlandishly tall headdress, which, coupled with her extreme age, made her look like a character out of a historical play.

"He decided it was best that he return home to Amsara. I have had no news of him since."

Lady Saizura snorted. "No doubt he has given his father a complete description of your castle and its defenses, Sakehera. I'd be concerned, if I were you!"

Jelena's eyes flashed with anger. "My cousin is an honorable man! He would never betray anyone he considered a friend, not even if his own father asked him to. If Duke Teodorus attacks Kerala, it won't be because of anything Magnes told him!" Jelena glared at the old noblewoman defiantly.

"Hee hee! The girl has spirit, Majesty! I'll give her that much," Saizura cackled. "Pity she is not okui."

"She is our king's daughter, Lady Saizura, and my daughter-in-law! That should make her good enough to meet even your standards!" Sen growled.

"Peace, Lord Sen...my lady!" the king intervened.

Raidan studied his niece's face. Her lower lip trembled a little, and her eyebrows drew downward at their inner corners. She surreptitiously rubbed her belly, as if in pain. Despite her apprehension, she was managing to maintain her composure. Raidan doubted that his own son Raidu could do as well.

"Fathers," Jelena continued, emphasizing the plural and looking at Keizo and Lord Sen in turn, "And my lords and ladies. I know what I am, and what I'm not. Many of you are not comfortable with my presence, and probably wish that I'd never found my way here, but I did. I've no desire to overturn any laws that are *fair*, nor do I wish to take away something that is not mine. All I want is to know my father, and my family history, and to learn the history of the elven people." She fell silent.

"Well spoken, Niece," Raidan said. He scanned the faces of the others, and saw cautious acceptance on a few, but most looked decidedly non-committal. He had expected as much. If it came down to a battle of wills with his brother, then he could count on the necessary support of the majority of the Council.

It seems that my niece will be no real threat after all.

* * *

"She held up well. Even I felt a twinge of pride," Raidan admitted. "She seemed a little pale, though, and she kept pressing her hand to her belly." He sat for awhile in silence and watched Taya at her little writing desk as she jotted down notes in a small book bound in scaly red leather.

Raidan didn't inquire about the nature of her work. He assumed it to be magical, and he preferred to stay out of all business pertaining to the sorcerous arts.

Taya sighed and put down her pen. She closed the little book with a snap and laid it aside. "The girl is pregnant. Amara Sakehera told me this morning," she said.

"Will this complicate things?" Raidan asked.

Taya shook her head. "No...not really, though Amara will no doubt wish to delay the Sundering until after the child is born." She paused, then added, "It would be the compassionate thing to do, but I'm not sure we'll have that luxury. Of course, as Mistress of the Kirian Society, I will have the final word on when the ritual will be performed. Amara must abide by my decision."

Taya rose from her chair and came to sit beside Raidan, who slid over to make room for her upon the small couch. The scent of jasmine, inextricably linked to all Raidan's erotic thoughts about his wife, infused the air. "What about Keizo?" he asked.

"You must not tell your brother any of this!" Taya responded sharply. "I realize this puts you in a very difficult position..."

"Yes, it does!" Raidan exclaimed. "You are demanding that I withhold something so important that, by doing so, I'm committing a terrible betrayal! This is the life of my brother's only child!"

"A life that you would not hesitate to take yourself if you felt it necessary!"

Raidan stared into his wife's eyes and saw the iron-willed Mistress of the Kirian Society staring back at him.

"You must do this, Husband," Taya murmured. "Greater things are at stake here than the life of one girl...The very existence of the material world."

Forty five years of marriage had taught Raidan many things; the most important lesson being the absolute superiority of Taya's instincts over his own.

He slowly nodded. "If you say that I must lie to my brother...that I have no choice but to do this thing...then I will do it, because I trust you completely."

Despite the seriousness of their conversation, Raidan found the smell of his wife's perfume distracting. He gazed at Taya and marveled again at his great fortune. Most married couples counted themselves lucky if they even liked each other. He had received in Taya a gift beyond price—a best friend as well as a wife. He pulled her close and kissed her.

"What was that for?" she asked.

"Do I need a reason to kiss my wife?" He brushed her cheek with a forefinger.

"No, of course not," she replied softly.

"How could I ever live without you?" he whispered.

"You'll never have to find out."

* * *

Two days later, Raidan stood beside Keizo before a glittering assemblage of the elite of Sendai as the king formally claimed Jelena as his own.

"I hereby proclaim her to be my legitimized child, a true daughter of the House of Onjara, and I now elevate her to the rank of Princess." Keizo's voice rang out clear and strong, reaching even those who had to stand at the back of the vast, State Audience Chamber.

Jelena, looking a little overwhelmed in her formal court gown and makeup, nevertheless stood tall by the king's left hand.

"She shall be known from this day forward as Princess Jelena Onjara Sakehera of Alasiri." The king beckoned and Jelena knelt before him. He held out his hands to Raidan, who placed within them a coronet of white gold worked all around its circumference with a motif of griffins, each one clutching a moonstone in its claws.

The king placed the coronet on Jelena's head. "Rise up, Daughter, and take your rightful place at my side," he intoned. He took Jelena's hand and helped her to her feet. She swayed a little, recovered, then moved to Keizo's left.

The ceremony ended with a fanfare of horns, blown with melodic precision by the court heralds. The formal procession through the streets of Sendai would now commence, so that the common people could see their new princess. Jelena would ride in an open litter, flanked by members of the King's Guard. Raidan and the king would ride before her, Sen Sakehera and her husband Ashinji directly behind. Raidan had heard his niece protested mightily about the arrangements, insisting that she wished to ride her own horse, but the king had held firm. Keizo had confided to Raidan just this morning that his daughter was with child, and would deliver next spring. Raidan duly congratulated his brother, keeping to himself the fact that he already knew.

The restless crowd parted before them as the royal party moved slowly toward the tall double doors leading out of the hall, which stood open to admit the hazy fall sunshine. Brightly caparisoned horses, held by grooms in formal livery, stamped and snorted on the gravel, harnesses jingling. Members of the King's Guard stood at each corner of a litter upholstered in pale green silk, ready to hoist the conveyance onto their shoulders. Two additional guards would walk along either side.

Raidan carefully hid his amusement as Jelena frowned at the sight of the litter. She allowed the guards to help her in, then spent several moments arranging the many layers of her gown. Raidan suspected her efforts were not to create an artful display of the sumptuous fabrics, but simply to get them out of her way so she could recline more comfortably against the pillows. After she had composed her garments to her satisfaction, she adjusted the griffin coronet on her brow, then looked about her as if searching for something.

Someone, Raidan realized, as Ashinji Sakehera appeared at her side. He crouched down and the two of them bent their heads together, whispering earnestly to each other.

Your fortunes have risen quickly, young Sakehera. I doubt this sits well with your brother, Raidan thought.

"Your Highness, at your pleasure!"

Raidan looked away from the lovers to see that a groom had brought his horse. All around him, the procession formed up, preparing to move out across the parade ground and down the main avenue into the city. Even at this distance, the prince could hear, like waves crashing against the shoreline, the muted roar of the crowd gathered along the street.

Keizo had already mounted his horse and sat waiting. Raidan swung into his saddle and the king signaled to the litter bearers. Ashinji Sakehera stepped away as they raised Jelena and her litter to their shoulders. He grabbed her hand and kissed it, then went to mount up beside his father. Raidan maneuvered his horse into position next to the king, and they moved off.

The procession wound its way slowly through the streets of Sendai. The largely okui crowds greeted their king and his newly legitimized daughter with polite cheers and muted applause.

All of that changed the moment they entered Jokimichi.

The hikui folk had turned out as if for a festival day. All the shops and houses were hung with streamers and brightly painted banners. The people greeted Jelena with tumultuous cries, surging forward in a desperate attempt to touch her.

At first, Jelena appeared too overwhelmed to move. She sat as still as a painted statue, one manicured hand pressed to her lips. Then, as if awakening from a dream, she turned her head from side to side, and Raidan could see tears flowing from her eyes, carving streaks through her heavy white court makeup. She leaned forward and thrust her hand over the side of the litter, like a woman dangling her fingers over the gunwale of a boat.

An old man seized her fingers, kissed them, then just as quickly released them. Another and yet another person grabbed her hand, each one pressing it fervently to adoring lips.

The King's Guard made a move to close in and put a stop to things, but Jelena shouted at them to maintain their places. Keizo nodded his head, signaling to the bewildered guardsmen that they should obey his daughter.

"It appears that the hikui folk have already taken your daughter into their hearts!" Raidan had to shout in order to be heard above the crowd.

"So it would seem!" Keizo replied. "Would that the rest of our people were as accepting!"

"Give them time, Brother! The people love you, so they will love your daughter because she is yours!" Raidan spoke to reassure his brother, though he, himself did not really believe his own words, and he could see the uncertainty written on Keizo's face. The king had always paid close attention to popular opinion, even before he had come to his throne. Raidan felt certain that his brother had noticed the lukewarm reception given to Jelena by the majority of the okui in the city. The prince did not think it realistic to expect that Jelena would be able to win over the okui people of Sendai, despite her likeability and determination.

The procession flowed like a colorful snake out of the hikui district, then turned around and began the slow ascent back toward the castle. Raidan glanced over his shoulder at Jelena, who now leaned back against her pillows, eyes closed. She looked so young and vulnerable, and despite the ruin of her makeup, exquisitely pretty. Raidan could now understand Ashinji Sakehera's attraction to her.

The crowds had become once again mostly okui folk, curious to see the hikui girl from the east whom the king had declared an Onjara princess. They cheered, but Raidan knew they directed their devotions toward Keizo and not his newly proclaimed offspring. The prince was well-pleased.

It seems that ambition will be served merely by awaiting the inevitable turn of events, he thought.

13

Dark Ambition

Within a cold, shadow-haunted chamber, far below the light and warmth of the inhabited levels of Sendai Castle, the King's Companion knelt before a small altar of rough-hewn stone. Scattered about the room lay the tools of the sorcerer's trade—thuribles, rock crystal orbs of various sizes, wands, and an extensive collection of vials, bags, bundles, and bottles—all crammed together on plank shelves affixed to the plastered stone walls.

Sonoe had chosen her workplace with care—an abandoned storeroom deep within the warren of chambers that made up the undercroft of the castle. Hers was a secretive business.

The altar stood in the exact center of an intricate circular pattern of lines painstakingly etched into the hard-packed clay of the cellar floor. Viewed from above, a discerning eye could see the many smaller patterns that made up the larger arcane construct. At each point where two or more lesser patterns intersected, a small beeswax taper burned.

Sonoe focused her mind on the task at hand. She removed the gold pins holding her fiery tresses in place and shook them free. She then un-tied the sash of her thin silk robe and let it slip from her shoulders to the floor. Her bare skin—pale as fresh cream in the candlelight—roughened with gooseflesh in the chilly air, but she ignored the discomfort.

She removed the black stone pendant that hung about her neck and placed it on the altar, then paused to steel herself against what she knew she must soon endure.

The spirit will no doubt wish to...abuse me first, she thought. *I mustn't break, mustn't show any weakness...No matter what it does to my flesh.*

Casting a pinch of incense upon the glowing coals in the small iron thurible, she inhaled the pungent fumes and felt a rush as the mildly narcotic smoke entered her body. Her mind drifted into the still place at the center of her being—that part of her wherein dwelt the essence of her Talent. She drew on the well of energy that fed her power and directed it outward, so that it could be shaped according to her will.

Her fingers tingled and sparked as she picked up the small blade lying beside the thurible, and with a quick, sure stroke, she made a shallow cut across the ball of her left thumb. She squeezed and a crimson bead of blood appeared. Carefully, so as not to spill a single drop, she let her life force drip, along with her blood, into a silver chalice. *One, two, three...*

After she had counted six drops, she bound her slashed thumb in a strip of clean linen. The first part of the spell was complete.

Next, she poured a measure of wine into the chalice. "I maketh this draught from the blood of my veins and the life force of my body, so that it may be a worthy offering," she murmured, stirring the wine with an ivory rod.

She cast another pinch of incense onto the thurible, then lit two red candles.

She raised her arms. "I entreat thee, O Nameless One! Thy servant Sonoe awaits your dread touch. I am ready to receive thee, Master!"

She let all of her mental shields drop, and waited.

The black stone now glowed from within, emitting an eerie, blue light. Sonoe could feel the approach of the ancient spirit, the one who had dwelt in darkness, imprisoned, for a millennium, and now hovered on the verge of freedom. He had first come to her in a vision, whispering promises of power beyond all imagining, the power of an empress who would rule at his side.

The stone served as a link, and she, Sonoe, acted as the living tool by which the Nameless One would obtain the one thing essential to his plan.

The Key.

He came like the wind before a storm, surging along the link forged between them by the combined strength of their magics. He slammed into her body, hurling her onto her back with brutal force. She felt her legs forced apart and then the sensation of some*thing* entering her. Though she had anticipated this, still she screamed in pain and fury as the Nameless One assaulted her. She felt as if she were impaled upon a spear of ice, the frozen organ of a frost giant.

It seemed as if the rape went on for hours, but in reality, it lasted no more than a few heartbeats.

The Nameless One withdrew and hovered before her, radiating malevolent satisfaction.

In form, he appeared as a black mist, ever-shifting, though always maintaining the rough outline of a man. Twin orbs, glowing like baleful red coals, occupied the space where the eyes of a living man would have been.

His voice rang in her head like the peal of a huge, brazen bell.

You are mine, to do with as I please.

Sonoe licked dry, cracked lips. She struggled to rise, wincing in pain, but the spirit lashed out and forced her into a servile crouch.

You will always be on your knees before me, unless I give you permission to be otherwise, or unless I wish you on your back.

Sonoe shook with fury and fear in equal measure. "When you first came to me, you promised me power! You said that you would make me an empress, but instead, I find that I am to be your slave?" She glared up at the Nameless One through a curtain of mussed hair.

A rough sound, like the grinding of metal upon metal, rent the air. Sonoe flushed in humiliation at the Nameless One's scornful laughter.

The moment you forged the mind link with me, you became my slave, Sonoe. But do not despair. Though you are my slave, you shall indeed share my triumph and my power. No other shall be set above you, save me. I shall reshape reality to my will and we will rule over all things, side by side.

Sonoe's anger began to cool, then hardened into steely resolve. "I submit then, willingly, Master," she murmured.

Again, the metallic grinding of the Nameless One's laughter tore at her ears and her mind.

Submission does not come easily to you, beautiful one, but you will learn, and it will be my pleasure to teach you.

Sonoe felt her breasts and thighs caressed by an unseen, icy hand. Though bitter bile rose in her throat and threatened to choke her, she remained still.

The one who harbors the Key. Tell me of her.

"She sleeps in the arms of her husband, in chambers near the king's private quarters," Sonoe answered in a rough voice. "I have scanned her and tasted her energy! It is...delicious!" Sonoe found herself becoming aroused at the memory of how the Key had felt. She had experienced nothing like it before — intoxicating, exhilarating, yet terrifying all at once. She had immediately craved more, but there had been a barrier, like a layer of clear ice, preventing more than a cursory touch.

The vessel knows nothing of what she harbors?

"She knows she has Talent, and she knows some facts about the Key. I couldn't prevent my...colleague, Amara Sakehera, from telling her. The girl is her daughter-in-law, after all." Sonoe paused.

You must be careful. I need not tell you the dire consequences if you are discovered.

"I am well aware of the risks!" Sonoe hissed in annoyance. If any of her fellows in the Society discovered her duplicity, not even the king himself could save her. But none of that mattered. The Nameless One offered a prize worth any amount of risk.

You must be prepared to kill them all to gain control of the vessel.

Sonoe knew full well that "them" meant her fellow Kirians, as well as anyone else who might interfere. Amara Sakehera she could deal with easily, but Taya Onjara was another matter. As for the rest of the Kirian Society, the one person who had the power to stop her—the former Mistress of the Society, Chiana Hiraino—mysteriously disappeared years ago. The only remaining members—Iza Fudai and Keyak Hyuga—were both retired from practice.

"I can do whatever it takes," Sonoe declared. "But you must be ready to do your part when the time comes!" She watched the spirit's misty form grow ever more insubstantial as the power that sustained the link between them weakened.

My strength is fading, otherwise you would be writhing in agony for your insolence. The link must be severed soon, so listen carefully. First, you must befriend the girl, earn her trust. Only then will we be able to gain control of her. I shall...keep watch...on...your... progress...!

"I understand...Master," Sonoe replied.

The Nameless One severed the link.

Sonoe knew the spirit had withdrawn to his prison beneath the icy wastes of the Kesen Numai Mountains to rest and rebuild his strength. She felt like a spent wineskin. The dull pain between her legs served as a brutal reminder of the price for her ambition. She crawled over to where her robe lay and pulled the thin fabric over her naked and bruised body, then slowly climbed to her feet. How she would explain her condition to Keizo she had not yet decided, but he knew that, at times, her work as a high level mage could be hazardous. He would not question her too closely.

With her remaining strength, she conjured a magelight, then extinguished the guttering tapers and slipped the black stone pendant around her neck. Lifting the offering chalice to her lips, she drained it to the dregs. Her magical sense detected not a trace of her blood left in the wine. The Nameless One had taken it all.

With the magelight drifting before her, Sonoe began the long walk back to the king's private quarters.

14

A Question Of Loyalty

I've just received an urgent message from my steward." Sen Sakehera waved a small piece of paper in the air like a flag. "Several reports have come in, leading him to believe that a sizable fighting force is gathering just beyond my borders at Amsara Castle."

Raidan had never before seen Sakehera so agitated. Raidan and Keizo, along with Sakehera, now met in the king's private chambers each morning, to eat breakfast and review any reports that had come in from the previous day. Six weeks had come and gone since Keizo had presented his daughter to the people, and during that time, the plans for the defense of Alasiri had begun to take their final shape.

"So. It begins," Keizo said quietly. "But why so soon? Winter will be on us in a matter of weeks. Surely, the humans don't mean to attack us in the snow!"

"No, the Soldarans are not stupid; on the contrary, they are very clever," Raidan pointed out. "This move is meant as a diversionary tactic. We expected they might try this very thing."

"Of course," Keizo said, nodding. "The Soldarans know we will have to send a force out to deal with them... The empress is trying to distract us, split our forces and disrupt our plans for the defense of Tono next spring."

"My steward also reports that there've been some isolated attacks," Sakehera continued. "Crops destroyed, livestock slaughtered or stolen... but so far, nothing more organized." He paced around the room, pausing at last to gaze out of a window. "The duke's been a good neighbor up 'til now," he said, "but, when all's said and done, he's a Soldaran nobleman and must obey his empress. Our peaceful coexistence is over, I s'pose."

"I see no other alternative but to send your own troops back to Kerala, augmented with a contingent from the regular army. Kerala and its people must be protected," Keizo said. "Unfortunately, I simply can't spare you, Sen. Your son will to have to lead the troops in your place."

"Sadaiyo may be my Heir, but he was not trained as an army officer. Leading a unit of Kerala guardsmen is one thing, but..." Sakehera spread wide his hands, as if offering an apology for his son's perceived shortcomings.

"Then I'll put my son-in-law in charge," Keizo said. "He is a trained officer with years of experience."

"No, Brother," Raidan interjected. "Sen's Heir should lead the force back to Kerala. It wouldn't be proper to give command to his younger brother, even if he is more qualified. Let them both go, but send your son-in-law as his brother's second. That way, rank is maintained and you have an experienced officer to keep an eye on things."

"Yes, of course. A sensible solution," the king agreed. He turned a rueful face toward Sakehera. "My daughter will not be at all pleased when she learns that she's to be separated from her husband," he sighed.

"No. Neither will my son, especially now, with his first child on the way," Sakehera agreed. "But they both realize what's at stake here. They know their duty." The Commanding General came away from the window and sat down at the table where a servant had just finished laying out the morning meal. "My sons have never had anything other than enmity between them, much to my sorrow," he said, rubbing his chin pensively. "It's entirely my own fault. Truth is, I've always loved Ashinji best. Of all my children, he's the one that comes closest to the person I wish I could be. I just pray Sadaiyo can put aside his bitterness..." He shook his head. "No, no. Both my sons will do what's required of them."

"Of course they will. They both have my complete trust, old friend," Keizo assured. Sakehera nodded in gratitude. "With any luck, this operation should take only about two months time, three at the most," the king continued. "The first snowfall will put an end to it, if we don't succeed in driving the Soldarans back before then."

Raidan drummed his fingertips on the dark, polished wood of the table. "There's another pressing matter, I'm afraid," he said. "I've gotten several more reports from Tono about the human plague. There's been an increase in the number of cases of the disease striking elves, and what's worse, Odata thinks some of her troops have come down with it."

"Damn!" Keizo exclaimed. "If this plague takes hold in a serious way among Odata's people, we are in very deep trouble. I don't need to tell you what devastation an unchecked illness can wreak on an army."

"I'm researching a preventative," Raidan stated. "I've been studying the writings of a certain human physician who has come up with a very interesting theory, which I intend to test... on myself if I have to."

"That sounds too dangerous. I can't allow you to risk your life in such a manner. I rely on you too much!" Keizo replied forcefully.

Raidan raised his hands in a gesture of appeasement. "I promise I won't take any foolish risks, Brother, and I swear I'll do nothing until I have learned more about Nazarius' theory."

"What does this theory say?" Sakehera asked. "How can the disease be prevented?"

"Nazarius proposed that the essence of the disease itself can be utilized in producing a kind of natural blockage," Raidan answered. "Unfortunately, Nazarius himself died before he could test his theory."

The king shook his head. "This all sounds so fantastical. How can a sickness prevent itself from afflicting a body?"

"Your question reveals just how little we know about the workings of illnesses. It's why I've devoted myself to science...to find out the answers."

The king appeared unconvinced, but Raidan knew the futility of arguing any longer. His brother remained firmly mired in the traditional view that magic and science existed as separate entities, rather than the more rational view that each stood as two different aspects of the same discipline. To Keizo, magic would always be the superior path.

"We need to have our force on the road to Kerala as soon as possible," Keizo said.

"They can leave by the end of the week," Sakehera answered.

A heavy silence fell over the room. Raidan knew that each of them shared the same dire thoughts which no one wished to speak aloud.

A shout, followed by the sound of a young woman's laughter— lighthearted and joyful—floated up from the yard below.

"Our children are down in your private sparring yard, hitting each other with practice swords," Sakehera commented. "I wonder how wise that is, given Jelena's condition." Raidan noted the fatherly concern in his voice.

"I've known my daughter barely two months," Keizo said, "but I've come to learn that she is very much an Onjara. When she sets her mind to something, nothing will deter her. She has insisted on serious weapons training...to aid in the defense of Alasiri, she says."

"Keizo, we need to formulate plans for what we might do if...if it looks like the Soldarans will prevail." Sakehera's voice was grave.

"Don't you think that is a little premature?" the king shot back. "We haven't even had so much as a skirmish yet! You're selling us short if you're already talking of defeat before the war's even begun!"

"Sen's right, Brother. Our forces are outnumbered at least three to one. The Soldarans have the most formidable army in the known world. He's just trying to be realistic. We need a backup plan should the unthinkable happen and the Imperial Army succeed in breaking through our lines at Tono." Raidan paused, then added, "I also believe we should plan to utilize magic as part of our overall defense plan."

Keizo cocked an eyebrow. "I thought you were a man of science, Brother. Now, you advocate using magic?"

"I believe we need to use every weapon at our disposal. The humans have no magic; therefore, they will be unable to mount any defense against ours. It could give us the advantage we need to counter their superior numbers."

"Yes, yes, that's true!" Sakehera agreed.

Keizo laid his hands flat against the table and looked up with troubled eyes. "The amount of skill and energy required to conjure the kind of powerful workings we are going to need will be enormous. It will take several high level sorcerers, and even then, the risks to each of them of death or insanity will be significant...Still, I agree with you."

"We should consult my wife," Raidan replied. "She, better than anyone else at court, will know exactly what needs to be done."

"I will hear from Taya tomorrow, then, during the council meeting." Keizo paused, then added, "I plan to allow Jelena to attend as well. It's high time she started learning the skills of statecraft. The future has become too uncertain. I want her to have at least a basic knowledge, in case..." Keizo frowned and would not meet Raidan's eyes.

"In case...what? What are you trying to say, Keizo?" The unspoken part of the question hung like a dark shadow between them. The king stood and went over to the window. He stared out over the sunswept rooftops for awhile, hands folded behind him, rocking back and forth on his heels. A stray breeze lifted a tendril of silver hair and blew it back over his shoulder.

"I'm not trying to say anything, Brother, other than I wish my daughter to be prepared for any eventuality," he said at last, turning from the window to face Raidan. "Both of us will necessarily have to risk our lives on the battlefield when the time comes, as will your son Raidu. It may come to pass that Jelena will be the only one of our blood left who can carry on. I want her to be ready."

Raidan felt the heat of anger rise within him, but he ruthlessly quelled it. As much as he hated to admit it, Keizo was right. He remembered Taya's admonition that he do nothing, even if Keizo took the unthinkable step and proclaimed Jelena his Heir. There were larger forces at work, and Raidan had to give them time to play their part.

"Keizo, I want to go talk to my sons, tell 'em they're heading home and what they're to do when they get there...If I have your leave?" Sakehera asked. Despite their lifelong friendship and the familiarity that came with it, Sakehera never forgot that Keizo was his sovereign first and foremost.

"Yes, yes, of course," Keizo consented. "And when you see my daughter, please tell her to come to me as soon as is convenient. I'll be in my study."

"I will. Raidan," Sakehera said, nodding his head in farewell. He rose from his chair and departed.

"Brother, I know you too well," Keizo said after Sakehera had left the room. He returned to his chair and poured himself another cup of tea before continuing. Raidan remained silent, waiting. "I've known since the day our brother Okame died, when I ascended the throne and you became my Heir, that you've desired the crown for yourself, or if not for you, then for Raidu."

"I won't insult you by pretending otherwise," Raidan replied. "But I have always stood behind you and supported you as a brother should. I've never allowed my ambition to cloud my judgment."

"True enough. I rely on and trust you most of all, but I suspect that if I try to set my daughter above you, you will fight me, even to the point of open rebellion."

Raidan's eyes narrowed as he regarded Keizo, who stared back at him with eyes as hard and cold as glacial ice. He chose his next words with great care. "Brother, when have I ever given you cause to question my loyalty? I hold the good of our people before all else, just as you do, Keizo. The last thing I want is a civil war, which is what will surely happen if you try to name Jelena as your Heir."

"Is that a threat?" Keizo asked in a conversational tone, but Raidan could see tightly controlled anger in the rigid lines of his brother's body.

"No! It is merely a statement of fact. I happen to know over half the Council would oppose you, and in the ensuing fight, factions will inevitably form among the lesser nobility, further weakening us at a time when we need to be strong and united. And let us not forget the people!" Raidan stabbed the air with a forefinger, for emphasis. "Most, if not all okui will refuse to accept her as Heir, whereas the hikui will embrace her; in fact, they already have! Jelena would serve as a very potent symbol for them and encourage them to demand equal legal status."

"Don't you think the people will accept my daughter because she is mine? She is a true Onjara; the White Griffin proved it!" Keizo replied heatedly.

"Keizo, you should have married and gotten yourself a legitimate heir!" Raidan shouted. "I don't know why you never did, because if you had done so, we wouldn't be in this situation now! I would have gladly stepped aside for a legal child of yours, but for a bastard *hikui*..." He stopped and closed his eyes, unable to continue as his anger threatened to boil over and consume him.

"You dare speak to me thus?" Keizo asked in a low voice.

Raidan's eyes snapped open and he sucked in a deep breath. "Let's stop right now before I...before *we* take this too far." He leaned forward, his face close enough for Keizo to strike if he so chose. "Zin...*Brother!* I don't wish to fight you, but...I beg of you. Don't do anything that all of us will regret. At least hold off making any decision until after we settle things with the Soldarans."

Keizo's jaw worked, as if dangerous words fought to free themselves from the confines of his mouth. He clenched and unclenched his fists, and for one tense moment, Raidan thought his brother would punch him in the face after all. He prepared to dodge the blow, but it never came. Keizo sat back in his chair with a grunt and turned his face away. He rested his chin in his hand.

Raidan sighed with relief. "Keizo, I..." he began, but the king interrupted him.

"Leave me. I need to think." He refused to meet Raidan's eyes.

Without another word, Raidan got up and departed.

15
Danger In The East

Y ou did very well with the sword today, love," Ashinji said. "Your cousin Magnes would be proud."
"I know you held back, Ashi, even though I've asked you not to," Jelena replied with mock irritation. "You won't hurt the baby. The swords are dull and besides, you aren't aiming anywhere near my belly."

The two of them had spent the morning in the king's private sparring yard; after a quick bath, they had returned to the Sakehera family quarters for a lunch of cold meat, cheese, and bread. After helping themselves, they settled into their favorite window seat overlooking a small garden courtyard directly below the tower apartment.

Jelena's weapons training now kept Ashinji busy most mornings. Within the short period of time he had been schooling her, she had made rapid progress. He felt Jelena pushed herself out of fear of the near future, but also from her desire to master some basic skills before her body grew too ungainly.

"I can't help worrying, but..." he raised a hand to forestall her protest, "it doesn't mean I don't think you should learn how to defend yourself." His undeniable need to protect her had to coexist with his desire to help her become strong and self-confident. Sometimes, he found it difficult to balance the two.

Five months into her pregnancy, Jelena glowed with robust health. The nausea that had plagued her early on had subsided; her appetite had increased to the point where she now ate more than he did. Ashinji gazed into his wife's face and noted how it had grown rounder, softer. Even with her mouth full of food, he found her irresistible.

Jelena is carrying our child, he thought, smiling. She stared back at him quizzically.

"What? Do I have sauce on my nose?" She reached up to wipe her face.
"No, love. I'm just thinking about how lucky I am."

Jelena laid her hand on her swollen midsection. "I'm the lucky one," she replied.

They continued their meal in companionable silence; ever attuned to her mood, Ashinji gradually became aware of a subtle change in his wife's demeanor.

"Something's troubling you. What is it?" he asked.

Jelena sighed and took a sip of wine from her tankard before answering. "I visited Sateyuka yesterday," she said.

"Your friend the weaver." Ashinji had yet to meet Jelena's new friend, but he approved of their acquaintance.

"Yes. Going down to Jokimichi, remembering what happened to Sateyuka and her family...it made me angry all over again, Ashi."

"Have you spoken to your father about how you feel?"

Jelena shook her head. "No. Until now, I felt I didn't know him well enough to speak to him about such things. But we have grown much closer in the last few weeks. My father is a good man and a good king, but I think he ignores the plight of the hikui...not because he's uncaring, but because to change the laws would mean going against tradition."

Ashinji picked his next words with care. "I know you'll be angry when you hear this, but...perhaps now is not the time to distract your father with this." Jelena looked at him sharply. Ashinji took her hand. "I don't mean to say I think it's right that a hikui should be less than any okui person under the law, but if the Soldarans succeed in overrunning Alasiri, none of that will matter. We'll all suffer, okui and hikui alike."

"I know what you are saying is right," Jelena conceded, "but I still must tell him how I feel. I'm sure he'd want to know."

"Ah, children!" Sen called out as he swept into the room, interrupting their conversation.

"Hello, Father," Ashinji rose to greet his father. "You look troubled."

"I have news, Youngest Son." He regarded Ashinji with a solemn expression.

"Father, what's happened?" Ashinji asked, frowning. He moved closer to Jelena and slipped an arm around her waist.

"There's trouble back home," Sen answered. "Soldaran troops are gathering at Amsara Castle. We have good intelligence that says they're planning an attack on Kerala within the month."

"No!" Jelena exclaimed. "My uncle can't..." She stopped herself with a fierce shake of her head. "What am I saying...of course he can!" She swore a string of oaths in Soldaran. Sen's eyebrows shot up.

"Easy, Wife," Ashinji soothed, stroking her arm. "How large is the duke's army, Father?"

"At least two thousand strong, by the best estimates of our scouts, and nearly half of that is heavy cavalry. And it's not the duke who leads them."

"Who, then?" Jelena asked. "Surely not my cousin Magnes! He would never...Wait, wait. It must be Thessalina. She's always been the captain of the ducal forces. But then that means..." She grabbed Ashinji's forearm and he winced at the strength of her grip. "Something has happened to my uncle, Ashi. He's ill, or...or...." She paused, then added, "He would never allow Thessalina to lead his troops into battle if he could do so himself."

"A woman does, indeed, appear to be in charge," Sen confirmed.

"Have there been any reports of my cousin Magnes?" Jelena asked.

"I'm sorry, my dear, but the scouts don't know what your cousin looks like. There's really no way to tell if he's even at Amsara."

"I know you're worried about Magnes, Jelena," Ashinji said. "Let's pray that he somehow finds a way to get through this trouble unscathed."

"The king wants a force of our own in Kerala to stand ready to repel any sorties the Soldarans make across our border," Sen continued.

Ashinji frowned. "Why would the empress choose to launch an invasion so far to the east...and why now? I thought her plan is to attack through the Tono valley next spring."

"Think about it, Son. The empress knows that by sending an army out to the east now, she can split our forces and weaken us by making us fight an exhausting defensive action. This way, she wears us down before the main fight even starts."

The harsh squawk of a raven drifted in through the open window. The sound filled Ashinji with foreboding. He shivered and pulled Jelena close against him. He could sense her puzzlement. "I assume Sadaiyo will lead our guards back to Kerala?" he asked.

"Our guard and a contingent of regular troops, yes," Sen replied, then added, "You'll go along as his second-in-command." Ashinji felt Jelena stiffen in his arms. She pulled away and sank back onto the window seat, her face gone pale.

"My heart is telling me to beg you not to send Ashi away," she whispered, looking at Sen, "but my mind understands what is at stake. I know where my husband's duty lies." The pain and fear in his wife's voice cut like knives; still, Ashinji had never been so proud of her.

"Spoken like a true princess," Sen replied. "Your bravery honors us, my dear."

"I don't feel very brave right now." Jelena put an impatient hand to her face and dashed away the tears leaking from the corners of her eyes.

"When do we leave, Father?" Ashinji asked.

"Two days from now. I'll be staying in Sendai. The king can't spare me just now. The full council meets tomorrow. There's still a lot of planning to be done, and in light of these new developments.... Well, I've got to go find your brother, and I pray to the One that wife of his controls her temper when she hears Sadaiyo's going away without her!"

"I'll be ready, Father," Ashinji assured. Sen nodded and squeezed his shoulder, then headed for the door.

Ashinji sat on the couch beside Jelena. She looked so young and frightened, like a little girl who faced the loss of her entire world.

"Jelena..." he began, but she laid a finger to his lips, stilling his words.

"Please don't say anything, Ashi."

He gathered her into his arms and held her while she cried.

* * *

That night, Ashinji dreamed of fire. Flames shot up in bright walls all around him, yet he could not run fast enough to escape. The sounds of pursuit—the thud of horses' hooves, the hoarse shouts of men—echoed in his ears; suddenly, he found himself surrounded by shadows, all featureless, save one. He knew, with terrible certainty, that if he could recognize that face, he would be able to save himself.

'Help me!' he cried, but harsh laughter drowned out his plea. The eyes of the one he should have known burned like stars—cold and distant. Ashinji realized at that moment he was lost. A high-pitched keening, like the wail of a damned soul tore at his ears. He looked down to see an arrow had sprouted from his chest. Bright blood, red as roses, spurted, and he fell, down, down, into darkness...

...and woke with a start, clammy with sweat. His heart hammered against his ribcage and his limbs shook with the knowledge that he had just experienced not a dream, but a vision of his future. He turned to look at Jelena, who lay facing him, sleeping soundly. As he watched, she sighed and muttered, then rolled onto her other side, away from him.

He lay back and took a deep breath, trying to will his body to relax, but to no avail. He knew he would sleep no more this night.

When Jelena awoke the following morning, she found him sitting in the window, staring out over the rooftops, his eyes narrowed against the red glare of the rising sun.

* * *

"Little Brother, your first duty as my second-in-command is to hold my stirrup while I mount." Sadaiyo grinned in more of a wolfish display of his teeth than an actual smile.

"Good morning to you, too, Brother," Ashinji replied, determined to keep a rein on his temper. "The company is assembled and ready to move out as soon as you give the order."

"Lord Ashinji!" a familiar voice called. Ashinji turned to see Gendan approaching at a brisk walk, helmet tucked beneath one arm; Aneko trailed him by a few steps. The Captain of the Kerala Guard bowed crisply to Sadaiyo, acknowledging his presence, as did Aneko, but both gave their entire attention to Ashinji as Gendan spoke.

"It's good to see you, my lord," the captain exclaimed.

"Likewise, Gendan," Ashinji replied, then turning to Aneko, he said, "Jelena has missed you. She wanted to visit you at the barracks, but..."

"I understand, my lord," Aneko replied, smiling. "Things have changed a lot. My good friend Jelena is no longer as free as she once was. Such is the fate the One has decreed for her."

"You must be anxious to get back home to see your wife, Gendan," Ashinji said. "I'm sure it's been hard being separated from her these past months."

Gendan nodded. "Kami's a strong girl, my lord, but no woman should have to endure childbirth without her man beside her. Your father, Goddess bless him, has given me permission to stay at Kerala 'til after Kami delivers."

"My father is a compassionate man," Ashinji replied, studiously ignoring Sadaiyo.

"I have work to do," Sadaiyo grumbled, clearly irritated at not being the center of attention. Both Kerala guards bowed their heads as he stomped off.

"Jelena should be here any moment," Ashinji said. "She's probably with my father and the king. She'll come out with them to see us off."

Ashinji observed Gendan discreetly watching his brother. The captain frowned as Sadaiyo berated a soldier for some minor infraction. His eyes flashed as they shifted to Ashinji. "May I speak freely, my lord?" he asked.

"Of course, Gendan. You needn't ever be afraid to tell me what's on your mind."

"I know why 'tis Lord Sadaiyo leads this expedition, rather than you, my lord, and we'll all obey him, as is our duty, but..." He paused, lower lip caught between his teeth. Ashinji remained silent, waiting for the captain to collect his thoughts and continue. Gendan leaned forward, his voice barely above a whisper. "Just know, should you need us, the Kerala home guard'll stand behind *you*, my lord."

Aneko nodded in agreement. "We will always have your back, Lord Ashinji," she said.

Ashinji tugged at his earlobe, unsure of how to respond to Gendan's words. Kerala's captain had made it clear where his loyalties lay, and the part of Ashinji that despised the kind of man his brother was, felt deeply moved. The other part that honored familial duty pricked him with guilt.

Ashinji's father had placed him under his brother's command, in a position of trust. He was honor-bound to obey Sadaiyo's orders, whatever he might personally feel about his brother.

Shouts and cries of "*The king is here!*" rose above the throng of soldiers and horses milling about the parade ground.

Gendan tapped Aneko's arm. "We'd best be gettin' back to our places." He then looked pointedly at Ashinji. "Remember what I said, my lord."

Ashinji watched as the two Kerala guards hurried away and were swallowed up by the crowd, then turned and headed toward the castle's main entrance. Soldiers stepped aside to let him pass, many of them offering him words of greeting. Since becoming the son-in-law of Silverlock, Ashinji found himself in a position where he had never expected to be—he was famous.

And rich, in his own right. As a wedding gift, the king had given him the best thing he possibly could have—financial independence in the form of his own land. Just yesterday, Ashinji had received the first financial reports. The estate of Goura was small, but profitable, and would be even more so once a competent manager could be found to run it. It lay about two day's ride northeast of Kerala Castle, just over the border in neighboring Manza, the demesne of Lord Dai, Sadaiyo's father-in-law.

The family that had once held Goura had died out, leaving the estate vacant. Ordinarily, any vassal estate in which the family line became extinct would pass to the ruling lord to be disposed of as he or she saw fit. Most of the time, the land would be given to a younger child of the lord. No doubt, the king had compensated Lord Dai well for the land.

Misune probably would have received Goura, Ashinji thought. *No doubt Sadaiyo has already pointed out to her how I've been given what should have rightfully been hers.*

He reached the broad, shallow steps leading up to the castle's main entrance just as his father, the king, Prince Raidan, and Jelena all emerged. He waited for them to reach the bottom stair, then bowed his head. "Your Majesty, your Highness." He looked up and caught Jelena's eye.

When he had left her behind in the warm haven of their bed before sunrise, he had made her promise she would eat something before she came down to see him off. He raised his eyebrows questioningly.

"Yes, I ate," Jelena replied, laughing, but her voice caught and he saw tears glittering in her eyes. Despite her brave face, put on for his benefit, he sensed her fear, though she held it well in check. She came and stood beside him, linking her arm with his.

"Where is your brother, Son?" Sen inquired, eyes scanning the crowd.

"I'm not sure," Ashinji replied. He looked over his shoulder. "He was..."

"Here he comes now," Prince Raidan said.

Sadaiyo emerged from the throng, looking harried and followed by an equally harried aide. He sketched a bow before the king and the prince. His eyes flicked over Ashinji and away again, as if his brother wasn't worth his attention.

"The army is ready to form up and move out, your Majesty," Sadaiyo reported.

"Very good," Keizo replied. "You may give the order any time."

"Father, have you seen Misune?" Sadaiyo inquired, his voice rough with irritation. Sen shook his head.

"Haven't seen her, Son. I'm sure she'll be here before you leave, though."

"She'd better be," Sadaiyo grumbled. He turned to Ashinji. "Go and give the order." He bowed again and dashed off into the crowd, shouting for his aide to bring his horse. The king, Prince Raidan, and Sen had all moved off a little way and stood in a close huddle, their expressions intense. Ashinji slipped an arm around Jelena's waist and pulled her close so he could speak to her without having to raise his voice. He put a hand under her chin and tilted her face up so he could gaze into the warm hazel of her eyes.

He opened his mouth but no words would come, as if his tongue had lost all ability to form meaningful sounds.

I love her so much, it hurts, he thought. *I can't burden her now, not when we are about to part, with the vision I've been given of my future.*

She gazed expectantly at him, love flowing out of her body like the blue fire she harbored within herself. It felt so sweet, and yet the pain of knowing he might not live to see her again made it almost unbearable.

His throat ached with unshed tears.

"Jelena," he began, then paused to catch his breath.

"What is it, my love?" she whispered.

He rested his forehead against hers. "There's too much to say and not enough time for all of the words," he said. "Let me try and mindspeak to you." She nodded and closed her eyes.

He rarely used his ability to mindspeak. It always made his head hurt when he tried, but any amount of pain seemed worth the effort to convey his innermost feelings.

He entered her mind as gently as he could, amazed anew at the brilliance of it. The blue fire burned at the core of her being, mysterious and powerful, but he shied away from it, wary of its strength. He opened himself to her and let the love that filled his soul pour from him like blood from an open wound. He gave every drop he could, and when he could give no more, he withdrew.

Jelena cried out as he staggered, momentarily weak as a kitten. She clutched at him, trying to hold him up while he willed his knees to lock and take his weight. The weakness passed, but he knew the ache in his head would linger for hours.

"Ashinji!" Jelena whispered fiercely. "Ashi, look at me!" He met her eyes and winced at the intensity of her gaze. "Ashi, you promise me that you'll come back to me—*to us!*" She grabbed his hand and pressed it against her belly. "This is your child in here, a child that needs its father! Promise you'll come back!"

He closed his eyes.

"*Promise!*" she cried.

He kissed her, and though he tried, he could not keep the desperation out of it. Jelena sobbed once, then with a mighty effort, stifled her tears. When at last she lifted her head, she had fully regained her composure.

"I swear, my love, that I will do everything in my power to return to you and our child," Ashinji murmured. Jelena nodded, and as she reached up to touch his face, he grabbed her fingers and pressed them to his lips.

"*Captain Sakehera!*" Sadaiyo bellowed. Ashinji sighed and turned to face his brother, who approached the steps on the back of a bay stallion. "You've had long enough to make your farewells! Get to your horse and give the order to form up! *Now!*"

"Go," Jelena said, pulling herself up straight and proud, like a true princess.

"Lord Ashinji, your horse!" Homan, first sergeant of Peregrine Company and Ashinji's aide, came forward, leading Ashinji's favorite black charger Kian. Homan held the animal's head while Ashinji mounted, then handed up his captain's helmet. Jelena moved over to stand at Ashinji's foot. She rested a hand on his stirrup. He looked down into her beautiful face.

"We'll be waiting for you," she said. He pulled the helmet down on his head and buckled the chinstrap, glad his face was now hidden from her. He did not want her last memory of him to be one in which he wept.

16
Toward A Dark Horizon

Misune made her appearance just before Sadaiyo gave the order to ride out. Lifting the hem of her bright yellow gown, she swept down the steps and strode briskly towards Sadaiyo's horse, golden lion's eyes flashing and mouth set in a petulant frown.

Ashinji felt a twinge of sympathy for her.

She is a skilled warrior, after all, he thought, *and if she weren't pregnant, she'd be riding out with us.*

Ashinji watched from a discreet distance as his brother and sister-in-law exchanged a few tense words. He couldn't hear what they said, but from the looks on their faces, and by the way Misune stomped off, he deduced their parting had been less than tender.

He took one last glimpse of Jelena, who had moved to stand between his father and the king, before urging his horse forward into place beside his brother.

The grille of Sadaiyo's helmet obscured his facial expression, but his movements as he readied himself to ride were sharp and angry. Ashinji refrained from any comments; long, bitter experience told him that to say anything now would only invite a vicious verbal attack. Instead, he checked his gear and waited for Sadaiyo to give the order.

At last, Sadaiyo was ready. He raised a gloved hand in the air and swept it forward. Shouts ran up and down the lines as the signal passed through the ranks. The army began to move.

The grinding crunch of gravel beneath hundreds of hooves, the mingled smells of horse and leather, the hard blue sky above—all of Ashinji's senses were heightened, the knowledge of his impending death acting as a stimulant to his nervous system. Every scent, sound, and color seemed impossibly acute, crystalline and pure. The urge to look back over his shoulder to see Jelena one last time proved almost too much to bear, but he dared not.

I might not be able to leave, he thought.

The army snaked down through the city, making its way toward the gates. The people lined up along both sides of the street, watching somberly as it passed, over eight hundred strong. Ashinji, seeing the apprehension in their faces, realized they knew this represented only the beginning of what could prove to be a brutal, devastating war.

Sadaiyo remained silent until they had ridden beyond the outer gates and out on the broad road leading east toward Kerala. "So, Little Brother. Our father has finally found a way to force us to work together." His tone, as usual, dripped with sarcasm.

"You are in command, Brother. I'll follow your orders because that is my duty," Ashinji answered. "All I ask is that you don't allow your feelings for me to get in the way of your judgment. Too many lives are at stake."

"If you mean my deep brotherly love for you, don't worry," Sadaiyo retorted. He urged his mount forward and soon, his bigger, faster stallion had pulled ahead of Ashinji's black gelding. Ashinji was content to let his brother ride ahead.

As the morning wore on, the sun climbed higher and the day grew unseasonably warm. A late fall heat wave was not uncommon this far south— one last taste of summer before winter's chill descended upon the land.

I know what a chicken roasting in an oven must feel like, Ashinji thought. He finally loosened the chinstrap and pulled his helmet off, resisting the urge to hurl it away from him. Instead, he hung it from the pommel of his saddle.

Looking over his shoulder at the ranks, Ashinji saw how the troops slumped in their saddles, wilting beneath the merciless sun. He made a decision.

Sadaiyo still rode a slight distance ahead with his aide, forcing Ashinji to urge his horse into a jog to catch up. As he moved alongside, Sadaiyo acknowledged him with the merest flicker of a glance.

Ignoring the implied slight, Ashinji spoke. "Perhaps it's time to call a halt, Sadaiyo," he suggested. "We've been riding steadily for at least three hours, and in this heat, the troops and horses will need more rest and water."

"No," Sadaiyo answered. "I've got to get this army to Kerala in ten days' time, and unless I push hard, we won't make it."

"The troops will be in no shape to fight if they are pushed to exhaustion and they start dropping from the heat," Ashinji pointed out. He kept his voice calm and reasonable. "Call a halt, Brother. It needn't be a long one." From the corner of his eye, Ashinji saw Sadaiyo's aide staring intently over the tops of his own mount's ears, pretending not to listen, but Ashinji knew better. The last thing he wanted was a public disagreement with Sadaiyo. Morale would suffer if the troops witnessed their leaders at odds.

Ashinji couldn't see his brother's face, but by the slump of his shoulders, he knew Sadaiyo had reconsidered and given in to good sense.

"Very well," Sadaiyo answered through clenched teeth. "A brief stop. Give the order."

The relief of the troops was palpable. The air rang with laughter and shouts as they pulled off their helmets and many upended water bottles over sweating faces. Ashinji poured water into a leather cup and held it up to Kian's muzzle so he could drink. The horse eagerly sucked the cup dry and nosed Ashinji's hand for more. He allowed the gelding one more drink before putting the bottle to his own lips.

Sadaiyo had removed his own helmet and now stood in the shade of a large old oak tree beside the road, deep in conversation with a man dressed in the plain garb of an estate worker. As Ashinji approached, he heard Sadaiyo tell the man to convey his thanks to his mistress. The man, after bobbing his head several times, turned and hurried off. Ashinji saw him mount an ugly mule and set off at a cumbersome trot down the road.

"Who was that?" he asked, pointing at the receding figures of man and mule.

"A servant from Enzan Estate," Sadaiyo answered. He took a drink from his water bottle and wiped his mouth with the back of his hand. "Enzan's only about another three hour's march down the road. The Lady sent him out to invite us to camp on her lands. She's even promised to feed all the senior officers...and put you and me up in the manor."

"Amazing how quickly news of an army on the move travels," Ashinji commented. He dropped to the ground and lay in the tough grass, folding his arms behind to cradle his aching head, still sore from mindspeaking with Jelena. "It will be nice to eat something other than camp food, but I'll be sleeping under the stars tonight with my company," he stated.

Sadaiyo rolled his eyes. "Suit yourself," he replied. "I, for one, won't pass up the chance to sleep in a real bed."

"It will be strange, sleeping without my wife beside me," Ashinji said quietly. Sorrow struck at his heart like a hammer blow. An image of fire obscured his vision for an instant. Sadaiyo said nothing. "You must feel the same way," Ashinji added, looking up at his brother's handsome profile. "I know it's none of my business, but..." He paused, trying to read Sadaiyo's mood, then decided to forge ahead. "I couldn't help but notice that you and Misune parted on less than happy terms."

"You're right. It is none of your business, but since you are so curious, I'll confide in you. Misune was furious that she had to stay behind. I tried to reason with her, but..." Sadaiyo threw up his hands in exasperation. "There's just no reasoning with her sometimes! She's like... a thunderstorm or a whirlwind!"

Ashinji hid a smile behind his hand. Clearing his throat, he offered words of sympathy. "I'm sure once she calms down she'll realize that a campaign is no place for a pregnant woman, not even one of her considerable skill at arms."

Sadaiyo snorted. "I doubt it...But what of your wife, Little Brother? How did the princess handle you leaving her?"

Ashinji thought he detected the slightest hint of distain in Sadaiyo's voice when he said the word *princess*. "Jelena is strong, and incredibly brave. She'll be all right. She has the king and our father to support her. And she'll need their support, especially...after whatever happens... happens."

Sadaiyo's eyebrows lifted in puzzlement. "What are you talking about?" he asked.

Ashinji looked away, out over the stubbled fields shimmering in the midday sun. "Nothing. I just meant...we'll be risking our lives in battle. Anything could happen."

"I don't know about you, but I plan on coming back alive," Sadaiyo stated. "I've got a son on the way, and I intend to be there on the day he's born."

"A son?"

"That's right. The child's a boy. Misune can already sense his Talent. He's going to be a grand mage, I'm sure of it." Sadaiyo grinned. Ashinji felt his throat constrict with tears he dare not shed, tears for his own child who might have to grow up without a father.

Damn it! Visions are shades of what might be, not of what will be! I can't give in to this! I've got to fight to change what I've been shown!

Ashinji rolled over and climbed to his feet. Restlessly, he paced around the hoary bole of the ancient tree, rubbing at his temples.

Sadaiyo regarded him with mild curiosity. "What's gotten into you?" he inquired. "Nervous about facing the humans?"

Ashinji shot his brother a withering glance. Sadaiyo never missed an opportunity to needle him. "No," he replied and turned to walk away toward the road where his sergeant Homan waited, holding his horse. He felt the strain of keeping a lid on his anger slowly but steadily wearing him down, and an entire day had not yet passed. *How will I survive another nine?* he thought.

"You look troubled, my lord," Homan commented. "Anythin' I can do to help?" The sergeant spoke with the slow drawl of the Arrisae Islands. Ashinji trusted him completely, but certain things were too personal to share, even with a trusted officer.

He shook his head. "Thank you, but there's really nothing you, or anyone other than myself, can do about my particular set of problems." He gazed down the dusty road. "There's a good meal waiting for us at the end of our day's march, I've heard."

Homan grimaced. "Field rations are only for keepin' the body from starving. No one really likes 'em. A hot meal'll be welcome. I s'pose there'll be a soft bed for you and Lord Sadaiyo, eh?"

"I'm certain my brother will take every advantage of Enzan's hospitality, but I'll sleep with Peregrine Company."

Homan nodded in approval. "You've always shared everythin' with us, Cap'n. The good and the bad."

Ashinji shrugged. "I'm a soldier, just like the rest of you."

But not really, he admitted to himself. *Not since Jelena's ascended to her lofty position and pulled me up with her.*

Even though they all tried to pretend as if nothing had changed, he could sense the difference in the way the men and women under his command viewed him, now that he had become Keizo Onjara's son-in-law.

Before, he had shared an easy camaraderie with his company, the Peregrines. They followed his orders, not only because they had to, but because they genuinely liked and respected him. Ashinji knew none of that goodwill had changed, but now a distance existed between him and his troops that had everything to do with his new social status. Though unavoidable, it still saddened him.

Homan snapped to attention, and Ashinji turned to see Sadaiyo approaching, dangling his helmet carelessly by its chinstrap.

"Time to go," he said as he brushed past, signaling for his horse.

"Pass the word along, Homan. We're moving out," Ashinji ordered. Homan nodded once in acknowledgement, then turned and began to shout out the order to mount up. His words echoed down the line and the army quickly rose up and fell in. On Sadaiyo's signal, they resumed the march.

The sun hung low in a hazy sky when they finally reached Enzan Estate. The estate was large and prosperous, and the road leading to the manor wound through fields planted with row upon row of grapevines. Fruit hung heavy in plump, purple clusters on the gnarled vines, awaiting the harvest.

A figure stood in the road ahead of them, waving. As they drew closer, Ashinji recognized the man who had been sent to meet them several hours earlier. Sadaiyo held his arm up, signaling the column to stop.

The man approached and bowed low. "If it please you, my lords, my lady has bid me lead you to the ground where the army is to camp tonight." Sadaiyo waved impatiently, indicating that the man should proceed. The servant bowed again and trotted off, leading them down a side road that curved away deeper into the vineyards.

Dusk had fallen by the time they left the vineyards and entered a large, open meadow. A single, massive oak tree stood near the center, like a well-armored sentry on guard duty. The manor house stood at the far edge of the grassy expanse, windows gleaming a soft gold from the light of many lamps. Sadaiyo reined his horse to a halt and dismounted. He handed off the stallion to his aide and turned around in a circle, surveying the ground. Ashinji waited, still mounted, for his brother's command.

"Give the order to set up camp, and I want you and the other senior officers to assemble under that tree as soon as everything's settled," Sadaiyo directed. "I don't intend to keep our hostess waiting any longer than necessary."

The camp sprang up quickly. By the time Ashinji had passed the word to those officers who ranked high enough to dine at the lady's table, most of the common troops had shed their armor and now attended to evening duties—grooming horses, starting small cooking fires, cleaning tack, laying out bedrolls.

Ashinji checked in with Peregrine Company before leaving to join the other senior officers.

"I feel sorry for you, Cap'n," Homan drawled. "While you're up at the manor eatin' whatever poor fare the lady can scrape together, we'll all be out here feasting on dried fish and journeycake!" A gale of laughter erupted all around. Ashinji grinned and for a brief moment, he felt the ease he had known with his people before he had been lifted so high above them by circumstance.

"I'll try not to feel too envious," he replied. "I'll be back after dinner, so save some beer for me."

"And a little something stronger, my lord?" Homan winked and held up a small metal flask. Ashinji recalled, with wistful clarity, the night he had shared a flask of muato with Magnes Preseren.

I wonder where Jelena's cousin is now, he thought. *Will we have the misfortune to come face to face on the field of battle? If I'm forced, can I fight, to the death, a man I call 'friend'?*

Goddess! Maybe the face I saw in my vision...belonged to Magnes! Can it be possible that my friend—my kinsman—will be the instrument of my death?

"My lord...Are you all right?"

Homan's question broke Ashinji's melancholy reverie.

"Yes, Sergeant, I'm fine...just thinking, is all."

"We'll see you later, then, Cap'n."

"You surely will," Ashinji replied. He waved in farewell and strode off into the darkness toward the great oak tree.

"There you are!" Sadaiyo called out as Ashinji arrived at the meeting place beneath the spreading branches of the old tree. "You've kept all of us waiting!"

"Sorry," Ashinji murmured, glancing around at the six men and two women who made up Sadaiyo's senior command. Like Ashinji, they all held the rank of captain, and, with the exception of Gendan, had served in the regular army for many years, two as far back as the reign of Keizo the Elder.

Gendan nodded in greeting. "My lord," he said.

"Are the king's officers treating you well, Gendan?" Ashinji asked quietly.

"Errrr...yes, Lord Ashinji, well enough, I reckon, though some of the troops are a little snotty to my guards. Guess they figure army regulars rate above a lowly provincial guard unit." Gendan sniffed, clearly indignant.

"The Kerala Guard is far from lowly, and soon, the regulars will know your true worth, as I do," Ashinji replied.

Gendan scuffed his boot in the litter of dried leaves and last year's acorns. "Thank you, my lord. Means a lot t'hear you say that," he said.

A liveried servant arrived to escort the group of officers to the manor. As they proceeded across the meadow, now trampled down by the passage of hundreds of boots and hooves, Sadaiyo fell in beside Ashinji. "Why so broody, Little Brother?" he inquired. "Could it be that, like me, you miss the sweet company of your wife?"

Ashinji regarded his brother with surprise. Though he couldn't discern Sadaiyo's expression in the darkness, he thought he detected a note of sympathy in his brother's normally sardonic voice.

"I miss Jelena very much," he replied, careful to keep his own voice neutral. He didn't trust Sadaiyo not to use any of his tender emotions against him, and he would never divulge the true reason for his bleak mood.

"Well, a fine meal, good wine, and a willing girl will lift your spirits!" Sadaiyo chuckled. "But, of course, you'd rather sleep alone, outside, on the hard ground." He laughed again.

Ashinji slowed his pace in order to allow Sadaiyo to walk ahead, determined to avoid his brother's direct company as much as possible tonight.

When they reached the manor, the lady herself greeted them at the door. Lady Kara was an elderly widow, and still attractive even though age had left its inevitable traces upon her face. A knee-length tunic and wide trousers of fine white cotton enhanced her graceful figure, and she wore her hair in a towering, old-fashioned coiffure. Three middle-aged women flanked her on either side, and by the close resemblances of all their faces, Ashinji deduced they were Lady Kara's daughters.

"Welcome to Enzan, my lords," the lady greeted them in a warm, melodious voice, inclining her head. For a moment, Ashinji caught a glimpse of the beautiful young woman she had once been. "My humble home is honored by your presence."

"Lady Kara, it is we who are honored by your gracious hospitality," Sadaiyo replied, taking the lady's hand and pressing it to his lips. Lady Kara smiled, a look of satisfaction on her face, clearly taken in by Sadaiyo's courtly gesture.

"Please, come inside. I've had a meal prepared for all of you. Nothing fancy, mind. We're simple country folk, after all, but there's plenty of food and it's hot." She turned and led the way into the house, her daughters falling in beside her.

The meal proved to be anything but simple. The long trestle table creaked beneath platters of roasted ducks in citrus sauce, rabbit pie, and tureens of baked trout from the local stream. Pots of boiled fennel root, a fresh salad of greens grown in Lady Kara's own garden, and baskets of bread complemented the meats, and to wash it all down, several fine varietals produced at the estate's own winery.

Despite the splendid quality of the food, Ashinji found it impossible to summon up much interest. He ate just enough to avoid offending their hostess, and allowed himself a single goblet of wine, steadfastly refusing any refills.

Two of Lady Kara's three daughters had managed to position themselves on either side of him, and now gazed at him like hungry cats contemplating a nest of baby mice. Their sister had ensconced herself between Sadaiyo and her mother, where she now conducted a not-so-subtle seduction campaign. Sadaiyo basked in her attentions, clearly enjoying himself.

Ashinji wondered why the three women, despite passable looks and a decent fortune, had yet to find husbands.

"You've hardly touched your food, Lord Ashinji. Is it not to your liking?" asked the sister on his left. She regarded him from a heart-shaped face graced with full lips and sparkling blue eyes.

"Everything is delicious, Lady Tamina," he replied. "I'm just not very hungry." He lifted his wine goblet to his lips and took a small sip. Tamina leaned in close and the scent of roses caressed Ashinji's nose.

"You seem sad, my lord. Such a handsome young face should never look so mournful." She reached up to coquettishly twirl a loose strand of black hair between her thumb and forefinger.

"I miss my wife," Ashinji replied, and though he tried, he failed to disguise the pain in his voice.

The sister to his right boldly caressed his forearm. "You must love her very much, my lord," she murmured. "But a wife who is far away can't keep her husband warm at night, can she? It's perfectly understandable that a man, even one who loves his wife, would wish to take some comfort where he could... Ease the loneliness of the road."

"My sister Shuzen is right," Tamina purred in agreement.

A woman's throaty laugh momentarily distracted him. Ashinji looked away from Shuzen in time to observe Sadaiyo engage Lady Kara's oldest daughter in a firm kiss. He turned away in faint disgust, only to be skillfully ambushed by Tamina, who slipped one hand between his knees and grabbed his chin with the other. Boldly, she pulled his face to hers and kissed him. He grunted in surprise, and tried to push her away but she held fast. From the corner of his eye, he could see Lady Kara smiling in approval.

"Lady Tamina, please!" Ashinji gasped, after he managed to disengage his lips from hers.

Tamina smiled. "Oh come, now. Why so shy? You're wife's not here. You're free to play, and you can have both of us."

"Our sister Uebaru gets your brother, of course, because he is the eldest and so is she, but Tamina and I are much better lovers than she is," Shuzen purred. She tweaked Ashinji's ear.

This is all too much, he thought. *I've got to get out of here before I explode!*

Ashinji rose from his seat. Conversation halted and all eyes fastened on him. "Lady Kara, I humbly apologize but I'm not feeling very well. I think I should leave now."

He could see that Lady Kara saw through his feeble excuse, but he didn't care. For an instant, intense regret and annoyance flashed across her lined face, but she quickly recovered.

"Of course, Lord Ashinji," she replied, the gracious hostess once more. "I am so sorry you are...indisposed."

"My lord, d'you want me to come with you?" Gendan asked, half-rising from his seat, a look of concern on his weathered face.

Ashinji shook his head. "No, Captain. Stay and enjoy yourself."

Neither Tamina nor Shuzen bothered to disguise their anger at being rejected. Both raked him with withering looks, then turned their backs.

Ashinji bowed to Lady Kara and fled the room.

As he escaped out into the crisp, smoke-scented air of the fall night, the sound of renewed revelry followed him, mocking him with unbridled gaiety.

The moon rode high and full, bathing the countryside in quicksilver light. Fine gravel gave way to packed earth as he walked along the path toward the meadow where the army camped. He could hear the sounds of the camp off in the distance—the skirl of a flute, raucous laughter, the neigh of restless horses, voices raised in song. It filled him with intense longing and regret; never had he been more acutely aware of his own mortality than at this moment.

He paused on the moonlit path to drink in the sweet air. Closing his eyes, he visualized Jelena, standing before him, arms raised in love and welcome. In his mind's eye, he reached out to embrace her.

If only I could hold you one last time, he thought. *If only we could share one last kiss...*

I could go to my death a happy man.

17

Raging To The Heavens

Sadaiyo returned to camp at sunrise, looking a little haggard, but well pleased. Ashinji had been awake and working for some time already, supervising the distribution of rations to his company.

Sadaiyo sauntered up and greeted him with a cheerful grin. "Good morning, Little Brother. Sleep well?"

"Yes, I did," Ashinji lied.

"Well, I hate to brag, but I didn't get much sleep," Sadaiyo replied. "I didn't think I could possibly keep up with three...but somehow, I managed to... rise to the occasion." He chuckled lasciviously. "You know, you really hurt Tamina and Shuzen's feelings, not to mention Lady Kara's. You ought to have better manners." He raised a hand as if to forestall a protest. "But don't worry! I was able to, ah, smooth their ruffled feathers and sweeten their tempers."

"Sex has never been a blood sport for me, like it is for you, Brother," Ashinji retorted. He stared at Sadaiyo with weary eyes, wanting only to be left alone.

"Oh, Lady Kara and her daughters weren't interested in sport, my naïve little brother. They were deadly serious." Sadaiyo grinned again.

"What are you talking about?" Ashinji demanded, irritation and fatigue roughening his voice. He hated Sadaiyo's word and mind games.

"Blood, Ashi. Heirs. In case you didn't notice, none of Lady Kara's daughters is exactly in the bloom of youth anymore. Enzan needs heirs or it will pass to the Crown upon the deaths of all the good ladies. I just stepped in and, uh, performed a little service for Lady Kara. With any luck, Enzan can stay in the possession of the family."

Ashinji stooped to stuff a bag of dried fruit into his saddle bag, unsure of how to respond. That Sadaiyo would do such a thing, without their father's permission, was outrageous, but not surprising. He looked up at his brother, considered several different replies, discarded them all, then settled for no reply at all.

Sadaiyo prodded Ashinji's saddle bag with his toe. "Better fill up an extra water bottle. We won't have time for a lot of stops today." He strode off. Ashinji watched him go, wondering what Misune would do if she knew. He believed Sadaiyo loved Misune as much as he could love any person other than himself, but Sadaiyo's idea of love clearly did not involve the concept of fidelity.

Homan trotted up. "Lord Ashinji, the company is ready to ride," he announced.

"Thank you." Ashinji stood and stretched the kinks out of his muscles. "Until my brother gives the order to form up, the company can relax," he said. Homan saluted and headed off in the direction of the horse lines.

The morning sun had just topped the trees, bringing with it the promise of another hot day to come. The trampled grass in the meadow gave off a powerful, pleasant aroma. Bees buzzed in lazy circles among the late wildflowers growing in clumps along the margins. Ashinji retreated to the shade of the stately sentinel oak to wait and think. He leaned back against the rough bark, letting the trunk support his weight.

What little sleep he had gotten last night had been plagued with chaotic dreams. The vision of his death still haunted him, even though he knew no prophetic dream told of what would happen, only of what might happen. He could change his fate, if only he knew which path to take and which ones to avoid.

That's the difficult part.

Ai, Goddess! You brought Jelena to me, chose me as her protector, and now, you show me my death? How am I to protect my wife if I'm dead? Why, then did you ever bring us together?

Raging to the heavens won't help, you fool!

The bray of a horn, signaling the army to mount and form up, rang out. Ashinji sighed, pushed away from the tree trunk, and stepped from under the sheltering branches into the brilliant sunshine. He glanced up at the white disk of the sun and wished for the respite of a rainstorm. His brightly lacquered armor felt like an oppressive shell encasing his body, and he longed to strip it off and plunge into the nearest body of water. Even the little algae-filled pond at the bottom of the meadow looked inviting.

Homan walked up, leading Kian. Ashinji climbed into the saddle and Homan handed him his helmet. "I think I'll ride bareheaded today, Sergeant," he said. "The company has permission to do the same."

"Thank you, Cap'n. I'll pass the word along."

Ashinji watched as the army coalesced into well-ordered ranks. Off in the distance, in the direction of the manor, he spied a splash of color. He focused his gaze until the splash resolved into the figures of four women, standing at the bottom of the path leading to the house. Sadaiyo, astride his stallion, cantered toward them.

Sadaiyo reined his mount to a skidding halt before Lady Kara and her daughters. He flung himself from the saddle and strode boldly to the first in line, who, by her height, Ashinji could tell must be Uebaru. They exchanged a few words, then Sadaiyo swept her into his arms and kissed her. He proceeded to do the same to Tamina and Shuzen. To Lady Kara, he bowed low and kissed the back of her hand.

What Sadaiyo had done for the Enzan family was not unheard of, but it usually happened only after a contract had been executed between all of the involved parties. Sen would be furious when Sadaiyo got around to telling him.

Sadaiyo remounted his horse, and with a final wave, turned and galloped back to where Ashinji waited along with Homan and Sadaiyo's aide Lanic. "Let's go," he said.

As the army wound its way out of the meadow, the four women of Enzan raised their hands in farewell.

* * *

Nine days later, the army crossed into Kerala. They rode straight for the castle, arriving just as the sun dipped below the horizon in a blaze of orange, pink, and red. Iruka, Kerala's steward, stood waiting at the outer gate to greet them. Ashinji and Sadaiyo dismounted and two stable hands came forward to take hold of their mounts' bridles.

Sadaiyo spoke first, forgoing any greeting. "Iruka, I know Kerala has no place to billet eight hundred extra troops. What arrangements have you made?"

"Welcome home Lord Sadaiyo, Lord Ashinji. It is good to see you both." Iruka bowed, his snow-white soldier's braid falling forward over his shoulder.

"There is room for at least a hundred in the lower yard, and another hundred can camp in the upper," the steward said. "It'll be crowded, but that can't be helped. The rest will have to make do out in the rear pastures. I had ample warning from your father, so there should be enough extra provisions laid by." Supremely capable, Iruka had served Lord Sen for more years than Ashinji had been alive, and before becoming Kerala's steward, he had been a sergeant in the army of Keizo the Elder.

"If it please you, my lord Sadaiyo, you may give me your requirements, and any instructions you may have now."

Sadaiyo turned to Ashinji. "Eagle and Kestrel Companies will camp at the castle. The rest of the army will go out in the pastures, and you'll ride with them to supervise. When the troops are settled, you may return to the castle."

"Yes, Brother." Ashinji's voice was cool but his eyes burned with anger. Sadaiyo knew full well Ashinji believed in sharing the living conditions of his company while in the field. By relegating the Peregrines to the pastures outside the castle walls, he had compelled Ashinji to join them. While his brother slept in comfort, Ashinji would have the hard ground as his bed.

Sadaiyo betrayed his satisfaction with a tiny smirk; he would never dare to gloat or laugh aloud at his cruelty in front of the troops.

Ashinji remounted Kian. "I'll see you tonight, then." He wheeled the black gelding and started back across the bridge to where the army waited, strung out along the far bank of the river like a large, shiny millipede.

"I'll save your old place at table!" Sadaiyo called out after him.

* * *

Three days later, Ashinji sat astride Kian under a hazy yellow sky, staring at a swath of forest in the distance. The force that had left Sendai thirteen days earlier now occupied a position a little to the east of the Saihama River fords, the only place where an army of any size could safely cross the river. Elven scouts had put the Soldaran forces about a day's march south of the fords.

"We beat them here, Little Brother!" Sadaiyo had crowed triumphantly upon their arrival, and even Ashinji had to admit the hard march out of Sendai had been a wise decision. It had gotten them to Kerala Castle ahead of the enemy, and given the troops some time to rest.

A field of golden-brown grass, waist-high and dried to hay in the relentless sun, stretched in a gentle slope down toward where the trees began. The hay should have been chopped weeks ago, but fear had kept the farmer who worked this land cooped up at home. Ashinji felt a surge of anger, for now, the hay would go to waste.

"We'll set up camp here and post guards at the fords," Sadaiyo ordered and his officers, including Ashinji, moved quickly to obey. As he rode Kian through the tinder-dry grass, Ashinji thought about the danger of fire, and the questionable wisdom of Sadaiyo's decision to make camp in this spot.

I couldn't disagree with him in front of the troops, he thought. *Dissent before the ranks looks very bad...Besides, he'd only ignore me.*

He decided to give an order forbidding any cooking fires. The troops would grumble at having to eat cold rations; still, he couldn't run the risk of a stray spark starting an unintentional blaze that would almost surely lead to disaster.

After he had seen to Kian, he spent some time arranging the postings to the fords, and making certain his order about no fires got disseminated through the camp. Only after he finished his duties would he see to his own needs.

By the time Ashinji could finally sit down and rest, dusk had fallen. Homan had already set up his camp chair and as Ashinji sank into it with a grimace, the sergeant held out a plate and cup. Ashinji took them with a murmured word of thanks. A hunk of cheese, two journeycakes, and a pile of dried berries rested on the plate, and a sip of the mug's contents confirmed that Homan had fetched some beer from the supply wagons. Ashinji sighed with gratitude and took a bite of cheese.

As he ate, his mind drifted back to his last evening at Kerala Castle, three days past, when he had paid a visit to the home of Gendan and Kami. The couple had invited him to help celebrate both their reunion and the impending birth of their child. Over a special meal prepared by Gendan himself, they had listened as Kami caught them both up on all the latest news and gossip. Though Kami's pregnancy had progressed without any problems, she had expressed great weariness of her physical state.

"I'm actually looking forward to my labor!" she had claimed. Upon hearing the news of Jelena's own pregnancy, she had wept with joy, and Ashinji had been genuinely touched at the depth of affection the young guard still felt for his wife.

That evening had been one of peace and friendship, of quiet good cheer and the deliberate banishment of all fear and uncertainty of the future. For a few short, precious hours, Ashinji forgot his anger and grief.

The thud of footfalls and the hail of a sentry broke into Ashinji's reverie, dragging his mind back into the present.

"Runner's here, Cap'n," Homan announced. Ashinji nodded and gestured to the messenger to approach. A slim young woman trotted up and bowed. In her hand, she held a folded piece of paper.

"My lord, I bring orders from the general," she said, a little out of breath from running.

So, he's calling himself 'the general' now, Ashinji thought. His eyebrow lifted in sardonic amusement. He set his plate and cup on the ground and held out his hand. The girl relinquished the paper, then stood waiting expectantly. Ashinji unfolded the paper and held it up, squinting.

"Here, Cap'n. Don't strain yourself," Homan said, raising a lantern over Ashinji's head so the light could illuminate the message.

"Thanks, Sergeant." Ashinji read in silence, then looked at Homan and said, "It seems that we are to hold the left flank tomorrow." He turned his attention to the runner. "No answer," he said. The girl bowed, then darted off into the darkness.

A ferocious itch developed just below the upper edge of his breastplate, a hair's width lower than his finger could reach. He gritted his teeth and tried to ignore the torment. "Goddess' tits, I wish we didn't have to sleep in armor tonight!" he grumbled.

"I hear you, my lord," Homan commiserated. "Best you be turning in soon, after you finish your dinner, o'course. The humans'll be here and spoilin' for a fight on the morrow. Your cot's all made up for you, whenever you're ready."

How wonderful it would be if I could just sleep tonight...no dreams of fire and death...just nothingness.

"Thank you, Homan. I think I'll take your advice, but not until I've walked a little." Ashinji stood and stretched. "I'm feeling a bit restless," he added.

"What, now, my lord? You've not finished your dinner."

Ashinji shrugged. "Not that hungry, I guess."

"I'll walk with you, if you like, Cap'n," Homan offered.

"No, no. You stay here... finish your own dinner. I'll not be long, and I won't go far."

"Very good, my lord."

Ashinji set off at a leisurely pace, threading his way between clumps of men and women, some sitting on the ground, others standing or reclining as comfortably as they could on the hard earth.

As he made his way through the darkened camp, he could see no details in the faces around him, but he kept his ears wide open, catching every snippet of conversation. He never paused, preferring to listen as he walked, and what he heard did not surprise him.

The troops were nervous—understandably so—but unafraid, and determined to hold the line against the enemy. The Soldaran Imperial legions were arguably the finest fighting force in the known world, but the army awaiting them across the border in Amsara consisted of local levies, not professional Imperial regulars. The Duke's force had the advantage in numbers only.

The Alasiri force, in contrast, consisted entirely of professional soldiers, all highly trained and well equipped. Ashinji knew both his father and King Keizo counted on the superior skill of the Alasiri regulars, along with the small contingent of Kerala guards, to offset the disadvantage of their lesser numbers. Despite his own confidence in the abilities of his troops, Ashinji had no illusions. The battle to come would no doubt prove brutal and bloody.

"Halt! Who goes there!" a familiar voice barked from the shadows.

Ashinji stopped in his tracks, realizing he had reached the edge of camp. "It's just me, Aneko, out for a walk," he answered.

"My lord!" Aneko exclaimed, materializing out of the darkness. "You shouldn't be out this far." She gestured with the tip of her spear toward where the Saihama River ran, chuckling and gurgling over its stony bed. "D'you remember the last time we were out here, my lord?" she asked.

Ashinji couldn't see her face, but he heard the smile in her voice.

"How could I not remember? I almost killed my future wife that day."

"You knew it even then, didn't you, my lord? That you and Jelena were meant to be together?"

"I did," Ashinji replied. "Although it took a great deal of work on my part before I could convince her."

Aneko laughed. "Lord Ashinji, Jelena loved you from the very moment she laid eyes on you. She just didn't believe that someone of your high station could love someone like her... a hikui, I mean. It's obvious now how wrong she was about you." Aneko paused, then added "She has been truly blessed by the One."

Ashinji shook his head. "No. I'm the one who's been blessed." He made no attempt to disguise the emotion in his voice. "Aneko," he continued. "There's something you must do for me."

"Anything, my lord," Aneko replied.

"If...if anything should happen to me..." Ashinji had to stop talking for a moment because his mouth had gone as dry as old bones. Aneko waited in silence for him to continue. He took a deep breath.

"Go to Jelena and tell her I was thinking of her and our child...every waking moment. Tell her that my love never faltered, even as I drew my last breath. Promise you'll do this for me, Aneko."

"Lord Ashinji, I promise, but you'll be able to tell her yourself!" Aneko whispered fiercely. Ashinji sensed her body shifting position in the darkness. "My lord, you must take care, watch your back. Kerala needs you too much. Your father needs you!"

My wife needs me even more, and I can't be there for her!

"Thank you, Aneko, for being a friend to Jelena," Ashinji said. "I think I'll head off to bed now, before I fall down from weariness." He turned to go.

"Lord Ashinji," Aneko called softly. Ashinji paused. "I know I speak for most everyone at Kerala when I say that we wish things could be different."

Though she had chosen her words with care, Ashinji understood the unspoken message behind them. He opened his mouth to reply, but Aneko had slipped away, leaving him alone in the dark of a moonless night, with only his thoughts for company.

18
Betrayal

Ashinji stood under a vault of glittering stars, surrounded by a sea of rustling, sun-dried grass. An acrid odor tickled his nose and he sneezed. Off in the distance, he heard shouts. The sick sensation of extreme danger streamed through his subconscious mind. A voice howled his name.

Lord Ashinji! My lord, you must wake up!

Ashinji's eyes flew open and he sat up with a gasp. Homan stumbled backward to avoid a collision with his captain's head and fell hard on his rump.

"Lord Ashinji!" he croaked, his expression grim. "The meadow's afire! They've set it alight, an' the entire camp's in danger!"

"Who, Homan?" Ashinji scrambled to his feet, heart hammering in his chest. He grabbed his sergeant's hand and hauled the man up.

"The Soldarans, Cap'n! You must hurry!"

Ashinji snatched up his sword and buckled it on, then grabbed his helmet. With a jerk of his head, he indicated that Homan should follow him. "Are they coming, Homan? Are they here?" Ashinji shouted as he and the lanky sergeant made their way through the maelstrom of running bodies toward Sadaiyo's tent.

"Dunno!" Homan gasped. "Might just be a small party sent ahead to burn us outta this field... Sow confusion amongst us so's we'd be too exhausted to put up a good fight tomorrow."

A reasonable deduction, Ashinji thought. *If the positions of our respective armies were reversed, I might have suggested just such a tactic myself.*

The two of them arrived at Sadaiyo's tent just as he emerged, shadowed by his aide, Lanic. "Little Brother, it seems the humans have gotten the jump on us," he said. For once, his voice contained not the slightest trace of condescension. "The meadow has been fired on three sides." Thick smoke now billowed across the elven encampment in stinging clouds. Ashinji's eyes filled with tears, and a coughing fit lurked at the back of his throat.

"How did they get past the sentries?" he rasped.

Sadaiyo made an impatient gesture with his hand. "That's just it. The fire started beyond the picket line. They must have known the flames would burn toward us. Damn it!" he cursed. "Get to your horse and form up your company. I want you to ride down to the fords and station yourself there quick as you can. If there's to be an attack now, it'll come from there!"

"Yes, Brother!"

Horns blared all over the camp. Sadaiyo's other captains arrived. Orders were given, and men and women scattered to carry them out. Ashinji and Homan rushed into the smoky darkness. The sky glowed with the eerie orange light that only a wildfire could produce.

"This way, my lord!" Homan shouted, waving his arms over his head, then pointing in the direction of the horse lines. As they waded through the swirl of bodies, Ashinji felt relieved to see that most of the activity, while frantic, appeared organized. The troops seemed focused, intent on getting themselves and their comrades out of danger.

Shrill neighs alerted them to the uneasy state of the horses. Ashinji quickly spotted Kian, a groom at his head stroking the big black gelding's nose. Kian's eyes gleamed like wet stones in the ruddy light of the fire. He appeared nervous, but not yet panicked.

"There, there, my friend!" Ashinji spoke soothing words as he approached the horse. Kian threw his head up and whickered. Ashinji took the lead rope from the groom's hand. "Bring my saddle and bridle," he ordered. The groom scampered off, returning quickly with the heavy war saddle in his arms, bridle draped over his shoulder.

While the groom held Kian's head, Ashinji tacked him up. As he worked, his mind feverishly attacked the problem at hand. The Peregrines would have to ride around the fire line to get to the fords. Once there, he would position them on the Soldaran side of the river, and pray they did not have to hold off the entire human army on their own.

Even so, Sadaiyo has given me an order and I'm duty-bound to carry it out... *The Peregrines must hold the fords until Sadaiyo can bring up all our forces!*

After checking the girth one last time, Ashinji flung himself onto Kian's back and snatched up the reins. Homan handed up his helmet and he pulled it on. "Mount up quick as you can and get back to the company. We need to ride out now!" He heard Homan call out "Yes, Cap'n" as he spun Kian around and tapped the warhorse's flanks with his heels, keeping a firm hold on the reins. He could feel the gelding's mounting excitement through his legs and hands. The big horse wanted to run, but Ashinji held him down to a brisk walk, unwilling to risk trampling a hapless trooper too slow to get out of the way.

All around, companies were forming up. Sergeants screamed orders and troopers shouted to one another. Bedding and dishes lay discarded on the ground, creating a dangerous jumble for Kian to pick his way through. Smoke and ash filled the air. Ashinji tried to stifle a coughing fit, to no avail. His eyes and nose streamed wetness down his face, but he could not wipe them without stopping to remove his helmet.

At last, the standard of Peregrine Company loomed ahead. A man ran up and skidded to a halt just in front of Kian, causing the gelding to snort and start in surprise. Ashinji recognized Goran, Homan's immediate subordinate.

"Lord Ashinji," he gasped, then doubled over in a fit of coughing.

Ashinji waited until he recovered, then asked "Is the company formed up?"

"Yes, my lord," Goran croaked. "We were awaiting your return."

"We're moving out now. Our orders are to get to the fords and hold them." Ashinji pointed over his shoulder. "Homan is right behind me. When he comes up, tell him to bring the company around to the north. There's a break in the fire there. I'll ride ahead to scout."

"You shouldn't ride out alone, Captain," Goran protested. "It's not safe! There could be humans swarming all over the riverbank by now!"

"I'll be careful," Ashinji replied. "If I see anything suspicious, I'll hold back and wait for the company." Goran looked unconvinced, but he didn't dare argue. Instead, he bowed in acknowledgement.

Ashinji clicked his tongue and Kian started forward. He steered toward the northern end of camp, the area farthest from the river.

It soon became clear to Ashinji what the humans must have done. A small party had forged ahead of the main body of the Soldaran force and had crossed the river under cover of darkness. The moon was new, so the only light would have been from the stars, perfect conditions for sneaking close to the elven camp without serious risk of detection.

Once the raiders had come in as close as they dared, they had spread out and fired the tinder-dry meadow simultaneously on three sides. After completing the job, the raiders fled back to the river to make good their escape.

Once Ashinji had broken free of the main body of the army, he spurred Kian into a rolling canter. The gelding snorted and tossed his head; the lather on his neck testified to his nervousness in the face of the fire. Still, he obeyed his master and carried Ashinji willingly enough.

The fire roared and crackled like a living thing as man and horse sought to circle around it. Thick clouds of smoke billowed all around, ob-scuring Ashinji's vision, but a momentary thinning allowed him to spot the break in the flames. He turned Kian's head toward the clear space and urged the horse forward.

Kian whipped past the fire line, hooves throwing up gouts of hot ash. With the flames now behind them, Ashinji steered the gelding to the west and south and gave Kian his head, allowing him to run.

Onward they raced, the red glare of the flames lighting their way. Up ahead lay the dark wall of shadow that marked the tree line along the far bank of the river. On the near side, the bank—rocky and overgrown with thick tussocks of vegetation—dropped sharply to the water. Ashinji pulled back on the reins and sat deep in the saddle, checking Kian down to a walk. The gelding, barely winded, pranced and jigged at the bit, eager to be off again.

Ashinji approached the river with caution, wary of the thickets which might conceal any number of dangers. At this distance from the camp and the fire, he could once again hear the normal noises of the night. Crick-ets chirped from deep within the tangled growth and cicadas shrilled rhythmically from the trees across the gurgling expanse of water. An owl hooted overhead.

Ashinji brought Kian to a halt and sat very still, listening. With a sigh of frustration, he unbuckled the chinstrap of his helmet and pulled it off. He imagined he could hear Homan scolding him for taking such a risk but he needed a few moments free of the encumbrance of the helmet. A stray night breeze ruffled his hair.

Kian snorted and threw up his head.

"What is it, my friend?" Ashinji whispered. A prickling sensation tick-led the back of his neck, and the air grew heavy with menace.

Too late, he realized his peril.

Out of the darkness they rushed, eerily silent. Kian trumpeted in alarm and reared, striking out with his front hooves. Ashinji clung to the saddle, struggling to free his sword from its scabbard, but too many hands pulled at him. Before he could react, they had dragged him to the ground.

Kian whirled and let fly with a vicious kick of his hind legs, scattering their attackers and allowing Ashinji to scramble to his feet and draw his sword. Instinctively, he assumed a defensive stance, his eyes and brain analyzing his situation with the speed of desperation. He cursed himself for a fool.

He faced at least a dozen attackers, all armed, probably one of the raiding parties sent ahead to fire the meadow. For some reason, they had lingered on this side of the river, perhaps to watch what their handiwork had accomplished. Now they had Ashinji surrounded and cut off from escape.

Without warning, Kian let out a shuddering groan and went to his knees. Ashinji gasped as the big horse flopped over on his side and lay quivering. He saw the pale sheen of entrails through a gaping wound in the gelding's belly, and horrified, he realized Kian, his mount and his friend, had been gutted.

Ashinji swallowed his anger and grief. He had no time for them now, for if he didn't think of some way to get out of this situation fast, he would soon join Kian in death. He raised his sword and shouted in Soldaran, "There are a hundred fighters hard on my heels! They will be here any moment!"

"This 'un speaks Soldaran!" one of the humans cried in apparent astonishment.

"Shoot 'im an' let's get outta here!" another voice demanded.

"I hear hoof beats!" cried a third.

Ashinji heard them as well, but it sounded like a lone rider, not Peregrine Company. His heart sank. Who else had been foolish enough to ride out here alone?

Could it be Homan, coming to search for me...? But no, *Homan would come with all of Peregrine Company behind him, as ordered. Where are they? Surely they should have been here by now!*

The humans all stood frozen, heads cocked like dogs, listening. The hoof beats had stopped.

"Ain't nuthin' but yer imagination, Caius," one of them spat. The others muttered in agreement.

Ashinji's eyes strained to see into the darkness. He knew he'd heard hoof beats. *I've got to warn whoever is out there,* he thought. "Hoy, soldier! There's an ambush here! Beware and help me if you can!" he shouted.

The humans flung themselves at him. He managed to dodge the first few blows but a solid swing from a blunt weapon connected with his back plate, knocking him to his knees. Reflexively, he brought his arm up to parry a sword blow.

"No, no! Take 'im alive!" a harsh voice barked.

Ashinji looked around wildly, seeking any opening that would allow him to live, and caught sight of the unknown horse and rider, standing a spear's toss away in the darkness. His heart leapt into his throat.

"*Help me!*" he screamed.

No! It can't be happening! I won't let it!

The rider shifted a little in the saddle as if trying to get a better view of the unfolding violence. At the same instant, Ashinji caught a glimpse of the rider's armored chest and the intricate designs lacquered onto its surface. Even in the dim starlight, he recognized the pattern.

"Sadaiyo," Ashinji whispered.

"*Help me, Brother!*" he screamed again.

A sharp blow to his shoulder, followed by searing pain, cut off his next cry. He looked down to find an arrow sprouting from the narrow, vulnerable space between the edge of his breastplate and his left pauldron.

"Sadaiyo...help," he gasped, and slumped to the ground.

As he lay bleeding, his body slipping into shock, his mind drifted along the threads of several thoughts. First, he felt admiration for the skill of the human archer, then profound sorrow for all he was about to lose, and finally, bitter hatred for his brother's betrayal.

"You idiot! I told you I wanted 'im taken alive!"

Ashinji struggled to raise himself off the ground so he could face his slayers with some semblance of dignity.

The humans closed in, weapons raised; intent as they were on killing him, none of them had spotted Sadaiyo. Through a gap between two of his attackers, Ashinji watched Sadaiyo wheel his horse and lash the animal's flank with the quirt-end of his reins. The horse snorted and sprang away, disappearing into the dark.

Ashinji choked back a sob and forced his face to settle into a calm, expressionless mask, determined to meet his death with bravery.

I'm so sorry, Jelena my love! I tried to survive for you...and for our child. I guess it's no longer up to me to be your protector. I'll see you again, when we are reunited in the loving embrace of the One.

The humans had formed a tight circle around him, looking down on their victim.

"Hurry up and do it!" Ashinji snarled in Soldaran.

A man stepped forward, raised the butt of his sword and swung downward. Ashinji's head exploded in pain and his mind dropped away into oblivion.

* * *

"Hmmm. You are asking for a very difficult manipulation, my lord. Very tricky."

"Can you do it, old man?"

"Yeeees...I can...but..."

"The memory must be completely erased and replaced by a new one, and the tampering must be undetectable."

"Memories cannot be erased, young man. They can, however, be walled away behind barriers and made inaccessible to the conscious mind."

"Can you render the barrier itself invisible, so that even a high-level mage can't detect it?"

"Depends on how high."

"The highest. A Kirian."

"Oh, my. That is high.... I can disguise the barrier, make it look like part of the background, so to speak. It will for all intents and purposes be invisible to all but the deepest probe, but if this Kirian you wish to hide from knows what to look for, it won't remain hidden very long."

"What about the replacement memory? Will it feel authentic?"

"Oh, yes. You, yourself will believe it to be true, and so will anyone casually scanning you. I must warn you, though, there is a chance, especially as time goes by, that the barrier will eventually break down and allow the genuine memory to reemerge."

"Yes, well...I don't care. I need only hide it for awhile. So, mage. We come to the last detail. Name your price."

"I can ask for no less than thirty gold, my lord."

"Thirty...! My entire monthly allowance is only twenty!"

"Nevertheless, that is my price, young man."

"Goddess' tits! If my life didn't depend on this...Very well. Thirty gold. Do I need to count it out for you?"

"Oh, no, my lord. I trust you. Now, I'll just put this away and you lie back and make yourself comfortable..."

* * *

Sadaiyo emerged from the mage's cottage, feeling a strange mixture of sadness and relief. He had come to the old man's home on the advice of Lanic, seeking respite from the tormenting guilt of witnessing Ashinji's death at the hands of a human raiding party, nearly three weeks ago.

The mage had helped Lanic in the past with some painful memories; for a reasonable sum, the old man entered a person's mind, softened the edges, removed the hurt, and soothed the guilt, thus allowing acceptance and healing.

Now, Sadaiyo could begin the process of forgiving himself.

As he rode back to Kerala Castle beneath a sky heavy with storm clouds, he thought of the last moments of Ashinji's life—he'd tried so hard to reach his brother, but the humans had rushed him and beaten him back.

There were just too many of them! I tried, Ashi, I really did...but by the time I could get a few arrow shots off, they'd already cut you down. I couldn't even retrieve your body...they dragged you away across the river. Ai, Goddess! How will I tell our parents? How will I tell your wife?

A cold drizzle pattered down from above, and Sadaiyo pulled the collar of his heavy, fur-lined cloak close around his neck. Tomorrow, he, along with a small contingent of troops, would leave Kerala and head back to Sendai to report on the actions at the border.

Within the last week, the weather had turned, and with the first frost, the Soldaran army had withdrawn to Amsara Castle. The bulk of the elven force that had marched out from the capital would remain in Kerala to serve as a deterrent against further incursions, but no one expected the humans to return before spring. Winter had brought an end to all military operations.

I'll be glad to get back to Misune, Sadaiyo thought. He spurred his horse and the stallion sprang into a gallop, throwing up clods of mud with each stride.

* * *

The old mage hunkered down by his fireplace, savoring the heat of the flames. In his wrinkled hands, he held a small glass sphere. The sphere glowed with a soft white light, like a large, illuminated pearl.

Good thing I thought to make a copy of this memory, he thought as he rolled the sphere gently between his palms. *Never know when it might come in handy. Always prudent to keep a little insurance.*

The old man chuckled and began recounting his coins.

19
Shattered

Eight weeks after Sadaiyo led his army out of Sendai, a small contingent returned to the city. A messenger arrived midmorning, sent ahead with news of the expedition's success. The human army had withdrawn to Soldaran territory, and Sadaiyo had left behind the bulk of his forces to guard the border. They would remain encamped around Kerala Castle for the entire winter and into the spring. The loss of their numbers would no doubt prove a serious blow to the defense of the Tono Valley, but the elves dared not leave their vulnerable southeastern flank unprotected.

Jelena heard the news as she finished her morning routine, assisted by Eikko, the hikui servant girl whom she had met soon after her arrival in Sendai. Eikko's duties had gradually shifted as she and Jelena had become better acquainted. Now, instead of helping Lady Amara with the twins, the young servant spent most of her time as a companion to Jelena.

A note, delivered from her father, informed Jelena of the company's imminent arrival. Brimming with excitement, she threw on her clothes and hurried down to the parade ground.

The weather had grown much cooler in the weeks since the army had left, and today, a chilly wind numbed Jelena's cheeks as she exited the castle's main entrance. Eikko, who followed dutifully after, clucked in dismay. She shook out the heavy woolen cloak she carried and flung it around Jelena's shoulders.

Jelena murmured her thanks and pulled the warm folds close about her body, shivering a little from both excitement and apprehension.

For the last few days, she had been unable to shake the feeling that all was not as it should be with Ashinji. She could not lay her finger on it; no unusual dreams disturbed her sleep nor had she any flashes of prescience. Nevertheless, she felt unsettled and out of sorts.

Part of it, she knew, could be attributed to her advancing pregnancy. The child had grown quite active in recent weeks. Perversely, she—Jelena's doctor had informed her that she carried a girl—seemed most energetic at night, when her mother wanted to sleep.

"Your Highness, you really shouldn't wait out here in this wind," Eikko admonished. "It's too cold. I know you want to be here to greet Captain Sakehera, but he won't arrive for a while yet." The hikui maid tugged gently on Jelena's sleeve, a liberty she never would have taken with an okui mistress. "Come back inside," she coaxed.

Jelena pursed her lips in irritation and snapped, "Stop fussing, Eikko!" Immediately, she regretted her ill temper. *Eikko is only concerned for my well-being and that of my daughter,* she thought. Chagrined, she apologized. "I'm sorry, Eikko. I didn't mean to be cross with you...I miss my husband so much and I want to be right here when he rides in."

"'Course you do, Highness," Eikko replied. "I understand." She flashed a quick smile.

"We'll wait just inside the door." Jelena waved toward the castle's entrance. "There's a bench we can sit on." Eikko nodded and the two young women retreated out of the chill wind into the relative warmth of the entrance hall, where they settled on the bench to wait.

They sat for a time in comfortable silence. Jelena tried to relieve her anxiety by practicing the meditation taught to her by Princess Taya. In recent weeks, the Kirians had stepped up her training, and Jelena was now proficient in many of the basics. She could mindspeak with ease, perform a simple surface scan on another person, and maintain a shield against unwanted mental intrusions by any non-mage-trained attacker. Her swift progress had surprised her.

Jelena's dreams of learning to control her Talent, and more specifically, the blue energy the Kirians referred to as the Key were being realized, but she now found herself in a strange and tense situation. Jelena had known for some time that Taya and Sonoe were, if not outright enemies, then rivals, for sure, and each one believed she knew best how to conduct Jelena's training. Consequently, they often clashed, and only the moderating presence of Amara kept a lid on things.

Ever since spotting Sonoe standing below her bedroom window, Jelena had felt uneasy in the presence of her father's Companion. The red-haired sorceress had offered no explanation for her behavior; in fact, she had said nothing at all about the incident. Soon afterward, however, Sonoe had be-come very solicitous towards Jelena, going out of her way to offer gestures of friendship. She did seem genuinely interested in Jelena in a sisterly way so, in time, Jelena's unease abated. Lately, she found herself more and more in Sonoe's company. It felt good to have the friendship of an older, more experienced woman.

"Are you warm enough, my lady?" Eikko inquired, breaking the silence and recapturing Jelena's attentiton.

"Uh...Yes, Eikko, thank you." Jelena turned to gaze with speculation at the hikui maid. "Eikko, do you have any Talent?" she asked.

Caught off-guard by the question, the other girl stammered, "I...I don't know, Princess...I mean...I've never thought about it." She shrugged her plump shoulders. "I s'pose I must have, at least a little. Our elven blood gives us all a touch. Both my parents, though, are hikui, as were their par-ents, so it's been a few generations since there've been any purebloods in my family tree. I suspect most of the Talent's been lost in us." She regard-ed Jelena with a puzzled expression. "Why, if you don't mind me asking, would you want to know?"

"I'm curious, I guess. There must be some hikui who have strong Talent," Jelena mused.

"If they dared show themselves, you can bet the okui wouldn't allow them to use their abilities. They might even be killed."

"You can't mean that, Eikko! There're laws against murder. Even the hikui are granted that protection."

Eikko snorted. "There're laws for okui and laws for hikui, Princess. Surely you know that by now."

Jelena sighed, realizing the futility in arguing the point; besides, Eikko's frank statement contained an undeniable kernel of truth. "I've been working hard on my father, Eikko, to get him to see the injustice of having a different set of laws for hikui," she said. "The good news is that he is listening to me. How could he not? I'm hikui and his daughter."

Eikko looked dubious. "Begging your pardon, Highness, but okui folk have lorded it over us since...well, since always! It'll take nothing less than a miracle to change 'em."

"Then get ready for a miracle, Eikko, because it's going to happen. I'm determined," Jelena replied.

The heavy main entrance doors of the castle stood ajar. From some-where outside, faint shouts drifted in on a chilly breeze that swirled around Jelena's toes. She shivered and pulled her cloak more closely around her. An instant later, a messenger burst though the doors and pelted across the broad hallway to the sweep of the staircase, heading up toward the king's private quarters.

Jelena sprang to her feet. "They're here! Ashinji's home!" she cried and rushed out into the cold, Eikko hard on her heels. The wind whipped back the cloak from her body and snapped loose coils of hair about her face as she stood gazing out across the parade ground toward the upper gates of the castle. The strange apprehension building within her crested until she now shook with anxiety.

Where are you, Ashi?

"Daughter, I see you're already here."

Jelena spun around to see the king descending the broad steps, Sen and Prince Raidan flanking him on either side. Sonoe, resplendent in a green velvet cloak lined with fox fur, followed Keizo. Jelena ran to her fa-ther and clung to him, on the verge of tears.

Keizo looked startled, then concerned. He folded his arms around Jelena and asked "What's all this now, child? Why are you in such a state?"

Jelena looked into her father's winter-grey eyes.

"I...I can't explain, Father. I just feel like something's terribly wrong with Ashi. I've felt this way for a while now." She shook her head in irrita-tion, angry with herself for her emotional weakness. She pulled away from Keizo's embrace and drew herself up straight. "I'm being silly," she stated. "Ashi is well and he's riding home to me."

"'Course he is, my dear," Sen chimed in. "If anything had happened to him...to either of my sons, I'm sure we'd have heard already." He looked back over his shoulder and muttered, "Hmm. I wonder where Amara and Misune are?"

"Misune is not feeling well, Father-in-law, and Mother stayed behind with her," Jelena explained. "She's had such a hard time, you know."

Despite Misune's excellent health, her pregnancy had not gone well, and she often could not rise from bed. Jelena actually felt sorry for her. She and Misune would never warm to each other, but of late, they had arrived at a peaceful coexistence, due, Jelena felt, to their shared condition.

"You're right, of course," Sen replied. "We men can be incredibly insensitive at times." He scratched his head, looking a little sheepish.

"Oh! I think I see them!" Eikko burst out, then covered her mouth with her hand and shrank back behind Jelena.

"Yes, here they come," Raidan confirmed, glancing at the hikui girl with a frown.

Jelena ran down the last steps to stand on the cold gravel of the parade ground, ignoring the chill seeping through the thin leather soles of her slippers. She focused her entire attention on the company of riders, just coming into view.

Three riders detached themselves from the vanguard and galloped ahead, sliding to a stop before Jelena, the hooves of their mounts spitting gravel. Sadaiyo, in his distinctive black-lacquered armor, dismounted first. He handed over the reins of his horse to the man on his right and approached Jelena. Something in the way he carried himself set off a wave of fear that rushed from her head down to her toes and back again, leaving her dizzy and a little sick.

Ashinji isn't with him!

Sadaiyo halted in front of her and pulled off his helmet.

"Where is my husband?" Jelena demanded.

Sadaiyo's eyes flicked to her face, then away. He shifted his gaze past her right shoulder, then bowed low.

"Lord Sadaiyo, you have returned safely and with success. I congratulate you and offer you the profound gratitude of our people." Keizo had come up behind Jelena, and now rested a hand upon her shoulder.

"Thank you, Majesty," Sadaiyo murmured. Jelena glared at him, willing him to look at her, but his eyes once again skipped over her face to focus on his father, who had come to stand at Jelena's left.

The terrible pressure built up within her gave way.

"*Where...is he?*" she screamed. Eikko gasped in dismay, and Keizo squeezed her shoulder hard, as if to steady her.

"Father...Sister-in-law," Sadaiyo began. The clatter of dozens of hooves rang in the air around them as Sadaiyo's company fell in behind him in orderly ranks. Still refusing to meet Jelena's eyes, he continued. "We were caught by surprise while encamped at the Saihama fords. The humans sent several small raiding parties ahead to set fire to the meadow where the army lay sleeping. My brother rode out—alone—toward the river to scout, according to his sergeant." Sadaiyo looked over his shoulder and indicated with a lift of his chin a man with the insignia of Peregrine Company on his tabard.

He paused, as if to gather his thoughts. "When I heard where he had gone, I knew Ashinji was in terrible danger, so I immediately rode after him," Sadaiyo continued. "I did find him...but..." His voice faltered and his eyes swiveled downward.

"But what, Son? Please, tell us!" Sen's voice shook.

Sadaiyo raised his head and addressed his father. "Ashinji had been ambushed by one of the raiding parties. By the time I got there, they had already dragged him off his horse. I saw them... hacking at him. He tried to defend himself, but there were just too many. I got off a few arrow shots before...before they saw me and started firing back. Ashi wasn't moving; I knew he was dead. I tried to get to him...I really did! I couldn't even retrieve his body because...because they tied a rope to him and dragged him away across the river.... I'm so sorry Father!" Sadaiyo lapsed into silence.

Jelena threw back her head and wailed.

Ashi is dead? No, that can't be true!

Her knees buckled, and she fell backward into the arms of her father.

"Are you absolutely sure that my son-in-law is dead?" she heard Keizo cry.

"My child...my son!" Sen moaned in anguish.

Rage, like a white-hot star, flared to life within Jelena. She struggled to her feet, then, without warning, launched herself at Sadaiyo, screaming, "*You're lying! You did this! You killed him!*" She swung a vicious punch at Sadaiyo's face, snapping his head back with the force of the blow. His nose exploded in a spray of blood. Cursing, he clapped his hands over his face and staggered backward, gore leaking through his entwined fingers.

Strong hands seized Jelena's arms from behind and pinned them to her sides. Everyone shouted at once, a crazy babble of voices. Jelena screamed again. "*I know you did this! I swear I'll make you pay!*" Her eyes burned dry and hot. The terrible rage within her had boiled all her tears away before they could form. Within her womb, Jelena's daughter began to kick frantically, as if she understood the awful tragedy that had befallen her and her mother.

Without warning, blue flame erupted in a brilliant geyser of energy from the tips of Jelena's fingers, blasting the gravel at her feet and causing those that held her to fall back in consternation. Her vision narrowed down to a dark tunnel with Sadaiyo's face staring at her, open mouthed, from the far end. Slowly, she raised her hands and stretched them toward Ashinji's murderer.

"Jelena, stop this now!" a voice cried.

Blinking in confusion, Jelena came back into herself to find Sonoe standing in front of her, blocking her view of Sadaiyo and preventing her from flinging the lethal energy that crackled from her fingertips.

"Jelena," Sonoe whispered. "I can't allow you to do this. You'll destroy yourself as well as him."

The blue fire sputtered and died. Jelena's hands fell to her sides and she drew in a deep, shuddering breath.

Gods, what did I almost do? Her entire body trembled.

"I want to see my wife," Sadaiyo mumbled through his bloody fingers.

Jelena turned and collapsed into Keizo's arms.

"Jelena, my sweet child," the king murmured. "I know the agony you feel right now, but surely... Ashinji was Sadaiyo's brother! It's unthinkable he could have had a hand in your husband's death. I'm certain what he says is true."

Jelena shook her head. "No, Father...He's lying...I know it! Sadaiyo hates Ashi... He always has!" She threw a wild look at Sonoe. "Truthread him!" she wailed. "Please, Sonoe! Do it now!"

Sonoe's eyes brimmed with tears. "I cannot, Jelena. It's...it's not proper for me to enter the mind of a nobleman uninvited."

Jelena pounded her fists against Keizo's chest. "Help... help me!" she moaned. Her entire world had just collapsed and she felt herself sliding down into the madness of overwhelming grief.

A thick silence had settled over the parade ground. Those troopers in the front ranks witnessing the drama as it unfolded stood still as statues.

"Lord Sadaiyo, I want a full report as soon as you can make it," Prince Raidan spoke up.

"Yes, Highness," Sadaiyo replied. He sniffed loudly and wiped his dripping nose with a cloth. "I ask permission to dismiss the troops, your Majesty."

"Granted," Keizo said. Sadaiyo turned to the two men behind him and gave the order.

Jelena closed her eyes and tried to retreat to the still point in her mind Taya had shown her, the spot of refuge and peace, but no peace or solace for her pain awaited her there. Ashinji, her husband and soul-mate, the father of her child, was dead and lost to her.

How will I survive?

"Come, Daughter. Let me take you inside, out of the cold. It's not good for you or the baby." With gentleness, Keizo took her by the arm and led her toward the castle doorway. Eikko, weeping piteously, followed a few steps behind. Jelena allowed herself to be led, unresisting. She didn't care where she went; nothing mattered any more.

As she passed through the massive portals of the castle, she paused once to look over her shoulder, in the vain hope that Sadaiyo's news was a horrible mistake and she would see Ashinji galloping across the parade ground on his horse Kian, alive and whole.

Instead, she saw Sen, his face contorted by grief, the agony of his loss like a gaping wound. He stood before Sadaiyo, eyes closed and hands clenched into fists, looking as though he would shatter at any moment. Sadaiyo laid a hand on his father's arm, but Sen flinched away, as if he found the touch of his surviving son too painful to endure. Shoulders slumped, Sadaiyo turned and walked away, leaving his father standing alone, inconsolable.

We both loved him almost too much, Jelena thought, and then all thoughts ceased, leaving her mind enveloped in cold, bleak despair.

* * *

Now is the time to strike, when she is most vulnerable!

"No, Master, not now! She is too well protected. Taya has her wrapped about with so many wards, I can barely sense her anymore."

Sonoe stood at the center of the Summoning Sigil etched into the floor of her cellar work room, the Nameless One floating before her like a miniature storm cloud.

She twirled a lock of hair around her forefinger, then flung it away in frustration. "I've tried breaking through, but they're just too strong and well-crafted."

A surge of energy—blue-black and deadly cold—lanced out from the spectral form and struck Sonoe between the eyes. Agonizing pain tore through her skull. She screamed and fell to the hard-packed earth, writhing and clutching her head.

Your efforts have been pathetically weak so far! I am beginning to regret my choice of you as a tool. You are proving yourself to be unequal to the task, woman.

"No, no!" Sonoe gasped. She levered her body up into a submissive crouch, hands still pressed to her throbbing skull, and gazed through narrowed eyes at the entity she had chosen to serve. "I am equal... *more* than equal, I swear! I am making good progress with her; she considers me her friend. She trusts me. If I move too fast I will arouse too much...suspicion...Ai, Goddess!"

The pain ceased, and Sonoe moaned in relief. She wrapped her arms around her body to stop it from shivering. Several of her warding candles had sputtered out; she re-ignited them with a wave of her hand.

I am growing impatient. Every moment you delay, each hour that passes without the Key in my possession...my enemies gain that much more time to gather their strength and plan their opposition. The nebulous entity twisted slowly in on itself, then extended a tendril, snake-like, to loop around Sonoe's body, caressing her as gently as a lover. A second tendril wrapped around her neck and began to squeeze.

The sudden increase in pressure around her throat cut off Sonoe's cry of alarm. Her thoughts swung wildly from pleas to curses and back again as darkness blurred the edges of her vision. She struggled, to no avail. The Nameless One held her fast in a grip as solid and cold as iron.

Just as quickly as he had struck, he released her. She slumped onto her back, choking and gulping for air.

A reminder of my strength, which grows as each day passes. I am still not strong enough to break free completely, but the chains my enemies imprisoned me with so long ago are weakening.

Sonoe sat up, rubbing her neck. Cautiously, she climbed to her feet, her eyes never leaving the slowly writhing spirit-form—the only manifestation the Nameless One could manage at present. Despite his apparent fragility, he nevertheless still posed a deadly threat, as he had so effectively demonstrated.

"I need more time to find a way around Taya's protections," Sonoe said. "Taya is not the only one shielding the girl. The king himself is using some of his Talent to block access to her, although he is unaware on a conscious level of what he is doing. Also, I can't work openly. I must move with stealth or I'll be discovered."

The Nameless One lashed out again but this time, Sonoe was ready. The energy washed harmlessly around her, blocked by her own protective shields. A wave of pure hate—putrid and corrosive—flowed from the entity like poison from a festering wound.

Sonoe choked back the bile rising in the back of her throat. "Master...*please!*" she gasped. The Nameless One withdrew in on himself and hovered, a dense ball of smoke. Sonoe stood waiting, tense and wary as a lioness confronting a thunder lizard. She could sense his strength waning. Soon, he would be forced to sever their link and retreat to his prison. She felt a flash of annoyance.

He's like a petulant child...one with enough power to destroy my mind if I'm not constantly on guard!

"Master," she cajoled. "Jelena trusts me. Now that her husband's dead, she will reach out to me even more. I shall be there for her like the loving older sister she never had. The closer we become, the easier it will be for me to find a way to break down the wards that guard the Key."

Very well. Do what you must. The voice in her head sounded faint and hollow. *I grow weary and must rest.*

In the heavily guarded place in her mind where Sonoe sequestered all thoughts she didn't want the Nameless One to know, she indulged in a mental sneer.

He's squandered most of his energy lashing out at me. As painful as that was, it's far better than what he usually does.

Sonoe was a proud woman, accustomed to giving orders and having them obeyed. She would never consider herself a slave, and she suffered all the indignities the Nameless One heaped upon her for one reason only.

Power.

Sonoe had a plan—a secret strategy she kept hidden away behind mental shields that not even the Nameless One could pierce. *Let him use me now,* she thought, *but when I'm ready, the tables will be turned and the master becomes the slave.* The power of the Key was too seductive, too all-encompassing. She could not allow the corrupt spirit of a long-dead sorcerer king to wield it for his own twisted purpose.

Sonoe had determined to take the power for herself and rule the known world as its benevolent queen.

But I will rule alone.

"Go and rest, Master," she said, her voice softened with just the right amount of servile sweetness. "I will contact you later."

The spirit formed no words in her mind, but Sonoe felt him fuming at his own weakness. She waited as his essence drained away, like dirty water sluicing down a gutter, then heaved a sigh of relief and rubbed at her bruised neck.

Poor Jelena, she thought. *I must go to her at once.*

A wave of genuine sadness washed over her, catching the young mage by surprise. Fiercely, she shook it off.

You're getting soft, Sonoe! Stay focused, she chided herself. After extinguishing all the candles with a finger snap, she left her work room to the dark and the spiders.

Part III

20

Captured

Whoa! Hold on to 'im, lads! He's wakin' up!"
Slowly, consciousness returned, and with it, pain.
What's happening?
"This one's special. Look at his armor!"
Voices...Soldaran...what...where am I?
"I've never seen such armor before. It's...it's painted."
Ashinji opened his eyes.
I'm alive!
"Look! He's awake!"
Ai, Goddess! Feels like an axe blade's split my head open!

A wave of nausea swept over him, and he had just enough strength to roll over onto his side to retch. This action brought a new, agonizing discovery. The arrow that had pierced his left shoulder remained, embedded deep in the muscle.

Ashinji flopped onto his back again, desperately fighting the red fog of pain that threatened to overwhelm his mind and send him hurtling back into the dark. His body begged him to let go, to seek the release of oblivion, but his mind stubbornly refused.

I'm alive. I've got to keep fighting.

"I claim his armor. I'm the one what struck the blow that felled 'im."

"Hey, there! That's not right! We all helped capture him. We split 'is stuff, fair 'n square!"

"You shouldn't get anything, Lew, you idiot! It was you what almost killed him with that arrow, even after the cap'n said to take him alive!"

"Shut up, all of you! He may still die. Just look at him. He's lost a lot of blood. Anyway, there'll be no squabbling. Jan's right; we all had a hand in his capture. His gear gets split between us, but seeing as I'm senior, I get first pick."

Ashinji's mind worked feverishly, despite the pain, to assess his situation. *I'm on the ground, surrounded by at least eight men,* he thought. He recognized the voice of the burly human standing at his feet, a lantern clutched in one beefy hand. This man had directed the attack, and the authority in his tone marked him as their leader.

The man stooped and lifted Ashinji's sword off the ground. He hefted the blade in his free hand. "I'll take this, I think. I've heard the elves make better swords than we do." He swung the blade over his head in a wide arc. "Good balance," he commented.

"He's watching us, Cap'n. D'you think he understands what we're saying?"

"You bonehead! 'Course he does...you heard him yell at us in Soldaran, remember?" He held the lantern up so its light dazzled Ashinji's watering eyes. "Hey, tink! You understand us, don't you?"

Ashinji debated the choice of whether he should feign incomprehension, in the hope of learning something which could aid in his escape, versus attempting to bargain with the humans—offer them the promise of ransom if they returned him to Kerala. He chose the latter course.

"My name is Ashinji Sakehera," he said, his voice little more than a whisper. "My father is Sen Sakehera, Lord of Kerala. He is very rich and will pay you far more in ransom than what my gear is worth."

"See, he speaks Soldaran real good! How about that?" the captain exclaimed. "Well, Ash-een-gee...Sakee...heery, just how are we supposed to get word to your high and mighty father, eh? Shall we ride up to his gate and announce ourselves? I don't think so. In fact, I have a better idea."

"What we gonna do with him, Cap'n?"

The captain stroked his chin, regarding Ashinji with frank speculation.

"Well, just look at him, lads. Look at that face. Fine and pretty as he is, I reckon with a little paint and a nice gown, he'd make a right proper girl. What do you say to that, eh, Pretty Ash-een-gee?"

"There must not be enough human women around here for you to rape," Ashinji retorted, the bitter brew of rage and pain making him reckless. The captain aimed a vicious kick at his gut. The blow connected with devastating force, and Ashinji folded up with a grunt.

"Now now, Pretty! See what you've made me go and do!" Coarse laughter rang in Ashinji's ears.

"We gonna castrate him an' sell him to a brothel?" More laughter.

"No, you idiot!" the captain spat. "We're taking him straight to her Ladyship. She'd have my balls for her belt if she found out we captured a tink officer and didn't bring him in for questioning."

So that's it, then. I'm to be taken to the enemy encampment and subjected to interrogation.

Ashinji sighed with relief and closed his eyes. He had no illusions about his situation, but at least the danger of summary execution had passed, for the present.

"Wha' about that arrow?" someone asked.

Ashinji peered groggily at the slender shaft of wood protruding from his shoulder. The arrow had broken off at midpoint, leaving the iron tip buried in his flesh. If one of the humans tried to remove it, he might bleed to death.

"No! Leave the arrow alone!" he gasped, terrified that they intended to draw it out right then and there.

"Pretty Ash-een-gee's right. We'll leave the arrow for the surgeon to deal with. We wouldn't want him bleeding out on us now, after all the trouble we went through to capture him alive." The captain gazed up at the sky. "C'mon lads. Dawn's not far off and the tink army is still just over the river, no doubt missing Ash-een-gee here. We'd better get moving. Lew, Conor, get him to his feet."

Rough hands seized Ashinji by his arms and hauled him up. He bit back a scream as the humans' brutal handling kindled the dull throb in his shoulder to fiery agony. He swung his head from side to side in an effort to shake off the swoon that threatened to take him.

"How're we gonna get him back to camp, Cap'n? He don't look like he can walk too good."

"Hmm." The captain paused, then declared, "He'll have to ride. I'll carry him with me, on the front of my saddle. We'll need to strip off his armor first, though."

So, this is the final humiliation—to be dragged into the enemy camp stripped, wounded, and completely helpless," Ashinji thought. *Sadaiyo, did you hate me so much that you hoped I would suffer before my death, or did you wish a clean, quick end for me? Either way, the result will be the same.*

Because they had no familiarity with elven armor, the humans did a clumsy job of removing it from his body, and despite his efforts to remain stoic, Ashinji could not hide his suffering. His captors wrung several cries of pain from him, clearly taking delight in his agonies. When they had finished, Ashinji sagged in the arms of the captain, clad only in his blood-soaked under-tunic and breeches. As a final insult, the captain pulled his wedding bracelet from his wrist and yanked the service rings from his earlobe.

Dazed and semi-conscious, Ashinji could not resist as the captain hauled him up into place at the front of his saddle.

The man steadied him with one well-muscled arm. "Hold on, Pretty. I'll have you kneeling before her Ladyship by and by."

Ashinji squeezed his eyes shut and prayed for a quick release.

* * *

The captain reined his bay gelding to a jerky stop. He let go of his grip and Ashinji slid from the saddle to land hard upon the ground, where he lay until one of the humans hauled him to his feet. Two men stood on either side of him, supporting his weight with their bodies so he wouldn't collapse.

"Conor!" the captain barked. "Go and tell the bosses we're back and we've got a present for her Ladyship." The man called Conor, wiry and slim as a racing hound, took off to carry out his orders. The captain came and stood before Ashinji. "Her Ladyship'll be very keen on learning all of your secrets, Pretty. I suggest you cooperate. She's not a girl who takes too kindly to nonsense."

A crowd had formed around Ashinji and the returning raiders. Even in his current, pain-fogged state, Ashinji could sense the humans' feral excitement at having an enemy, wounded and helpless, among them. He could almost believe the scent of his blood stoked their lust for his murder.

"Captain Sirrus!"

The crowd parted to make way for a woman. She strode forward to stand before the captain, who snapped a brisk salute.

"Your Ladyship," he responded.

She wore the mantle of authority with the ease and confidence of one accustomed to command. Clad in the armor of a noble, she carried herself like a lifelong soldier. Her thick, dark hair hung in a loose braid down her back and a slim circlet of gold rested on her brow. Even in the crazy mix of light and shadow made by torches and lanterns, Ashinji had no trouble guessing her identity, for she closely resembled her brother Magnes.

"So, it's true, then. You've captured one of their officers," she said. "The information this man has could prove to be of extreme value, provided we can somehow communicate with him." She paused, then added, "Well done, Captain."

Captain Sirrus ducked his head in acknowledgment of the praise. "He can speak Soldaran, Ladyship," he pointed out, then stepped aside so his commander could approach Ashinji.

She stood for several moments, saying nothing, regarding Ashinji with cool appraisal. He stared back, trying to conceal how awful he felt. To let her see any weakness in him now would be disastrous. Her gaze flicked down to the splintered arrow shaft protruding from his shoulder.

"That looks like it hurts," she said.

"It does, but I can manage."

The woman frowned, a quick twist of her full lower lip. "I doubt that very much," she countered. "All men are much the same, whether they're human or elf, I think. You needn't try to impress me with your bravery." She reached out and swiped a forefinger across Ashinji's brow, then held it up in front of his face. "Cold sweat," she said. "I know what an arrow wound feels like. Your face is as white as fresh curds."

"Thessalina Preseren, my name is Ashinji Sakehera."

The woman started in surprise. "How do you know who I am?"

"Your brother Magnes is my friend," Ashinji replied.

Thessalina's eyes narrowed. "You know my brother?" she asked sharply. "Then you must be...you're the one he talked about...the elf nobleman who took in my tink cousin!"

"Jelena is my wife," Ashinji stated. Magnes' sister seemed taken aback by this piece of information, as if the fact that she and Ashinji had a familial connection disturbed her. "If Magnes is here, I'm certain he would wish to see me," Ashinji added.

"My brother Magnes disappeared some months ago," Thessalina revealed. "After our father died. No one knows where he went or if he'll ever return. For the time being, I am acting as his regent." Her face clouded over. Ashinji felt resentment flowing from her like a gray fog. His heart sank. Contacting Magnes had been his only real hope of escape.

"Captain Sirrus, you and your men will be rewarded," Thessalina said. "Have the prisoner brought to my tent straightaway." She spun on her heel and walked away.

"You heard what her Ladyship said!" Captain Sirrus barked. He motioned to the two men holding Ashinji's arms and they hustled him forward, unmindful of his wound. By the time they reached Thessalina's large tent at the center of the camp, fresh blood seeped out around the embedded arrowhead, and Ashinji was breathless from stifling his screams. His captors released him, and, too weak to stand, he collapsed to the rug-covered canvas floor.

"Gods!" he heard Thessalina exclaim. "Fetch the surgeon at once!"

"Yes, my lady!" Footsteps pounded out of the tent. Ashinji felt a hand cradle his head. He opened his eyes to find Thessalina bending over him.

"Can you hear me?" Her dark gaze pierced the fog shrouding his mind.

"Yes, I can hear you," he whispered. "May I please have some water?" Thirst had become almost as harsh a pain as that of his wound.

"Bring me some water!" Thessalina ordered, and someone handed her a leather canteen. She uncorked the spout and, supporting Ashinji's head in one hand, she held the bottle to his lips. The tepid water tasted of cowhide, but Ashinji drank until Thessalina pulled it away. "Not too much. You'll make yourself sick," she murmured.

"Help me up, please," he croaked. Thessalina slipped an arm beneath his uninjured shoulder and assisted him into a sitting position. She then squatted beside him, staring intently into his face. Neither one spoke for many heartbeats.

Finally, Ashinji broke the silence. "What are you going to do with me?" he asked, returning her gaze.

"Your Soldaran is excellent. How and why did you learn to speak our tongue?" she responded, ignoring his question.

"Languages come easily to me. I had a tutor who taught me the basics, and my father has many books written in Soldaran. As for the why...Is it not wise to know one's enemy as intimately as possible? What better way than to learn his language?"

Thessalina sighed and bit her lower lip. "I've never actually seen a full-blooded elf before, let alone talked to one," she said.

Ashinji's chuckle turned into a wince. "Your brother said something similar to me when we first met," he replied.

"Your commander made a foolish mistake, settling his army in a field of dry grass. Did he not think we'd try to burn him out?"

"My commander is..." Ashinji stopped himself before the words *not an experienced officer* escaped his lips. *No. I can't let her know of any weaknesses,* he thought. Instead, he said, "Your raiders were lucky...to get past our pickets. It will not happen again."

Thessalina's eyebrows shot up like the wings of a bird. "Lucky, you say. I say otherwise...We will cross the river at dawn. Our numbers are far superior to yours, and your soldiers will be worn out from fighting the fire."

"Our force is made up of seasoned professionals. They will hold their own, I have no doubt. We defend our homeland, do not forget." Ashinji paused, fighting a fresh wave of nausea and dizziness. He coughed, then whispered, "We will resist you...to our very last breaths."

"I expect you will," Thessalina replied.

"What...will you...do with me?" Ashinji asked again. He could barely keep his eyes open now.

Thessalina did not answer for several heartbeats. Finally, she said, "I don't know, yet."

"My lady, the surgeon is here." A soldier stood at the tent's entrance with another man, clad in a leather apron, beside him. Thessalina motioned for the surgeon to enter. He crossed over to where Ashinji sat and hunkered down to examine the broken arrow.

"Have him brought to the hospital tent, my lady," the surgeon directed. "Should be a simple matter of drawing out the tip, as long as it's not barbed... none of the archers uses barbed heads, do they? Anyhow, I'll draw out the tip, flush the wound, and apply a poultice. I suppose his kind can get wound poisoning and fevers like we can, but tinks are tough...or so I've heard." His voice oozed contempt. Thessalina nodded her head in dismissal and the man stood and departed.

Ashinji could feel the last of his strength trickling away with each fresh drop of blood that escaped his body.

Thessalina looked down at him with what might have been a measure of sympathy. "We'll talk later, if you survive." She snapped her fingers. "Take him," she ordered. The same two guards who had brought him before their commander came forward and hoisted Ashinji to his feet. They saluted, then half-dragged, half-carried their captive from the tent. Ashinji struggled to support some of his own weight in order to relieve the excruciating pressure on his wounded shoulder, but the guards mistook his efforts for an escape attempt.

"Quit wigglin'! You'll not get away from us, tink," the man on his left growled. He tightened his grip, cruelly digging in his fingers.

Human faces, distorted with hatred, derision, savage glee, and every other kind of ugliness passed by in a blur as the guards hustled him through the camp. Ashinji felt like a wounded animal, paraded before the masses in a sick spectacle. He tried to conceal his fear, but he was just too beaten, too drained.

In a curtained-off area at the back of the large, empty hospital tent, the surgeon stood waiting, hands on hips, an impatient scowl twisting his thin lips. Two younger, larger men stood on either side of him, each clad in a heavy leather apron matching his own. A long wooden table filled the remaining space.

"Here," the surgeon ordered, pointing. The guards pushed Ashinji down on the table, maintaining their grips upon his arms. "You two can go. My lads'll handle him now."

On his signal, the surgeon's assistants surged forward. One secured Ashinji's arms, the other grabbed his ankles.

"Put in the gag," the surgeon ordered, then proceeded to slice off Ashinji's bloody tunic with a small knife. One of the assistants stuffed a wad of filthy cloth into his mouth. The surgeon bent down to peer into Ashinji's eyes. "Try not to move," he murmured, acknowledging for the first time that he treated a man and not a beast. He straightened and disappeared briefly from Ashinji's view, returning with a pair of pliers and a slender blade. "Hold him steady, lads," he commanded. A tiny smile played about his mouth.

He seized the broken arrow shaft with the pliers and yanked.

Ashinji uttered a single, agonized scream, then the darkness claimed him, and he felt nothing more.

21
No Choice But Surrender

Ashinji awoke to find himself clad only in his breeches, lying on a blanket atop a loose pile of straw. A thick bandage swaddled his left shoulder. As he blinked slowly to clear his vision, his surroundings swam into focus.

Light's pretty dim, it must be near sunset. That means I've been out at least a day...Ai Goddess, the attack! It's over now, of course...Sadaiyo held them off, surely...Sadaiyo had to have...he had to!

Struggling against the pain that threatened to send him back into the embrace of the darkness, he levered himself up to a sitting position and looked around.

An awning of dirty canvas swayed overhead, supported by two poles driven into the ground at its front edge. The back and sides were secured to a three-sided enclosure made of the slender trunks of sapling trees. Loosely woven matting attached to the saplings served as a screen; whether to foil curious eyes or keep him ignorant of what lay beyond his prison, Ashinji could only guess.

A pair of guards sat on stools at the front of the enclosure, their backs to him, the slump of their shoulders speaking eloquently of their boredom and absolute belief in his helplessness. Ashinji, much to his surprise, found himself taking offense at the guards' offhand attitude toward him, then the absurdity of such feelings struck him and he couldn't help but laugh.

I am helpless, he thought. *And wounded. And totally alone.*

One of the guards heard Ashinji's bleak expression of mirth. He twisted around on his stool and peered into the gloom of the makeshift cell. "Hey Trip, I think he's awake," he said to his companion.

"Hey, tink! You awake in there?" the other guard called out.

Ashinji considered feigning continued unconsciousness, but he was desperately thirsty and he hoped these two had orders, at the very least, to see to his basic needs.

"Please, may I have some water?" he asked, and silently cursed the weakness of his voice.

"Go get him some water."

The one called Trip heaved himself to his feet, and grumbling under his breath, stumped off. The remaining guard continued to stare into the enclosure, searching the shadows. "We'd all heard you spoke Soldaran," he said. "Her Ladyship'll be happy you're still alive. Soon as Trip's back with the water, I'm off to fetch her."

Ashinji didn't bother with a reply. Instead, he lay back on the crude mattress and curled up on his uninjured side. *I might still be alive now, but for how long?* he thought. His entire left arm and shoulder throbbed with brutal intensity. A ferocious headache and queasy stomach only compounded his misery. He knew a poisoned wound could bring an ugly death, and he felt sick with dread.

Even with their far more sophisticated knowledge of anatomy and physiology, despite the advantages of medical sorcery, elven doctors could not stop the advance of putrefaction once it had progressed past a certain point. Ashinji had little confidence in the Soldaran camp surgeon's ability to save him if his wound turned bad.

Trip returned carrying a waterskin. He had to stoop to enter the enclosure. With a sniff, he dropped the waterskin next to Ashinji's head. Too weary and sick to move, Ashinji closed his eyes. He could feel the human's presence like a dim light flickering over him.

"Why you staring at him like that? C'mon, get outta there!" Trip's fellow guard growled.

"Just curious, is all," Trip muttered. "'Aint never seen a tink up close before. Think the priests are right about 'em?"

"I don't know, and I don't care. Now come out and sit down. I'm going to fetch her Ladyship."

Ashinji both felt and heard Trip's retreat to his stool outside the enclosure. He opened his eyes and reached for the waterskin. It took every bit of energy he had to lift himself upright, uncork the waterskin, and raise it to his lips. Despite his raging thirst, his stomach rebelled after only a few small sips and he had to stop drinking lest he vomit up what little water he had managed to consume. He lay down to wait.

For a time, his mind drifted in retreat from the emotional anguish of all that had befallen him. He wanted to let go completely, but the thought of never seeing Jelena again held him back.

"Ashinji Sakehera."

The sound of his name brought him out of the fog. He rolled over and saw Thessalina crouched at his side, eyes narrowed, lips twisted in a frown.

"You look worse now than when my men first brought you in." She made a low rumbling sound deep in her throat, a noise Ashinji interpreted as an expression of anger. "That surgeon is little more than a butcher, but he's all we've got out here."

"If the wound stays clean, I will live," Ashinji replied. Each word took a tremendous effort to form. "Tell me...tell me about the attack," he whispered.

"Your people fought bravely, just as you said they would. Your general proved more clever than I'd expected, considering his first blunder. He had the superior position and so was able to hold us off. I finally had to call a retreat."

Ashinji nearly sobbed with relief. He struggled to sit up, but Thessalina pushed him back down with gentle hands.

"Don't," she said. "Just lie still and listen to me....My commanders wanted me to force you to talk, and at first, I agreed, but now..." She sighed and rubbed her eyes. "Now, I find that I lack the stomach for it."

Ashinji stared at her, confused. He had expected Thessalina to demand all his knowledge of Sadaiyo's tactics and the size and deployment of the elven forces. He had also expected threats of torture. Thessalina's confession took him by surprise. She seemed strangely conflicted, almost as if she felt sympathy for his plight.

Her dark eyes searched his. "Even if I had given the order to torture you, you wouldn't have told me anything useful anyway, would you?"

"No," Ashinji answered.

"I thought as much...By all the gods, I'm going to pay a heavy price for this decision," she said.

"What are you going to do with me?" Ashinji asked, for the third time.

Thessalina remained silent for a long time. When at last she spoke, Ashinji heard what sounded like regret in her voice. "I can't send you back to your people. My commanders won't allow it. They'd have you killed first. I dare not go against them any more than I am already. They only choose to follow me out of respect for my father, not for any special loyalty they have for me. My position is still very tenuous, and this act of mercy," she shook her head as if in disbelief of her own actions, "will infuriate them.

I'm risking a lot...but I must do what I think is right. I won't be responsible for your murder. If that means I'll have to fight to keep my command, then so be it. I have a few allies...and the power of the duchy behind me." She paused, then added, "I...I'm really very sorry you and my cousin will be separated." She seemed genuinely surprised by her last words.

From everything Jelena had told him about Thessalina, he had expected no quarter from her.

Maybe she's not quite the stony-hearted bigot Jelena thinks she is.

"I can't let you go, but I can't keep you prisoner, either," Thessalina continued. "We are about to push our offensive and I won't have time to think about or deal with you so I've arranged to have you taken off my hands." She stood and the top of her head just brushed the underside of the canvas awning. "A slaver named Marcus is in the area. He specializes in...exotic types. I'm selling you to him."

Ashinji shivered as the meaning of her words sank into his tired mind. "You...you are making me a...*slave?*"

Thessalina nodded. "Look at it this way. I'm giving you a chance...a chance to live. If you're very, very lucky...well, only the gods know." She spun on her heel and made as if to leave, then paused and turned back to gaze down at him. "The priests tell us that elven beauty is a trap to catch the unwary," she said. "They say that your kind weave spells to ensnare us so you might steal our souls because you have none. They say elves are jealous of humans because we have souls...and we are superior for having them."

"Do you believe what your priests teach you about my people?" Ashinji asked.

"I thought I did," Thessalina replied, and then she left.

Ashinji rolled onto his side and let his mind slip back into blankness, too exhausted to think about the meaning behind Thessalina's final words.

* * *

"This is the prime specimen you told me about? My lady Thessalina, with all due respect...he looks terrible!"

"That may be so, but he's young and strong. He'll heal."

Ashinji woke with a start from a crazy dream in which a huge, black, four-legged beast with the upper torso of a man screamed at him to watch his back. He moaned aloud at the shock of pain that coursed from his shoulder down through his arm. He tried to flex his fingers but his hand had grown too swollen to close.

"Ah, he's awake. You say he speaks Soldaran?"

"Fluently."

"And how do you say his name again?"

"Ash-een-gee."

"You must be Marcus," Ashinji murmured through dry, cracked lips. "My new owner."

He opened his eyes to see a tall, powerfully built man stooping over him. A thick head of curly black hair and a full beard framed the man's broad face.

"That's right, Ash...Ashinji. Lady Thessalina has told me a few things about you." He shot Thessalina an exasperated look. "She didn't tell me you looked like shit, though!"

"Do we have a deal or not Marcus? I can always sell him to Celene, you know." Thessalina planted her hands on her hips, impatience evident in every line of her body.

"Temper, temper, my lady. Let's not be too hasty, now. I said I was interested and I still am, but in light of his, ah, condition, I'm going to have to reduce my offer. Cost of nursing him back to health...the risk I take that he might die of that wound...well, you understand."

"I understand that you'll make a handsome profit on him when you re-sell him in Darguinia!" Thessalina's dark eyes flashed.

"Yes, well. I won't make anything if he dies. I'll give you twenty imperials."

Ashinji wondered how much twenty imperials would purchase—a good warhorse, perhaps, or a decent suit of armor? He found it a very curious experience to be haggled over.

Thessalina frowned. "An elderly house slave might be worth only twenty. He's a trained fighter. I know for certain you'll get at least fifty for him, maybe more. I want forty or I'm sending for Celene."

Marcus chuckled appreciatively. "You've missed your calling, my lady. You were born to be a trader. Take thirty five and we'll shake on it." He held out a beefy hand. Thessalina extended hers and they shook.

Marcus hunkered down beside Ashinji and fixed him with a penetrating stare. His brown eyes, much to Ashinji's surprise, held no contempt.

"I've never had any ill feelings toward your kind," the slaver began. "So, you'll not get any special abuse from me. Matter of fact, I believe in treating my stock well, keeping them fit and healthy. I don't make any money on sick slaves. You're in no condition to try anything foolish, like an escape attempt, so I won't bother to warn you against it." Marcus stood up as far as the low ceiling would allow. He turned toward Thessalina. "I'll come and collect him first thing tomorrow morning." Thessalina nodded curtly and followed the slaver out of the enclosure, leaving Ashinji alone with his thoughts.

The dream that had haunted him—of fire and pursuit and a face he knew he should recognize but couldn't—it had all come to pass in a few terrible, life-altering moments. The image of Sadaiyo turning his back and riding away to abandon him to death would be burned into his mind's eye forever.

* * *

Later that evening, Trip brought him a bowl of soup and a cup of beer, but Ashinji felt too sick to eat. He knew his body needed nourishment in order to heal, but the smell of the food twisted his gut into knots. He begged Trip to take it away, and with a disinterested shrug, the guard complied.

Later still, the surgeon appeared like a blood-spattered apparition, waking Ashinji from a restless doze. He bent down and pressed his blade-thin nose against the bandages that swaddled Ashinji's shoulder, then raised Ashinji's arm and ran his fingers over the swollen flesh.

He clicked his tongue and shook his head.

"Too much swelling. Not a good sign," he said. He laid a hand against Ashinji's forehead. "Fever as well. But the wound has no odor. Puzzling. Perhaps it's due to your inhuman constitution. I have no experience treating your kind, so I don't know what to expect." He clicked his tongue again. "Willow bark, golden seal, and feverfew, I think. Yes, hopefully, they'll do the trick. I'll send one of my assistants with a draught." He turned to go, then paused and said "I suppose you're in a lot of pain. I'll send some poppy juice as well."

Ashinji shook his head. "No. No poppy juice." The drug would take away his pain, but it would also cloud his mind more than the pain already did. He couldn't afford to have his thoughts impaired any further.

"Suit yourself, then," the surgeon growled.

After he departed, Ashinji wondered if he had imagined the blood upon the man's apron.

* * *

"Hey, tink...wake up."

Ashinji felt the sharp prod of a booted toe in his ribs. He rolled over to see Trip standing over him, hands on hips, his body silhouetted against the bright sunlight pouring into the enclosure.

Blinking against the glare, Ashinji sat up and rubbed his face with his uninjured hand. He made a mental assessment of the state of his body, and realized with relief that the surgeon's draught had been effective. The swelling in his arm had noticeably decreased and he found that he could now move the fingers of his left hand. A tiny spark of hope kindled in his breast. Perhaps he would escape death awhile longer.

"Gods, you smell strange, tink," Trip commented. He wrinkled his nose in distaste.

"I need to...to..." Ashinji began, but the guard finished his sentence.

"Take a piss, sure. 'Course you do. I'll take you to the latrines." He stepped back and waited.

It seemed as if every bone and muscle in his body hurt, and as Ashinji struggled to his feet, he wondered how he would find the strength to make it all the way to Darguinia. He swayed, weak as a newborn lamb, and would have fallen had not Trip lunged forward to catch him.

"Here, lean on me," the guard muttered, and swung Ashinji's right arm over his shoulder.

After two days in the relative dimness of his makeshift prison cell, the sunlight outside seemed painfully bright, momentarily dazzling Ashinji's eyes. He allowed Trip to lead him to the latrine pits, where he had no choice but to relieve himself before a curious crowd of onlookers. Hot with shame and fury, he stumbled away on Trip's arm, the catcalls and hoots of derision like the lash of a whip upon his bare back.

Marcus was waiting for him, along with Thessalina, when he returned.

"Hmm. I think he looks a little better," the slaver commented.

"The surgeon will be here shortly to change his bandages and then you can take him," Thessalina replied. She stepped closer to Ashinji and looked into his eyes. "My army attacked your forces again, last night under cover of darkness, but your general was ready for us. Once again, I had to call a retreat." She searched Ashinji's face for his reaction.

"My brother is a capable commander," he replied.

Thessalina's eyes widened with surprise. "Your brother commands the elven forces? Perhaps I was too hasty in selling you to Marcus here," she said. "Your brother, no doubt, would have paid me a handsome ransom for your return... much more than I'm getting from this old fox!" Marcus snorted and rolled his eyes.

Ashinji shook his head. "I thought your commanders would have killed me first, rather than let me return to my people."

Thessalina tossed her glossy mane. "Enough gold changes even the most resolute of minds. I would have had to share the ransom with them, of course."

"My brother would not have bargained with you in any case," Ashinji said.

"Why not?" Thessalina lifted one eyebrow.

Ashinji did not reply, but his expression must have given her some clue, for she frowned and said "I am truly sorry for you, Ashinji."

"My lady, I've come to tend the elf." The surgeon strode up, followed by an assistant carrying a leather sack. He exclaimed with satisfaction when he saw Ashinji conscious and standing. "The draught worked. Excellent." He snapped his fingers. "Bring him in here so I can work," he ordered, indicating the enclosure.

Ashinji sat down on the dingy straw and tried to remain still as the surgeon first removed the bandages then proceeded to clean the wound, but the man made no effort to be gentle. By the time he finished, Ashinji had nearly reached the end of his endurance. Sweat-soaked and shaking, he shot the surgeon a bitter, angry glare as the man wiped his hands on a rag and stood. "I'm finished. You can take him now," he called out. To Ashinji, he snapped, "On your feet."

Marcus entered the enclosure, a pair of manacles dangling from his hand.

"C'mon now, Ashinji. Time to go," the slaver said cheerily. The manacles clinked as they swung against Marcus' thigh.

For in instant, Ashinji considered running, then just as quickly gave up the idea. Even if he could find the strength to run, he would be cut down before he could take three steps.

"My father is Lord of Kerala, Commanding General of the Armies of Alasiri," he whispered. "I am the son-in-law of the king. Do not do this to me, please!" He despised himself for begging, but he had nothing else left.

"I know you've got a pedigree, Ashinji, but none of that matters anymore," Marcus said. "You're a slave now, that's all. The sooner you accept it, the easier things'll be for you. I s'pose I could try to sell you back to your dad...that is, if you really are who you say you are...but why should I take the risk? There's a war on, and your people just might kill me first and ask questions later. No..." He shook his head for emphasis. "I'll make a very handsome profit selling you in Darguinia, with no risk to my life." His voice hardened. "Now, get up and hold out your hands."

Surrounded by his enemies, too weak to fight or flee, Ashinji had no choice but to surrender. Slowly, he climbed to his feet and extended his hands to his new master.

"Wait," Thessalina spoke up. Marcus turned toward her, eyebrows raised. "He can't go all the way to Darguinia half-naked," she said. She looked at Trip. "Go find a tunic," she ordered. "And a pair of sandals as well." They waited in silence for the guard to return. Ashinji scanned the faces of the humans around him, trying to summon an emotional reaction, but he found he could not. He had gone numb.

Trip returned with a tunic and a pair of shabby sandals.

"I will need help," Ashinji said. "I cannot raise my arm over my head."

The guard hesitated.

"Well, go on! Help him!" Thessalina barked, stabbing the air with her forefinger. Trip jumped to comply, and assisted Ashinji in donning the clothing. The dingy brown tunic hung loosely from his body and the sandals were too large, but the mere fact that he no longer stood half-naked among the enemy acted as a balm to his shredded dignity. Marcus came forward and closed the manacles over his wrists, testing them with a tug to make sure they were secure. He then attached a leather leash to Ashinji's right wrist.

"Lady Thessalina, it has been a pleasure conducting business with you," Marcus said, grinning. "I hope the rest of your business goes just as well."

Thessalina waved her hand in a gesture of dismissal. "Just go," she said. "I gave one of your assistants a pass that will let all of you stay the night at Amsara Castle. Show it to my steward."

As she turned to leave, Ashinji called out to her. "Lady Thessalina, if my friend Magnes should ever return home, will you please tell him what became of me?" Thessalina halted. Slowly, she turned to face Ashinji. As their eyes met, Ashinji reached out with his mind to taste the flavor of her psychic energy. He detected determination, ambivalence, anger, and something else....

Thessalina abruptly looked away. She opened her mouth to as if to speak but the words seemed to balk on the tip of her tongue, resisting all of her efforts. Defeated, she spun around and hurried away, as if fleeing something she dared not face.

Marcus huffed and scratched at his beard.

"I think she likes you," he said.

22

The Heart Of The Empire

Marcus drove up to the outer gates of Amsara Castle just as the sun disappeared below the horizon. Ashinji had spent much of the day sleeping on a pile of musty blankets in the wagon bed; the cessation of the wagon's bumpy movements roused him from a restless doze. He raised his head.

The two soldiers standing guard at the gates came forward to challenge Marcus, who then explained he had permission to stay the night.

"Let's see yer proof, then," one of the guards demanded.

"From her Ladyship's own hand," Marcus stated, and with a flourish, produced his pass.

"Give it 'ere." The guard snatched it from Marcus' fingers and held the small square of wood up to his eyes, squinting. After a moment's inspection, he said, "Looks alright, I reckon. Drive on, then. You c'n park over by the east wall."

"Much obliged," Marcus replied and snapped the reins to get his sturdy dun mare moving. He drove into the outer yard and pulled the horse to a stop at the designated spot.

The people of Amsara Castle had settled in for the evening, but the arrival of strangers, especially at this time of day, piqued their curiosity. The children approached first. By the time Marcus and his two hired hands had climbed down, a sizable gathering of the castle's youngest inhabitants had the wagon surrounded.

Ashinji lay very still, hidden from view, listening to the whispers and giggles that skittered around him. The piping sound of the children's voices evoked memories of his two little sisters, Jena and her twin Mariso—so much alike, they could sometimes fool their own brother if they put their minds to it. The thought of never again hearing their bright laughter or seeing their sweet faces aglow with youthful mischief filled his heart with sadness.

Marcus unhitched the horse from the wagon while his men unloaded the gear they would need for the night. The older of the two, a short, stocky fellow with silver-laced black hair cropped above his ears, tried, with little success, to shoo the children away while his partner, a blond bear of a man even more powerfully built than Marcus, got to work erecting a small shelter against the castle wall.

A chilly wind skirled down from the stone heights of the castle towers and gusted through the yard. The last light of the dying sun had faded now, leaving the stars to shine forth in all their crystalline brilliance. The smell of autumn permeated the air. Ashinji, clad only in the thin, rough cotton of his borrowed tunic and breeches, shivered. *It's going to be a cold night*, he thought.

Marcus climbed into the back of the wagon, a set of leg irons in his hands. He grabbed Ashinji's ankle and fastened the shackle around it, then attached the other end to a stout ring embedded in the wood of the wagon bed.

"You'll be safe enough here, I think," he said, then climbed down and stumped off. Ashinji sighed and wrapped himself up in a blanket, then lay down and tried to sponge his mind clean of thoughts.

A few moments later, he felt rather than saw a small body creep into the wagon. A hand grasped the edge of the blanket and gave it a sharp tug.

Ashinji looked up to find a boy, thin-faced and crowned with a shock of sandy hair staring at him, eyes wide as saucers. The child made a little choking noise in his throat and backed away. Ashinji watched as he scrambled off the wagon and fell into the arms of his comrades, who all began chattering at once.

"Get away from there, you brats!" Marcus bellowed.

The children scattered like sparrows before a hawk, shrieking as they ran. Cries of *"tink, tink!"* echoed against the walls.

Marcus climbed back up in the wagon bed, growling like an angry lion.

"Damn brats," he spat. He held out a small wooden cup. "The doctor told me to give you this three times a day for the next three days." Ashinji propped himself on his elbow and took the cup from Marcus' hand. He drained the bitter liquid in one gulp, fighting the urge to gag. He recognized the draught as the same concoction that Thessalina's camp surgeon had given him the night before.

"Are you hungry?" Marcus asked.

"Yes," Ashinji answered, surprised at just how hungry he did feel.

"I'll bring you some grub, then." Ashinji pulled the threadbare blanket back over his shoulders and lay down to wait for the promised food.

He knew he had fallen asleep only after the soft whisper of a female voice in his ear woke him. He rolled over and peered out through the slats of the wagon's side to see a woman staring back at him.

Short and stout, the woman wore the plain garb of a servant. Several tendrils of iron-gray hair had escaped the kerchief covering her head and hung down to frame a face on which every line and groove told of a lifetime of toil and worry. She kept glancing around her as if she feared discovery.

"*Psst,*" she hissed. "C'n ye understand me? Are ye awake?" She wrung her hands together. "Oh, please, talk t'me if ye can!"

Despite his fatigue, Ashinji sat up and leaned against the side of the wagon so the woman could see his face. "What is it you wish to speak to me about, Grandmother?" he inquired in a gentle voice, addressing her as he would an elderly elven woman.

"Oh, ye can understand me!" she gasped. "Please...might ye know of...of a girl, my little girl...well, she weren't my child by blood, no. I never gave birth to her, but I did deliver her into this cruel world, I did."

A glimmer of recognition lit the edges of Ashinji's mind.

"She was...well, her sire was one of yer people. My girl had to run away. She ran north, t' find her dad. P'raps you seen a half-breed girl up in yer country, lookin' for her dad?"

Ashinji saw in his mind's eye a memory of Jelena sitting on a couch, her legs tucked beneath her and a sweet bun in her hand. She spoke to him of her childhood, and the human woman who had raised and loved her.

"I do know of your girl, Claudia," he answered.

"Ye know my name!" Claudia cried. Her hands flew to her face.

"Jelena has told me all about you."

"Ye...y've seen my little girl? Oh, please tell me everything! I've missed her so much!" In the cool starlight, tears glittered on Claudia's seamed cheeks.

"Jelena is well. She found a home and a family, and she thrives."

Claudia reached through the slats of the wagon and groped for Ashinji's hand. He took her work-roughened fingers in his and squeezed them reassuringly.

"How d'ye say yer name, kind sir?" Claudia asked.

"Ashinji," he replied.

"Ash...een...gee," Claudia drew out the syllables as if savoring the sound of the elven phonemes. "'Tis a fine, grand name."

"Jelena calls me 'Ashi', mostly."

"How do ye know my little girl?" Claudia asked, still holding tight to Ashinji's hand.

"We are husband and wife."

Claudia drew in a sharp breath. "Ye be my baby's man! Oh...What misfortune has brought ye here and separated ye from my Jelena?"

Ashinji could not bear to speak the whole truth—it hurt too much—so he related only the bare-bones facts of his ambush and capture, leaving out the stunning betrayal that had made it so much easier.

Claudia was weeping softly now. "My poor, poor baby...How will she ever bear it?"

Ashinji swallowed against the ache in his throat caused by his own grief. "When she is told that I am dead, she will be devastated," he said. "But Jelena is strong. She has family now to shelter and support her. She also has our child to think about. She will survive."

"Jelena is with child! My baby is goin' to have her own baby," Claudia whispered. "Oh, but what is to become of ye?"

"Marcus the slave trader is taking me south, to Darguinia. There, he will sell me and after that, I do not know."

"'Tis an evil thing, 'tis!" Claudia raged. "After all my poor Jelena suffered, she finds a bit o' happiness only to have it ripped away from her! If only there was somethin' I could do...but I'm just an old woman." She covered her face and Ashinji watched helplessly as her stooped shoulders shook with grief.

"Claudia... Jelena will survive. I know she will. Her love for our child will keep her strong. And if the One permits it, I will find a way to return to her.... But there is one more thing I must tell you, Claudia."

"What is it, dear Ash-ee?"

"Jelena found her father. He is the king of my people."

Claudia gasped. "Praise all the gods," she whispered. "My little baby is...a...a..."

"Hey, what's going on over there!" Marcus called out.

"Quickly, Claudia! You must go now," Ashinji said.

Once more, Claudia grabbed Ashinji's hand and kissed it. "May the gods bless an' keep ye, dear Ash-ee."

She turned and scurried away across the yard, disappearing in the shadows just as Marcus returned to the wagon, a bowl and cup in his hands. "I thought I heard voices over here. Were you talking to someone?"

He set the bowl and cup down by Ashinji's hand. The chain attached to his ankle rattled as he shifted position, reminding Ashinji of his new station. "Just an old woman from the castle, curious about what a tink looks like up close." The pejorative left a foul taste in Ashinji's mouth the moment it left his lips.

"Huh! Well, I suppose the riffraff 'round here don't get too much excitement. Anyway, there's your dinner. I'm guessing your kind eat the same things as what we eat." Marcus jumped off the wagon and Ashinji followed the sound of his boots as they retreated back toward where he and his men had set up their lean-to. He strained to make out the words of their desultory conversation, but they sat too far away. Eventually, he gave up and turned his attention to his food.

He raised the bowl to his nose and sniffed. The pleasant aroma of a meat stew provoked a growl from his stomach. Marcus had failed to provide him with a spoon, so awkwardly, he wedged the bowl between his knees and used his good hand to feed himself.

The cup contained sour, thin beer. He drained it in one gulp, and after sucking the gravy off his fingers, he wiped his hand on a corner of one of the blankets that made up his pallet. He then lay down on his back, wrapped himself up, and stared at the star-spattered sky overhead.

The blond bear-man came back later to collect the cup and bowl and to unchain Ashinji just long enough for him to relieve himself against the castle wall. After he had finished attending to the needs of his body, Marcus' assistant re-secured him to the wagon for the night.

Shivering, Ashinji buried himself beneath the pile of musty blankets and tried to quiet his mind enough to fall asleep. Despite his best efforts, the memory of Sadaiyo's betrayal kept rising up, unbidden, to torment him.

Never in his worst nightmares had Ashinji ever imagined that Sadaiyo's jealousy would lead to such an act.

Somehow, I've got to survive and return to hold my treacherous brother accountable.

Sleep came to him at last, shortly before dawn.

* * *

Marcus rousted his men at sunrise, and had them pack their gear for a speedy departure. Ashinji looked for Claudia among the knot of castle dwellers gathered in the yard to see them off. He caught a glimpse of her kerchief-covered head at the back of the crowd. As the wagon trundled out through the castle gates, he saw Claudia break free of the group to stand apart, hands clasped together before her as if in prayer.

How you must have mourned when you awoke that day nearly a year ago to find your Jelena gone, he thought. *I hope, now that you know Jelena is safe, you can find some peace of mind. Farewell, Claudia.*

Claudia raised her hand and waved.

* * *

Fourteen days later, filthy and in chains, Ashinji entered the heart of the Soldaran Empire.

Darguinia had grown up around a natural, deep-water harbor. The flows of two mighty rivers emptied tons of silt into its murky waters, keeping the dredgers busy year round. The city functioned as the hub of a vast network of trade routes that supplied it with every conceivable commodity from all corners of the far-flung empire.

The main slave market, located in the city center near the Grand Arena, was the largest in the empire, according to Marcus. There, a buyer with enough imperials in his or her purse could purchase living chattel to suit any purpose, from field hand to housemaid, gladiator to pleasure slave. Separate, smaller markets set up within the main precincts dealt in specialty items, such as skilled artisans, children, and exotics. Marcus intended to offer Ashinji up for sale at the latter.

The arrow wound in his shoulder had healed well, leaving Ashinji with only a small, puckered scar and some residual pain. He attributed his relatively easy recovery to the fact that he had done nothing for the last two weeks other than eat, sleep and watch the scenery roll by. The further south they traveled, the warmer and drier the climate had become. The landscape had changed accordingly, shifting from lush grassland and broadleaf forests to low, scrubby vegetation, dry meadows, and stands of tough-looking, waxy-leafed trees.

The wilderness had gradually given way to farmland; Ashinji noted how the fields of late summer wheat and rye lay sere beneath the relentless sun. Marcus had clicked his tongue in dismay. "There wasn't enough rain last spring, and the summer's looking to linger past its welcome," he'd said. "A poor harvest'll mean hunger in the cities for sure, and that means big trouble for the empress."

The slaver had been true to his word and had fed his captive well and prohibited his assistants from abusing Ashinji physically, although the two men had delighted in verbally baiting him at every opportunity. Ashinji had little trouble ignoring them, having mastered the art of shedding hurtful words years ago under the harsh tutelage of his brother.

As Marcus deftly maneuvered the wagon through the steady stream of traffic heading into the city, Ashinji observed everything around him with keen interest. He knew he could not escape—at least not any time soon—but he had faced his death and had survived, an outcome he had not expected. His survival ran counter to the prophecy of his dream, proving that the future remained fluid, and could be shaped by his own determination. If given the opportunity, he would attempt escape; therefore, he needed to commit to memory every detail he could of the way in and out of Darguinia.

The broad road upon which they traveled ran for a time through a sprawling shantytown. Everywhere he looked, Ashinji observed masses of humans shoving, walking, crawling, squatting, eating, selling, buying, sleeping, and dying.

Ashinji had always been aware on an intellectual level that the human race outnumbered the elven, but the reality of how much so now became shockingly, terrifyingly clear.

We elves are in serious trouble, he thought.

Ashinji could only stare at the crowds and wonder how Alasiri would ever prevail over such odds.

As the wagon rolled on, the shacks and shelters of the shantytown gave way to small houses and businesses made of wood and brick. The dirt road turned into an avenue paved with a smooth hard surface Ashinji could not identify. When he dared to ask Asa, Marcus' salt and pepper-haired assistant about it, the man answered "It's concrete, ya stupid tink!"

The sun had crept past its zenith when the road finally passed the massive public buildings of the city center. Despite the fear that gnawed at his gut, Ashinji still felt impressed at the grand scale of everything. No elven scholar had ever denied the engineering and architectural abilities of the human race, and among all human peoples, the Soldarans were universally acknowledged as the best builders.

The Grand Arena hove into view like a mighty ship, its massive walls of white stone rising to dizzying heights, dwarfing the other structures around it. Marcus drove out onto a road encircling the huge round building and turned the horse's head to the right, following the curve of the wall eastward. He began to whistle a cheerful tune.

No doubt he's anticipating the profit he'll make on me, Ashinji thought.

After following the road for a short distance, Marcus drove the wagon through a set of tall stone gates. The words, "Grand Slave Market" written in High Soldaran script, decorated the plinth.

Ashinji watched in horrified fascination as they rolled past an auction in progress, one of several going on at once in various areas of the market. A young woman stood on a raised platform, naked except for the chains on her wrists and ankles, blank eyes staring through a curtain of tangled black hair. A crowd of men ringed the platform, all shouting and gesturing with their fingers. Another man, dressed in gold-trimmed robes, stood beside the girl, prodding her thighs with the butt of a leather whip. When the handler spun the girl around, bent her over and kicked her legs apart, Ashinji turned away in disgust.

The scene he had just witnessed, coupled with the noise and heat, left Ashinji shaking and nauseous. He leaned against the side of the wagon and struggled to breathe, a mere hairsbreadth from panic.

There's no way I'll let Marcus strip and parade me naked in front of a howling mob of humans. I'll find a way to kill myself first!

The wagon stopped in front of a smaller, walled-off area. Marcus set the brake and jumped down from the driver's seat. He scrambled onto the wagon bed and stood, hands on hips, looking down at Ashinji. "Your new life is about to begin, Ashinji," he announced. "This is the exotics market. Mostly humans from faraway lands with different colored skins are sold here, but half-breeds and some non-humans end up here as well. You'll be a special prize. Not too often a pureblooded elf ends up in your circumstances. The bidding should be spirited!" His eyebrows lifted in amusement.

Ashinji remained silent.

"First things first," Marcus continued. "We've got to get you cleaned up." He snapped his fingers and his assistants came to attention. "Take him to the wash yard. I'll be along shortly," he ordered.

Marcus' assistants escorted Ashinji to an enclosed yard deep within the exotics market area. Stone troughs lined the walls on three sides. The cobble-paved yard sloped inward toward a large circular drain hole in the center. A crowd of people, some washing themselves, others being washed against their will with varying degrees of struggle, filled the space.

Asa grabbed a wooden bucket and filled it with water from one of the many small taps spouting from the walls over the troughs. "Don't just stand there, Lacus you lazy dolt!" He glowered at Blond Bear. "Get his clothes off!"

Lacus stepped forward and Ashinji raised his hands. "I can undress and wash myself if you free my hands," he said. Lacus looked at Asa, his broad face full of uncertainty.

Asa frowned, then said "Yeah, go ahead. Where can he run to, eh?"

Hands free, Ashinji peeled off his filthy clothes and dropped them into the trough. He looked at Asa. "Soap?" he asked, and the man went off to find some. While he waited, he unbraided his hair and raked his fingers through its greasy length, grimacing in disgust, acutely aware that others in the yard were beginning to take notice of him.

Asa returned and pressed an irregular yellow lump into Ashinji's hand. Ashinji turned his back to the yard and began washing the two and a half weeks worth of accumulated grime from his hair and skin. When he had finished, his skin smarted from the harsh soap, but the sheer bliss of a clean body raised his spirits as much as they could be in this horrible place.

Lacus produced a clean tunic from the pack he carried slung over one broad shoulder. With a grateful sigh, Ashinji slipped the unbleached cotton over his still-wet body. He dunked his dusty sandals in the trough to rinse them and slipped them back on his feet, then fished the old tunic and breeches out of the murky water.

"Leave those," Asa ordered, and Ashinji let the water-soaked garments slip out of his hand to land with a wet plop on the cobbles at his feet. "Hold out your hands," Asa commanded and fastened the manacles back on Ashinji's wrists.

As they left the wash yard, Ashinji glanced about and saw the many gazes turned on him.

Goddess, please! Help me get through this! he prayed. *Help me survive and get home to Jelena and our baby!*

He looked at the sky and caught sight of a pair of white birds winging their way across the roofs of the market. They swerved and alighted onto the wash yard wall. Their bead-like eyes seemed to follow Ashinji as he passed below their perch.

Seeing the birds, he didn't feel quite so afraid anymore.

Perhaps these birds are a sign from the One, he thought. *I am Ashinji Sakehera, son of Sen and Amara, Lord and Lady of Kerala. Jelena Onjara Sakehera is my wife, and I am son-in-law to Keizo Onjara, King of Alasiri.*

I am no slave!

He would hold these truths in his heart, and survive.

23

The Grieving Season

Winter tightened its grip on Alasiri. The trees had shed their leaves and stretched bare branches to the gray skies like bony hands grasping toward heaven. The flocks of migratory birds that had passed overhead in countless numbers throughout the late fall had vanished, fled south to their breeding grounds in the human lands. The summer-sleek hides of horses and cattle had grown rough and shaggy, and the sharp wind off the high Kesen Numai Mountains sang of the coming snow.

As the season deepened, so too, did Jelena's grief. For a time, she withdrew completely from all life at court, sequestering herself in a small set of rooms near the Sakehera family quarters. Unable to bear Sadaiyo's presence, Jelena had refused to return to the home of her in-laws, and so the king had given her a private flat of her own to live in, along with Eikko.

Keizo came to see her every day, as did Amara and Sen. She would sit with them for a time, but then beg them to leave her, so she could retreat to the haven of her bedroom to lie alone with her sorrow. Sonoe came as well, sometimes with Keizo, sometimes on her own. For reasons Jelena did not quite understand, only Sonoe seemed able to give her any comfort.

Sonoe had been there, standing with the king, when Sadaiyo delivered the news that ended life as Jelena had known it. During the few moments it had taken for Sadaiyo to speak, Jelena's world had imploded, leaving her a widow and her unborn daughter fatherless. She could recall little of that terrible day, but one of the few memories that stood out had been the unexpected tenderness of Sonoe's attentions.

Her father's arms had cradled her in those first few hours of agony, but later, when she had begged to return to her room, his Companion had accompanied her and had stayed with her through the long, dark night.

Jelena had found herself clinging to the older woman as she would to a sister, accepting the comfort Sonoe offered without question or hesitation. All the suspicions she had harbored against Sonoe vanished like dew at sunrise, and now, after so many weeks of closeness, she shared a bond with the flame-haired sorceress both deep and strong.

Sonoe now came to Jelena's rooms each morning and saw to it that she got out of bed, went to the bath house, got dressed, and ate. If not for her friend's persistence during those first few days, Jelena doubted if she would have had the strength to move at all.

With each passing day, the pain, though still intense, grew a little easier to bear. Slowly, Jelena learned to live with her grief.

This particular morning, Sonoe was late, and Eikko, perhaps not having the heart to disturb her, had left Jelena alone to linger awhile longer in bed. Thin, wintry sunshine spilled like ice water across the coverlets, and Jelena sighed in annoyance at herself for forgetting to remind Eikko to draw the curtains last night. The light made it impossible to sleep, as did the movements of her daughter.

Jelena tossed the covers aside and slid awkwardly out of bed. She drew a fur-lined robe over her nightgown, and with a hand pressed to her aching back, she shuffled over to the little water closet to relieve herself. That done, she settled into the window seat, pulling her robe close about her to ward off the chill that seeped through the glass. Her unborn daughter dealt her another kick to her ribs.

"Easy, easy, little one," she whispered in Soldaran. "Why must you be so hard on your poor mam?" Jelena almost never spoke in her native tongue anymore, and at times, she missed the sound of it.

Where is Sonoe?

Jelena felt a twinge of worry. She looked out the window, letting her gaze wander over the rooftops glazed with frost. A flutter of black against the blue tiles caught her eye. A large raven had dropped from the sky to land on a dragon-headed rain spout directly across from her window. The bird looked as though it watched something below its perch. Jelena craned her neck to try to get a look at what the bird saw.

In a little courtyard below Jelena's bedchamber, Sonoe and Princess Taya stood face to face in what seemed to be a tense confrontation. Even from so great a distance, Jelena could sense the animosity that crackled between the two mages like a lightning strike. Sonoe spoke and Taya reacted as if she had been struck. Both women threw up their hands simultaneously and each took a step back and away from the other. Jelena cried out in alarm.

From the other side of the bedchamber door, she heard Eikko call out, "Princess! My lady, are you ill?"

"I'm fine," Jelena answered, tearing her gaze away from the stand-off below. She pushed herself up from the window seat and moved to open the door, but before she reached it, Eikko had bustled in.

The hikui girl scanned Jelena with a practiced eye. "You cried out, my lady, and it frightened me!" She looked both relieved and accusatory all at once.

"I was startled, that's all, Eikko. I just saw my aunt and Sonoe down in the courtyard and they seemed to be having a nasty argument," Jelena explained. She moved past Eikko into her sitting room.

"I'm sure they'll settle it, Highness, one way or another. You shouldn't let it worry you," Eikko said, as she followed her mistress out of the bedroom. Jelena sat on the couch before the fireplace, and Eikko quickly moved to throw a fresh chunk of wood onto the glowing embers of last night's fire.

But it does worry me, Jelena thought, well aware of the bitter rivalry between her aunt and Sonoe, but still ignorant of its origins. Neither mage had offered an explanation, nor had either one asked her to make a choice between them.

One day, they might, and then what?

"Shall I bring you your tea, Highness?"

A soft rap upon the outer door interrupted Jelena's reply. Eikko hurried over to admit a rather flustered Sonoe. The mage pulled off her green velvet cloak and dumped it into Eikko's arms, then swept into the sitting room and dropped on the couch beside Jelena. She held herself stiffly upright, eyes closed, jaw locked tight. Her long, graceful fingers clinched into fists on her lap.

"Sonoe, I saw you with my aunt. What happened?" Jelena asked in a low voice. She stared at her friend's profile and waited.

With an explosive sigh, Sonoe relaxed. She opened her eyes, turned toward Jelena and smiled. "It's nothing that I haven't had to deal with many times before, pet," she answered. "The princess and I have...old grievances. Grievances which I have long since put aside, but she seems unable to move past. I try to live peacefully with her, for your father's sake, but, well..." She shook her head and reached out to gather Jelena into her arms. "I am sorry if you were worried," she whispered.

Jelena felt Sonoe's warm, comforting energy envelop her like a soft blanket.

"I...I wasn't worried, not really," Jelena fibbed. Sonoe chuckled. The baby jumped and both Jelena and Sonoe gasped, then burst out laughing.

"That little one of yours... she grows stronger every day," Sonoe said. "I can feel her Talent, Jelena. It blazes like the sun. She will be a great beauty and an even greater mage one day."

Jelena looked down at her bulging belly and tried to imagine what her child would look like. "I pray every night, Sonoe," she said, "to Hani, the Soldaran goddess of Beauty. I ask her to let Ashi's face come again into the world when our daughter is born."

"Eikko!" Sonoe called out.

"Yes, mistress?"

"The princess is ready to go to the bath house now."

Eikko disappeared into Jelena's bedroom and emerged a few moments later carrying a heavy cloak of fine, golden brown wool and fur-lined leather boots. She flung the cloak over the top of Jelena's robe and bent to assist her mistress with the boots.

"Now you're ready to go out into the cold," the maid pronounced after she'd done up the last bootlace.

"I'll wait here for you," Sonoe stated. "Don't dawdle. Your father is expecting us for breakfast."

Jelena smiled. "I have an announcement to make that he'll want to hear. I've decided on a name for my daughter."

Sonoe beamed with delight. "I won't ask you to tell me now, because I know you'll want to tell your father first," she said. Her emerald eyes shone with affection. Jelena wondered anew how she could have ever been afraid of her father's Companion.

Jelena waited for Eikko to pull on her own cloak, and then the two young women descended to the courtyard and hurried toward the bath house, their breath swirling in gouts of steam about their heads. As they walked, Jelena glanced over her shoulder to see Sonoe standing in the sitting room window, looking upward, head cocked, as if listening to something.

That's odd, Jelena thought as she followed Sonoe's line of sight to the peak of the roof directly opposite the window. The enormous raven she had seen earlier still clung to the frost-slick tile. The bird opened its beak and uttered a harsh cry.

The sound sent an icy finger of dread trailing down her spine, and she shivered. Why the caw of a raven should affect her so, she couldn't fathom. She looked back toward the window, but Sonoe had disappeared.

"Princess! Do come along, you'll catch your death out here!" Eikko pleaded through chattering teeth.

"Coming," Jelena replied. She glanced once more at the roof. The raven remained motionless, a black form silhouetted against the blue sky.

Many Soldarans believed that ravens harbored the souls of executed criminals, bent on mischief and mayhem. Claudia had always discouraged such thinking, believing it to be nonsense; nevertheless, ravens had always made Jelena uneasy.

Pulling her cloak tighter around herself, Jelena turned her back on the bird and followed Eikko's retreating form. From behind, she heard the flap of wings and a heartbeat later, the raven swooped by, low and fast, then angled up over the roof tops and disappeared. A single, blue-black feather floated down to touch the ground at Jelena's feet. She sidestepped to avoid treading on it, her gut twisting in irrational fear.

Ashinji would think her silly, and in her mind, she could hear the sound of his good-natured laughter, sweet and mellow. A sharp pang of sorrow opened the ever present wound in her heart as fresh tears wet her cheeks.

I've got to stop crying every time I think of you, Ashi. I know you'd want me to get past the pain and move on, for our child's sake!

By the time she reached the bath house, she had stopped crying, but she felt like the hurt would never truly end.

24
The Power Of A Name

"Keizo, Jelena has something important to tell you," Sonoe said as she slipped into her accustomed place at the dining table, to the right of the king. Almost without conscious thought, she arranged her robes to artful effect and settled into the attitude of seductive attentiveness she always adopted when in the presence of her royal lover.

Jelena came to her father and accepted his paternal kiss, then took her place across from Sonoe. The two of them had Keizo all to themselves this morning, for which Sonoe felt greatly relieved. The thought of having to face Taya again, after their run-in earlier....

The old bitch is getting suspicious, she thought. *I must tread carefully, very carefully, indeed. Things are at a crucial stage, now. I can't afford any mistakes!*

"What is it you want to tell me, Daughter?" Keizo asked. His voice, as usual, was calm and measured, but the sparkle in his eyes betrayed his eagerness to hear Jelena's news. Before she could speak, however, the servants arrived with the meal.

Sonoe watched Jelena surreptitiously as the servants laid out the food. The magic of the Key within Keizo's daughter bled through every pore of her skin, as beautiful and bright as the sun. Sonoe felt intoxicated by its energy. How could any serious mage not wish to possess such power?

The Nameless One thinks he controls me, and that I will meekly assist him in obtaining the Key! I'll let him believe he has the upper hand, for now. But when I turn the tables on him...then we'll see who controls whom!

"Shall I pour you some tea, my dear?"

"Uh... yes, please," Sonoe answered, turning her attention back to Keizo and smiling as he filled her cup. He always seemed to derive pleasure from serving her with his own hand, and she derived enormous satisfaction from letting him do so.

"Now, Daughter... Tell me your news," Keizo commanded after he had poured tea for them all.

"I've decided on a name for your granddaughter," Jelena said, smiling. "Ashinji and I didn't have much time to discuss names before he... left for Kerala. I've picked one that would please him as well as me."

She lowered her head for a heartbeat, and when she looked up, her eyes glittered with unshed tears. "Ashinji's grandmother, Lord Sen's mother, was named Hatora. I've decided Hatora will be our daughter's name."

Keizo nodded in agreement. "Hatora is a fine name. I'm sure my old friend will be well pleased with your choice. It is fitting that you should honor the memory of your husband in this way."

"Thank you, Father," Jelena said.

"Jelena my pet, I thought we might go riding after breakfast...that is, if you feel up to it," Sonoe suggested.

"That sounds like a fine idea. My daughter needs to get out and get some fresh air," the king concurred. Jelena looked hesitant.

"You need to get out," Sonoe insisted. "You've been in seclusion for long enough. We'll ride down through town and go out beyond the gates for a little way, just to the Meizi Road." She looked to Keizo for support.

"Yes, excellent. I'll send for a pair of guards to accompany you."

Sonoe cursed inwardly, but knew better than to argue. Keizo usually allowed his mistress to come and go as she pleased, unescorted.

He must feel Jelena needs extra supervision due to her fragile state. No matter; I'm more than a match for a couple of guards.

"Yes...yes, it would be nice to get out. I'm sure poor Willow is going crazy for lack of exercise," Jelena conceded.

"It's settled, then." Sonoe lifted a sweet bun to her lips and took a bite.

"What are your plans for today, Father?" Jelena inquired.

"After breakfast, your uncle, your father-in-law, and I will meet. We must finish the last details of our strategies for the upcoming war. A full council is scheduled in two days, and the plans must be ready by then for presentation and review." Keizo sighed and the benign cast of his face hardened into grimness. "I know it doesn't seem so now, but spring will be upon us before we know it. We must be prepared for what is to come. Our very survival as a free nation depends on how accurately I and my advisors can predict the Soldarans' tactics."

"We have one big advantage over the humans... our magic," Sonoe added.

"Yes, we do," the king replied. He reached over to brush a finger along her cheek. "As a member of the Kirian Society, you will play an important role in the planning and execution of our magical defense. I hate to think of you in danger, my love, but there is a good chance you will find yourself on the front line when this conflict begins."

Sonoe saw genuine love and concern for her in his storm-gray eyes. Her heart skipped a beat and she berated herself for her weakness. She had never intended to allow any soft emotions like affection to cloud her judgment when dealing with the king. But despite her intentions, she found, after so many years living with him, that she had grown extremely fond of Keizo.

Which makes what I ultimately intend to do to him and his daughter all the more difficult, she thought. *But not impossible. Any sacrifice will be worthwhile if it means I gain the power of the Key.*

She noticed that Jelena had pushed aside her plate. "Are you finished already, Jelena? You've hardly eaten a thing," she chided gently.

The girl glanced at her half-eaten breakfast and shrugged. "I'm just not very hungry right now," she said in a small voice.

"Well, a nice ride in the fresh air will do wonders for your appetite," Sonoe replied. "Shall we go?"

After a round of farewell kisses, Sonoe and Jelena left the king to finish his own breakfast in solitude. Two guards waited for them at the stable entrance, as expected. In a very short time, they were mounted up and heading into the town, Jelena astride the gray mare she called Willow, and Sonoe on her favorite bay gelding Susei. One guard rode at the fore to clear the way, the other followed behind his two charges.

The streets bustled with morning traffic. A few of the townsfolk paused to watch as Sonoe and Jelena rode by, but most continued with their business, either uninterested or oblivious. Sonoe often went abroad in the town, so her presence incited little attention, and very few of Sendai's okui population could identify Jelena by sight. To most observers, Keizo's daughter looked like just another hikui woman—a bit more well-to-do than most, but otherwise unremarkable.

They had to keep a tight rein on their mounts as they moved through the busy town, but once the little group had passed through the outer gates, the horses eagerly picked up the pace. Sonoe and Jelena urged their mounts forward, and the guards both fell back to a discreet distance.

The two women rode for a time in companionable silence.

Eventually, Jelena spoke. "Sonoe, I know it's probably none of my business, but why hasn't my father married you? You've been with him for so long, it seems...well, somehow unfair."

"It's simple really, Jelena, love. Your father won't marry me because I'm common-born," Sonoe replied.

"Oh...I...I couldn't tell. You're so...so refined, so noble!"

Sonoe laughed, secretly pleased. "I'm really just a farm girl from Ayame. When I was still quite young, my parents sent me off to work as a servant on the estate of a local mage. My mother recognized that of all her children, I had the most Talent. I think she hoped my master would see my potential and decide to take me on as an apprentice. Lucky for me, he did."

Of course, I helped things along by letting him spread my legs whenever he wanted!

"My first master taught me all he knew, but I soon realized it was only the tip of a vast mountain of knowledge. I needed to get to a place where I could receive more advanced training," Sonoe continued. "Master Bansa recognized that I had surpassed his abilities, so he arranged for me to travel to Sendai where I could enter the mage school run by his order, the Kan Onji, also known as the Red Order."

Sonoe basked for awhile in the glow of nostalgia. Bansa had been quite elderly when she had come to him, but that hadn't stopped her from seducing him. He had taken her virginity with surprising vigor, and had proved to be a skilled and imaginative lover as well as a kind master.

"Master Bansa paid for my first few months at the school, but he was not a wealthy man, and so I had to start working for my lessons."

"As a servant?" Jelena asked.

Sonoe burst out laughing.

"Did I say something funny?" Jelena sounded a little miffed.

"Jelena, my sweet girl. You are just so...so innocent in many ways," Sonoe replied. "I earned my keep flat on my back! Or on top... or on my hands and knees... however it was required of me."

"Oh," Jelena answered in a small voice.

"Don't look so shocked. There's no shame in what I did. I chose my first profession freely, and it allowed me to pursue my true vocation. Now, I'm a well-respected member of the Kan Onji, a Kirian, *and* King's Companion. I've done quite well for myself, and I did it without having the power of a noble family behind me."

"I...I didn't mean to give you any offense, Sonoe," Jelena said. "I was just remembering my own situation back in Amsara. I wasn't given any choice when my uncle arranged to sell me as a concubine to a much older man. I felt desperate, trapped. I couldn't imagine spending my life as a slave, so I ran away."

"And you found love and family. The Goddess has blessed you."

"Yes, I guess She did. Even though Ashinji and I had so short a time together, I'm still grateful. He is...was the love of my life."

"And soon, you'll bear his child...Yet another blessing."

"Does it sadden you that you have no children of your own, Sonoe?"

"Yes, sometimes. But your father has said he wants no children between us, so I take steps to see to it that I don't conceive. Perhaps, now that he has you and your child, he will relent and allow me to have a baby of my own."

They had ridden out beyond the last clusters of houses that made up the suburbs of Sendai and now traveled in open countryside. The road that ran to the town of Meizi, seat of Prince Raidan's fiefdom, stretched ahead of them, lined on either side by ranks of ancient oak trees. A chilly wind played in their gnarled branches, rattling the old wood with a sound like dry bones.

The screech of a raven echoed from high above. Jelena's head jerked upward like a startled deer. She peered at the pale sky, frowning.

It is time!

The cold voice of The Nameless One sounded in Sonoe's head like the faraway whisper of death. She twisted in her saddle to note the position of the two unsuspecting guards bringing up the rear, their bodies relaxed and swaying along with their mounts' strides. She crooked the index finger of her right hand, and her horse tripped and went down on one knee, sending her tumbling from the gelding's back to the roadway. Jelena cried out in alarm and the guards shouted in dismay.

Sonoe groaned as she raised herself on her elbow.

"Sonoe, are you hurt?" Jelena asked breathlessly, kneeling down on the hard dirt of the road.

How did she get off her horse so fast? Sonoe wondered.

"Lady Sonoe!" the two guards cried as they flung themselves from their horses and ran to her.

"I'm not hurt... Just had the wind knocked out of me! Don't fuss!" Sonoe grumbled in a show of irritation and hurt pride. She extended her hand to the nearest guard. "Help me up," she commanded.

"Yes, my lady," the man replied and seized her hand.

Sonoe pounced on the man's unprotected mind and squeezed. He made a little choking noise in his throat and fell forward on top of her, unconscious.

"What th..." the other guard exclaimed, but before the rest of his words could leave his mouth, he, too, collapsed. Jelena screamed in fear.

Sonoe pushed the guards' limp bodies aside and grabbed Jelena's wrists.

"Jelena, hush!" she commanded, and before Jelena could pull away, Sonoe had the girl's head between her hands. She looked deep into Jelena's eyes and plunged through their hazel depths, past the girl's superficial consciousness toward the center of her mind. She saw the Key, glowing like a lamp at the bottom of a well. She encountered no resistance, which surprised her.

What has Taya been teaching her? Why is she not fighting me?

Sonoe slammed against an invisible barrier with enough force to throw her out of Jelena's mind and rock her back on her heels. Intense pain shot through her head and she groaned aloud through gritted teeth. Jelena slumped forward, moaning.

Damn you, Taya!

The barrier had been so skillfully laid that Sonoe had been unable to detect it. Only an adept of equal or greater skill than her own could have constructed such a beautifully made shield.

"S...Sonoe...wha...wha..."

Sonoe touched two fingers to Jelena's temple and felt the girl subside into her arms, head lolling. She eased her to the ground.

The flutter of wings alerted the mage to *his* arrival.

The raven alighted on the roadbed a short distance away and hopped closer until it stood a couple of paces from Jelena's head. It looked sideways at the girl's slack face out of one jet-bead eye. This particular bird still appeared fresh and healthy, so Sonoe knew the Nameless One had just recently taken control of it. It uttered a small croak.

"The Crown Princess has been busy," Sonoe said aloud, disgust roughening her voice. "She has put up a third level shield around the Key. I can't crack it without killing the girl."

Then kill her! She has to die anyway!

"I can't kill her now!" Sonoe retorted. "How would I explain her death? Besides, we don't have another vessel prepared, and without a proper vessel, the magic of the Key will be lost! Is that not what you told me?" Sonoe had to struggle against her mounting fury. In the part of her mind she kept hidden, she savored the knowledge of the weapon she would use against him when the time came.

A gust of sulky energy wafted through her mind like the fetid odor from a latrine pit.

I grow weary of my prison. It has been a thousand years since I last walked the earth as a flesh and blood man. I long to see, to smell and hear, to taste...everything!

"You must be patient, my lord," Sonoe said. She held out her arm and the raven hopped onto it. "I'm already working on a way to bring the girl to you. I found an ancient book in the king's library. It's a lost chronicle of the Kirians. In it, I found references to a translocation portal somewhere within the precincts of Sendai Castle. If I can find it, I might be able to reactivate it. There is a portal within the ruins of the Black Tower. If both can be reactivated, I can bring the girl directly to you."

The portal within the Tower remains energized, though the power has waned over the centuries. The last time it was used was over three hundred years ago, when two of your order came to check on me.

"Taya Onjara is Mistress of the Kirians now."

Though that office should belong to me, Sonoe thought.

"She watches me very closely now, especially since I've gained the girl's trust." Sonoe frowned. "Amara also keeps a close eye on the girl, and both have had a hand in her training. They are preparing her for the Sundering, though neither has told Jelena the full truth of what will happen. They will send her, unwittingly, to her death and console themselves with the righteous knowledge that they have saved the world! Cowards!" Sonoe spat. "If they had any nerve at all, the two of them would seize the power of the Key for themselves!"

And you, of course, would not dare to entertain such a betrayal!

The black stone pendant hidden between her breasts exploded with a sudden burst of heat, searing Sonoe's skin and wringing a startled cry of pain from her lips.

"No, Master, no!" she gasped, clutching the stone. "Please, you are burning me!" The stone grew cold again and Sonoe sighed in relief and irritation.

One of the guards stirred. The raven spread its wings and clacked its beak.

"You must go now, so that I can revive them all before too much time has passed and they notice something's amiss," Sonoe said.

Without warning, the raven lunged at her face and sliced her cheek open with its razor-sharp beak.

Sonoe screamed and flung the bird from her. Cursing, she pressed a hand to the bleeding wound. "Why did you do that?" she cried.

So that when you gaze upon the scar that mars the beauty of your face, you will be reminded of who owns you.

The raven launched itself into the air. It turned on a wingtip and sped off in the direction of Sendai, leaving Sonoe sobbing with rage.

When she had at last mastered herself, she reached over and tapped each of the guards on their temples. They groaned as they regained consciousness. Sonoe lay down on the ground and brushed Jelena's forehead. As the girl's eyes fluttered open, the mage slipped into her mind and sponged away all traces of her intrusion.

The two guards climbed to their feet, looking bewildered.

"My lady!" they cried in unison.

"Are you hurt?" the older of the two asked, bending over Sonoe, his face a mask of concern. He seemed to have no idea that he had been unconscious.

"I'm just bruised," Sonoe snapped.

"My lady, your face is bleeding!" the other guard exclaimed.

Jelena sat up and looked around, clearly puzzled.

"How did I end up on the ground?" she asked to no one in particular. Her gaze alighted on Sonoe and she yelped in alarm. "Sonoe, are you all right? Your horse fell!"

"Yes, yes, I'm fine. Just a little cut on my cheek is all. I must have fallen on a rock. Help me up," she commanded, holding her hands out to the guards. "It's not like Susei to be clumsy." She walked over to where the bay stood, tail swishing.

"He's got a scraped knee," the younger guard commented. "Must have stepped in a pothole or something." He began scanning the roadbed as the other guard helped Jelena to her feet.

"You should let me wash that cut for you," Jelena said, coming up behind Sonoe.

Sonoe turned to face Jelena and forced a smile. "Thank you, pet," she said. She stood still while Jelena ministered to her, all the while seething with anger.

You'll be the slave, and I shall be your mistress! You think you rule me now, but what you don't know is that I possess the tool which will give me complete power over you! All I have to do is speak the word when the time is right!

She had stumbled across it quite by accident. While digging through a chest of old scrolls she had found in the dustiest, dimmest corner of the library storeroom, her hand had encountered a tiny book.

Its leather binding was crumbling with age and the ink upon the parchment pages had faded almost to illegibility, but she'd instantly recognized the hand of Master Iku Azarasha himself. How the book had survived so long, she couldn't fathom. She had taken the book, realizing she'd discovered a treasure of immense value.

She had worked in secret for many days, and after much effort, she managed to raise the faded ink enough to read the contents of the book. What she read astounded her.

The little book turned out to be a personal account of the last battle between the sorcerer king Onjara and his daughter and successor, Queen Syukoe. It also described the Ritual of Sundering that broke the king's power and sent him down to defeat and undeath. Master Iku had meticulously recorded everything about those events, including the names of everyone who had taken part.

Sonoe had unwittingly found the only weapon she would need to subjugate the ancient spirit.

His true name.

25
Ashinji's Choice

Mistress de Guera! Always a pleasure to see you!"
Marcus placed his clasped hands to his heart and bowed his head in greeting as a woman and three men approached.

"Marcus. I got your message, and I was intrigued. Where is this extraordinary merchandise you wish to show me?"

"He is right over there, Mistress, sitting against that post.... Ashinji! On your feet, now!"

Upon hearing his name, Ashinji looked to where Marcus and the woman stood waiting, but couldn't bring himself to move. The trauma of his situation had momentarily paralyzed him.

"You heard the boss!" snarled Lacus. He aimed a kick at Ashinji's ribs, but a sharp word from Marcus halted his foot in mid-swing. Slowly, Ashinji climbed to his feet. He moved to stand before Marcus and the woman, pushing tendrils of wet hair out of his face with his shackled hands.

The woman gasped and her eyes widened. "Is this...is he...?"

Marcus bobbed his head. "Yes! He is, indeed, Mistress."

"But...however did you get him?"

"I bought him in Amsara from the duke's daughter. She's leading a small campaign against the local elven warlord. This one was captured in battle by some of her soldiers."

"He's beautiful," she breathed.

Ashinji studied the woman closely while she and Marcus discussed him as they would a stallion or bull. She still possessed much of her youthful vigor, even though the lines at the corners of her dark eyes betrayed her maturity. Her lustrous black hair framed her face in a complicated coiffure; her fine clothes and jewelry spoke of her wealth and position. The three men—two flanking her and one at her back—wore plain but well-made clothing. Ashinji guessed they were high-ranking servants in the lady's household.

"He says he's noble born, the son of one of their lords," Marcus continued. "He speaks excellent Soldaran."

The lady looked impressed. "Is this true? Do you speak our language?" she addressed Ashinji, then cocked her head to one side and provided the answer to her own question. "Yes, you do. I can see it in your eyes. What is your name?"

"Ashinji Sakehera...Mistress," Ashinji replied softly.

"Ashinji," the lady said, rolling his name on her tongue as if savoring a sweetmeat. "The sound of it is so...so like you," she added. "Exotic and sensual." Her dark eyes smoldered.

"He's young, fit, and a trained warrior, Mistress. He will do well for you, however you choose to use him," Marcus said. "Do you want to see him stripped?" The lady nodded in affirmation.

Ashinji's gut churned. Wild thoughts of escape flashed through his head, but in his heart, he knew them to be futile. He remembered the human girl, bound and naked on the auction block. Asa the blond bear came forward, hands grasping, but Ashinji fended him off.

"I'll do it myself," he growled and awkwardly wriggled out of his tunic. He raised his chin in defiance as Mistress de Guera's eyes took in his naked body from head to toe. Her gaze lingered for several heartbeats below his waist then swept up to pause at his left shoulder.

She raised a perfectly manicured finger and pointed. "Is that a new scar I see there on his shoulder?" she inquired.

"Uh, yes, Mistress, it is," Marcus answered. "He was shot during his capture. I first saw him right after the camp surgeon had cut the arrow out of him. He was in bad shape, but I gladly took on the task of nursing him back to health." Marcus smiled broadly. "As you can see, the wound healed beautifully, and he's fully recovered."

"So it seems." Mistress de Guera's tongue darted over her lips. "You may cover yourself...Ashinji." Ashinji felt a wave of relief as he pulled the rough tunic back down over his body. He had experienced humiliation in the past at the hands of his brother, but Sadaiyo's worst could not compare to what he had just endured. He struggled to hold his head up, though his cheeks burned with shame and fury.

"As I've said, Ashinji, here, is a trained fighter. He'd be an excellent draw as a gladiator," Marcus pointed out.

"Yes, he would. The people are always hungry for the exotic, the novel. Aruk-cho is still one of my biggest money-makers. The crowds turn out in droves to see him whenever he appears. A pureblooded elf is something no one has yet seen in the Grand Arena." Mistress de Guera stepped forward, and before Ashinji could dodge or pull away, she seized his head between her hands and stared straight into his eyes. He froze.

"Perhaps I have another use in mind for him," she murmured. A little piece of Ashinji's mind, detached from all the horror, noted that he and the lady stood at the same height. A fragment of memory flashed across his mind's eye— one of the many moments when he had been this close to Jelena, preparing to savor the taste and feel of her warm, soft mouth. Unbidden tears welled in his eyes.

Mistress de Guera held him thus for what seemed like an eternity. The scent of roses swirled around them.

"There is such sadness in you, Ashinji," she said.

"Do you wonder why, Mistress?" he replied in a ragged voice.

She shook her head. "No, of course not." She trailed a finger across his lips and stepped back. "Name your price, Marcus."

"I couldn't part with him for less than two hundred imperials, Mistress," Marcus replied, rubbing his palms together.

"I want him, Marcus, but I won't be robbed. I'll give you one hundred."

Marcus threw up his hands. "Mistress de Guera, for you and only you would I sell him at a discount, but I have to recoup the extra expense it took to get him here. I had to pay for the medicine and the special food that restored his health out of my own pocket, you know. Give me one-fifty and I'll make some profit, at least."

The lady rolled her eyes. "Your sad story doesn't interest me, Marcus. One twenty five."

"One-forty, Mistress. Please, have some compassion! You must admit he's worth every copper."

"One-thirty, and not a sol more."

"We have a deal, my lady," Marcus purred. He grinned and held out his hand. Mistress de Guera huffed and shook her head, but she took Marcus' hand and shook it. A tiny smile flickered over her lips as she glanced toward Ashinji.

So, it's done, Ashinji thought. *At least I've been spared the humiliation of a public auction.* He watched as one of Mistress de Guera's servants stepped forward and removed a leather pouch from his belt. He handed the pouch to his mistress, who opened it and carefully counted out the agreed upon price and dropped the coins into Marcus' waiting palm.

"I'll need proof of ownership," the mistress said. Marcus rummaged around in his belt pouch and produced a folded piece of paper.

"I trust, since this was a private sale, we can, ah, avoid full disclosure to the market clerks?" He held out the paper. "I'd prefer to pay as little tax as possible."

"Of course," the lady agreed, unfolding the paper and perusing the contents. "Well, this all seems to be in order." She refolded the paper and tucked it into the wide belt at her waist.

"It is always a pleasure doing business with you, Mistress de Guera," Marcus said with a grin. He turned to face Ashinji. "I know you can't appreciate this, but I did you a big favor by selling you to this lady. I could've sold you to one of the brothels or to a torture house. At least now, you'll have a chance to win your freedom. Good luck to you, Ashinji. I mean that. Hold out your hands."

Ashinji obeyed, because he could do nothing else. Marcus removed the shackles from his wrists, but another of the mistress's servants stepped up and snapped a fresh pair on almost before Marcus had taken his off. He then attached a stout chain lead and deferentially placed the handle into the hand of his mistress.

Mistress de Guera gave the chain a gentle tug. "Come along, Ashinji," she ordered and turned to walk toward the front gates of the main market. The three servants closed up around Ashinji, both to shield him from curious eyes and to block any possibility of escape.

A sedan chair awaited just outside the gates, a quartet of burly slaves crouched beside it, sweating in the midmorning sun. Mistress de Guera mounted, assisted by one of her servants, and the slaves hoisted the chair to their shoulders. Another servant secured the leash attached to Ashinji's manacles to the back of the chair, then unfurled a large parasol and held it over his mistress's head. The procession started off. Ashinji looked back once over his shoulder to see Marcus and his two assistants standing beside the gates, watching.

To his astonishment, Marcus waved. Ashinji turned away in confusion.

Waves of heat rose from the dusty road. Ashinji's damp hair dried quickly and now hung down his back in a tangle. He longed for a comb and some almond oil.

Strange how such little things seem so important now, he thought.

Mistress de Guera remained silent and aloof in her chair. The slaves set a steady pace toward the stone bulk of the Grand Arena. The servants walked in silence as well, ignoring Ashinji. He felt like a ghost, floating along in their midst.

They approached the Arena from the rear, entering a vast complex of annexes that sprawled out from the main structure like the wings of a great bird. The bearers turned down a wide alley between rows of high brick walls broken at regular intervals by tall, wooden gates. They halted outside one set of gates which resembled all the others, except for a brass plaque attached to one post. Ashinji could not read the words engraved upon them—they were too small for him to see from where he stood—but he guessed that they identified this particular place.

Two of the servants scurried forward to push open the gates and the slaves bore Mistress de Guera through. Ashinji had no choice but to follow.

He found himself walking across a small, grass covered quadrangle toward a set of inner gates. One of the servants shouted and the gates swung open to reveal a much larger, sand-floored enclosure.

The yard lay empty under the glare of the sun. Wooden posts sunk into the ground at regular intervals stood around the perimeter. An awning of canvas ran the length of one side. Beneath the awning, Ashinji could see the deeper darkness of open doorways. At the far end of the yard, opposite the gates, stood a two-story building, surrounded by a brick wall of its own. A small arched gateway pierced the wall, blocked by what looked like an iron grille. The chair bearers made for the house and set their mistress down before the gate.

Mistress de Guera spoke for the first time since leaving the slave market.

"Send Aruk-cho to me in a quarter turn," she ordered. She climbed out of the chair, straightening her skirts as she alighted.

"Yes, Mistress," the youngest of the servants answered, then turned on his heel and sped away.

"Bring him," Mistress de Guera said, indicating Ashinji with a flick of her wrist. The older of the remaining servants untied Ashinji's leash from the chair and pulled him along in the mistress's wake. They passed through the iron gate— which had been cleverly fashioned into the semblance of a climbing rosebush— then across a small, fragrant garden humming with bees and through an arched doorway into the cool interior of the house.

It took a moment for Ashinji's eyes to adjust to the dimmer light inside the dwelling, but when he could finally discern his surroundings, he saw a large open room full of low, wooden furniture, ornate carpets underfoot, and gauzy hangings softening the walls. The far end of the room opened onto a courtyard.

Mistress de Guera settled gracefully onto a padded bench. "Leave us," she commanded, and the two manservants promptly withdrew, though Ashinji had no doubt they would remain within earshot should their mistress require them. "You may sit, if you wish." She indicated the carpeted floor. Ashinji considered what it would mean if he sat at this woman's feet, decided it was pointless to worry about such things any longer, and sat.

"Tell me about yourself," she said.

"I am the second child of Sen and Amara, Lord and Lady of Kerala. My father is the Commanding General of the King's Army of Alasiri. I have a wife, who I love more than my own life, and a child on the way who I may never see." His voice broke, and he had to pause, lest he cry out in anguish. Mistress de Guera sat in silence, waiting, as he mastered himself enough to continue.

"I have an older brother and three younger sisters. My wife's father is Keizo Onjara, King of Alasiri...I am not sure what else you wish to know."

"When Marcus said you claimed to be a nobleman, he didn't say you were a prince." Mistress de Guera leaned forward and Ashinji caught the scent of roses.

"I am not a prince," he corrected her. "I am married to the king's daughter."

"How did you learn to speak Soldaran so well?"

"Languages come easily to me. I know Sharan and a little bit of Qoum, as well."

Mistress de Guera sighed and leaned back. "I hear the pain in your voice, Ashinji. You miss your home, your family... your wife. You fear you will never see any of them again, and truthfully, you probably won't. Still, there is a chance for you to survive and to make a place for yourself here.

I'm going to give you a choice, the last one of any consequence you'll get as a slave. You can go to my stable and earn your keep and possibly your freedom as a gladiator. You'll be treated just like all the rest of my fighting slaves. Or... you can live in this house, with me, as my personal slave."

Ashinji studied Mistress de Guera's face but her visage remained smooth, almost expressionless. Tentatively, he reached out with his mind to brush the surface of her consciousness and encountered only calm anticipation.

"If you choose to live in my house, you'll be allowed to come and go as you please," the mistress continued. "I'll dress you in clothes befitting your position, and you'll dine at my table. You'll share my bed as well." She arose, cat-like, from the bench and stood over Ashinji. Gently, she began to caress the top of his head, running her fingers through his tangled hair.

"I can make your life here very easy, beautiful one," she whispered.

"Jelena, my wife, is my soul-mate, Mistress," Ashinji answered. "I could never bring myself to betray her, not even to save myself pain and hardship... I must choose to be a fighter."

Mistress De Guera continued to stroke Ashinji's hair for few more heartbeats. "Very well," she sighed, then stepped back and regarded him with disappointment. "I can't say I'm surprised, though I did hope... I can keep you in my house by force, but I won't. I'd rather you come to me willingly. Corvin!" she called out. The senior manservant appeared. "Is Aruk-cho here yet?" she asked.

"He's waiting outside the gate, Mistress," Corvin answered.

"Give Ashinji here over to him."

"Yes, Mistress." Corvin stepped forward and grabbed the back of Ashinji's tunic. He gave it a sharp tug. "On your feet, slave," he ordered.

Fighting a surge of anger, Ashinji complied.

"Ashinji, look at me," Mistress de Guera commanded and he raised his eyes to meet hers. "My offer remains open. Should you change your mind, just get word to me." She waved her hand and Corvin gave his back a firm shove, propelling him toward the entrance to the house.

Ashinji exited, blinking, into the heat and heavy fragrance of the garden. A bee darted past his ear and he swung reflexively, hitting himself in the face with the chain that bound his wrists together. Cursing, he rubbed his jaw.

Corvin guffawed. "I hope you swing a sword better than you do a chain, tink!"

"I would not come within striking distance of me when next I hold a weapon, if I were you, human," Ashinji responded in a low voice. Corvin sniffed, but held his tongue.

They approached the gate and Corvin stepped in front of Ashinji to push it open. "Aruk-cho!" he called out. "The Mistress has got fresh meat for you!"

Ashinji stepped through the gate onto the hot sand of the yard. Something large and dark stood beyond.

Ashinji gaped in astonishment.

An *akuta*!

26

A Gladiator's Life

Ashinji had first learned about the race of horse people from an old book in his father's library, but until now, he believed they had died out many years ago. In the ancient past, the akuta had been staunch allies of the elves.

Built like a man from his torso upward, with powerfully muscled arms and broad shoulders, the akuta stood at least a head taller than Ashinji. Just below his waist, where the hips and legs of an elven man would have been, the four-legged body of a horse began. His hide glistened like black satin in the sun. A thick mane of black hair sprouted from his head and cascaded over his shoulders to brush his withers.

A heavy leather harness crisscrossed his upper body and attached to a thick, metal-studded belt encircling his man's waist. Leather guards covered both forearms. An enormous, curved sword hung at his side.

The akuta's fathomless black eyes narrowed as he caught sight of Ashinji.

"My heart grieves to see you here, friend," he rumbled in a voice like distant thunder.

"I had no idea any of the akuta still lived," Ashinji replied. "Are there many more of you?" He stared in awe at the creature, remembering his dream of several weeks ago.

"We are far fewer in number these days, but we hold our own, much like our old friends the elves do. I am Aruk-cho of the Wakani Clan."

"I am Ashinji Sakehera."

"I will see to Ashinji now, Corvin. You may go." Corvin's chin shot up and a look of offense twisted his plain features. Without a word, he turned on his heel and stamped back through the gate, disappearing into the garden.

Aruk-cho produced a set of keys from a pouch on his belt and unlocked the manacles on Ashinji's wrists. Sighing with relief, Ashinji massaged where the metal had chafed his skin.

"Follow me," the akuta directed as he headed off across the yard toward a long, low building, the manacles swinging from his hand.

"How did you end up here, Aruk-cho?" Ashinji inquired. He had to scramble to keep up with the akuta's long, rolling stride.

"I was a slave like you, once. I made the mistake of going up against the chieftain of my tribe. I lost, and so found myself in bondage, sold to the Soldarans. That was many years ago."

"Are you a gladiator?"

"I was, but I earned my freedom. Now, I run this yard for Mistress de Guera, and, occasionally, I fight for prize money. Everything will be explained to you soon." He paused in front of an open doorway. "Here is where you will sleep." The akuta had to duck in order to pass through the door. Ashinji followed and found himself in a long barracks. A scarred wooden table filled the center of the space, and an empty fireplace gaped like an open mouth in the wall opposite the door. Shelves lined the walls at the back, each just long and deep enough to hold one body. The sound of snoring filled the hot, still air.

Aruk-cho stamped one massive hoof upon the hard-packed clay floor.

"Up...Up with you!" he bellowed. "Rest time's over!" He turned to Ashinji. "Everyone in this room is new, like you. Most were brought over from the market just yesterday." The sleepers began to stir from their shelves, muttering and sniffling. "All of you, out in the yard, now," Aruk-cho ordered, pointing through the open barracks door. "The mistress will be along shortly to address you."

Ashinji followed Aruk-cho back out into the shimmering heat of the yard, then stood and watched as his fellow neophyte slaves emerged from the barracks. He counted ten others, all young and apparently fit. Six of them Ashinji recognized as native Soldarans by their skin color and facial features. He knew the rest were human, but of types he had never before seen.

Two of the men had skins the color of a bay horse, with broad, flat noses and hair that hung in long ropes to their waists. Another had skin the color of honey, with narrow, dark eyes and jet-black hair gathered in a topknot at the crown of his head. Ashinji found the last man the most curious of all, for as far as he could tell, this human had no body hair—he even lacked eyebrows—and his pale skin had been seared red by the relentless southern sun. By the way he squinted and hunched his shoulders, Ashinji could tell the direct sunlight pained him much more than it did the others.

Aruk-cho had gone into the barracks directly across the yard and had re-emerged leading a straggling procession of female slaves. He ordered them to form up into rows behind the men. All six of them were Soldarans.

"Hey, you!" a voice hissed to Ashinji's right. He swiveled his head to see one of the Soldaran males, a boy just coming into manhood, sidle up to stand beside him. "Can you understand me?" the boy asked.

"I can. What is it you want?"

"You're an elf," the boy stated.

Ashinji sighed. "Yes," he answered.

"My ma was half-elf! See? I got pointy ears." The boy pushed his ruddy brown hair away from the side of his head to display bluntly tapered ears. He grinned. "My ma named me Seijon, after her pa. What's your name?"

"Ashinji Sakehera. Seijon is a very old elven name. It belonged to one of our greatest kings, many thousands of years ago." Ashinji could see the boy's elven blood in the cast of his features, though he could pass for a full-blooded human if he hid his ears.

"I never thought I'd get to meet another one of my grandpa's people," Seijon said.

Another? Ashinji thought.

"I never knew my pa," the boy continued. "He took off before I was born. It was always just my ma an' me." The boy's voice contained no trace of bitterness.

"Be silent!" Aruk-cho ordered. "The mistress approaches." Seijon stifled a giggle and made an exaggerated show of shutting up. Mistress de Guera strode toward them, trailed closely by Corvin. She halted beside Aruk-cho, who bowed his head in respect.

"The new slaves are all assembled, Mistress," he rumbled.

Though Ashinji stood in the front row, Mistress de Guera ignored him. She cleared her throat and began to speak. "My name is Armina Marcela Luiza de Guera. As of this day forward, I control your lives completely. I decide when you eat, when you sleep, when you fight, when you rest. In short, I own each and every one of your bodies, and later this afternoon, you'll all receive my mark of ownership upon your shoulders. I'm not so foolish or naïve as to believe I own your souls. That is the one thing you still can call your own."

Mistress de Guera paused to sweep her penetrating gaze over her new property. "I was born on a farm in Thalacia," she continued. "At the tender age of twelve, my father sold me to a Thalacian horse trader. Too many mouths to feed, and as I was only a girl, all my real value was located between my legs. So off I went. The trader kept me awhile, and after he knocked two kids out of me, he sold me to a Soldaran agent looking for young, healthy females for the arena. I was big and strong for my age, a good candidate for gladiator training.

"Eventually, I ended up here, in Darguinia, a slave like all of you, put up for sale at the central market. I had the good fortune to be purchased by Antonius Sisco himself...yes, I see some of you know of him."

Several of the Soldarans nodded.

"Sisco was a legend! The greatest trainer of all time," Seijon whispered to Ashinji.

"Sisco trained me personally," Mistress de Guera continued. "He made of me a finely crafted fighting machine. I was magnificent. None had seen my like before, nor have since." She spoke matter-of-factly, without a hint of arrogance, almost as if she praised another person.

"I reigned as Female Champion for three years. During that time, I never lost a match, and by virtue of my skill, I earned my freedom. The day I retired from the arena, I became Sisco's wife and partner. We were married for twenty five years and I gave Sisco five sons and three daughters. This yard you find yourselves in is the business we built together."

She paused, and bowed her head for a moment, then raised it. "I lost my dear husband two years ago. The yard is mine now and mine alone, though one day, all that Sisco and I have built will be our legacy for our children."

"I tell you all this because I wish to inspire you," Mistress de Guera said. "If you are talented and very, very lucky, you can survive your time here and earn enough money to buy your freedom. It is possible. I did it. I began with nothing, and now, I'm one of this city's most respected citizens."

"And so I will make this pledge to you all. Put everything you have into this, fight bravely, obey me and my trainers without question...do all of this for me, and when you die, you will be treated with honor. But, if you live...after two years, I will free you, and gift you with a handsome sum for start-up money. You'll be able to go home if that's what you wish, or stay and make a go of it here."

She slowly scanned the ranks of expressionless faces before her. "Aruk-cho will explain the rules of the yard now." She nodded toward the akuta.

"Everyone gets up at daybreak, except on off days, when you can sleep in if you wish," Aruk-cho began. "Practice starts after breakfast and will run until midmorning, when you get a half-turn break, then resumes until midday. You eat, then you get free time for three turns. You can rest, if you wish, or occupy yourself with personal tasks. Practice matches begin at three turns past midday and go until sunset, then you're finished for the day.

"All slaves are on five days, off two. If you live long enough to earn your freedom and you choose to stay on as a prizefighter, you fight as many days as you wish. The Grand Arena runs six days a week. We are but one yard among twenty, but we are also one of the top five; therefore, our contract gives us a lot of days in which we must fill the seats.

"Four days out of six, our yard runs points matches. These are non-lethal, and the fighters earn points for style and skill. They are usually timed, or sometimes go to first blood. Those slaves who are less skilled will fight these matches exclusively, until I decide when he or she is ready to advance. You advance by improving your skills. The better you get, the more points you earn. Points get you rewards. At first, it will be extra privileges, and later on, it will be money.

"The other two days, we run lethal matches. These matches are always between yards, and they end only when all fighters on the opposing side are either dead or so badly wounded, they can no longer fight. Only those slaves who are the most skilled will be put into these matches. If you mortally wound an opponent, or if you, yourself are mortally wounded, the kill is required to be swift and clean. Unnecessary cruelty will be punished by loss of points and esteem. The people come to the arena to see feats of skill and bravery, not butchery.

"You will only be required to fight one lethal match per month until I can see that you stand a decent chance of survival, then you'll fight one every ten days."

He paused to make sure he had each slave's full attention, then continued. "There are special matches put on for Festivals. Whether or not you fight in these depends on your skill and seniority. These matches always carry very large purses and you can earn a lot of money and points, but they are almost always filled up with prizefighters. Only a few slots are generally available for slaves. Always, these matches are lethal.

"Finally, there is the Great Festival of Cheos, Lord Of Heaven. This is the biggest festival on the calendar and it lasts an entire week. The Grand Champions are decided during this series of matches. All fighters, both slave and free, who have accumulated enough points are eligible to participate. The matches run as eliminations, with the winners advancing to the next rounds. The finals are held on the last day. The winners, one man and one woman, will each be named Grand Champion. If he or she is a slave, freedom is the reward, along with a handsome purse."

Aruk-cho paused again and pushed at the sand with a forefoot. He looked to Mistress de Guera, who just nodded. He continued. "So, that is how things are. Not as bad as you imagined, I'm sure. As slaves go, you are the lucky ones. You will get far better treatment here in the de Guera yard as gladiators than almost anywhere else, including the brothels. It is in the mistress's best interests to keep her stable well fed and fit. Only healthy, skilled fighters make her money. Not all yard owners are as wise as our mistress. Do your best for me and for her and you can count on both of us to do our best for all of you. *Dismissed!*"

Ashinji turned to follow the others back to the barracks.

"Wait, Ashinji!" he heard Aruk-cho call out behind him.

"I'll go and grab you a bunk next to mine," Seijon offered. The boy's whole body quivered with excitement, reminding Ashinji of Jena and Mariso. He sighed and nodded in assent. Seijon's face broke into an ecstatic grin and he dashed off toward the barracks.

"The boy has attached himself to you, I see," Aruk-cho commented.

"So it would seem," Ashinji replied dryly. "Do the Soldarans often sacrifice their children to their blood sports?"

"Seijon will not be participating in any lethal matches. The mistress purchased him as a house slave some months ago, but he kept pestering her to let him learn to fight. Just yesterday, she gave in and sent him to me."

"What is it you want of me, Aruk-cho?"

"There is someone here that you should meet. Come with me."

Intrigued, Ashinji followed the akuta to the far end of the yard where another barracks stood.

"This is where the veteran females bunk," Aruk-cho explained. He paused before the curtained entrance. "Gran!" he called out. "Gran...There is someone here to see you!" The curtain twitched aside and an old woman poked her head out, squinting in the sunlight.

27
The Key To The Conspiracy

Silence and the musty smell of places long shut away from the sun surrounded Prince Raidan. As he strode along, the lantern in the prince's hand cast crazy shadows on the frost-rimed stone walls; his breath rose in thin puffs of steam from his lips and nostrils.

The prince had chosen the location for his secret conferences with care. This part of Sendai Castle had been closed up and abandoned years ago during his father's childhood. As a boy, Raidan had stumbled upon a hidden doorway into the block of rooms by accident, during an expedition of discovery. He had revealed his secret to no one, not even his brothers.

Raidan reached the end of the corridor and paused at what appeared to be a blank wall. Raising the lantern to eye level, he located and twisted aside a round metal disk covering a spy hole. He placed one eye to the hole and looked into an adjacent corridor. A group of people stood in a nervous clutch opposite Raidan's position.

Good. They're all here, he thought.

He fitted his fingers into a set of depressions in the stone and triggered the releasing mechanism, then pulled the hidden door open. He stepped through and motioned for the others to enter. Silently, they obeyed, and followed the prince as he led them to their meeting room.

Raidan had already prepared the room beforehand. Several lanterns dangled from wall hooks, their flames flickering in the drafts from the ventilation shafts set high in the walls; braziers burned in each corner, providing some small respite from the biting cold.

After everyone had taken their seats, Raidan sat for several moments, silently studying the faces of his supporters. He thought about the underlying motives that had driven each of them to endanger all they had to stand behind him and against their king.

Morio of Ayame and Coronji of Tohru, brothers-in-law and unrepentant racists, would both rather see Alasiri plunged into civil war than accept a hikui as their queen. Saizura of Kinat, the oldest of Alasiri's great lords, worried more about propriety than purity. She objected to Keizo's daughter because the girl had been born outside of a legal marriage.

Seitan of Ograi owes his position to me, thought Raidan. He had convinced the king to name Seitan as Lord over an older sister who had proved herself unfit to run the fiefdom after the death of their mother. *Seitan will support me unquestioningly.*

Odata of Tono worried most about the reaction of the hikui populace to the naming of a hikui Heir. She feared the impetus it would give to the hikui movement for social equality.

Ebo of Suiren had agreed to back Raidan for one reason only. Recently widowed and without an Heir, her price for her support had been simple—a child sired by an Onjara. Raidan had accepted, and his middle son, Kaisik, would perform the service upon his next birthday, when he would officially come of age. The boy was handsome, cheerful, and above all, obedient—a stark contrast to his brooding older brother, Raidu. Ebo would, no doubt, find him more than acceptable.

"Let me begin by thanking you all once more for your support," Raidan said. "I pray each day that there will be no need to call upon it. I, more than anyone else in this room, wish to avoid open confrontation with my brother, especially during this time of extreme danger to our nation. Civil conflict right now would only aid our enemies and hasten the demise of the elves as a free people."

"Yet, you clearly are willing to take the risk, if necessary. Why else bring us all here?" Morio responded with a voice roughened by years of pipe smoking.

"None of us wants war among ourselves, but neither do we wish to see one of impure blood ascend the throne of Alasiri. There must be a better solution," Ebo added.

"She's a bastard, plain and simple! How could Keizo have elevated her to such a high station?" Saizura fretted. "He should have just dealt with the girl quietly, provided her with a settlement and sent her packing back to Kerala." The elderly Lady of Kinat sliced the air scornfully with her bird's claw of a hand.

"My brother, so far, has given no indication that he intends to name my niece Heir over me. However, she and Keizo have become very close, and before she lost her husband, she was demonstrating a keen interest in statecraft. Even I have to admit she showed great promise. Now, she is too wrapped up in her grief to do much more than get through each day. And, of course, there is her child to consider."

"Perhaps...an accident could be arranged," Coronji suggested. "It would certainly take care of things. I volunteer to do the job." His lips curled in a tiny smile, and Raidan thought of a snake anticipating the feast of a mouse.

The prince's eyes flashed. "Whatever else she is, she is an Onjara and not some common by-blow that can be disposed of in a back alley!" His anger, he knew, arose from the fact that Coronji had dared speak openly of the very thing the prince himself had already considered.

"I apologize if I have given any offense, Highness," Coronji said, but his tone indicated he believed Raidan's outrage to be little more than pretense.

"Tell us your plan, Highness. Just what do you intend to do if the king should decide to elevate his bastard over you?" Odata queried.

"My plan is simple," Raidan replied. "If Keizo decides to name Jelena his Heir, he will tell me first. He owes me that courtesy. I will then inform him, without naming any of you, that I have the support of over half the council, standing in opposition to his decision. I will also point out that the elven people won't accept a hikui as queen, no matter that she is the daughter of their beloved Silverlock.

"My brother has ruled Alasiri wisely and well. He always takes into consideration the will of the people when making any decision that affects them, and this decision would have a profound effect. I believe he will understand this, and reconsider."

"And if he doesn't?" Odata pressed. "You said yourself that Silverlock and the girl have forged a very deep bond. Is there a possibility that he may not listen to reason?"

"Yes, there is," Raidan answered slowly, "and if he won't, then I'll threaten him. Faced with the defection of half his lords and their levies, he'll have to see the folly of his course. The loss of so many troops will be devastating to the army. The Soldarans already outnumber us. Sen Sakehera is an excellent commander, but even he couldn't mount a defense with so few bodies. Keizo will realize he is risking the defeat and conquest of all of Alasiri. He won't allow that."

"You seem so sure, Highness." Seitan, who until now had remained silent, finally spoke up. "You know the mind of the king far better than any of us, but are you *certain?*"

Raidan scanned the tense faces around him. He could feel the emotions of each blowing back at him like the dry wind off a wildfire: fear, anger, resignation.

Am I sure of my brother? he thought.

No, not entirely, but I am sure of myself.

If Keizo will not listen, there's only one thing I can do to save Alasiri. It's extreme, but desperate times call for extreme measures. I'll kill Jelena with my own hand, if necessary, then step aside, and the Kirians' plans be damned. Raidu will become Keizo's Heir.

"Yes, I'm sure," he said.

* * *

Raidan made his way back to his apartments through the late night stillness of the castle. The prince had always thought of Sendai Castle as something more than an inanimate structure; it felt like a living organism, with stone flesh and wooden bones. All of the myriad souls who made their homes within its walls were like the impossibly tiny disks he observed floating in his own blood when he examined it with his lenses. He didn't know the exact function of the mysterious disks, but he knew they must somehow keep his body alive, just as all the maids, cooks, gardeners, grooms, and countless other workers kept the castle 'alive'.

He paused outside the entrance to listen and thought he could hear the great fortress slowly, slowly, exhaling.

"What, still awake, Wife?" Raidan said as he entered the day room and saw Taya sitting on the couch, a thick book in her hands. She laid the frayed volume down on her lap and silently watched as he crossed the room to settle at her side. "You look troubled," he murmured, then brushed her lips with his. She sighed. "What is it?" he asked.

"You've come from a meeting with your supporters."

"Yes," he replied.

She frowned, angry now. "Husband, you are playing a dangerous game! If Keizo discovers you've been plotting against him..."

Raidan held up his hand to silence her. "I am not plotting against my brother. I'm putting into place a plan that just might avert a civil war."

"Your plan calls for killing Keizo's daughter. That, Husband, you cannot do. It would mean utter disaster!" Taya's green eyes blazed with warning.

Raidan felt his temper give way. "Damn it, Taya!" he growled. "What would you have me do? Stand by passively while my brother disinherits me and our son? No, let me speak!" he demanded as Taya opened her mouth to respond. "You know I trust you completely, but the time has come when blind trust is not enough. I must have a sound reason for staying my hand. Jelena harbors important magic, and the Kirians need her for a vital ritual, one that will safeguard our world as we know it...This much you've told me, but I *know* there's more to it!" He met Taya's hard-eyed stare with one of his own. "If you want my cooperation, Wife, then tell me the entire truth now."

Taya rested a hand on the book in her lap. She stared down at its faded brown leather cover for several moments before she spoke. "I will tell you everything now, because you have a right to know, but from this day forward, you are sworn to our cause."

Raidan took a deep breath to both calm and prepare himself. He waited expectantly for Taya to begin.

"This book," she tapped the cover for emphasis, "used to belong to a former head of our Society, someone who was once very powerful but is now departed. It is one of the oldest volumes of the chronicles of the Kirian Society that we have. It helped me put together the pieces of the puzzle, so I now know who, or I should say *what*, Jelena is."

Raidan frowned. "I don't understand. Jelena is my niece..."

"Yes, this is true...Your niece, Keizo's daughter. But she is also something more," Taya continued. "The girl we know as Jelena Onjara is a flesh and blood vessel—a container, if you will—for something very old and extremely powerful. This I've told you already."

Raidan nodded. "The Key."

"Yes," Taya replied. "Jelena's life force is intermingled with the energy of the Key, which is why she must die in order for us to remove it." She paused for a moment, eyes pensive, before continuing. "Iku Azarasha, Master of the Kirian Society over a millennium ago, was a mage of extraordinary Talent. He was the greatest Kirian of his age...perhaps of any age. It was he who first constructed the energy pattern that allowed the Kirians to master teleportation." Taya shook her head in frustration and regret. "Sadly, the knowledge of how to construct new portals has been lost to our generation, though we still know how to use the existing ones. There are two right here in Sendai Castle."

"Wait." Raidan interrupted. "You said Master Iku and the Kirians hid this Key inside Jelena, but how...how could a group of mages who lived a thousand years ago put a spell into a girl who is a mere eighteen years of age?"

"Patience, Husband. I'll explain that part later," Taya replied.

She lifted the frayed cover of the book and thumbed through the yellowed pages with great care, pausing at a spot about midway through. "This section chronicles the only time Alasiri was ever torn by civil war," she explained.

"I'm familiar with the story," Raidan commented. "We all are. My ancestor, one of the first Onjara kings, battled his daughter for the throne. He lost and his daughter had his name expunged from all official records."

"Yes," Taya confirmed, "but there is much more to the story than is widely known. For instance, why was the name of your ancestor wiped away, as if to delete his very existence?"

Raidan shrugged. "Vengeance?" he said.

"That's the official reason, yes." Taya paused, her eyes darting across the pages. "Princess Syukoe went to war against her father because of his plan to unleash a magical cataclysm upon the material world. The king was a powerful sorcerer in his own right, with a Talent that may have surpassed even Master Iku's. The Kirians discovered what the king meant to do, and they set about trying to stop him. Master Iku was once the king's most trusted councilor, but he threw his support behind the princess once he learned the full extent of the king's plan.

"The king constructed a spell so powerful, it qualified as a Great Working. Such magic is hazardous in the extreme to anyone who attempts it. Many steps and safeguards are necessary to avert disaster, and even so, there is a significant failure rate. Part of the Working involved the very ring your family has used as a symbol of its royalty."

"The White Griffin." Raidan looked down at the copy adorning the third finger of his left hand. As a scion of the House of Onjara, he was entitled to wear an exact replica of the actual White Griffin, until the day came when he took the throne and replaced his copy with the real thing.

Taya nodded in affirmation. "The other part consisted of a smaller component spell, separate from the larger Working, but integral to its function. The Kirians separated this small piece of magic, this Key that unlocked the main energy of the Working, from its original vessel, the White Griffin Ring."

"And then they somehow placed it in Jelena." Raidan nodded in understanding. "Just what was this Great Working supposed to do?" he asked.

"The exact nature of the king's Working is not recorded here," Taya sighed in frustration, "but whatever it was, Master Iku and the other Kirians deemed it so evil, they were willing to risk insanity and death to stop it from being carried out. According to this account, the Kirians joined for a Great Working of their own, and even after reading of it, even with the evidence of its success living and breathing before my very eyes, I still have trouble believing such a thing could ever have been accomplished!

"After the Kirians separated the Key to the king's Working from the Griffin Ring, they somehow...*reached forward a thousand years in time* to this age, and hid the Key within the body of a living Onjara descendent: Keizo's daughter, Jelena."

Raidan stared hard at his wife's face, searching for any evidence that she had the slightest doubt about her conclusions. He saw none.

"There is more to the story," Taya said. "After Princess Syukoe defeated her father, she removed his name from all official records, not for revenge, but to prevent any adept with sufficient power and skill from using it to raise and control his spirit."

"I don't understand," Raidan stated. "Are you saying the king was not slain?"

"The unnatural prolongation of life can be achieved by certain dark means," Taya explained. "These are subjects never discussed with the uninitiated, and I shouldn't discuss them with you, really. Through such magic, a practitioner can literally become immortal, though it's an existence quite unlike life as we know it. The chronicle confirms the Kirians were unable to destroy the Nameless One completely. Only his body could be killed, but his spirit remained very much alive. The Kirians had to confine their enemy through magical means. They had to destroy all knowledge of his true name in order to prevent anyone with sufficient ability from releasing and controlling him." Taya paused, then said slowly, "The true name of a thing is the ultimate key to its power."

Taya laid the book aside and rose to her feet. She crossed the room to stand by the hearth and held her hands to the flames. Her auburn hair gleamed in the firelight and the heavy silk robe she wore couldn't quite hide the lush outlines of her body beneath. Raidan felt his own body stir in response.

After a moment, she continued. "Jelena harbors the Key to the Nameless One's Great Working, a spell deemed so terrible, so utterly evil, that the greatest magical minds of the time were willing to risk everything to stop it. The Kirians were entrusted with the task of insuring that no one could ever make use of it again..." Taya's voice trailed off.

"If the Nameless One, as you call this...this entity, is safely locked away, how can it be a threat? Jelena is well protected by a cadre of powerful mages," Raidan said.

Taya shivered and for the first time in many years, Raidan saw fear in his wife's eyes. His heart skipped a beat.

"The wards that keep the Nameless One confined are beginning to disintegrate—why, we don't know," Taya said. "The spirit is awake and gaining in strength. Soon, he will be strong enough to break free, and that we must not allow, not under any circumstances."

"And he no doubt wants his Key back," Raidan said.

"The Nameless One is searching for the Key as we speak, and when he locates it, as he most assuredly will, he'll realize that its energy is inextricably bound to Jelena's life force," Taya replied. "He will need to seize her body and somehow bring her to him so that he can remove the Key from her. I've done my best to protect the Key by sealing it away behind magical wards, but any adept with enough skill could, given time, break them down. The Nameless One will try, and eventually succeed. Once he possesses the Key, he can use it for its original purpose."

"Goddess' tits," Raidan swore softly.

The two of them said nothing for a time.

Finally, Raidan broke the silence. "What are the Kirians planning to do?" he asked.

"We are training the girl in the use of her Talent, but this is just a pretense. Our true mission is to prepare her for the Sundering. The Kirians must remove the Key from Jelena before the Nameless One finds her and secure it in a different vessel—preferably the White Griffin itself—which was, after all, its original vessel. Afterward, we must somehow find the necessary strength to re-imprison the spirit."

"You don't sound entirely certain you can do this," Raidan said, frowning with worry.

"Our Society is not what it once was, Husband," Taya sighed. "We are greatly reduced in both numbers and strength. Our chances of success would be much improved were we not missing one of our most Talented members, but unfortunately, she has been gone for some time and her whereabouts are unknown. Those of us who are left will have to somehow find a way."

"Is there no way to perform this...this Sundering without killing Jelena?" Raidan asked. Curiously, he found the prospect upset him.

"Not that I know of," Taya replied. "The only way to release the energy of the Key is to release Jelena's life energy from her body."

"Have you told any of this to Jelena? Does she realize she will have to die?"

"Jelena knows only part of the truth. We haven't yet told her that her death will be necessary, but I've seen her courage. She won't fail us when the time comes. What I fear is that we won't be up to the task...that we will fail her and her death will be for naught." Taya returned to the couch and sat beside Raidan. She laid her hand atop his. "Do you see now, Husband, why you needn't stain your hands with the blood of your brother's child? Jelena's blood will be on our hands," Raidan knew she meant the Kirians, "and if we are successful—pray Goddess that we are—then we will bear the brunt of Keizo's wrath."

"All of this must be very hard for Amara Sakehera... Sonoe as well," Raidan commented.

Taya's eyes narrowed. "Sonoe has become very close to Jelena of late... too close." Taya tapped her cheek with a forefinger. "I've never trusted her, as you well know, despite our long association. I believe that if she could find a way, she would extract the Key and use its power for her own purposes."

"I find that difficult to believe!" Raidan exclaimed, mildly shocked at his wife's allegations. "Sonoe has been devoted to my brother for many years. Such a betrayal seems totally out of character. Really, Wife, you need to let go of this old grudge."

"Believe what you will," Taya replied.

Raidan slipped his arms around his wife's waist. He could feel the power of her Talent humming within her like a hive of bees trapped beneath her robe. He kissed the back of her neck and spoke soothingly into her ear. "Time for bed, my love. We can put aside all of this until tomorrow."

Taya swiveled in his embrace and kissed him. "You are right," she agreed.

Arm in arm, they rose and retired to their bedchamber.

* * *

Later that night, as Taya lay sleeping beside him, Raidan stared at the bedroom ceiling, thinking.

It seemed that no matter which way his mind turned, the same conclusion confronted him, dressed in all of its grim repercussions. He tried to imagine Keizo's horror and grief upon learning the how and why of his daughter's death.

But what greater horror will befall all of us if Taya and her colleagues fail? If there were any way to spare you that pain, I would, Brother, but there's just too much at stake!

The elven people were beset on all sides, from both known and unknown enemies. Though not especially pious, Raidan nevertheless found himself wondering what terrible crime the elves had committed to cause their One Goddess to forsake them.

He continued to stare into the darkness until daybreak.

28
Allies And Enemies

Gran, this is Ashinji. He has just arrived," Aruk-cho said. "I will leave you two alone. You will, no doubt, have much to discuss." The akuta turned and lumbered off. The old woman disappeared from the window and a heartbeat later, she emerged from the doorway of the barracks.

"Ai, Goddess...I am so sorry to see you here, my son," she said in Siri-dar. She held out her hand to Ashinji, who clasped it in his. "Who are your kin, young Ashinji?" Gently, she removed her hand from Ashinji's grasp and patted his shoulder.

"My parents are Sen and Amara Sakehera, Lord and Lady of Kerala," he replied.

The old woman gasped. "Amara Sakehera is your mother?"

"You know my mother?"

The old woman bobbed her head. "Amara and I were colleagues, many years ago." She waved her hand, indicating that Ashinji should follow her. "Come. We'll go sit, and you can tell me your tale. We still have some time before the afternoon training session begins."

She led him to where two rough stools leaned against the barracks wall. Ashinji waited for her to sit before he settled beside her.

"Once upon a time, I was known as Chiana Hiraino," the old woman said.

"Are you kin to Tesuka Hiraino, the famous historian?" Ashinji asked.

"Tesuka was my father. You've studied his writings in school, no doubt. Well, Chiana Hiraino no longer exists. The woman you see before you now is known simply as 'Gran'. The Soldarans tend to call every woman past her childbearing years by this name. It's a term of affection for them."

Gran was, indeed, well into her elder years. A fan of creases set off her clear blue eyes, and silver frosted her pale blonde hair. Bony hands, roughened by hard work, rested in her lap; still, her lean body gave the impression of strength rather than frailty.

Ashinji wondered how the daughter of such a renowned man as Tesuka Hiraino had come to be in this place.

"Are you a slave, Lady Chiana?" he asked.

Gran chuckled. "Yes, my son, I'm a slave, and please, don't call me by my old name. I'm "Gran" now, and just that. Now, tell me how you ended up here."

Ashinji gave her an abbreviated account of the battle that had ended in his capture, omitting the part Sadaiyo's betrayal had played.

"I'd heard rumors the Soldarans had already launched an attack on our homeland," Gran said, "and now I know the rumors are true."

"The empress sent an army into Kerala, with the express purpose of splitting the Alasiri forces in order to weaken us. Now, King Keizo will have to keep part of his army in my father's demesne, tied up defending the border."

"I remember the day Sen Sakehera married your mother," Gran said. Her eyes grew wistful as she recounted the memory. "By the One, but he was handsome! I can see a lot of him in you. Your mother gave up a great deal to be his wife."

"You said you and my mother were colleagues once."

"Yes, indeed. We went to school together. We are both graduates of the Kan Onji, also known as the Red Order."

"You're a sorceress? But then..."

"I *was* a practitioner once, but I gave that all up long ago," Gran interrupted. "So did Amara, but for very different reasons." Her voice had taken on a note of sadness, and Ashinji sensed something painful hidden behind her simple statement. Gran reached out and laid a hand on his forearm. "Your Talent is quite strong, young Ashinji, but it is still largely dormant. No...wait." She paused and her eyes fluttered closed for a moment, then opened again. "Your Talent is *not* dormant. It has been blocked, and by someone quite skilled."

"Blocked? Are you certain?"

"Quite certain," Gran replied." Do you have any idea who might have done this to you, and why?"

"Yes, sadly, I do. My mother."

Gran frowned. "But why would Amara block her own child's Talent, particularly one as strong as yours is?"

"I'm second-born. The House of Sakehera always pledges its second-born child to the king's service. I've been a soldier my entire adult life."

"Ah," Gran nodded. "And I remember that in your mother's family, only the girls receive any formal magical training."

"Yes, that's right," Ashinji said. "So, you see, I never had any chance of developing my Talent much beyond the basics, even had I wished to. I think my mother must have blocked me in order to make it easier for me to accept my fate."

"I sense this has caused you pain, my son," she said. "Have you any sisters, then?"

"I have three sisters, but none of them have been sent to mage school... at least not yet."

"Such a pity you were not sent to the Red Order," Gran replied, shaking her head. "You could have been a formidable mage. Still, there is much you can learn, even now. I can't remove the block without hurting you, but I can teach you how to use the Talent you do have to help you survive this place. Even blocked, you are still stronger than you realize."

"I have a wife and a baby on the way, Gran. I need to survive for them." Ashinji paused, then added, "Somehow, I have to find a way to escape."

"Ai, son," Gran sighed. "In all the years I've lived in this yard, I've not once seen any slave escape, save through death."

"I don't understand why you're still here, Gran. Surely, a sorceress of the Red Order is too powerful to be held against her will."

"Mistress de Guera has offered me my freedom any time I choose to take it, but I have declined," Gran replied.

"But...but why?" Ashinji asked, astonished.

"That is a long story, young man, and one day, perhaps I will tell it to you." Gran's tone and the set of her jaw warned Ashinji not to push any further. "Now, tell me about your wife. Who are her kin?"

"My wife's name is Jelena..." Ashinji began, but Gran interrupted him.

"Jelena...that's not an elven name," she said.

"No, it isn't. She's Soldaran-born."

"You married a *human*?"

"Jelena is hikui. Her mother was the sister of the human lord whose lands border Kerala to the south." Ashinji told Gran of Jelena's childhood as a drudge in her uncle's house, her reasons for fleeing north into Alasiri, and of how they had found each other.

"Your wife sounds like a remarkable young woman. Did she ever find her elven kin?" Gran asked.

"Yes, and when she did, it was almost more than either of us could adjust to. She had always been told her father came from a noble family, but just how noble proved to be a great shock. Jelena is the daughter of our king."

"Silverlock's daughter! Keizo Onjara sired a child on a human woman?" Gran had drawn herself up on her stool and her face wore an expression of consternation.

"Yes. The king met Jelena's mother before he came to the throne."

"Tell me, does your wife have any Talent?" Gran peered intently into Ashinji's face.

"Yes, she does, but she's unable to use it much. My mother, as well as Jelena's aunt and her father's Companion are both giving her some training..."

"Her aunt...Do you mean Taya Onjara?"

"Princess Taya Onjara, wife of Crown Prince Raidan, yes." Aware, now, that Gran's interest in Jelena had become much more specific, Ashinji asked, "Why all of these questions about my wife?" He felt uneasy.

She's behaving as if she needs to find out something about Jelena that's of vital importance to her...but how could that be? Until this moment, she had no idea my wife even existed.

As if sensing his growing discomfort, Gran settled back onto her stool and patted Ashinji's knee. "Don't mind my nosiness. It's just been so long since I've spoken to another elf. I've been trying to teach that imp Seijon some Siri-dar, but all he cares about are the curse words and the vulgar names for private body parts." She smiled, but her eyes remained troubled.

They sat in silence for a time.

Gran finally spoke. "You'll find that life here isn't so bad, as long as you follow the rules. Mistress de Guera takes good care of all of us. I, myself, have special privileges. The mistress allows me to come and go as I please. I'll bring you special treats from the market now and then!"

"How can life as a slave be anything but bad?" Ashinji did nothing to hide the bitterness and anger in his voice. "My wife must surely believe I'm dead by now. She faces the birth of our child without me by her side. My brother..." He stopped himself before spitting out the angry words that burned his tongue, and glanced at Gran. Her eyes narrowed, but she remained silent. "What hurts the most is the realization that my child and I might never know each other."

Gran leaned forward and placed both hands on Ashinji's shoulders. "Hold on to that anger, young Ashinji! It will keep you alive... that, and the hope of returning home to your family some day."

"Two years is a long time."

"I know, but I'll help you, and so will Aruk-cho. Though his first loyalty is to the mistress, he is a good man, and you can trust him to be fair. The other trainers, well, they are all human. Thank the One that Aruk-cho is in charge."

"Mistress de Guera offered to take me as her concubine," Ashinji revealed. He laughed ruefully. "I turned her down. Perhaps that wasn't such a smart move."

"The mistress has an eye for beautiful young men, and it's a fact that humans find us especially attractive, even while they revile us for being without souls."

"Jelena has told me much about the religion of the Soldarans. It's at the heart of their hatred for us, this idea that we have no souls. It makes us inferior beings in their eyes."

"Not inferior, no. They view us as tainted with evil, and therefore capable of tainting any Soldaran who comes in contact with us. It's all very contradictory, you see. The average Soldaran will dutifully spout all of the racist nonsense he or she has been taught in church when asked about elvenkind, and yet, if they thought they could get away with it, many would gladly couple with us."

"Hmm," Ashinji nodded, then a thought struck him. He leaned forward, excited. "Gran, you said you were a sorceress once, a very powerful one, yes?"

"Yes," Gran replied cautiously.

"Then that means you are skilled at mindspeech. I've heard that trained mages can communicate with each other by mindspeech over great distances. Gran, can you contact my mother and let her know I'm alive?"

Ashinji felt the tiny spark of hope that had flared to life within him die when Gran sorrowfully shook her head.

"Mindspeech works best over short distances. The farther apart two people are, the harder it becomes. It's true that trained mages can communicate with one another, even when separated by great distances, but in order to accomplish this, an amplifier of some kind must be used. Otherwise, it's impossible." Her pale eyes brimmed with regret. "I haven't the necessary tools or materials to construct an amplifier. I'm sorry, Ashinji."

Ashinji lowered his head to hide the bitter disappointment on his face. "I had hoped..." His voice trailed off and he covered his smarting eyes with his hands.

"I know...I know," Gran murmured.

"*Gran!*" A female voice, full of pain, cried out from the interior of the barracks.

Gran slowly rose to her feet. "That'll be Vasta. Sounds like the poppy juice is wearing off. She took a nasty sword cut to her forearm in the Arena yesterday. Very deep. The healer spent a long time stitching it up." She sighed and brushed back a stray lock of silver blond hair. "I serve as the yard medic for the women, among my other duties. Simple things, mostly, like tending wounds and dispensing medicines the healers have left. But I'd best go in now. We'll talk more later."

Ashinji stood and as he turned to go, Gran called out to him. "Look after Seijon. He's a good boy, really, who just needs a decent role model. The humans fill his head with nothing but nonsense about our people. Your presence will help counter a lot of it."

"I'll do what I can," Ashinji promised.

* * *

Later that day as the westering sun bathed the yard with ruddy light, Ashinji, along with the other newcomers, received a wooden practice sword and paired up with a veteran so the trainers could assess the skills of each new slave.

Ashinji's sparring partner threw down a casual insult by way of introduction then sprang to the attack. Ashinji countered each blow with ease, and in a matter of moments, he knew all he needed to about his opponent's style. He hung back on the defensive, letting the larger, heavier human tire himself. Then, when he had wearied of the game, he disarmed the man with a deft maneuver. The human cursed as his sword went spinning out of his hand.

Ashinji had to restrain himself from whacking the man across the top of his shaven head. Instead, he dropped his guard and stepped back, inhaling a little more deeply to catch his breath.

"Aruk-cho said you were a professional soldier," the trainer who'd been observing the sparring remarked. A tall, lanky, hard-bitten man with a weathered face and big hands, he sauntered forward, a lopsided grin distort-ing his already uneven features. He hawked and spat on the sand at Ashinji's feet. "You're good, tink. The best I've seen in a long time. It pains me to admit it, but 'tis so. From now on, you're swordmaster to the newbies."

"C'mon, Joktan, you can't be serious!" Ashinji's erstwhile sparring partner protested. "You know I'm supposed to get that job!"

"Shut yer hole, Leal!" Joktan growled. "I am and it's done, so deal with it!" The two men glared at each other for several tense heartbeats.

"You promised me," Leal muttered, backing down. He shot a venom-ous look at Ashinji, who met his furious eyes without flinching.

"I do not want the job. Give it to him," Ashinji said, keeping his gaze firmly affixed on Leal's face.

"You think I'd let you off the hook so easily, tink? Forget about it! The job's yours. Neither of you has got any say in this."

Ashinji swiveled his head slowly to face Joktan. He stared at the trainer for a moment, then said, "My name is Ashinji." He pronounced each word with deliberate force, saving special emphasis for his own name. "Not...*tink!*" Anger propelled the slur from his mouth like a projectile.

"Yeah, sure, whatever..." Joktan sniffed. "As long as you teach the rest of these sorry shitballs how to handle a sword, I'll call you 'sweetheart' if you like." Raucous laughter erupted among the other slaves. Only Leal remained grim-faced and silent.

I've made a dangerous enemy, Ashinji thought, *and I've only just arrived!*

Joktan clapped his hands and the laughter ceased. "That's all for to-day," he announced. "Veterans, Aruk-cho has posted tomorrow's matches on the board. Two points melees and one lethal. Check before you go to bed, idiots! Newbies, report to the infirmary before dinner, so you can all get your fine new marks. The mark of de Guera means a lot in this town! You should all be proud to bear it." He paused, as if trying to remember something important, then exclaimed, "Shit! Almost forgot! It's the last Torsday of the month tomorrow. You all know what that means!"

"Yeah, it means we all get laid!" a male voice called out.

"You wish you were gettin' some!" a female voice responded.

More laughter.

Ashinji sighed and looked over his shoulder, searching for Seijon. He spotted the boy at the back of the crowd, jumping up and down in an effort to see over the taller bodies blocking his view. Seijon must have seen him at the same moment, for his face broke into a huge grin and he waved.

Joktan dismissed the slaves, who began dispersing, women to their side of the yard, men to the opposite. Ashinji remained standing in place while the others drifted past.

Leal swung in close and bumped Ashinji hard enough to stagger him. "Watch your back, tink," he growled. The human's voice dripped with menace.

"Leal's insane," Seijon said quietly as the big man stalked off toward the barracks reserved for the veterans.

Ashinji shrugged. "He does not scare me."

"Well, he should. I saw him beat a girl to death 'cause she wouldn't do what he wanted. One of the girls who comes for pleasure. The mistress was furious! She had to pay off the girl's owner for the loss. Leal spent a week in the hole for that one and lost all his points for the month."

Ashinji didn't know what "the hole" was, but he guessed it to be some form of punishment. He looked down at Seijon's face and saw a flicker of raw emotion pass across it like a cloud across the noonday sun.

"Was your mother a prostitute, Seijon?" he asked, his voice gentle.

The boy nodded. "She died when I was a little kid. Some man hurt her bad...so bad she spit blood before she...well, it was a long time ago." He refused to meet Ashinji's eyes.

"Not so long ago, I think." Ashinji laid a hand on the boy's shoulder and squeezed, thinking about Gran's request. "When do we get fed around here?" he asked.

Seijon looked up and smiled. "Soon! The food's real good here, and we get all we want. When I first came, I couldn't believe it, so I used to hide stuff, like when I lived on the streets. I don't do that anymore."

The food proved similar to typical elven cuisine, though a bit heavier and oddly spiced. The main course consisted of a thick stew, rich with fatty meat. Boiled root vegetables and grain, baskets of coarse brown bread, greasy yellow cheese, and jugs of decent quality, dark beer rounded out the meal.

While they ate, Seijon kept up a steady stream of questions, which Ashinji did his best to answer. Appalled at the amount of falsehoods the hikui boy had been fed concerning elves, he determined, if nothing else, to serve as a living rebuttal to all the lies.

The other men in the newcomer's barracks proved more curious toward Ashinji than hostile. He could see their interest writ large on their faces as he spoke of Alasiri and his former life. In the company of the new slaves, at least, Ashinji felt the first stirrings of a strange kind of camaraderie.

After the evening meal had been eaten and the remains cleared away, Ashinji took a stool outside to sit and savor the cool evening breeze. Seijon followed and hunkered on the ground with his back against the wall.

The sounds of muffled laughter and a snatch of song drifted on the dusty air. Somewhere in the compound, a man sneezed. From across the yard, in the direction of the women's barracks, a female voice cried out, whether from pain or pleasure, Ashinji couldn't tell.

"Ashinji," Seijon murmured, "D'you think you'll ever get to go back home to Alasiri?"

"I was not so sure a short while ago, but now...Yes, I believe I will see my home and family again," Ashinji replied, and he surprised himself with the surety of his resolve.

"Will you take me with you?" In the waning light of dusk, the hikui boy's eyes looked like huge, dark stones in his lean, humanish face.

"When the time comes, Seijon, we will speak of it. It is too soon now."

The sound of approaching hoofbeats heralded the arrival of Aruk-cho. The akuta greeted Ashinji in Siri-dar. "Good evening, my friend. I have come to find out how you are doing." He halted just beyond the awning and stood with one back foot flexed, horse-like. His long black tail swished gently to and fro.

"I'm as well as can be expected, I think," Ashinji said. He glanced down at the fresh mark on his right shoulder—a stylized lily flower seared into the skin by a red-hot branding iron. "Gran's salve has eased the pain of this burn quite nicely...By the way, I must compliment you on your command of Siri-dar."

"Can I have a ride Aruk-cho?" Seijon jumped to his feet, bouncing like an eager toddler.

"Not now, young one," Aruk-cho replied. "I have work to do. Perhaps tomorrow evening." The ghost of a smile played about the akuta's fierce countenance. "Gran instructs me in your tongue when time permits," he said to Ashinji. "She has attempted to school that one as well," he indicated Seijon with a lift of his chin, "but he is very impatient, as all young ones are."

"Joktan has made me swordmaster for the new slaves. I am to train every one who needs basic instruction," Ashinji said.

"So Joktan told me. He is a man who sees very little to praise in this world, but he praised your technique when he spoke to me. This is a good thing, Ashinji. Your usefulness will keep you out of harm's way much longer. Slaves with skills that are needed in the yard face far fewer lethal matches."

"I made an enemy through no fault of my own," Ashinji said with a rueful shake of his head. "The human called Leal seemed to expect that he would get the job. He has threatened me already," He tugged at his bare earlobe, missing anew the feel of the rings he used to wear there during his old, lost life.

"Yeah, Aruk-cho! You've got to do something about that crazy shit-head!" Seijon cried. "Give 'im nothing but lethal matches 'til someone finally guts 'im!" Ashinji no longer wondered at the boy's obvious hatred for Leal, given that a man like Leal had murdered his mother.

"I do not fear Leal, Seijon," Ashinji said reassuringly. "He is a good swordsman, but I am better."

"He won't come at you with a sword. It'll be a knife in the back, in a dark corner," the boy muttered.

"The young one is right. Leal is treacherous, and much more clever than he looks. Watch yourself at all times. Now, I must go. The mistress has tasks for me to complete before I can seek my bed."

Ashinji bid the akuta goodnight, and watched as he melted into the darkness.

"Get Leal before he gets you, Ashinji," Seijon whispered.

"It is time for bed, Seijon," Ashinji replied.

That night, Ashinji dreamed of a faceless man, standing over him with a knife, poised for the downward stroke that would end his life. Ashinji opened his mouth to scream, but his tongue froze, unable to form any sound. Just as the glittering blade began its descent, a huge black shadow blotted out the light and the faceless man vanished.

Ashinji woke with a start. The vertigo that always gripped him after a prophetic dream left him queasy. He lay back on his bunk and stared at the ceiling, drawing in deep breaths to slow his galloping heart.

Perhaps Seijon is right; I should get Leal before he gets me...No! I will kill only in self-defense.

He covered his face with his hands.

Jelena, my love, I miss you so much!

He slept no more that night.

29
A Vision, A Tale, And A Plan

The march of days passed inexorably onward and, as Gran predicted, Ashinji soon settled into the rhythm of life in the de Guera yard. The weather gradually cooled as fall melted into a winter so mild, Ashinji barely noticed the difference.

Ashinji's job as swordmaster to the unskilled new arrivals kept him out of the lethal matches, as Aruk-cho had promised, but after about a month at the yard, he found himself on the regular roster for the many points matches run each week.

On the day of his debut in the Grand Arena, he caused a sensation. The Darguinian public had never seen anything like him before, and they responded with immediate and near frenzied excitement. He beat his opponents in all three matches, and left the blood-stained sands with only a shallow cut across his sword arm and the thunderous applause of the crowd ringing in his ears.

From that day forward, Ashinji battled in the Arena five days a week. On some days, he fought in the pouring rain, and on others, beneath the weak glare of the winter sun. At first, he used a variety of weapons, including the short, heavy stabbing sword favored by the Soldaran fighters, but quickly settled on a lighter, longer blade forged in the desert country of the Ahzani. The Ahzani weapon came closest to the feel of an elf-made sword.

His opponents proved a mixed lot; he faced an even assortment of good to excellent fighters, some of whom might have killed him, given the right combination of luck and timing. He constantly gave thanks to the One that his position in the yard spared him from the lethal matches, though he had no illusions that his situation could not, nor would not, eventually change.

All of the fighters, both slave and free, wore armor of some sort. Mistress de Guera issued each of her slaves a stout coat of leather sewn over with small squares of steel, steel-plated leather arm and leg guards, and a metal helmet with an open face. None of it matched the quality of his elven-made armor, but Ashinji knew it was better than nothing.

He never left the Arena without a cut or two, but luck and skill kept him from more serious injury. Every day, he mourned the loss of his old life and longed for the comfort of Jelena's arms.

He often dreamed of her. Sometimes, she smiled and seemed happy; other times, her face glistened with tears. Only once did he wake with the queasy feeling in the pit of his stomach that always accompanied a prophetic dream. In his vision, he saw Jelena, hugely pregnant and in the midst of labor. She lay with her head cradled in the lap of a beautiful, red-haired woman. Something dark and menacing fluttered around the woman's head like shreds of mist. Jelena wailed as a birth pain wracked her body. Ashinji could only watch in disembodied horror as the flame-haired woman thrust her index finger straight down Jelena's throat.

All the next day, Ashinji moved about in a fog of fear. He felt certain the face he'd seen in his dream— though indistinct—belonged to King Keizo's Companion. Sonoe had a well-known reputation as a powerful mage, and Ashinji knew of her involvement with Jelena's magical training. If Sonoe bore Jelena any ill will, she had never revealed her true feelings. Ashinji had no cause to distrust her—until now.

That evening, he sought out Gran and told her of his dream.

"'Tis a pity such a Talent as yours was never developed, Ashi. You would be a force to be reckoned with!"

As was her custom every evening after supper, Gran sat outside the women's barracks on a three-legged stool, back against the wall, smoking a pipe. She fanned the air before her face in an effort to disperse the pungent smoke given off by the burning herb. "I've been meaning to give up this filthy habit," she grumbled.

Ashinji, perched on another stool beside her, stifled a cough as the fumes stung his throat. "I need to know for sure the woman I saw is a danger to my wife, Gran."

"Visions are tricky things, young man. Many times they show only what *might* happen, not what *will* happen. Their language is often symbolic, as you well know. This red-haired woman might not be an actual person, but rather an avatar of someone or some*thing*."

"No, no." Ashinji shook his head. "She is an actual person...the official consort of King Keizo, and a trained mage."

"We will try an old technique for delving into the deepest parts of the mind." Gran took a drag on her pipe and allowed the smoke to trickle from her nostrils in long streamers before continuing. "I will be as gentle as I can, but it will hurt, and you'll have a nasty headache afterward." Her pale eyes met his.

Ashinji nodded.

Gran dumped the still-burning herb from her pipe onto the ground and tucked it into a skirt pocket. "I might see things you wish to keep private, Ashi. Does that worry you?"

"No, Gran. I trust you," Ashinji replied. He leaned forward and Gran placed her cool hands on either side of his head. He closed his eyes.

Ashinji's mind had been probed before, but only by his mother. Those superficial scans had been more of a discomfort than truly painful, but this was an entirely different experience. He felt his body squirming even as he fought to remain still while Gran pushed ever deeper. Her mind felt cool, logical, superbly ordered, and very, very powerful. Ashinji had never felt such immense Talent before. He heard himself groan as Gran pulled forth the memory of the red-haired woman and held it up for examination.

The face resolved itself into a clear picture of Sonoe. Even though he had expected it, Ashinji's gut still twisted with dismay. Why would Sonoe wish to hurt Jelena? It made no sense to him.

The feel of Gran's mind changed as the memory of Ashinji's vision became clearer. Her thoughts crackled with alarm, which only fueled his own anxiety. The pain of the probe intensified and it required all of his strength just to remain still.

"Gran...please, enough!" he gasped through gritted teeth.

Abruptly, the pain ceased. He opened bleary eyes to find Gran still drawn close, her hands gripping his head.

She peered into his eyes. "Are you all right?" she inquired.

"I have a bad headache, as promised, but otherwise... yes."

As Gran massaged his temples, a look of profound sadness flitted across her face.

"What's wrong?" Ashinji asked.

Gran shook her head and sniffed loudly. "Just an old woman's memories, coming back to haunt her. You remind me of someone very dear to me, someone I lost a long time ago." She sat back with a sigh. "It's not important. What is important is that I know this Sonoe, or more precisely,

I know of her. She was a student of the Kan Onji when I served there as provost. Even as a student, she stood out for her brilliance and ambition. I always knew she'd go far, but..."

"King's Companion is not what you would have expected for her?" Ashinji smiled wryly.

Gran sniffed again and raised an eyebrow. "She came to us with almost no money and so was obliged to work for her keep and training. She did very little manual labor, as I recall."

"The darkness I saw hovering around Sonoe...what does that mean?"

"I don't know," Gran admitted. "It could mean that she, herself, is evil, or she is being influenced by an evil, outside force."

"I know she's a very powerful sorceress, Gran. Do you have any idea what she's doing—or might do—to my wife?" Ashinji paused. "Goddess' tits! Jelena's blue fire... That must be what she wants!"

"What is this 'blue fire'?" Gran asked.

"It's some kind of an energy form within Jelena, but it's not part of her Talent. Do you think Sonoe knows what it is?"

Gran countered with a request. "Tell me everything you know about this energy form your wife harbors."

"Well..." Ashinji hesitated then continued, "I don't know much at all, really... only that it's always been there, according to Jelena. She has no idea what it is or how to control it. She assumed it was a normal part of her elven heritage and hoped to learn more about it after she came to live among us. The few times when she and I have shared a mindlink, I've seen it in her. It always looks like a blue ball of light."

"Do you know of the Kirian Society, Ashi?" Gran asked.

"Yes. They're an ancient order of mages. My mother is a member...or she used to be."

"Before I had to leave Alasiri, I was the Mistress of the Society," Gran revealed.

Ashinji silently digested this information while Gran continued. "Once, we Kirians wielded power enough to shape political and social events to our will. We were the moral guardians of the realm. The kings and queens of Alasiri listened to and heeded our counsel. Now, sadly, we are but a pale shadow of the Kirians of old." She stared out into the darkness as if her eyes could pierce the veil of time and see into the past.

"This is all very interesting, but what does it have to do with Jelena and Sonoe?" Ashinji's anxiety made his voice sharp.

Jelena is in danger and I can't protect her as long as I remain a captive! he thought.

"Patience, young man," Gran admonished. "I'm telling you all of this so you will better understand what must be done. Now, listen. What I'm about to tell you is known only to the Kirians, and has been safeguarded by our order since ancient times. I'm only telling you because you are directly involved.

"When we first met, you told me of your wife, a hikui daughter of the house of Onjara. It set off alarm bells in my mind. I didn't want to believe it at first, but it fit the prediction too well to be dismissed."

"What prediction?"

"You know the story of the ancient king whose daughter defeated him and erased his name from all official records?"

"Every elven child learns about Queen Syukoe in school," Ashinji answered.

"Well, what is not taught is the real reason why she did what she did... and what was done to the king whose name is no longer known. This is the truth of it...."

* * *

Ashinji sat hunched on his stool, head in his hands, trying to make sense of what Gran had just told him.

That men and women could command the kind of power necessary to...to punch through the barrier of Time itself... His mind reeled in disbelief.

After a long silence, he straightened and turned narrowed eyes upon Gran. "This Key you speak of—this magic those ancient mages put into my wife—it's intertwined with her life force, you say."

"Yes, it is," Gran replied.

"And the Kirian Society, or what's left of it, must remove and safeguard it from this...this thing you call the Nameless One, who is, in fact, the undead sorcerer king Onjara." Gran nodded. Ashinji continued. "If this Key is so closely bound to Jelena's life force, won't removing it..." His voice faltered as realization crept up and pounced. "Removing it means killing her, doesn't it?" he whispered.

"Ashi, there are greater things at stake here than your wife's life." Gran's voice was harsh. Ashinji opened his mouth to reply, but the old mage cut off his furious retort before he could launch it.

"Just listen to me, young man! If the Nameless One regains possession of the Key, it will mean the end of everything! His essence is a thousand-year distillation of pure malice, and he wants nothing less than the complete destruction of the material world as we know it. He must tear down reality first, in order to refashion it into his own twisted version. To do that, he needs the Key. He *must* be denied, whatever the cost."

"Please tell me there's a way to do this without killing my wife in the process!" Ashinji begged.

"I will not lie to you," Gran replied. "There is a risk that Jelena will be lost, but the loss to the material world and every creature in it is incalculable if the Nameless One should gain possession of the Key, or if it should fall into the hands of a living mage powerful and ruthless enough to use it."

"Gran...*please!* Tell me there's a way!"

"Ai, Ashi... Son," Gran murmured. Her expression melted into tenderness and tears glittered in her eyes. "Your wife's death is not a certainty, only a possibility...I wish I could give you more reassurance, but I can't."

Ashinji stood up, overturning his stool, and began to pace. Gran watched silently.

"How is any of this going to happen?" he asked. "We're both slaves, Gran. We're hundreds of leagues from home, trapped in the middle of the capital of the Soldaran Empire, surrounded by countless numbers of humans... none of whom would lift a finger to help us escape!"

"That's not entirely true," Gran said. "There is someone who might be willing to help us. Two someones, in fact."

"Who, then?"

"One is a healing brother of the Eskleipan order. He used to come twice a week, but I haven't seen him for quite a while. He went out of his way to make my acquaintance the first time he came. He claimed to have a hikui relative. Calls himself Tilo. I shall inquire after him when next the Eskleipans come."

"Who's the other human who might aid us?"

"Not human, Ashinji."

"Aruk-cho!"

Gran nodded. "His first loyalty is to Mistress de Guera, but he just might be willing to help in an indirect way. Stop pacing and look at me, young man."

Ashinji halted.

"Ashi, there is something else I need to tell you, something about me. Please sit down." Ashinji did as Gran bid.

"You once asked me why I've chosen to remain here as a slave. I'm going to tell you the reason now. I remain to serve penance."

"Penance? For what crime?" Ashinji's eyebrows shot up in surprise.

"Crimes, Ashi. Arrogance, greed, selfishness...a lust for power so great, it cost those dearest to me their very lives."

"I don't understand."

"I was a very powerful mage once, Ashi. I enjoyed respect, prestige, all that came with my station, but it wasn't enough. I wanted more." In the dim light of the single lantern hanging on a hook by the barracks door, Gran's face looked grim and haunted. "I, in my overweening pride, thought that I could re-create the energy pattern needed to construct a Portal, a means by which the Kirians of old could travel great distances without having to trek overland. Only one Kirian has ever been able to create the proper energy pattern, and he has been dead a thousand years. The strength of Talent needed is enormous. Such a feat qualifies as a Great Working.

"I was warned not to attempt it, but this only spurred me on. I needed to prove my greatness! What a fool I was..." Gran stopped speaking. Her hand fluttered up to her face and touched her cheek as if the sensation of a long-ago kiss still lingered there.

"My attempt failed, with spectacular and horrifying consequences. The home I shared with my husband and children was reduced to rubble. Everyone in the house died...my family, our servants...everyone. Except me. I survived, barely. When I emerged from the ruins, I was quite insane. Much later, I learned that a local farmer found me, injured and wandering the fields near where my home once stood. The Red Order, as was its duty to one of its own, even one such as me, took me in and healed my body. They also, after many months, succeeded in healing my mind.

"When I came to my senses, my shame and guilt so overwhelmed me, I tried to kill myself, but my colleagues stopped me. The agony of living with what I'd done...Ai, Goddess! Nothing to me seemed punishment enough. My husband and my children were all dead by my hand, my professional reputation lay in ruins... I had nothing left. That was when I decided to spend the rest of my life doing penance for my crimes."

Gran fell silent, and Ashinji could see what a tremendous struggle she fought with her memories. He waited patiently until she found the strength to continue.

"I set out with only the clothes on my back and a little food, and I walked—yes walked—across Alasiri and down into the human lands. At the first settlement I came to, I stole a horse, openly, so that I would be pursued. I hoped when I was caught, I would be killed outright.

"The men who finally captured me did not kill me, though. They were soldiers from the local garrison. They took me back to their fort. Since I was too old to be a concubine, they set me to work cooking and cleaning for them. I wasn't very good at it, as you can imagine, so they beat me a lot those first weeks... but I welcomed all of the abuse they heaped upon me.

"After several months at the fort, a stranger arrived—a dealer of slaves. The captain of the garrison, only too happy to get rid of me since I was no good as a cook, sold me to the dealer, who brought me here, to Darguinia. Mistress de Guera bought me from the slave market on the first day I arrived. I'm still not entirely sure why. Pity, perhaps. I've been here ever since."

Gran ceased her narrative and fell silent.

Ashinji extended a hand and laid it atop her folded ones. Such an air of sadness hung about her that Ashinji momentarily forgot his own grief.

"You told me I reminded you of someone you'd lost. Who?" he asked.

"I had five sons. My youngest was about your age when he died. You remind me of him. His name was Taka..." Her voice broke, and a single tear slid from her left eye and trickled down her cheek.

Ashinji could think of nothing to say. Mere words could not serve in the face of such overwhelming tragedy. He continued to hold her hands, waiting until she could speak again.

"Ashinji, the Kirians must regain control of the Key. Any other possibility is unthinkable," Gran continued at last. Her face settled into an expression of fierce determination. "I now have a reason to return to Alasiri... and you must come with me."

"We'll need all the help we can muster," Ashinji said. "This human, Tilo. You have no idea when he's coming back?"

"No. In the meantime, I'll speak to Aruk-cho. Better that I approach him first. He will need a bit of persuading, but I'll bring him around."

"I did sort of promise to take Seijon with me if I ever tried to break out of the yard." Ashinji rubbed his jaw in annoyance. "I'm beginning to regret it. He's barely old enough to hold a weapon, much less fight with one. I'm afraid I'll just get him killed. He doesn't deserve such a fate, Gran."

"That boy is a lot tougher and more resourceful than you think. He had to be, to survive on the streets. Don't waste time worrying about him. He can handle himself well when he needs to. Besides, I couldn't bear to leave him behind, either."

Now that they had made the decision to escape, Ashinji felt an odd kind of peace descend upon him, even though he recognized the long odds for success.

So much of this depends on sheer luck, he thought. *If Aruk-cho will help us, if this human called Tilo returns and is also willing to help...maybe, just maybe, I'll hold Jelena and our child in my arms again.*

He refused to think of what might be required of them once they were finally reunited.

Part IV

30
Birth Day

Winter had begun giving way to spring, and in Alasiri, that meant rain. The daily precipitation saturated the ground and turned the roads to mud, making even the shortest trip a tedious slog. The gravel-paved streets of Sendai did not fare much better. The unusually heavy rainfall soon overwhelmed the network of channels and gutters that normally kept the city from flooding.

Another soggy, gloomy day, Jelena thought as she made her way through mid-afternoon traffic enroute to Sateyuka's house. She took special care to detour around the many pools of standing water, acutely aware that one misstep could send her crashing to the slick ground. Wrapped from head to toe in a gray wool cloak, scarf, slouchy hat, and gloves, she traveled in complete anonymity. If anyone happened to glance at her, she would look like just another pregnant hikui woman.

In Sateyuka's peaceful home, Jelena could shed the persona of royal princess and just be herself. She treasured the quiet, private time she spent with her friend.

Sateyuka greeted Jelena at the door with an affectionate kiss on the cheek, then helped her guest to remove her heavy outerwear.

"Go on into the sitting room and thaw out! Your skin is like ice," she exclaimed. "I'll just take these wet things into the kitchen to dry." Jelena did as instructed and with a heartfelt sigh, she lowered herself awkwardly onto the couch before the fireplace and stretched her feet toward the flames.

"Oh, here, let me help you get your boots off," Sateyuka offered as she entered the room, a heavily laden tray in her hands.

"No, please, Sateyuka. You don't have to do that!" Jelena protested as her friend went to her knees and grabbed a foot.

"Don't be silly, girl. How else are you going to get these off, eh? Big as you are? When's the last time you saw your own feet?"

Jelena giggled. "It has been awhile. I'll be seeing them soon, though. My doctor says the baby can come any time now."

"By the look of you, she'll be a big baby. There, now... Doesn't that feel better?" Sateyuka placed Jelena's boots on the hearth. The smell of steaming leather filled the small room.

"Ahhhh," Jelena sighed. "That does feel nice."

"I have your favorite," Sateyuka sang. She brought the tray over to where Jelena reclined and set it down on a small table. "How the confectioner was able to find lemons at this time of year... well, I just don't know, but here they are."

"Sateyuka, you are too good to me." Jelena smiled and bit into the crisp little ball of pastry. The sweet-tart taste of lemon burst delightfully on her tongue.

"Nonsense! You're like a daughter to me. You should know that by now."

"I do," Jelena replied. "That day I first saw you in the marketplace, I knew I had to follow you and find out who you were. It was as if the gods, or the Goddess, wanted us to meet."

"She knew you'd need a special place—a haven—where you could escape the unique pressures of your life."

"I know you're my friend, Sateyuka, but sometimes, I feel guilty coming here. To Jokimichi, I mean. I've been living in my father's house for almost a year now, and still, nothing has changed for the hikui people. They're still denied equality under the law—a law my father can change, yet does not! I get so angry at times...with him, with my uncle...with all okui. Every day, I see how the hikui servants are treated at the castle, and I can't help but wonder if, secretly, they resent me because I have all the rights and privileges of a full-blooded elf."

Sateyuka set down her teacup and patted Jelena's hand. "My dear, I can't speak for all the hikui of Sendai, but I can tell you what many of my friends and neighbors are saying about Princess Jelena. They say the princess is kind, loving, and gracious... a young woman of exceptional character. Jelena, our people love you, and want only the best for you. They view you as a symbol of hope for all hikui."

"I can't help but feel I've let all hikui down." Jelena stared morosely into the dark green depths of her tea. She wasn't sure she wanted to be the symbol of hope for an entire group of people—the burden seemed too enormous.

"You've done no such thing, sweet girl. No reasonable person expects you to change, single-handedly, an unjust system that's been in place since Alasiri has been a nation. You don't realize the enormous value of you simply being who you are. In the short time you've been living in Sendai, the attitudes of the okui are starting to change. Oh, it's subtle, but it's real. I can feel it, and so can others."

"How do you mean?" Jelena asked.

"I overheard two okui merchants talking in the market the other day. One actually wondered aloud whether it seemed fair to continue to deny hikui artisans membership in the guilds when so many of them were as skilled, or more so, than their okui counterparts. It may not sound like much, but it's definitely a start."

Jelena massaged her belly and closed her eyes, focusing her thoughts inward on her soon-to-be born daughter, Hatora. Most okui mothers could touch the minds of their children while they floated safe in the womb, but Jelena had yet to feel the consciousness of her own baby. Disappointed at first, she had soon become resigned to it, though she still tried from time to time.

"I pray that when my daughter is my age, she will live in a different world than we do, Sateyuka."

"I pray for that also."

Without warning, a sharp pain rippled across Jelena's belly. She grunted in surprise.

"What is it?" Sateyuka came to the edge of her chair.

"I'm not sure," Jelena said slowly. "I've never experienced labor before, so I don't quite know what to expect. It felt like a labor pain...I think." She screwed up her face in concentration, focusing on the sensations of her body.

Yes, something most definitely feels different!

"Jelena, if you're starting your labor, you can't walk back up the hill to the castle alone. I'll come with you." Sateyuka rose to her feet. "Let's get your boots back on now."

"Nothing's going to happen for hours, Sateyuka. I'm sure I can get home on my own. Please don't put yourself out."

"Stop it right now. Of course I'm coming with you, and I'll have no more arguments!"

Jelena shut up and allowed her friend to help her to her feet and into her still-damp boots. She waited by the front door while Sateyuka went to fetch their outerwear. As she waited, another ripple of pain coursed through her. She groaned through gritted teeth, clutching the door post for support.

No doubt about what's happening now!

"You're having another cramp," Sateyuka stated as she emerged from the back of her house carrying Jelena's things, a dusky purple cloak thrown over her own heavy dress. Jelena nodded, feeling a little light-headed from the pain. Sateyuka helped her don her cloak, then threw open the front door and grabbed Jelena's arm. "Hold on tight and lean on me if you need to. Let's get you home."

Mercifully, the rain had stopped, though gray clouds still scudded overhead. A cold, wet breeze splattered droplets against their cloaks as they walked. No one paid any attention to them, for which Jelena was thankful. Once, an elderly well-dressed okui man—rushing along with an air of importance—collided with Sateyuka, knocking her backward.

"Watch where you're going, clumsy hikui!" the man growled as he swept past.

Jelena stifled the urge to yell out a retort. "So much for changing attitudes!" she commented ruefully.

"I said the changes were subtle," Sateyuka replied, smiling. "How are you doing?"

"Fine, so far. No more pains...yet."

Jelena's body spared her any further contractions until just before she and Sateyuka passed through the outer gates of the castle complex. Jelena leaned heavily on her friend until the spasm subsided. She gulped several deep breaths and managed a weak smile. "If it hurts like this now, I don't know how I'm going to stand it when things really get going!" she said.

"You'll do just fine, sweet girl. Let's go, now."

The guards standing to either side of the massive portals snapped to attention when the two women came into view. Recognizing the king's daughter, they allowed her and Sateyuka to pass through unchallenged, as did the guards at the inner gates.

"I'd be honored if you would attend me, Sateyuka. I was planning to ask you before now, but I didn't expect Hatora to come today!"

"I'm the one who's honored, but are you sure? You must already have many women to attend you as well as your doctor. Perhaps I'd only get in the way." Sateyuka gave Jelena's hand a squeeze.

"I want you with me," Jelena replied, "but if you can't, I'll understand. I know you have your own business and family to attend to, and they need you more than I do."

"If you want me with you, then I'll stay. I must send a message to my daughter, though, so she knows where I am."

"Yes, of course."

In truth, Jelena would have many attendants during the birth, but besides Eikko, none would be hikui. And though she considered Eikko a friend, Jelena wanted the presence of another hikui who was not also a servant.

The two friends walked through the main entrance of the castle, the crisp snap of the guards' salute echoing off the stone as they passed. Jelena led the way through the quiet, elegant halls toward her apartments. As they walked, Sateyuka stared about her, wide eyed. Seeing her friend's awe brought back Jelena's own memories of her first days spent within these walls, before she knew for sure she belonged here.

Jelena paused just outside the doors to her private quarters.

"I'm surprised to see no guards here," Sateyuka commented.

"My father tried posting some, but I kept sending them away. I finally convinced him there's simply no need. I'm just not that important."

"Jelena, that's not true," Sateyuka chided. "To your family, especially..."

Jelena smiled. "All I meant is that I'm not important politically. Welcome to my home, dear friend. I should have invited you here long ago. Please forgive me?"

"There's nothing to forgive, sweet girl," Sateyuka replied.

Jelena pushed open the doors, calling out a greeting as she did so. Eikko came scurrying from the back room, a little breathless, as usual.

"I didn't expect you back so soon, Highness. I was just getting...Oh!" Eikko halted in mid-sentence upon catching sight of a stranger accompanying her mistress.

"Eikko, this is my friend Sateyuka the weaver, the one I visit down in Jokimichi," Jelena explained. "Sateyuka, this is Eikko, my companion." Jelena refused to call Eikko her servant.

"H...How do you do?" Eikko stammered, clearly a little flustered. "Highness, if I'd known you were bringing a guest, I'd have tidied up a little better and ordered some tea from the kitchen! I..."

"Don't worry about that, child," Sateyuka interjected soothingly. "We have much more important business to attend to right now. The princess has begun her labor."

Eikko gulped, then let out a little squeak. Her eyes widened in so comic a fashion that both Jelena and Sateyuka burst out laughing. At that precise moment, Jelena realized, for the first time since she had learned of Ashinji's death, she felt truly happy again.

"Summon a messenger, Eikko. Sateyuka must get word to her family that she's staying with me and...Oh, yes! Send word to Sonoe and my mother-in-law."

"Yes, Highness! Ohhhh, this is so exciting!" the young hikui girl squealed.

Jelena felt serene, strong, and unafraid of the ordeal to come.

Soon, I will hold you in my arms, Hatora. Any amount of pain will be worth enduring because I'm bringing you into the world.

Jelena had finally accepted Ashinji's death, but despite what she knew to be true, she had yet to lose a sense of connectedness to him. Her soul still felt joined to the unique spiritual essence that had defined Ashinji as a person, so much so, that she could almost believe he still lived.

Jelena steadfastly clung to that connection—the only thing that had kept her sane during the long, terrible winter.

Another pain caught her by surprise, wringing a startled cry from her lips. A gush of warm liquid sluiced down her legs to puddle on the matting beneath her feet.

"I think my daughter's coming very soon!" she gasped.

"Come with me now, my dear. Let's get you undressed." Sateyuka took her by the elbow and steered her toward the bedchamber. Jelena allowed Sateyuka to help her strip down to her shift, then sat on the edge of the bed while her friend massaged her back. The pain gradually subsided.

Jelena chuckled as she brushed a stray coil of sweat-dampened hair from her face. "Hatora wants to be born before anyone is ready for her. Do you think my daughter will always be so headstrong?"

"Your daughter will possess all of the best qualities of both her parents," Sateyuka replied, smiling. "I never got to meet your Ashinji, but I feel as if I know him from all that you've told me. He would be proud of you."

Yes, he would, Jelena thought.

* * *

"Now, Princess! Push hard!"

Gritting her teeth, Jelena bore down and delivered her daughter into the waiting hands of the doctor. Exhausted after hours of labor, she relaxed into the mound of pillows piled at her back and let her mind drift.

For a while, the world dissolved into a soft blur. The angry wail of her newborn daughter and the delighted cries of the women surrounding her floated through her consciousness like clouds across the summer sky. She saw Ashinji, standing before her, his head cocked as if listening for something. The sensation of his presence felt so strong, she cried out to him.

"Jelena, wake up... It's time to meet your daughter."

Jelena raised her head and found herself tucked into bed. "I must have fallen asleep," she murmured. She struggled to sit up and Eikko came forward to adjust the pillows. Some time between the birth and now, she had been washed and dressed in a clean shift. A wad of absorbent padding had been tucked between her legs to catch the last of the birth fluids.

She felt weary to her bones, but the sight of the doctor, standing beside the bed, holding a blanket-wrapped bundle, caused all weariness to vanish in a flash. Eagerly, she held out her arms.

At the first sight of her child's face, Jelena gave in to tears. She could already see Hatora had inherited all of her father's beauty.

Oh, Ashi, I wish that you could see our daughter and hold her in your arms!

"It's time to give your daughter her first feeding, Princess," the doctor said. "Here, let me help you." She pulled open the loose neck of Jelena's shift. "Just lay her head against your breast...Very good...That's it...let her take the nipple..."

Jelena marveled at the strength a healthy suckling newborn could exert on a breast. The sensation felt a little uncomfortable at first, but as she got used to it, a contented pleasure settled over her.

"Where is she? Where is my granddaughter!"

Sen's booming voice preceded his arrival at the bedchamber door.

"Sen, she's my granddaughter, too, you know!"

Jelena smiled at her father's exasperated reply.

"Your Majesty, Lord Sakehera, please come in," the doctor called out.

Keizo swept through the door, Sen hard on his heels. Eikko and Sateyuka immediately dropped into low bows. Sonoe remained sitting at Jelena's side, one hand stroking the new mother's hair. Amara stood and beckoned with a wave of her hand.

"Come and see your granddaughter, the two of you!" she said. As both men approached the bed, the blast of male energy rolling before them made Jelena dizzy. Keizo bent down and kissed his daughter's forehead.

"Well done, my girl. Well done." He gazed proudly at the nursing baby. "She's an Onjara, no doubt about it. Just look her!"

"Hah!" Sen exclaimed. "She looks like a Sakehera, my *old* friend!"

"Both of you are arrogant fools; Hatora is barely out of her mother's belly! She doesn't look like much of anything, except a wrinkled little plum," Amara scolded.

"The birth went well, your Majesty," the doctor said.

"How are you feeling, Jelena my dear?" Sen asked, his face alight with joy.

"Tired, but happy," Jelena answered. "I think Hatora's going to look more like Ashi than me. At least I hope so."

Sen blinked back tears. "Finding you was my son's greatest fortune."

"Two new grandchildren in the space of a month!" the king exclaimed. Misune had given birth to her son just four weeks previously. "You must be bursting with pride, eh, Sen?"

"Oh, yes," Sen replied. "'Course, my son Sadaiyo has been preening like a damn peacock! He has every right, though, 'cause my grandson is perfect!"

"Enough, you men. Jelena needs her rest!" Amara chided. "You can come back later."

Keizo laid a hand on his friend's shoulder. "Come along, old friend. I believe we've been dismissed. We'll go back to my apartments and drink a toast."

With much congratulatory back-slapping, Sen and the king departed.

"Hmmph...You'd think they were the ones who'd birthed this baby!" Amara sniffed, but her eyes brimmed with affection.

"Well, that's it for now. I'll be on my way as well." The doctor bustled around, collecting her things. "Lady Amara, please make sure the princess takes a draught from this bottle later tonight. It's a combination tonic and cleanser. It will help her to eliminate any residue left over from the birth." The doctor handed Amara a small glass vial. "Mix ten drops in a half-glass of sweet wine and a little water." She turned to Eikko. "Change your mistress' padding just before you go to bed, then again four hours later. I'll be round first thing tomorrow morning to check on mother and child."

"I'll see to it," Sonoe volunteered.

Amara nodded and handed her the vial. "You'll stay the night with her, Sonoe?"

"Yes, of course," Sonoe replied. "You go on to bed, if you wish."

"It has been a long day," Amara said. "I still have to see to my other daughters, though, before I can rest." She bent over to kiss Jelena's cheek. "Sleep well, dear. Come, Doctor. I will see you out."

After Amara and the doctor had left, Jelena relaxed back into the pillows and allowed Sonoe to place the now satiated and sleeping baby in the intricately carved wooden cradle by the bedside. The cradle had been a gift from Prince Raidan, and had come as a complete surprise. Jelena never expected anything from her aloof uncle, and his gesture had raised her hopes that someday, she might have a warmer relationship with him.

"Jelena," Sateyuka called out softly. Jelena opened her eyes with a start, realizing she must have dozed off again.

"Oh, Sateyuka! I'm sorry! I know it's late. You're welcome to stay the night, of course."

"Thank you, my dear."

"Everyone must be famished," Jelena murmured. The sudden hunger pangs roiling her stomach surprised her.

"I'll send down to the kitchen for some food," Eikko said and bustled from the room.

"I'll sleep in here with you and the baby tonight, Jelena," Sonoe said. "The weaver can sleep in the sitting room."

Jelena knew she should be annoyed at Sonoe's high-handedness, but she was just too tired. "I want both my best friends with me tonight, Sonoe. Sateyuka can stay in my bedchamber."

"Jelena, I don't wish to cause any inconvenience..." Sateyuka protested, but Jelena cut her off.

"It's already settled. Eikko can make you up a pallet by the window." Sonoe's eyes narrowed and her lips tightened, betraying her irritation, but Jelena chose to ignore it.

Sonoe will just have to deal with it!

"I think I'll rest now. Wake me when the food arrives."

"Of course," Sonoe murmured, bending over to kiss her lightly on the cheek.

As Jelena drifted off to sleep, the image of Ashinji once again appeared before her mind's eye. For an instant, he seemed so real, Jelena tried to touch him, but then he vanished, lost to her once again. She dreamt no more of him that night.

31

Duplicity, Concealed

Sonoe waited until everyone else in the room had fallen asleep before she acted. Silently, she slipped from Jelena's bed and moved to neutralize the two hikui. She gazed with contempt at the hikui weaver lying unconscious at her feet. The servant girl, Eikko lay sprawled by the door, also unconscious. Neither hikui knew what had hit them, nor would they remember anything when they awoke.

With a wave of her hand and a quick, whispered incantation, she warded the bedchamber door.

Now, I can work uninterrupted, she thought. Her hand crept up to touch the place where the stone—the power focus linking her consciousness to his—lay hidden beneath her robe. It felt warm, beyond what ordinary body heat would make it, a sure sign that one of his creatures lurked nearby.

I don't have much time until one of his infernal birds shows up...I must get in and out before then.

She prodded the weaver in the ribs with her toe. The woman lay unmoving. Sonoe nodded in satisfaction.

She climbed back into the bed, carefully maneuvering Jelena so the girl's shoulders rested in her lap. She then laid her hands on either side of Jelena's forehead and closed her eyes. With great care, she extended her consciousness down through the layers of Jelena's mind.

Fresh memories of Hatora's birth lingered at the surface. Sonoe flashed by, ignoring them. Deeper in, a memory of Ashinji Sakehera—fresh, and recorded in the part of Jelena's mind that registered visual images—caught her attention.

How very strange, Sonoe thought. *Jelena's husband is dead. She can't have seen him—not recently, anyway. Interesting puzzle, but I've no time to solve it just now.* She plunged deeper, pushing toward the pulsing blue light lodged at the core of Jelena's being.

She stopped short of the cunningly wrought barrier that had so painfully stymied her during her last deep probe of Jelena's mind. This was what she had come to examine.

Delicately, she extended sensory tendrils along the surface of the barrier. It rippled a little, yet appeared unbreakable.

Damn you, Taya!

Sonoe's rival had effectively sealed off the Key from all access.

I must find a way to break through the barrier; otherwise, I can't directly examine the energy signature of the Key itself.

Sonoe's plan to capture the Key for her own use depended on her gaining knowledge of its unique energy pattern.

The Nameless One obviously knows—he crafted it himself, after all. I must learn the pattern as well, and soon. His impatience continues to grow. I won't be able to stall him much longer.

Sonoe hovered above the cool blue star in frustrated rage.

There must be a weakness in the barrier somewhere!

She dared not flail against it for fear of killing Jelena prematurely and releasing the Key.

Think, Sonoe, think! If there is no weakness already, then you must make one yourself. Drill a hole, so to speak...Yes, of course! That's how, but I'll need another practitioner.

Swiftly, she withdrew, a little too fast, for Jelena jerked and stopped breathing for a few moments. Sonoe stabilized her with a touch and returned her consciousness to normal sleep.

She slipped out of the bed again, rearranged Jelena's pillows, and stood a few moments gazing down at the sleeping girl. She then looked at the baby, asleep in her cradle, and for a few heartbeats, tears stung her eyes.

If Keizo could marry me and make me his queen, would it all be enough?

Sonoe took a deep breath and banished the emotion that threatened to weaken her resolve.

No.

The wooden shutters covering the room's only window rattled softly in their frames, followed by a sharp rap. The stone at Sonoe's breast radiated a sudden flash of heat. She moved to the window and threw open the shutters.

A huge, disheveled raven hopped through on a blast of cold, moist air. It croaked and cocked its head to the side, fixing a black eye on the sorceress.

No, not quite all black. A tiny red spark flickered deep within its center.
The bitch has whelped.
Obviously.
And the pup could turn out to be more trouble than its dam.
She's just a baby! How can she possibly be any threat to you?

The raven flapped its wings, then hopped onto the edge of the cradle and bent down over the sleeping child, its razor-sharp beak poised just above the tiny throat.

Sonoe held her breath.

Perhaps I should kill it now.

"Don't!" Sonoe whispered.

The bird fastened its gaze back on her and Sonoe moaned in pain. Even across the vast distance that separated them, even through the filter of another creature's mind, the strength of the Nameless One was daunting. What must he have been like at his peak? She had no wish to find out.

You dare to instruct me?

No! No, of course not, it's just...this child can't harm you in any way.

Not now. But if she is allowed to come into her full Talent, she will make a formidable adversary. She is an Onjara, after all, and therefore my sworn enemy. She will come after me because she will have no choice. It is her destiny.

How can you know that?

The Nameless One's stormwrack voice fell silent in Sonoe's head. She sensed him pondering her words.

I won't kill the child...not yet, anyway. We can use it to insure the compliance of the girl. She will readily sacrifice her life in exchange for its life when the time comes. You will bring both of them to me.

A thread of sound from the hall outside the chamber impinged on Sonoe's consciousness. She jumped up and ran to the bedchamber door, pressing her ear to the smooth wood.

She could just make out the voices of Amara's young daughters engaged in soft conversation. They had come, no doubt, to see the baby, though why the girls had not gone to bed hours ago, Sonoe did not know. She hissed in irritation and whirled to face the raven, still perched on the rim of Hatora's cradle.

Amara's daughters are right outside! You must leave before they make up their minds to come in here. They are certain to see the bird!

The torturous sound of metal scraping against metal bounced around in her head, causing her to wince. Oh, how she hated his laugh!

That would be a difficult one for you to explain, wouldn't it?

Please go!

Why haven't you found the transportation portal yet?

Sendai Castle is a very big place, as well you know!

The door opened a crack.

You must go now!

Find the portal soon, or I'll kill you and choose another to put in your place.

Sonoe did not doubt the threat for an instant.

The raven spread its wings and flapped clumsily across the room and out through the open window. Sonoe followed and leaned out over the sill to make sure the bird had gone before she closed the shutters. She then crossed back over to the door and pulled it open.

Lani stood, fist raised as if to knock, mouth agape in surprise. Her twin sisters crowded at her back, peering around her like pups behind their mother.

"What is it?" Sonoe queried in a clipped tone.

"We...uh...We've come to see the baby," Lani answered, hesitant in the face of Sonoe's impatience. The two little girls nodded in unison.

"Well, Jelena and the baby are asleep, as should the three of you be! Does your mother know you're out roaming the halls so late at night?" Sonoe scowled and waved her hand in dismissal. "I thought not. Now, go away and come back in the morning!"

Lani drew herself up in a display of indignation. "You have no right to speak to me like that!" she said coldly.

Sonoe laughed. Eyes sparkling with equal parts amusement and irritation, she flicked her fingers and all three girls stiffened, then relaxed, blank-eyed.

"Now go back to bed, all of you. When you wake in the morning, you'll have no memory of what just happened." Like automatons, the girls turned around and shuffled off. Sonoe watched them go, then shut the bedroom door behind her.

A quick touch to the temples of the weaver and the maid restored each of them to natural sleep. As Sonoe lay back down beside Jelena, she checked the girl's mind to assure herself that all was well. Despite the lingering disgust and unease she always felt after one of The Nameless One's visits, she still managed to fall asleep.

At sunrise, Sateyuka groaned and stirred. The sound woke Sonoe, who climbed out from beneath the covers and carefully tucked them back around the still-sleeping Jelena. Throwing a robe over her thin nightgown, Sonoe padded over to where the maid Eikko snored loudly on her pallet by the door.

Leaning over the slack-jawed hikui, the mage reached down and shook the girl's shoulder. "Wake up, you silly cow!" she whispered. Eikko snorted and sat up, blinking. "It's morning. Send down to the kitchen for tea," she ordered.

"Umm, the princess usually has her tea at the eighth hour," Eikko mumbled. She scrubbed at her round face with plump fingers.

"I don't care, stupid girl! Get me some tea *now!*" Sonoe demanded. She could feel the girl's sullen anger, but the hikui dared not talk back or disobey. Instead, she climbed gracelessly to her feet and slipped out of the room.

"Where am I?" Sateyuka sat up and looked around her in confusion. Magical mind control sometimes caused short-term memory loss.

"You're in Sendai Castle, of course," Sonoe replied with a touch of condescension in her voice. "In the bedchamber of the princess. You came for the birth, remember?"

The hikui weaver frowned, then a look of relief softened her features. She nodded. "Yes, of course. I remember now. How is Jelena? Did she sleep well last night?"

"She did. Childbirth takes a lot out of a woman, or so I'm told," Sonoe replied. Sateyuka nodded in agreement. She stood and went over to where Jelena's newborn lay in her cradle. From the soft noises emanating from the cradle, Sonoe could tell the baby was awake. Sateyuka bent over the cradle and a look of such tenderness suffused her features that, for a moment, it looked as though she would burst into tears.

"She is so beautiful!" the weaver exclaimed.

"Yes, she is, and despite her impure blood, she'll be able to pass for okui. Very fortunate."

Sonoe felt and saw the flash of anger, quickly veiled, that the weaver let slip by her mask of politeness. She smiled inwardly.

No doubt this hikui believes she and the rest of her kind should have equal status with okui under Alasiri law. Amusing, really. But if Jelena succeeds in influencing the king, he might seriously consider altering the law.

That is not so amusing.

"Sateyuka, I'm so glad you're here."

Jelena had awakened, and now sat up in bed, her eyes riveted on the cradle that held her daughter. Love for the baby flowed from her, sweet and pure, like spring water. Sonoe felt a brief pang of longing, but ruthlessly suppressed it.

Sateyuka smiled. "Your daughter is hungry," she said, scooping up the infant and placing her into Jelena's outstretched arms. Jelena kissed the silky cap of dark hair atop the baby's head and snuggled back against the pillows. Pulling the neck of her shift open, she held Hatora's head to her breast.

"Hatora must know who I am already," Jelena said, her faced flushed with happiness. "Is that possible? She does have Talent, doesn't she? Sonoe, you and my aunt Taya and Mother Amara have all said so, and I did talk to her every day while she was inside me."

"Hatora's Talent is very strong. Of course she knows you," Sonoe replied.

A knock sounded at the door and it swung inward, admitting Eikko. She carried a tray laden with a teapot, cups, a small carafe of wine and a single glass.

"Umm, tea," Jelena sighed. "Is there food yet, Eikko?"

"It will be here soon, Highness." Eikko brushed by Sonoe and placed the tea tray down on a small side table. She wiped her hands on her skirt and, flicking a glance at Sonoe, turned to address Jelena. "Lady Amara sends a message to remind Lady Sonoe to give you your medicine. She'll be here shortly."

"She did not have to remind me!" Sonoe muttered, trying to keep the irritation out of her voice. She picked up the vial of medicine from the bedside table, removed the stopper and carefully counted out ten drops into the wine glass.

She then poured in a splash of wine and filled the rest with water. She handed the glass to Jelena, who took a sip and made a face.

"It's bitter!" she exclaimed in disgust.

"Yes, well, if it tasted good, it wouldn't work!" Sonoe said, laughing. "At least, that's what my mother always said to me."

"I never knew my mother," Jelena sighed. The ghost of an old sadness crept across her humanish features and lingered in her hazel eyes. "I loved Claudia, the woman who raised me, like a mother, but I always felt that a part of me was missing because I never got a chance to know the woman who bore me." She looked down at the suckling baby. "I never want my daughter to feel that pain, that emptiness, but I fear she will because she'll never know her father."

"But you're wrong, Jelena," Sateyuka said. "Hatora will know her father. You'll make sure of it, as will her grandfather Sakehera."

"The weaver is right, Jelena," Sonoe agreed. "You know Lord Sen is already head over heels in love with this baby!"

Jelena smiled. "Yes, he is, isn't he? It's because he misses his son so much. Ashi and he shared a very special bond. It caused a lot of trouble between Ashi and his brother. I just hope..." Jelena's words trailed off into silence.

"You hope what?" Sonoe prompted.

Jelena hesitated a moment, then continued. "I just hope Sadaiyo doesn't view my child as a threat to his son. If my father-in-law shows any favoritism toward Hatora because she's Ashinji's daughter, Sadaiyo might make things very difficult for her."

"How can he, Jelena? Hatora is of royal birth," Sateyuka interjected. "She is totally protected—she's the king's granddaughter. You have no reason to fear your husband's brother, or anyone else for that matter." Sonoe noticed Sateyuka looking at her with a guarded expression. Bitter waves of resentment lapped at Sonoe's mental shields, all directed at her.

Sonoe cared not a whit. "Again, the weaver...Sateyuka, is it?...is correct," she said. "You should listen to your friend, Jelena. She is obviously a very wise woman."

That should sweeten the cranky old cow's mood a bit.

The weaver pulled up a chair and placed it beside the bed, positioned so she sat facing both mother and child. She threw a glance over her shoulder at Sonoe, sharp as a dagger.

So much for flattery, Sonoe thought.

The servant girl Eikko now passed around the tea. As she handed Sonoe her cup, the mage performed a quick surface scan of the girl's mind and mentally nodded in satisfaction. She could find no trace of last night's occurrences in the hikui's memories.

"I think Hatora's had enough," Jelena announced. She covered herself back up and handed off the infant to Sateyuka, who lifted the child to her shoulder and began patting the tiny back. Jelena unsuccessfully tried to stifle a huge yawn. "I'm still so tired," she mumbled. "I think I'll rest my eyes for awhile. Wake me when breakfast comes." Almost before the last word had passed her lips, she had fallen asleep.

The weaver rose from her chair to replace the baby in her cradle, then sat back down, ramrod straight, face impassive, all but openly daring Sonoe to try to make her leave Jelena's side.

Sonoe sighed. "So, Sateyuka. Do you have a family?" she asked, attempting to make conversation.

"Yes," the weaver replied, and snapped her mouth shut as if to prevent the escape of any more words than were strictly necessary. Her eyes refused to move from Jelena's slumbering form.

"I'm not your enemy, weaver," Sonoe said.

"Perhaps not," Sateyuka replied. Her expression became thoughtful as she at last turned to look at Sonoe. "But if it weren't for Jelena, you and I could never sit in the same room together. I stand against all that you believe in."

"I believe okui must lead and hikui must follow," Sonoe replied. "Our blood gives us that right."

"And yet, you treat Jelena as okui."

"That is different and you know it!"

"Oh, is it? Explain to me how this is so!" Sateyuka's eyes flashed in challenge.

Sonoe shook her head. "This argument is pointless. Perhaps it would be wise for me to withdraw for a while. I'll be in the sitting room if Jelena needs me."

Outside the door, Sonoe came face to face with Amara. "I've left the weaver to watch Jelena," Sonoe said. "She's fed the baby already and is asleep again."

Amara nodded, "Good."

Sonoe glanced over her shoulder at the closed bedchamber door, then switched to mindspeech. *I'm worried, Amara. Now that Jelena is a mother, I fear her concern for her child will interfere with our plans.*

I, too, have considered this, but once Jelena knows the full truth, once she knows what's at stake, I'm confident she'll put aside all personal concerns and submit to her fate.

I wish I could be as sure as you are. The love she has for her daughter may be too strong. I fear she'll be unable to willingly leave the baby behind.

We will assure my daughter-in-law that Hatora will be raised in the protective fold of strong families, both my own and the Onjaras... No. She will go bravely.

"I think I'll return to the king's quarters. Jelena won't wake for awhile yet," Sonoe said aloud. "The weaver watches over her like a she-wolf does her cub." Sonoe's expression made clear her distain.

"Something is happening," Amara said softly. "Last night, I had a very disturbing dream."

"Oh?" Sonoe responded carefully.

"I felt the presence of our enemy, as if he were very near. He is growing stronger each day, Sonoe. We must begin preparations for the Sundering. I had hoped to delay it a while longer, but circumstances are forcing our hand. War with the Soldarans will be upon us soon, and I think we must perform the Working before then."

"I agree," Sonoe answered. "Our entire attentions must remain focused on the defense of Alasiri once the Soldarans attack. But aren't you forgetting one very important thing?"

"No, I'm well aware of our lack of a full complement. The only solution I can think of is to recruit practitioners from outside the Society to make up the difference."

"Risky, but perhaps necessary," Sonoe agreed. "I know of several who might serve."

"I'll leave it to you, then," Amara said. She opened the bedroom door and disappeared inside, closing it softly behind her. Sonoe nodded in satisfaction.

Yes, leave everything to me, she thought.

32

A Secret, A Threat, And A Surprise

*A*shinji!

Jelena?

Ashinji looked around in confusion. He felt certain he had just heard Jelena call out to him.

How is that possible?

"You all right?" Seijon poked him in the ribs with the blunt tip of his practice sword.

Ashinji shook his head and refocused on the boy. "Yes, I thought...well, never mind. The combination I just taught you, show it to me again."

He spent another hour with the boy, putting him through several more drills before he called an end to the session.

"You're improving by leaps and bounds, Seijon. I think you'll be ready to move on to live steel before long."

The hikui boy beamed. "I think I'm ready now!" he exclaimed.

Ashinji shook his head. "Not yet! Don't be so eager; it's a big step. Once you start with a real sword, you're going to get cut. That's guaranteed. Think you're ready for real pain?"

Seijon snorted. "I was knife fighting in the street long before I ended up here. I know what it's like to get cut."

Ashinji regarded the boy thoughtfully, remembering what Gran had told him of the young hikui's brutal childhood.

"Go and get cleaned up. It's almost dinnertime," he directed. "Give me your sword." Seijon nodded and handed him the practice blade, then scampered off toward the bath house.

Ashinji lifted his arm, sniffed, and grimaced. He gathered up the pile of assorted practice weapons and went to stow them away before heading for the bath house.

The Soldarans did not share the elves' reverence for cleanliness, but they did wash sometimes, usually after strenuous exercise. The slaves' bath house, a fairly simple affair, consisted of two water pumps set up on concrete pads at either end of a walled-off area of the yard, just behind the barracks. Stone-lined drains carried waste water away, and a canvas awning provided shade during the summer and protection from rain during the rest of the year.

Seijon had already stripped and hung his clothes on a peg driven into the wall. Ashinji noted with mild surprise how well-muscled the boy had become over the past few months.

No wonder his blows are so hard! Perhaps Gran is right, and I won't need to worry over his safety when the time comes for us to try our escape.

Ashinji had yet to tell Seijon of his and Gran's decision to leave. He didn't want to get the boy's hopes up in case they couldn't figure a way out, and the less he knew, the better. It reduced the risk to all of them.

Ashinji pulled off his tunic, breeches and sandals, and hung them next to Seijon's. A chilly breeze skirled around the interior of the bath house, lifting the awning and setting it to thrumming against the ropes holding it in place.

"I think it's going to start raining again," Ashinji commented. He glanced upward at the flapping canvas.

"Yeah," Seijon responded. Water gurgled and splashed from the wide mouth of the pump.

Ashinji undid his braid and raked his fingers through his hair several times. It had grown so long, he had taken to looping his queue around his neck when he fought.

I'll ask Gran to trim it when I see her this evening.

Seijon stepped back so Ashinji could douse himself. He leaned forward and let the cold water sluice over his head and shoulders. His mind skipped back, alighting on the memory of the first time he and Jelena had taken a bath together. The smell of her hair, wet and scented with herbs, the feel of her hot skin against his—he ached all over with longing and the grief of loss. The comforts of the bath house at Kerala Castle were a far cry from the cold water of the de Guera yard.

He stood up, gasping, and pushed his dripping hair away from his face.

"Hey, look who's here! It's the tink and his little doxie."

Seijon reacted as if struck. Trembling, he shrank back and muttered, "Shut up, Leal."

"What's the matter, doxie? Truth hurts? The whole yard knows you let him give it to you in the ass."

Leal strutted into the bath house, his tunic streaked with sweat. A fresh welt twisted like a petulant mouth across the top of his shaven head, testament to his last bout in the arena. He snorted and launched a gobbet of spit that just missed Seijon's face.

"Leave him alone, Leal," Ashinji said quietly, and moved to stand between the man and the boy.

"What are you going to do if I choose not to?"

The awning flapped and boomed overhead. The first patter of rain sprayed the canvas.

Leal closed in, stinking of sweat and violence.

Ashinji stood his ground, unflinching. Even naked, he had no fear of this man, for he knew all his weaknesses. He felt confident he could beat him in hand to hand combat, if it came down to that.

"I've no wish to fight you, Leal. Don't we fight and risk our lives enough in the arena?" Ashinji kept his eyes locked onto the human's, which glittered in the half-light like a feral dog's.

Leal snarled, revealing a mouth full of crooked teeth. "You think you're better'n us mere humans, don't cha? Well, I c'n kill you any time I want, tink."

Ashinji did a quick surface scan of Leal's thoughts. The big human's primitive rage roiled through his mind like molten rock, but a single image leapt out without warning.

At the same instant, Seijon cried in fear, "Ashi, he's got a knife!"

Reflex, honed by years of combat training, saved his life. Ashinji threw himself down and to the left, narrowly avoiding the arc of Leal's vicious thrust.

Quick as a cat, Ashinji sprang back, pushing Seijon roughly aside. The boy screamed something, but Ashinji ignored him, all of his attention focused on his opponent.

Leal rushed forward, bellowing like an enraged bull, knife raised. Ashinji met his charge and grabbed the arm holding the knife. As the human's momentum carried him past, Ashinji ducked beneath Leal's shoulder and threw his weight toward the ground.

Leal went down, an inarticulate cry bubbling from his lips as Ashinji, still holding the other man's arm, twisted it hard up and back.

"Drop it!" Ashinji growled, planting his foot on Leal's neck. When the human did not immediately comply, Ashinji forced his arm upward until the man shrieked in pain and the knife dropped from his twitching fingers.

"Let me up!" Leal gasped. "You'll dislocate my shoulder!"

"Give me one good reason I shouldn't do precisely that, you pathetic, cowardly ape!" Ashinji's heart pounded his ribs like a sledgehammer.

Leal fell silent, lying passively on the muddy concrete.

"Ashi, if you hurt him, the mistress'll punish you!" Seijon gasped through chattering teeth.

"I'm aware of that," Ashinji shot back. He continued to maintain the pressure on Leal's arm and shoulder. "When I let you up, you'd better leave, Leal." The man nodded mutely. Ashinji released the pressure and sprang back, kicking the knife against the wall. Seijon scuttled over and scooped the blade into his hand.

Slowly, like a bear rousing itself from sleep, Leal climbed to his feet. He turned to face Ashinji and Seijon, who stood back, tensely watching him. For a few moments, time froze as the three of them regarded each other.

As Leal stared hard at him, Ashinji saw the promise of his death in the other man's eyes.

A flash lit the sky and the rumble of thunder broke the spell.

Without another word, Leal turned and stalked out of the bath house into the rain. Ashinji relaxed and let out his breath in a whoosh. He turned to face Seijon, who stared after Leal with a look so full of hatred, it took Ashinji aback.

"I wish you could have killed him, Ashi. I'd kill him, if I was strong enough!" The bitterness in the boy's voice caused suspicion to grow within Ashinji's mind.

He has been strangely subdued these last few weeks...not like himself at all.

"Seijon, has Leal hurt you in the past?" Ashinji kept his voice soft and gentle.

Seijon reached for his clothes and began to dress. He refused to meet Ashinji's gaze as he answered, "Yeah, when I first came to the yard."

Ashinji donned his own clothing before turning to Seijon once again. "You can tell me about it. It might help. You should know I'm your friend and would never judge you."

The boy swallowed hard. His face flushed and his eyes filled with tears.

"I've never told anyone. Not even Gran," he whispered. Ashinji reached out and slipped his arm around Seijon's shoulder.

"No one ever did anything like that to me before, even when I lived on the street. I was lucky, I guess." The soft patter of spring rain filled the spaces between Seijon's words. "My first night here, Leal caught me as I walked back to the barracks in the dark. He dragged me behind the weapons shed...and he...he..." The boy hiccupped and his shoulders began to shake.

"It's all right, you don't have to say any more, Seijon. I understand," Ashinji murmured.

"No, you don't!" Seijon cried as he broke away to face Ashinji. "It happened more than once! It's still happening!"

"Goddess' tits," Ashinji whispered, horrified. It all made sense now.

Seijon nodded. "Leal makes me...He says if I don't, he'll kill you and Gran! I couldn't let him do that, Ashi!"

Ashinji took the boy in his arms and cradled him until the torrent of tears had subsided. He then held Seijon out at arm's length and stared directly into the boy's golden eyes.

"Seijon, you must never, ever believe that by your suffering, you are protecting me, or Gran. We can protect ourselves, far better than you know. This outrage stops now!"

"What are you going to do, Ashi?" Seijon asked, his voice trembling.

Ashinji considered finding Leal and killing him on the spot, but he rejected that idea.

No, I'll do this the right way.

"The two of us are going to Aruk-cho and you're going to tell him exactly what you told me. He will deal with Leal, of that you can be sure."

Seijon bit his lower lip, looking so child-like, it reminded Ashinji of just how young the boy really was.

"Come on, then. Let's go and find Aruk-cho."

With his arm still around Seijon's shoulder, Ashinji guided the boy out into the rain.

* * *

A day after Seijon had related his story of abuse to Aruk-cho, the yard-master had Leal thrown into the small, windowless cell located beneath the storerooms known as "the hole." There he stayed for an entire week, fed only on thin gruel and water. When he emerged, sullen and withdrawn, he made a conspicuous effort to avoid all contact with both Seijon and Ashinji. The rumor flying around the yard had him stripped of all his points accumulated so far that year.

Seijon's personality changed almost immediately. The cheerful boy Ashinji had met on his first day at the yard had re-emerged. By removing the terrible burden of his abuse, Ashinji had freed his soul.

Two weeks after the incident in the bath house, Gran came to Ashinji with exciting news.

"He's coming back! Tilo's coming back to the yard, maybe as soon as tomorrow!"

Ashinji, who had been diligently applying needle and thread to a rip in his tunic, paused to look up at Gran's flushed face.

"The Eskleipan brothers just left awhile ago. They said Tilo's been overseeing their temple clinic. Anyhow, he's back on rotation for the yards. When he comes, he'll want to see me. We'll both meet with him then."

"How risky is this going to be, Gran?" Ashinji asked. He held up the shirt to inspect his repair.

"Everyone in the yard knows Tilo and I are friends. It won't be risky at all, least not at first. Later on, when we need to discuss an actual plan, well..."

Ashinji sighed. "We have no choice, really. Don't forget the dream I had about my wife and Sonoe."

Gran nodded. "Time is wasting," she said.

"Not to mention, as soon as the rains let up, the Imperial Army will march north and Alasiri will be under attack," Ashinji added. He stared out across the yard at several of the female slaves engaged in a group sparring match. The clang of steel ringing against steel floated on the damp air.

I wonder if Jelena has given birth to our child yet... I might have a son now... or a daughter.

"What's your schedule tomorrow?" Gran asked.

"I'm fighting two points matches during the afternoon session."

"Good. Tilo should arrive after midday. When he finishes his rounds, we'll have plenty of time to talk."

"I hope you're right about this Tilo, Gran."

"I know I'm right."

* * *

Ashinji trudged from the Arena, the cheers of the crowd roaring in his ears. He unbuckled his helmet and pulled it off, teeth gritted in pain. Gingerly, he examined a long cut on his left forearm. It oozed blood, messy but not too deep.

His injury would make a good excuse to meet with Gran's human friend Tilo.

After his return to the yard, he washed the sweat, dirt, and blood from his body and sought out Gran. He found her in the infirmary. She stood next to a cot occupied by a slave who'd taken an injury during practice, talking to a tall, dark-haired human dressed in the brown robe of the Eskleipan Brothers. The man stood with his back to the door, so Ashinji could not see his face as he entered, but something about him seemed familiar.

Gran spotted him and beckoned with her hand. "Come in, come in. Tilo, here is the young man I want you to meet," she said in Soldaran.

So, this is Tilo.

Ashinji approached, raising his injured arm. "Perhaps you can give me something for my cut," he said.

The healer turned, mouth open as if to speak, but instead, he simply stared.

Ashinji stopped in his tracks, astonishment striking him mute as well.

"What's wrong?" Gran asked quizzically.

Ashinji had never expected to see this man again, especially not here, in this place.

He found his voice at last.

"Ai, Goddess...Magnes Preseren...it's you!"

33

Blood Feud

"Gods! Ashinji! I...I can't believe it!"

Magnes stepped forward and grabbed Ashinji by the shoulders, then pulled him into a warm embrace.

"You two know each other?" Gran exclaimed.

"Ashinji and I are family," Magnes answered.

"Magnes is my wife Jelena's cousin," Ashinji explained.

"Did I hear you right? Ashinji...you and Jelena are married?"

"Yes, you heard right, Magnes my friend. We are kinsmen in more ways than one now."

Magnes whooped and swept Ashinji into another bear hug. "When I left Kerala, I figured you two were heading in that direction." He paused, holding Ashinji at arm's length, then added, "Did my cousin ever find her father?"

"She did, my friend, and neither of us ever could have imagined who he turned out to be. Jelena is the daughter of Keizo Onjara."

"The...the elf king?" Magnes' eyes grew wide with astonishment. "My little cousin...*a princess!* Gods!"

Ashinji nodded, smiling.

The two young men embraced again, then turned to face Gran, their arms draped over each other's shoulder.

"So...Tilo is not your real name, then...Magnes?" Gran, who had been silently watching their reunion, now frowned in confusion.

Magnes nodded. "Yes, that's right, Gran. I left my old name behind for reasons...well, let's just say I need to remain Tilo for now." His face grew serious. "What in the world are you doing here, Ashinji?"

"I could ask the same of you. My story is a long, painful one, and I'm guessing yours is, too."

Magnes nodded. "How long have you been in the de Guera yard? Surely you're not a..." He let the word die on his lips.

"Yes, I'm afraid it's true. I am a slave. I was captured in a skirmish on the Kerala-Amsara border last fall, and I've been here ever since."

The man on the cot moaned softly and Gran cleared her throat. "Perhaps we should speak outside," she suggested.

Magnes checked the injured man one more time, then the three of them left the infirmary and made their way to the women's barracks, deserted at this time of day. Gran fetched three stools for them to sit on.

"Your sister Thessalina commanded the Soldaran force," Ashinji continued after they'd settled themselves in the shade of the barracks porch. "I learned from her that you had gone missing."

"Gods, Ashinji... I can't believe my sister had a hand in sending you here!" Magnes shook his head in dismay.

"There's much more to the story, my friend. To be fair to your sister, she could have ordered me killed, but she didn't. Instead, she had my wounds treated and made sure her troops didn't abuse me...physically, at least." The memory of Magnes' dark-eyed sister, and her strange reaction to him flashed across his mind's eye. "I think she believed she was doing the only thing she could to help me survive."

Magnes snorted. "By selling you into slavery?"

"I've been a gladiator for half a year now, and I am still alive."

"That's because you're a damn good fighter, and you have your Talent, even though you refuse to use most of what you have," Gran interjected. "I wish you'd show more interest in your magical abilities!"

"You said there was more to the story, Ashinji. How much more?" Magnes inquired.

Ashinji pondered a moment, then decided he had no good reason not to tell Magnes the entire truth.

When he had finished, Magnes reached out and laid a hand on his shoulder.

"I am so very sorry, my friend. To be betrayed like that by your own brother.... My sister and I have never been especially close, but I would trust her with my life."

"You are the first person I've told about my brother's part in this, Magnes," Ashinji said. "In truth, it's just been too painful to talk about... even to you, Gran."

Gran sighed and patted Ashinji's hand. "I've known all along, my son. I saw the memory when I first scanned you," she admitted. "I kept the knowledge to myself, knowing how much it hurt you to think of it. I knew when you were ready, you'd tell me."

Ashinji rubbed his smarting eyes. "The hardest part for me is knowing what the news of my death must have done to Jelena."

A stray wisp of cloud drifted over the sun's face, plunging the yard into cool shadow, perfectly mirroring Ashinji's darkened mood.

"I can only imagine what kind of story my brother concocted," he continued. "No doubt a tale full of his own brave attempts to rescue me." Ashinji's throat tightened in the old, familiar rage. "Though, how he can hide the truth from my mother..."

Magnes leaned forward, his brown eyes soft with sympathy. "Aren't we a fine pair?" he said. "The God of Misfortune must have seen us together and decided we were both worthy of his gentle ministrations."

"I've told you my sad tale, now it's your turn," Ashinji prompted.

The story of how Magnes' father cruelly separated him from the girl he loved caused Ashinji's heart to ache for his friend. Both he and Gran listened intently as Magnes spoke in a voice barely above a whisper.

"When my father told me how he'd arranged for Livie to marry another man, I just...I just lost all reason," he said. "I don't remember exactly how it happened, but when I came back to myself, I saw my father lying on the floor...dead. He had fallen and had hit his head on the edge of the fireplace mantle." Magnes swallowed hard and fell silent.

No one spoke for several heartbeats. Finally, Ashinji asked, "Are you certain your father is dead, Magnes? Maybe he had just fallen senseless from his head injury."

"I'm quite certain. No one, not even a man as strong as my father, could have survived such a wound."

"It was an accident. No one would have doubted you."

"I was afraid, Ashinji. I lost all sense, and when that happens, a man is liable to do anything. I chose to run. Not a day goes by that I don't regret my impulsive decision, but it's too late now. Accident or no, I'm still responsible for my father's death."

Gran patted Magnes on the knee. "You're a good, kind man, Tilo. I've watched you, seen how well you handle the sick and injured. I say you've done enough penance. You should think about going home."

"I can't, Gran. There's nothing left for me there. Besides," he paused for a moment, then said, "I quite like my life here. I've managed to find some peace... a little contentment. It suits me more than the life I was born to assume."

"I agree with Gran, Magnes. When I told your sister we knew each other, she reacted to your name not with hostility, but rather with sadness and confusion. I didn't understand at the time, but now I do. She only wants to know what became of you."

"No. I appreciate what you're saying, but no. Thessalina will be able to petition the empress to grant her the title of Duchess in another year. She will make a far better leader than I ever would. She has already proven that. I want her to have control of Amsara."

"You could always step aside. Why not release your sister from her grief?" Gran said.

Magnes shook his head, mouth set in a hard line. Ashinji sensed that he felt in no mood to be pushed any further.

Instead, Ashinji changed the subject. "Well, you may not want to go home, but I do." He pointed to Gran and then to himself. "In fact, we both must return to Alasiri, and soon."

"Of course. You have a wife and child waiting for you," Magnes replied. "But how will you do it? You're slaves in enemy hands. You're elves in a country of humans, which makes it impossible for you to fade into the general population should you manage to get out of this yard. And if you're caught, it might well mean your deaths."

"We know that," Gran said. "That's why we need all the help we can get. An accomplice on the inside, and one on the outside."

"We understand the risk you'd be taking, and neither of us would blame you for refusing, but you are the only human in all of Darguinia we can trust." Ashinji studied his friend's face and saw no hesitation.

"I'll do whatever it takes," Magnes said. "You saved my dear cousin's life. You gave her love and happiness, two things she desperately needed, and for that I will be forever grateful."

"Thank you, my friend," Ashinji said. The two young men clasped hands.

The brassy voice of a gong signaling the turn of the hour shattered the late afternoon stillness. Combatants who had participated in the day's final matches would return from the arena soon, be they alive and unhurt, wounded, or dead. The wounded would require Magnes' services, and if he had many injuries to tend, he would stay into the night, taking his evening meal in the barracks.

The three of them stood up, Gran massaging the small of her back as if it pained her.

"We'll discuss this further when I come back in a few days. In the meantime, I'll try to come up with some ideas on how we might do this," Magnes promised. "You mentioned needing an inside accomplice. Do you have someone in mind?"

A gust of wind, full of the scent of rain, blew across the yard and ruffled Magnes' dark curls. Overhead, gray clouds piled up, further dimming the light of the dying sun.

A large black shape moved toward them from the end of the yard where Mistress de Guera's home stood.

"We do," Ashinji replied. "And here he comes."

* * *

"Good evening, Aruk-cho," Magnes called out.

The akuta swung to a stop, tail swishing. He folded his heavily muscled arms across his chest and inclined his head in greeting. "I am glad you are still here, Brother Tilo," he said. "The mistress is having one of her sick headaches and needs more of your special remedy. She has run out."

"I'll bring it to her straightaway," Magnes replied. He turned to Ashinji and Gran. "I'll see you both later." He hurried after Aruk-cho, who had already started back toward the house.

"You never did have Tilo tend to your arm," Gran commented.

"Huh, so I didn't," Ashinji acknowledged. "Truthfully, I was so astonished to see him that I forgot all about it." He looked down at the long cut on his forearm, which began to throb with pain, despite having been totally quiescent for the past hour.

Ashinji sucked in his breath. "Ai, Goddess, that hurts."

"I have some salve in my kit. Wait here." Gran disappeared inside the women's barracks.

A few of the female slaves drifted past, on their way to the bath house. One of them, a tall redhead, flashed a brief, come hither smile as she sashayed by. Ashinji acknowledged her with a small wave. Her name was Leeta, and ever since she had arrived some three months back, she had been conducting a relentless campaign to seduce him.

It had been a very long winter in many ways. Ashinji had never been the sexual adventurer that Sadaiyo had been, but he always had access to willing partners when he wanted one. He and Jelena had been blessed with compatibility in the marriage bed, as well as out of it. This was, by far, the longest time in his life that he had gone without—made especially difficult when a female, even a human one, made it abundantly clear she desired him.

Leeta abruptly changed course and strolled to where Ashinji stood waiting for Gran to return. He steeled himself for the inevitable pass.

"Ashi," Leeta purred as she stepped in close and draped her arms around his neck. She smelled of sweat, leather, and the unique scent of human female.

"Leeta," he groaned, attempting to avoid her questing mouth and only partly succeeding. He wrapped his fingers around her forearms and tried to pry them loose.

Goddess, she's strong...and attractive...and I'm not made of stone!

He sighed and gave up.

Leeta's smile flashed full of mischief and lust. "Come help me get all my parts clean," she murmured. "I know how much you like clean." She pressed her pelvis hard against his.

If Leeta shared the common prejudices against his people with the majority of Soldarans, she never let on.

"As inviting as that sounds, you know I can't," Ashinji replied. Against his will, his body began to respond to hers.

Leeta rolled her blue eyes skyward. "Ashi, that little wife of yours is never going to know!"

"I'll know."

Leeta glared at him for a few heartbeats, then dropped her arms and stepped back. A few fat raindrops speckled the sand at their feet and splashed the tops of their heads.

"Better get to the bath house before it starts," Ashinji advised, pointing at the lowering sky.

Leeta sniffed and tossed her head. "You may not be human, but you're still a man, and no other woman in this yard has the guts to approach you, 'cept me. You know it's only a matter of time." She turned on her heel and strode off just as Gran returned.

"That one is determined to have you," she commented dryly.

"Well, she won't succeed," Ashinji grumbled as he tried to hide the evidence of Leeta's effect on him, but by Gran's wry expression, he could tell she was well aware of his...discomfort.

"Don't be embarrassed, Son," Gran reassured him. "You've been apart from the woman you love for many months now. The pressure inside you must be almost unbearable. It's a wonder you haven't exploded!" She chuckled. "It's so much harder for men."

"It is hard...Goddess, you have no idea!" Ashinji sighed.

"Let's go inside out of the rain and I'll fix your arm."

It took only a few moments for Gran to salve and wrap Ashinji's wound.

"I need to go and get a few of the practice swords out of the weapons shed so I can repair them after dinner," Ashinji said. He flexed his arm muscle to test the tightness of the bandage and found it to be comfortable enough.

"Tilo...I mean Magnes, should be just about done with the mistress," Gran replied as she tidied and replaced her supplies. "I'll go meet him at the house and we'll catch up with you at the dining hall."

Ashinji stepped outside and lowered his head against the downpour. He sprinted across the yard and slid to a stop beneath the shelter of the overhang that jutted out from the weapons shed roof. He pushed the door open and entered.

The shed held practice weapons only. The live steel always remained securely locked up when not in use, and only Mistress de Guera and Arukcho had direct access. Ashinji crossed to the far side of the small room where a number of blunted swords hung in racks against the wall. He removed one with a chipped blade and two with loose quillons and hoisted them all up on his shoulder.

His Talent saved him from immediate death...

...or perhaps it was his keen hearing, so much better than any human's. The sound of an exhalation, light as a feather, touched his ear.

A shiver of dread rippled down his spine. He *knew* he needed to dodge *now!*

The first blow caught him just below the right armpit, slicing across his ribcage and laying open skin and muscle in a long, gory tear.

Ashinji threw himself backward and to the side in a desperate attempt to avoid the killing stroke he knew would follow. His attacker's face remained hidden in shadow, but the malignant energy that emanated from the man like a poisonous fog proclaimed his identity.

No longer a matter of insults and petty harassment, Ashinji knew only one of them would walk away from this battle alive.

Ashinji aimed a swift kick at Leal's midsection. With a sharp grunt of surprise, the human doubled over, clutching his abdomen. Ashinji scrambled to his feet, teeth gritted against the pain, and made a dash for the door, but Leal recovered too quickly and blocked his escape.

In the open, where quickness and agility gave him the edge, Ashinji could beat Leal in hand to hand combat, despite the human's superior size and strength. In the cramped space of the weapons shed, he lost all advantage.

With a roar, Leal hurled himself forward, bearing Ashinji down to the ground in a fierce crash of falling weaponry. Ashinji struggled hard to twist free, but Leal held him fast, face down.

"I've got you now, *tink!*" the big man snarled, his breath hot and foul across the side of Ashinji's face. "Did you think I'd let it go, you gettin' me busted? Damn you! I lost a whole *year's* standing 'cuz of you! You an' that punk kid!"

Ashinji felt light-headed from pain and Leal's crushing weight atop his back, restricting his breathing.

"Let me up now, and I won't kill you later, human," he gasped. He knew his words would do no good, but anger and fear made him reckless.

"Fuck...you!" Leal muttered and plunged his knife deep into Ashinji's lower back.

A shockwave of agony rolled through Ashinji's body, convulsing him and cutting the lines mooring his consciousness to his flesh.

His spirit floated free and drifted upward until it came to rest on the ceiling of the weapons shed. From his new vantage point, Ashinji watched with calm interest what happened next.

Voices, raised in alarm, drifted through the open shed door. Leal heaved himself off Ashinji's limp form and spun around, knife dripping blood, clearly searching for a place to hide. He flung the blade from him and it skittered into a corner, sliding beneath a pile of broken harness. He glanced down at Ashinji's body, as if satisfying himself he'd made the kill, then bolted from the shed.

Ashinji knew he hovered near death, as close as he had ever come. Even when he had lain sick with fever from the arrow wound in his shoulder back in Thessalina's war camp—an entire lifetime ago, it seemed—his spirit had never left his body the way it had now.

This is a peculiar feeling, he thought, as he watched his blood pool around his sprawled body. He heard a voice screaming his name.

Seijon reached him first. The boy fell to his knees, crying hysterically. Next came Magnes. The look of horror on his friend's face shook him. The drumbeat of hooves upon the sand heralded the arrival of Aruk-cho. The akuta pushed his way in, forcing both Magnes and Seijon to scramble back to avoid getting trampled. Without a word, the yardmaster leaned down and scooped Ashinji's body into his arms and backed out of the confines of the shed.

"Take him to the infirmary!" Magnes shouted.

"Wait!" Gran cried out, rushing up and laying a hand on his forehead. She closed her eyes.

He felt like a giant hand had reached out to seize him, and now yanked him back toward the cold, bloodstained bag of flesh his body had become. He resisted at first, not wishing to be thrust back where there would be so much pain, but the memory of Jelena's gentle kisses persuaded him.

He slammed back into his body and awoke, screaming.

34

Race Against Death

Ashinji wailed, then lapsed into semi-consciousness. Gran staggered back, her face the color of milk.

"Quickly now, Aruk-cho! We've got no time to waste!" Magnes shouted. "Seijon, run and fetch Mistress de Guera!"

He raced off, the akuta trotting along at his side, Gran trailing a few steps behind. When they reached the infirmary, Aruk-cho gently laid Ashinji face down on a padded table at the back of the room. Wielding a small, sharp knife, Magnes carefully cut away Ashinji's tunic to reveal two stab wounds—one a long, shallow cut across his ribcage, and another wound in his lower back. The second injury was by far the more serious—a deep, ragged hole that oozed blood in sluggish gouts.

"I need something...a cloth or rag, to put pressure on this!" Magnes called out.

"Take this, healer." Aruk-cho thrust a wadded piece of linen into his outstretched hand, which he then pressed over the wound. Ashinji flinched and groaned. His eyes fluttered open and, for a few heartbeats, he gazed directly at Magnes, as if begging for release. Then, with a sigh, his lids drooped and he fell into a swoon.

Gods...Ashi!

A rush of powerful emotion—confusing, unsettling feelings he'd thought conquered and safely buried—surged through Magnes then, taking him completely by surprise. The sight of his friend's beautiful green eyes awash in tears of suffering filled him with agony of an entirely different kind.

Ashi! You can't die... I don't know what I'd do!

"He's in here, Mistress!"

Magnes looked up to see Seijon rushing into the infirmary, followed closely by Mistress de Guera. She pushed past Aruk-cho to gaze down at Ashinji lying on the table. "How bad is he?" she asked, her voice clipped and business-like, but her eyes betrayed her genuine feelings.

"Very bad, Mistress," Magnes replied. Wrestling his own fear into temporary submission, he added, "He's sustained a deep stab wound. I'm trying to slow the bleeding so I can assess what needs to be done to repair it."

"Gods," Mistress de Guera whispered. She turned to Aruk-cho. "I want the man who did this. Find him!" she snapped.

"I know who hurt Ashi," Seijon spoke up, his face puffy and red from crying.

"Who did this, boy?" Aruk-cho rumbled.

"That asshole Leal! I saw him attack Ashi. I ran to get help, but I was too late!" His face crumpled and he began sobbing once more.

Magnes caught the look that passed between Aruk-cho and his mistress.

"I'll return as soon as I can," the akuta promised, then he and Mistress de Guera departed. Magnes turned his attention back to the problem at hand.

How will I save the life of my friend?

"Gran, I know you have abilities...Talent, as your people call it...that are especially powerful," Magnes said. "You used it just now to bring Ashinji back from the dead, didn't you?"

Gran had never looked truly old to him until now. "No. I didn't bring Ashi back from the dead," she replied. "Not even I am that powerful!" She shook her head. "His spirit had floated free of his body, yes, but the cord that binds the spirit to flesh had not yet broken. All I did was pull his spirit back into his body."

Gran held out another wad of linen to replace the blood-soaked one Magnes had pressed to Ashinji's wound. He applied the fresh compress and tossed the used one to the floor.

Thank the gods the bleeding seems to be slowing!

After maintaining the pressure for a while longer, Magnes peeled back the compress and closely examined the two wounds. A plan formulated itself in his mind.

I'll stitch up the shallow cut completely, but the deep wound will need to drain. I'll close only the top part and leave a small opening at the bottom for fluids to escape.

"I need Fadili, my assistant," Magnes said, looking across the room at Seijon, who sat by the door, sniffling and wiping his eyes. The boy scrambled to his feet, nodded, and darted from the room.

Gran laid her hand on Ashinji's forehead, inhaled sharply, and shot Magnes a grim look. "He is very close to death, Tilo. Almost too close to pull back. I can hold him in his body, but I don't know for how long."

Magnes gazed into the face of his friend. Pale and still, it looked more like a death mask than the face of a living man, yet it had lost none of its beauty. A bright smear of blood stained Ashinji's cheek, standing out in sharp contrast like a rose on marble. Magnes' heart twisted painfully in his chest as he once again fought to master his strange and unruly emotions. He leaned over and whispered in Ashinji's ear.

"Ashi, if you can hear me, listen carefully. I won't let you die. I'm going to sew you up and then you will live. Jelena and your child need you. Focus on them!"

"He can hear you," Gran said. "Your words are helping!"

"I am here, Brother!" Fadili rushed into the infirmary, carrying the satchel Magnes used to transport all his equipment and medicines.

Seijon flew in a heartbeat later, hard on Fadili's heels. "Aruk-cho found Leal hiding in the *latrines!*" the boy gasped, breathless from running. "He tried to lie... said he didn't do anything, but there was blood all over his clothes. Aruk-cho threw him in the hole." He looked at Magnes, eyes pleading.

Magnes didn't have the heart to tell the boy, who so obviously loved Ashinji, that death could still claim their friend, despite all of Magnes' skills as a healer. Magnes himself didn't want to face that grim reality, but he had no choice.

Fadili and Magnes had worked together for many months now, and the young Eskleipan apprentice knew exactly what Magnes would need for any given task. Quickly, they fell into the rhythm of experienced partners.

While Magnes laid out all of the tools he would need, Fadili filled a copper basin with water and set it in the fireplace to heat. Next, he and Magnes stripped the remnants of their patient's blood-soaked tunic away. Gran remained at Ashinji's head, perched on a stool, her hands resting on his hair. She sat with eyes shut, unmoving, as if in a trance.

Fadili went to the hearth and fetched the basin of warmed water. Using clean strips of linen, he washed away most of the sticky gore clinging to Ashinji's skin. Magnes then studied the ragged margins of both wounds. The deep gash still oozed fresh blood, but far more slowly than before.

Got to close the big one first, he thought. Fadili had rinsed the basin and refilled it, then returned it to the fire to heat up once more. He now stood at Magnes' elbow, a small stoneware jar in one hand and another water-filled copper basin in the other.

The Eskleipans were considered medical eccentrics by the major Soldaran healing orders, snickered at by some, scorned outright as danger-ous rogues by others. During his time with them, Magnes had discovered that they practiced medicine more like what he had seen in Kerala among the elves. They revered cleanliness in all things; Magnes had learned that lesson very quickly under the demanding tutelage of Brother Wambo.

He held out his hands and Fadili poured a dollop of sharp-smelling liq-uid soap into his palms. The Eskleipans always washed with this special soap before performing any procedure. Leke Ndomo himself had formulated it many years ago; lately, Magnes had further refined the recipe. The simple act of hand washing saved many a life that would have otherwise been lost to wound rot. Why this was so, no one had yet figured out, but it worked.

After a thorough rubbing, Magnes rinsed the soap from his hands and dried them on a clean towel. Next, Fadili did a second washing around Ashinji's wounds with the medicinal soap, then rinsed the entire area clean with fresh water.

"Now, we're ready to begin," Magnes said. Fadili nodded in silent reply.

Magnes hadn't started out performing surgery. His interest lay in me-dicinal herbology, but spending a day observing the order's chirurgeon, Brother Jouma, at work, had sparked an interest in broadening his stud-ies. Now, he and Fadili performed all of the surgeries at the yards where the order held contracts.

Magnes had seen and treated many wounds during his time at the yards, both minor and horrific, but his stomach had yet to rebel and his hands had always remained steady. This time, though, proved different.

This man is my friend...my kinsman...

And...I...

No. I can't feel that. Mustn't let that out.

He drew in a deep breath to steady himself, and swallowed the bile burning the back of his throat.

Concentrate on the task. Only the wound matters.

Throughout the initial prep, Ashinji had remained motionless, but as Magnes probed the major wound, he began to stir.

"Gran, keep him still if you can," Magnes said as he inserted his index finger into the gash to ascertain its depth. Ashinji moaned and Gran muttered under her breath, as if in prayer.

"Look's pretty deep, Tilo," Fadili commented. "You'll want to do a two layer closure, I expect?"

"Very good, Fadili. Yes, both the inner layer of muscle and the outer must be sutured in order to minimize the risk of the wound opening up later... I'll need to put in a strip of linen to serve as a drain. I'm very worried, though. The blade passed through into the body cavity. It may have nicked an organ." Magnes withdrew his finger.

"This elf is your friend." Fadili made it a statement, not a question.

"Yes..." Magnes' voice caught for a moment. He cleared his throat. "It seems like an entire lifetime ago that we met. He is married to my cousin."

"I am very sorry, Brother."

Fadili's simple declaration of sympathy deeply touched Magnes. He nodded in acknowledgement. "I'm ready to start," he replied.

Magnes lost all sense of time as he immersed himself in the task of repairing Ashinji's torn body. His mind remained intensely focused and only peripherally aware of the other people in the room besides Fadili. Someone held a lamp aloft over the table to provide illumination. Voices buzzed softly over his shoulder.

From far away, a man screamed in rage and defiance.

With a deft twist of his fingers, Magnes tied off the last stitch and laid his needle aside. He exhaled noisily.

It's done.

He raised his arms above his head to stretch out his aching back, then slowly looked around.

The boy Seijon stood on a stool to his left, lantern in hand. Gran sat rigid as a stone effigy, both hands clutching Ashinji's head as if she alone prevented it from flying off his shoulders. Her eyes stared straight ahead, fixed and glassy. The scrape of a hoof upon stone alerted Magnes to the presence of Aruk-cho, just inside the doorway.

"Gran!" Magnes whispered. "Wake up!" He clicked his bloody fingers before her eyes. She sighed and, like a diver surfacing from deep water, emerged from her trance.

A shudder racked her thin frame. "Ai, Goddess!" she murmured. Her fingers relaxed and began stroking Ashinji's hair.

"Does he still live?" Aruk-cho called out from the doorway.

"Yes, he lives, but it was a very close thing," Gran rasped in reply. "I've never fought so hard to keep a soul from crossing over.... He's still very much in danger; the cord that binds him to his body is almost completely severed. It could snap at any time."

Without warning, she slumped sideways and would have fallen to the floor had not Fadili lunged to catch her. Gently, the young Eskleipan lifted her up and held onto her until she could sit unaided.

Magnes understood how she felt. He, too, was weary to the point of collapse. "Let's get him cleaned up and bandaged, Fadili. Seijon, stay where you are awhile longer. I still need the light. Yardmaster, I'm sure the mistress is impatient for news, if you don't mind."

"The mistress is...occupied at the moment," Aruk-cho replied cryptically. "When she is finished with her task, I am certain she will come to the infirmary herself."

Magnes recalled hearing a man scream. He shuddered, then banished the thought from his mind.

He and Fadili worked quickly to wash, pad, and then bind the freshly sutured wounds. Finally, they laid Ashinji on his uninjured side atop a clean, moss-stuffed mattress and covered him up to his chin with several layers of blankets.

"I've done what I can. The rest is up to you and your One Goddess," Magnes said. His eyes met Gran's. "I'll stay the night, of course. Fadili can return to the temple... let them know where I am."

"I'm staying too," Seijon piped up.

"As will I," Gran added.

"Are you certain, Gran?" Magnes asked. "You look completely exhausted."

"No more than do you, young man! I will stay, and there'll be no arguments."

Aruk-cho cleared his throat. "I will take my leave, then. I shall return in the morning. Many thanks to you, Brother."

"Aruk-cho, wait. I need to speak to you," Gran called out. "It's vital that you listen now to what I'm about to say." She stood up, and some of her weariness seemed to fall away.

The akuta carefully maneuvered his bulk further into the room until he stood before Gran, dwarfing her slender frame beside his massive one.

"I am listening, Grandmother," he rumbled.

"You and I have been here a long time, have we not?" she began. The akuta inclined his head in reply. "We both made a conscious decision to stay, though we are free to leave whenever we wish. I have always kept my reasons for remaining to myself. I can remain no longer. I must return to my homeland."

She wavered on her feet and Magnes jumped to catch her as she sagged.

"Gran, please sit down! You're about to collapse!" he scolded.

Seijon brought a stool over, and Magnes helped the old woman to sit. After taking a moment to catch her breath, she continued. "Something terrible is happening in the north, and I don't mean the coming war between my people and the Empire. I felt it stirring several years ago... an ancient and terrible evil that has for centuries been kept imprisoned by members of my order. That evil has grown stronger with each passing year."

"Before, I chose to ignore it. After all, I was no longer a part of the world of high magic. I gave up the practice of sorcery when I went into exile. But when Ashinji arrived, and I learned who he was—no, when I learned who his *wife* was, I realized that I could no longer remain out of the fight. My skills and strength will be needed by my colleagues, for only by combining all of our power will we have any hope of defeating what is coming."

"Gran, you told me long ago that you had been a sorceress and that you had given up your powers. The mistress will not stop you from returning home to take them up again if you must, but what part in all of this does Ashinji play?"

"Ashinji's wife is the key to everything...quite literally. She is an innocent, chosen before her birth by members of my order to be the bearer of a powerful magic. She has no idea what she harbors...no idea at all. But she must be protected at all costs from that which is coming. If the Key inside her is freed prematurely and falls into the wrong hands, it will mean the end of the material world as we know it... for humans, elves, for every living thing."

"I still do not understand, Grandmother."

"Ashinji must return with me to Alasiri; that is, if he lives. He has a vital role to play in the securing of the Key. It is his wife, after all, who harbors the magic. Aruk-cho, I am asking for your help. Your people and mine have been allies in the past. If...*when* Ashinji is well enough, help us to leave this place."

"You are asking me to abet an escape. Ashinji is legally a slave. I am the yardmaster here. The mistress trusts and relies on me." Aruk-cho's liquid black eyes slid from Gran's face to stare at Ashinji lying in his bed, silent and still. The atmosphere grew tense and heavy. Magnes studied the craggy lines of Aruk-cho's face, searching in vain for some clue as to what the akuta's thoughts were, but as usual, he had no luck. Aruk-cho remained a master of inscrutability.

"Aruk-cho," Gran continued, "I'm not asking you to aid us directly. You are an honorable man. I know where your first loyalty must lie. But Ashinji has to return home with me." She paused, then added, "I have some money saved. It's not enough to purchase Ashi's freedom, but I will gladly give it all to Mistress de Guera as partial compensation when we leave."

"I have some money also," Magnes interjected. "If it'll help buy my friend's way out of here, then I'll happily give it up."

Aruk-cho stood like a black granite mountain, large and motionless, except for the back and forth swing of his tail. At last, he spoke. "The mistress values Ashinji highly, and not just because of his skills as a fighter. She would not wish to lose him. And yet.... Gran, I have always known you are a woman of great power and knowledge, power that you keep carefully hidden. If you say there is an evil force that threatens our world, and Ashinji is needed to help defeat it, then I believe you. I will aid you however I can and hope the mistress will forgive me."

"I swear to you, Aruk-cho. When the time comes, I will protect you," Gran promised. "Thank you."

"I shall offer prayers for his life tonight, before I retire," Aruk-cho said, then as carefully as he had entered, he departed the infirmary.

Magnes waited until the yardmaster had moved out of earshot before he spoke. "You didn't tell Aruk-cho that you're taking the boy with you. Why not?" he asked.

Seijon, who had remained silent up til now, responded with a "Yeah, why not?" of his own.

"Because Aruk-cho has already been compromised enough!" Gran snapped. "He has agreed, at the very least, to look the other way while I steal one of his employer's most valuable pieces of property! If he knew I'm planning to steal the boy as well...The money I will leave behind won't come near to covering the mistress's losses for both Ashinji and you, imp!"

She wagged her finger at Seijon for added effect. "No, it's much better that he not be privy to everything."

"Sensible," Magnes agreed. "I also think it wise not to let him know I'll be in on the breakout. Fadili can be trusted to keep quiet." Fadili nodded for emphasis.

Gran sighed and rubbed her eyes. "Ai, Goddess I'm so tired," she whispered. She eased her thin body off the stool and down into the chair that Fadili had placed by Ashinji's bed. Tenderly, she caressed Ashinji's pale cheek and began fussing with the blankets.

Seijon and Mistress de Guera aren't the only ones who've fallen in love with Jelena's husband, Magnes thought. "Ashinji reminds you of someone who's close to you, doesn't he?" Magnes asked. A flash of insight had made clear the old woman's behavior toward his friend.

"Yes," Gran replied. "I had a son once, very much like Ashi." She said no more and Magnes didn't press, sensing the terrible weight of grief behind her words.

Fadili came up behind him and touched his shoulder. "Everything is clean and packed up, Tilo," he reported. "I'll return to the temple now, if you have no further need of me."

"Thank you, Brother," Magnes replied. "Tell Brother Wambo that I'll be back sometime tomorrow afternoon."

After Fadili had departed, Magnes pulled up another chair beside the bed and sat. Seijon had made himself a pallet on the floor at the bed's foot, and now lay curled up under a blanket with only the top of his head showing. Gran gazed at Ashinji's face.

"You miss him, don't you? Your son, I mean," Magnes said.

"I miss all my family," Gran replied. She reached out and laid a hand on Ashinji's forehead, closing her eyes. Magnes didn't realize he had been holding his breath until Gran's lids fluttered open. "Ashi is adrift... lost in the gray lands between life and death. All I can do is to continue to call to him, in the hope that he hears and heeds my voice."

"If he dies, what then?" Magnes asked. "Will you be able to do what you need to do without him?"

"I don't know. I'm not even certain that we can prevail, even with every weapon at our disposal, and Ashinji's death would make things that much more difficult."

"Then he has to live."

The night passed slowly. While Gran dozed and Seijon snored, Magnes remained awake, keeping watch. When the first light of dawn leaked in through the slats of the shutters, he rose, stretched the kinks from his back and reached over to press his hand to Ashinji's throat. A pulse—weak, but steady—beat against the sensitive tips of his fingers. He breathed a sigh of relief.

His friend still lived.

He bent over to whisper in Gran's ear. "Gran, wake up."

"Hmmmm, yes, yes, I'm awake," she muttered.

Her eyes flew open and before she could speak again, Magnes reassured her. "Yes, he's still alive."

"I know," she answered.

The infirmary door rattled in its frame, then swung open to admit Mistress de Guera. "How is he?" she demanded without preamble.

"Still alive, Mistress, but just barely," Magnes answered. Mistress de Guera advanced upon the bed and Magnes had to dodge in order to avoid a collision. She stood for many heartbeats, looking down at Ashinji, her face a mask of conflicting emotions.

At last, her eyes turned first to Gran and then to Magnes. "Leal admitted to stabbing Ashinji only after much...persuasion."

"What'll happen to Leal, Mistress?" Seijon asked, awake now, and sitting up on his pallet, hair tousled from sleep.

The mistress's full lips compressed and a tiny vertical crease appeared between her eyes. She reached beneath the blankets and withdrew Ashinji's hand clasped in hers.

She stood thus, unmoving, until Gran broke the silence. "Leal is dead, is that not so, Mistress?" the old elven woman asked. Mistress de Guera laid Ashinji's hand down on top of the coverlet.

"Yes, that is so."

Abruptly, the mistress spun on her heel and paced toward the door. Before she stepped through, she paused.

"My thanks, Brother Tilo, for your good efforts to save my slave. I am...appreciative." With that, she departed.

Gran shook her head. "The mistress has made a terrible mistake," she declared.

"What do you mean?" Magnes asked, though he already knew the answer.

"She has allowed herself to love a slave," Gran replied.

35

A Declaration Of Love

A month had passed since Jelena gave birth, and to celebrate the newest Onjara's first four weeks of life, the king commanded that a feast be given in the little princess's honor. At the same time, he would officially present his granddaughter to the people of Alasiri.

The day of the festivities dawned wet and blustery. The spring rains had been much heavier this year, a gift and aid from the One, many folk said. The longer the rains lasted, the longer they would delay the Soldarans' northward march.

Hatora remained calm and quiet throughout the entire presentation ceremony and the feast that followed. Even as her two proud grandfathers passed her back and forth between them like a game ball, she maintained an air of total contentment. Everyone present could see how much both the king and his oldest friend adored the granddaughter they shared.

The day after the feast, word arrived from the south. The Soldaran legions were on the move.

* * *

"Keep your eyes on your opponent's face, Princess! The eyes! Watch *his* eyes! Yes! Excellent!"

Jelena parried a blow aimed at her midsection, feinted left, then whipped her blade up and to the right, clocking her sparring partner on the side of his helmet, rattling him hard. He stepped back and lowered his own blade. With unsteady fingers, he fumbled at the strap that held his helm in place.

"Are you all right, Mai?" Jelena called out.

"He's fine, aren't you, boy?" Kurume Nohe, swordmaster and Jelena's teacher, answered. "My son has a very hard head."

Mai Nohe nodded in agreement as he pulled his helmet from his head and let it dangle from his hand by the strap. "Just a little dizzy is all, Princess. Don't worry yourself."

"I don't know, Mai. I hit you pretty hard." Jelena dropped her own sword and removed her helmet. "You look pale."

Mai laughed, his dark eyes gleaming. "Like my father says...I have a hard head."

Kurume Nohe and his son had been working with Jelena now for several weeks, taking up her arms training where she and Ashinji had left off before he'd ridden east to his death.

"You are making tremendous progress, Highness. One would think that you were born to this." Kurume nodded approvingly.

Jelena laughed in turn. "Hardly!" she exclaimed. "I was born into servitude in my uncle's house. I never would have been allowed near weapons of any kind had it not been for my cousin insisting I receive at least a rudimentary education. I learned the basics from him."

"You possess a natural ability, then. Frankly, I'm not surprised, considering your bloodline."

"Yes, well... natural ability aside, will I be ready to ride to war at my father's side?" Jelena caught Mai scrutinizing her from the corner of her eye. He seemed like he wanted to say something, but couldn't quite work up the nerve.

"I would wish for more time, but there's nothing like the forge of battle to temper a young warrior. You'll be ready." Kurume picked up Jelena's sword and held it out to her, hilt first. "I think you've had enough practice for today, Highness. We will resume tomorrow, same time."

"Until tomorrow, Master Kurume," Jelena replied, taking her sword and carefully sheathing it.

Kurume bowed, then turned and headed for the gate that led out of the king's private sparring yard. "You coming, Son?" he called out over his shoulder, never breaking stride.

"I'll be along shortly, Father. I want a word with Princess Jelena," Mai replied. "That is, if it's convenient, Princess."

"Of course, Mai. What is it you wish to speak to me about?" Jelena started walking toward the gate, helmet tucked beneath her arm. Mai fell in beside her. She kept her eyes focused straight ahead, afraid to look directly into Mai's face, afraid of seeing what she suspected might be there.

Please, Mai! Don't say it! Don't change things between us!

"I have a confession to make, Princess," Mai began. He hesitated, then stopped in his tracks, head lowered. Jelena had no choice but to stop walking as well. She waited for him to continue, dreading his next words.

"I...I have tried to control my feelings. Tried and failed!" Now that he had committed himself, words tumbled from Mai's lips like a river in flood. "It's been nearly a year since your husband died. I've waited, as was decent, because you've been in mourning, but now... now I feel like time is wasting! Alasiri will be at war soon, and if I wait much longer, it may be too late!"

"Oh, Mai," Jelena breathed.

Mai stood at about the same height as Ashinji, but where Ashinji had been fair, Mai was dark. His raven warrior's queue fell to his waist and his eyes, the color of aged wood, blazed with emotion.

"I love you, Jelena," he whispered.

Jelena squeezed her eyes shut to close out the sight of Mai's vulnerability. The ground beneath her did a slow roll, and she abruptly found herself clinging to his arm.

"Oh, Mai," she repeated in dismay as she pushed herself away from him. "I...I don't know what to say!"

"You don't have to say anything yet, just listen...Your husband was a good man. Many in the army admired Ashinji Sakehera, and not just those who served under him. I would never seek to take his place in your heart." He paused, then continued, "I'm common-born. You are a princess. It seems like an insurmountable obstacle, but it can be overcome, if only you can return my feelings, Jelena."

He stepped forward and swept her hand up in his. "Jelena, I promise that I'll love and cherish you as you deserve, and I'll love your daughter as if she were my own."

Jelena trembled. The strength of Mai's passion engulfed her— almost too much to bear, and yet...

Ashi is gone. I'll never see him again in this life; why hold on to a ghost? Mai is honest, kind, and nice to look at...and he loves me. Perhaps, in time, I'll come to love him, but if I don't...can I accept anything less than what I had with Ashi?

A sudden rush of anger from some deep, hidden place within her soul surged forth, taking her by surprise.

Damn you, Ashi! Why did you leave me like this? Why didn't you fight harder! Hatora and I need you!

"Jelena, are you all right?"

Jelena shook herself and nodded sharply. "Yes, yes, Mai. I'm all right. This is just a lot to take in. I mean, I suspected that you might...have feelings for me, but to hear you say it out loud...well, I need time to think."

Mai raised her hand to his lips and kissed her palm. "I'll give you time," he said, "but remember...none of us has as much time as we think we do." He released her hand and the two of them exited the yard. Jelena turned left toward the section of the castle where her apartments lay. Mai turned in the opposite direction.

"Mai, wait!" Jelena called out. He stopped and turned to face her, the hope on his face heartrending. "I promise I'll think about what you said, and I'll try not to keep you waiting too long. You deserve a quick answer."

Mai's eyes swiveled downward then back up to her face. "Thank you, Princess," he replied, then bowed and walked away.

Jelena stood watching his retreating figure, and tried hard not to cry.

* * *

"Lady Odata, has there been any more news from the south concerning the plague?" the king asked. Everyone seated at the large, rectangular table looked at the Lady of Tono.

"Sporadic reports, yes," Odata began. "It seems the disease went dormant over the winter, but with the coming of the spring rains, it has resurfaced. Most alarmingly, all of the new cases are occurring in okui."

Jelena's status entitled her to sit in on council meetings, though she had no right to speak without permission. Once she had shown an interest in matters of state, Keizo had encouraged her to do so, and for the last few weeks, she had never missed a session. She always tried to remain as unobtrusive as possible, dressing plainly and positioning her chair behind and to the left of her father's. After the first couple of times she attended, the council members appeared to forget about her presence altogether.

The king and his advisors knew they had little time left. The rains had stopped and the ground grew dryer by the day. The Soldaran forces were on the move. The elven army had to be ready to meet them.

Life in Sendai went on as usual, but an undercurrent of nervous trepidation flowed through the air like smoke—no panic yet, just a heightened sense of unease. It showed in the faces of the people as they went about their business and made their preparations for the gathering storm. Sendai had never in its long history suffered a siege, but the city had been built with numerous defenses, and according to a committee of experts put together by the king, it could withstand a prolonged blockade—six months, maybe seven—provided all storehouses were full.

The elves' biggest fear now, besides invasion, was the plague.

Keizo turned to his brother, who sat to his immediate right. "What do you propose we do?" he asked.

"I've decided to go down to Tono myself to personally investigate," Prince Raidan announced. "Secondhand reports are no substitute for firsthand observation."

"Do you think that's wise?" Keizo asked. "We don't know how the disease is spread, nor why it can now affect okui. What if you fall ill? I need you too much, Brother."

Jelena sipped at a goblet of wine, watching with keen interest the dynamic between her father and uncle. She understood exactly why Raidan wanted to go to Tono himself. Her uncle firmly believed in the ability of science to solve all mysteries and problems, and as a scientist, he would want to apply what he referred to as the scientific method to the problem of the plague.

Keizo, by contrast, held a traditionalist's view. He preferred to rely on Talent and its application through the use of magic.

"I've spoken to you of the theories of Nazarius, Brother," Raidan replied impatiently. "As long as I take precautions to avoid all bodily excretions from the plague victims..."

"Yes, yes, I know!" Keizo interrupted. "However, I don't put the same stock in those notions that you do."

The prince's eyes flashed with annoyance. "I'm a trained physician, Brother. I'm convinced my methods can uncover the cause of this plague, but I need to go to the source to apply them! I must examine victims, collect samples..."

"Majesty, I agree with his Highness," Sen interjected.

Both the king and the prince turned to face the Lord of Kerala.

"It's vitally important that we learn all we can about this illness and it seems to me the prince is the one best qualified to investigate."

"Don't fight me on this, Keizo," Raidan said in a low voice. The rest of the council looked on, faces impassive. Jelena watched her father's face slowly relax as he relented.

"Very well. Do what you must, but do it as quickly as you can."

"I will leave at first light tomorrow. I shouldn't be gone more than five days," Raidan promised.

After the matter of Raidan's investigation of the plague had been decided, the council spent the remainder of the session reviewing the battle plans. The complex logistics of gathering the combined forces of all Alasiri's fiefdoms were finalized. A plan for provisioning was already in place and supply lines established. The forces themselves still needed balancing and separation into two divisions—one under the command of Sen, the other to be commanded by the prince. The Sendai Home Guard also needed augmentation with additions from the main army. Sen would see to these details later, as the time drew nearer for mustering.

The king and his generals had worked out the final plan over many weeks of intense research and discussion. They had options available to cover all possible scenarios—from the quick defeat and rout of the enemy to a full scale invasion and siege of Sendai itself.

Not a single man or woman on the council wanted to contemplate the possibility that the heart of Alasiri might be invaded, but contemplate it they must. Their duty compelled them to plan for the worst and come up with ways to safeguard the future of the elven people.

Jelena listened attentively at first as each lord gave an accounting of the size and composition of his or her force, but her mind soon wandered. The image of Mai's face kept intruding on her thoughts, and with a painful start, she realized she now thought more about Mai these days than about Ashinji.

She knew she should look upon this as good and healthy—a sign that she at last felt ready to let go of the past and move on, perhaps to a new love. Still, she couldn't help but feel a small twinge of guilt and sadness, even though she realized she in no way betrayed what she and Ashinji had shared.

I promised Mai a speedy answer. That was five days ago. It's time to end his suffering.

Jelena rose from her chair and moved on silent feet to a small side door that exited into a secondary corridor. Before reaching for the handle, she glanced over her shoulder; no one seemed to have taken notice of her departure. She pulled on the handle and the door swung open on well-oiled hinges. She slipped through and hurried away.

36

The Longest Night

"Tilo, there you are!" Brother Wambo scurried toward Magnes from across the sun-dappled courtyard, skinny arms waving. Magnes waited for the elderly healer to catch up before he continued on his way to his dispensary. "Fadili told me of what has befallen your slave friend. I am sorry," Wambo offered in his thin, reedy voice.

Magnes nodded in thanks. "I was just on my way back to the de Guera yard to check on him."

"You look terrible, Brother," Wambo observed. "I daresay you could use a meal and a nap."

Magnes grimaced as he pushed his fingers through his unkempt hair. "It's been a rough night. When I left him this morning, my friend still lived, but that was several hours ago. I'm very worried. The worst of his wounds is quite deep. The knife pierced clear through the muscle layer and entered the body cavity."

"Eeee...Not good!" Wambo shook his head in dismay. "Your friend will most likely die, I'm afraid. Such is the fate of most arena slaves."

A momentary flash of irrational anger tightened Magnes' chest.

Ashi will not die! I won't let him! he wanted to scream, but instead, he reined in his emotions, then stopped in his tracks and regarded Wambo thoughtfully.

"Brother, do you remember discussing with me a plan to provide medical care to some of the outlying suburbs and villages around Darguinia?"

"Yes. You wanted to outfit a wagon as a traveling clinic. I thought it was a good idea; I still do. Anything we can do to combat the woeful levels of ignorance and superstition in the general populace is a good idea. Why do you ask?"

"I'll talk to you about it later. Right now, I've got to get back to the de Guera yard."

Wambo shrugged. "Eh, suit yourself, though I think you should eat something first. Good luck." He shuffled off, sandals slapping against the hard-packed clay of the courtyard.

Magnes continued on his way to the dispensary, intending to pick up some supplies before heading out. The traveling clinic idea hadn't been entirely his own. A suggestion by Fadili had planted the seed in his mind, and at first, the idea hadn't involved anything nearly as elaborate as a specially outfitted wagon. But the more Magnes had mulled over the details, the more he had been convinced of the merits of a wagon, and he knew just the person to finance the venture: Mistress Armina de Guera.

For years, the mistress had suffered from headaches of such ferocious intensity, they had left her completely debilitated when they struck.

The first day Magnes had come to her yard, several months ago, Mistress de Guera had been in the throes of agony, laid low by her head pain. His honey-sweetened tea of skullcap, ginger, willow bark, and valerian root had eased the pain and gained him an extremely grateful patron. Magnes felt certain the lady's ongoing gratitude would insure a swift affirmative to his request for money.

The irony of the whole plan lay in the fact that the very wagon the good lady financed would carry two of her slaves to freedom.

After packing a supply of fresh bandages and some packets of herbs he would need to treat Ashinji's wounds, Magnes started out for the arena precincts. The late afternoon sun shone through shredded clouds, blown apart by stiff spring winds.

As Magnes walked, people called out to him.

"Ho there, Brother Tilo! My wife's got another boil on her arse that needs lancing!"

"Brother, can ye come an' look at m' son's sore tooth?"

"Brother Tilo, the rash is baaaack!!!"

Magnes waved and kept walking. So many residents of the neighborhood now came seeking their services that the local temple of Balnath—their archrival—had sent several of their bretheren to spy on the Eskleipans as they went about their work. To Magnes, the priests of Balnath were nothing but reprehensible charlatans. They traded on the superstition and fear of the common people, preferring to keep them ignorant of even the simplest things they could do to protect themselves from disease, such as hand washing.

When Magnes reached the gate of the de Guera yard, the guard waved him through without challenge. He went straight to the infirmary and found Gran still sitting in her chair by Ashinji's bed.

"How is he?" he asked, advancing to the bed and dropping his satchel on the floor.

Gran heaved a weary sigh. "He's still adrift. All I can do is continue to call to him."

Magnes reached out and lifted one of Ashinji's eyelids. He observed no response, not even the barest flicker of awareness. He picked up Ashinji's wrist and felt for the pulse that beat there, slow, but steady.

That's one good sign, at least.

"I need to check the wounds and change the dressings," he said, replacing Ashinji's hand on the blanket.

Gran nodded. "I'll help you."

"I'll need a basin and some warm water."

While Gran went to fetch the water, Magnes began his work. He peeled back the coverlets to expose Ashinji's torso, swaddled in bandages. He pushed the unconscious man over onto his side in order to look at his back. A large brown stain discolored the linen, something he expected to see.

Doesn't look too heavy, though, thank the gods.

He dug in his satchel, retrieved a small knife, then began to cut the bandages. Carefully, he peeled away the soiled linen and bloody padding until his handiwork lay revealed.

The long, shallow slash across Ashinji's ribcage looked good. The neat black stitches stood out in stark contrast to the paleness of the patient's skin. The deep stab wound in the back, however, appeared red and swollen. Magnes leaned in close and sniffed. He breathed a sigh of relief.

No odor of rot...another good sign.

Gran returned with the water. While she held Ashinji up on his side, Magnes removed the sticky drain and washed the wound with an infusion of mallow root—excellent for inflammation. Next, he packed in a fresh strip of linen, applied a poultice of honeysuckle and comfrey and, with Gran's help, bound up Ashinji in a fresh wrapper of clean bandages. Together, they changed the covering on the mattress and resettled the patient under a pile of fresh blankets. Throughout the entire procedure, Ashinji remained completely unresponsive.

"Where is Seijon?" Magnes asked as he helped Gran clean up.

"I sent the boy to get a bite to eat. Poor little monkey. He's sick with worry. Ashi means the world to him."

"I think I've come up with a workable plan to smuggle Ashinji and Seijon out of the city." Magnes kept his voice low, even though he and Gran were alone.

"Tell me," Gran responded.

"It all hinges on Mistress de Guera. You know she looks kindly on me ever since I gave her a remedy for her sick headaches. I plan on asking her to fund a traveling clinic for the Eskleipans. The wagon will need to be custom made, of course. It'll have two storage bins beneath the main bed, plus a secret compartment Ashinji and Seijon can hide inside. You and I will simply drive the wagon out of town."

Gran's lips tightened in a frown. "The authorities may search the wagon at the city limits," she said. "Many transports get stopped and checked before they leave."

"I hate to ask because I know it's a touchy subject, but what about your Talent? Can't you use your abilities to...to...I don't know, somehow cloud the minds of anyone who might get suspicious?"

Gran sighed. "I swore many years ago never again to use my Talent to manipulate another intelligent being. My own terrible arrogance and belief that I had the right to control others led to...well, to the destruction of everything I held dear."

"This is an entirely different situation," Magnes pointed out. "You'd be using your Talent in the service of good. I don't pretend to understand all of it—evil spirits, a key, the end of the world—it's all very confusing, but you've said so yourself...Ashinji has a vital role to play in this. Seems to me that none of us has much of a choice anymore."

"You are right, my friend," Gran murmured. She squeezed her eyes shut as if afflicted with a sudden, intense pain. "Ai!" she moaned. "Even after so many years...the wounds are still fresh!" She buried her head in her hands, thin shoulders shaking with sobs. Magnes could only stand helplessly by, unsure if she would recoil at his touch or welcome it. Tentatively, he reached out and laid a hand on her arm. Her skin felt smooth and soft, like that of a much younger woman. She did not shrink away, but neither did she indicate she wished for any more contact. Magnes contented himself with trying to emote as much comfort and sympathy as he could.

At last, Gran wiped her eyes. "Most times, I can cope, but every so often... Thank you, Tilo—or is it Magnes now?"

"Best I remain Tilo for the time being...At least until we're out of Darguinia."

Gran nodded. "You must be ready for a little refreshment," she said. "I know I am. I'll go and see what I can find for us in the kitchen."

Magnes murmured his thanks as Gran left the infirmary. He stood for a few heartbeats, stroking his chin, and wondered if he would ever know the dark secrets that Gran kept locked away in the hidden storerooms of her soul.

Perhaps it's best I never find out. Gran and I are alike; both of us have painful secrets that weigh us down. I wonder...Is the blood of family on your hands, too, Chiana?

* * *

Magnes remained for the rest of the afternoon and into the evening, offering his services to any of the yard's residents, both slave and free, who needed them. Gran and Seijon kept a constant vigil at Ashinji's bedside, leaving only to tend their own bodily needs. Fadili showed up at sunset, stating his intention to remain and help for as long as Magnes needed him.

Just after moonrise, Ashinji grew restless and began to thrash and mutter. The fires of fever could be useful in small doses, but if left to rage unchecked for too long, they would consume the patient from within. Magnes, well aware of this, knew what he must do. The next few hours would prove crucial.

At Magnes' direction, a pair of slaves brought a tub into the infirmary and filled it with cold water. With Fadili's help, he first removed the bandages, then transferred Ashinji—still in the grip of delirium—to the tub and held him down while he struggled and raved. Gran positioned herself at his head and laid her hands on his temples.

"Quiet... quiet now, dear one," she whispered, and after a few moments, Ashinji's struggles subsided into sporadic twitches of arms and legs, though his eyes continued to jerk restlessly beneath closed lids.

Magnes watched and waited, and when he judged the patient had soaked long enough, he and Fadili lifted Ashinji out of the tub and held him up while Gran carefully blotted him dry. Together, they carried him back to the bed.

As Magnes redressed his wounds, Ashinji startled them all by abruptly sitting up. His eyes, round and glassy, focused straight ahead at an image only he could see. "Jelena!" he cried out in a voice made hoarse by illness. He then whispered a few words in Siri-dar and fell silent. A single tear rolled down his cheek.

"Ashi, can you hear me?" Magnes asked, but he got no response. Ashinji's consciousness clearly wandered in other realms. After a few more moments of wide-eyed silence, he slumped back on the bed.

"Jelena...That's Ashi's wife's name, right?" Seijon asked. The boy looked at Gran.

"Yes, it is," she replied, and Magnes immediately picked up on the troubled tone in her voice.

"Is there something wrong, Gran?" he asked.

"There is much that is wrong, but I'm in no position to do anything about it at the moment," she answered. "Right now, I must concentrate all of my energies on helping you keep Ashi alive."

By the time Magnes finished with the dressings, shivers wracked Ashinji's body. Gran piled on more blankets and they all settled in to wait.

The night crawled toward dawn. The moon, just past full, had slipped below the horizon when Ashinji once again grew restless with fever. Magnes and Fadili returned him to the tub for another cold soak.

"If the fever doesn't break soon, he won't survive," Fadili observed grimly. Magnes knew the truth of Fadili's words, but he still couldn't bring himself to voice his agreement.

Ashi is my friend...I'll be damned if I give up now!

Shortly before sunrise, Magnes roused himself and went to check on the patient. He sighed with relief.

The fever's broken, thank the gods.

He grabbed a cloth and wiped the sweat from Ashinji's forehead, then laid his hand against the skin, now cool to the touch. He lifted an eyelid and nodded in satisfaction. Ashinji had drifted out of delirium and into normal sleep.

The crisis is past...Now, it's just a matter of time.

"That was close," Magnes muttered. "Too close."

"Ai, that it was," Gran replied. She stirred in her chair, waking Seijon, who had fallen asleep while sitting on the floor beside her, his head cradled in her lap.

"Ashi!" the boy cried, scrambling over to the side of the bed.

"Quiet, monkey!" Gran scolded. "You'll wake him and Ashi needs his rest!" She softened the reprimand with a gentle pat on the boy's head. Seijon scrubbed at his tear-streaked face, gazing at Ashinji with love and relief in his eyes.

Fadili tried to hide an enormous yawn behind his hand. Magnes felt a pang of guilt. The young Eskleipan apprentice had been of tremendous help, giving his time and energy freely and without complaint.

Magnes rested his hands on the younger man's shoulders. "I can't thank you enough, Fadili. I know you didn't have to stay here all night, but I'm grateful you did. It made things so much easier."

Fadili shrugged and his generous mouth stretched in a tired grin. "You don't have to thank me, Tilo. We are brothers. This elf is also your brother, which makes him mine as well."

One last thing needed to be done before Magnes could return to the temple for a few hours of sleep. From the supplies in his satchel, he made up a mixture of willow bark, feverfew, and goldenseal.

"Brew this up as a strong tea and make Ashi drink it as soon as he wakes. He'll hate the taste, I'm sure, so put a lot of honey in it," he instructed, handing the packet over to Gran, who tucked it away within the folds of her skirt.

She nodded. "When will you return?"

Magnes raked a hand through his curls and scratched the stubble of beard sprouting on his chin and cheeks.

"This evening."

37

The Whirlwind

"C oncentrate, Jelena. Feel the dormant energy within the wick, take control of it...That's it. Now, kindle the flame."

"I'm trying, Sonoe, but I don't think it's working! Wait...I...yes!"

The little beeswax taper flared to life. Jelena gasped with delight.

"You did it, Jelena! Excellent! You see? I told you that you could." Sonoe laughed at Jelena's bemused expression. "You always underestimate your Talent, Jelena. You should never do that. Remember who and what you are. You're an Onjara, and believe me, you've got the Onjara ability. You mustn't be afraid to use it."

Jelena nodded in agreement. "I hear what you're saying, Sonoe, and I know you're right. It's just, well...until I came to Alasiri, I was a nobody... no, even worse, I was a despised nobody. It's been a long, hard struggle to let go of all that and to see myself as worthwhile. Ashinji helped me the most, but so has my father...and you, of course."

The windows of Sonoe's private sitting room were thrown open to admit the soft spring breezes that wafted up from the gardens below, bringing with them the sweet perfume of the season's first blooms. Sonoe and Jelena sat side by side on a silk upholstered couch, their bodies touching in the easy way of close friends. From across the room, gleeful giggles bounced through the air. Eikko and Sonoe's maid Chiba had charge of Hatora, and the two hikui girls happily passed the cooing baby from one pair of arms to the other. Sonoe's little dog Jewel spun and leapt around the girls in a frenzy of excitement.

Such peace, Sonoe thought. *Pity it all has to end.*

Her hand strayed to her bodice and pressed the black stone pendant secreted between her breasts.

Tonight, everything would change.

Sonoe reached out and laid a hand on Jelena's cheek. Despite all her efforts, she had failed to quash the genuine affection she felt for this girl.

It will make her death so much harder to witness. If only a way could be found to spare her...

Sonoe sighed.

Such thoughts are counterproductive. Jelena's fate was sealed long ago, and there's nothing anyone can do to change it.

"Kindling a candle flame seems like such a little thing, though," Jelena said. She reached out and snuffed the candle between her thumb and forefinger. "It's a far cry from the powerful magic you and the other Kirians wield. I feel like a mouse beside an oliphant sometimes."

Sonoe laughed. "Have you even seen an oliphant?"

"I've seen pictures...in books about the faraway south, out beyond the deserts," Jelena replied. "There are leagues and leagues of forests so dense, the sun never reaches the ground. The humans who live there, the Eenui, are small and very, very dark-skinned. They ride oliphants, or so the books say. Mai Nohe's father, Master Kurume, traveled to the Eenui lands, when he was a young man. It took him nearly a year to get there."

"Tell me about Mai," Sonoe prompted.

Jelena's eyes swiveled downward and a stain of color crept into her cheeks. "There's nothing to tell, really," she murmured.

"If that's so, then why are you blushing, pet?" Sonoe pressed, grinning. "You can't hide the truth from me, dear heart. You know better. I think the handsome young swordmaster has turned your head!"

"We are getting to know one another, yes. I promised I'd give him a chance to win me over, and he's certainly doing his very best!" A brief smile played across Jelena's mouth, to be replaced by a frown of anguish. "Oh, Sonoe! What am I to do? Mai is handsome, kind, steady...."

Sonoe pursed her lips thoughtfully. "I can hear a 'but' that you're not saying. Let me finish your sentence...'but he's not Ashinji'."

"Am I being hopelessly pathetic for hanging on to my dead husband for so long? Gods, Sonoe, what's wrong with me?" Jelena's voice rose with her inflamed emotions. "I'm lonely and my child needs a father! Any other woman in my position would gladly accept a man like Mai, but here I sit, pining after a ghost when a living, breathing, *wonderful* man wants to share his life with me!" Jelena huffed and flopped backward into the cushions.

"Don't be so hard on yourself," Sonoe soothed. "The love you and Ashinji shared was a very rare and beautiful thing, and it can't ever be duplicated. You're afraid that nothing else can ever measure up, but Jelena, there's your mistake. Don't even try to find the exact same thing you had, because you'll fail. Accept what comes along for what it is, and happiness will follow."

Such sage advice, Sonoe thought. *The ironic part is, I meant every word.*

Jelena nibbled on a fingertip, her humanish face a tablet upon which Sonoe could easily read all of her conflicting emotions. Clearly, Keizo's daughter felt a strong attraction to Mai Nohe, but her love for her deceased husband had not diminished one whit.

Poor Jelena! You so much want to be reunited with your beloved Ashi. Well, my sweet friend, your wish will be granted very soon.

"Jelena, I'm so sorry, but I've just remembered something that I need to do. I must go."

Jelena looked confused. "Now?"

Sonoe realized the abruptness of her departure would seem strange to the girl, but it couldn't be helped. She needed to get away from Jelena, and quickly. The closeness she felt for Keizo's daughter threatened to overwhelm her resolve.

"Yes. There's a very important errand I need to run. Society business. If I leave now, perhaps I won't get into too much trouble." Jelena nodded in understanding. "Stay here as long as you like," Sonoe added. "I'll have more tea sent up for you." She grabbed a light cloak, for where she must go would be chilly. "I'll see you at dinner."

She left Jelena and the maids to fuss over the new little princess, blissfully unaware of the coming storm that would soon alter all of their lives forever.

Sonoe paused in the hallway outside her sitting room door and cast a quick spell of concealment upon herself—a simple glamour, nothing more. She had no time for a true invisibility spell. Still, anyone who happened to glance her way would not recall seeing her.

Quickly, she made her way along deserted back hallways to the castle library. The place normally stood empty at this time of day, and today proved no exception. The mellow smells of polished wood and leather permeated the air. The library consisted of three interconnected rooms, each with its own collection of chairs and tables. Shelves lined the walls from floor to ceiling, each one containing many hundreds of scrolls, folios, and bound books. Narrow windows, glazed with expensive glass, pierced the wall space between the shelves, allowing in abundant natural light. Dust motes danced in sunbeams slanting to the mat-covered floor.

Keizo, never much of a scholar, rarely came here. His father, Keizo the Elder, had assembled most of the fine collection which now graced the shelves of Sendai Castle's library—a collection that included many of the most important texts ever written about the magical arts. Chief among them were copies of the writings of the greatest elven mage to have ever lived, Iku Azarasha, head of the Kirian Society during the reign of Queen Syukoe Onjara, over a thousand years ago.

In one of these books, Sonoe had found the last information she desperately needed.

To be precise, the information she had been diligently seeking had not actually been in any of the texts themselves. While pouring over yet another volume of Master Iku's meticulous accounts of the Kirian Society's business, Sonoe had discovered—scribbled in the margin beside a description of the proper activation spell for a teleportal—the words "see *Commentaries of Akan.*"

After a long stretch of frantic searching, she had located the *Commentaries*—a tiny, fragile volume bound in crumbling green leather. In it, an obscure scholar named Akan had recorded his opinions on the writings of Azarasha.

The bone-dry analyses of some long-dead academic held no interest for Sonoe, and she almost returned the little book to its dusty perch high up on a neglected shelf, but something caught her eye—what proved to be a fold-out drawing at the book's midpoint. Her eyes beheld a rendering of Sendai Castle as it must have appeared approximately two hundred years ago, when Akan wrote his *Commentaries*.

Sonoe had crowed in triumph when she realized what she had found. Only her discovery, several weeks earlier, of Master Iku's personal account of the defeat of the Nameless One, had been greater.

The drawing of the castle had been marked in two places with Xs within circles. Across the bottom of the page, Akan had written *Location of Sendai Portals* in his blunt, inelegant hand. One of the portals was located in a room just off the Great Hall, the other in the library itself. It made perfect sense to Sonoe that the Kirians would choose to place one of their portals in Sendai's library. They were scholars, after all.

The hardest part had been finding the library portal. It had taken her three days; the Kirians had hidden it well. When she finally did break through all of the wards and masking spells, the energy she dissipated in the process felt too fresh. She realized someone had been maintaining the magic. Only one other person in Sendai had the skill to do this, and since Sonoe hadn't known of the portal's existence until three days ago...

Damn you, Taya! What other secrets are you keeping from me?

No matter. If all went according to plan, that twisted, malevolent spirit of a long-dead king would be hers to command, not the other way around. At the proper time, armed with the most precious of weapons, Sonoe would finally turn on her master. Once she had accomplished that task, then her real work would begin.

After a quick mental scan of the rooms to assure that no amateur scholar sat studying in a cubbyhole somewhere out of view, Sonoe traversed the first two rooms on silent feet to the rearmost chamber. There, she entered an alcove lined with dozens of scrolls and reached up to the top shelf. Her questing fingers found a scroll that felt heavier than the others. She pulled down on it and the back wall of the alcove swung smoothly inward on well-oiled hinges—more proof that someone...no, Taya!—maintained this portal.

Sonoe slipped through the opening, pushed the secret door closed and plunged herself into total darkness. A whispered incantation conjured a silvery globe of magelight. The shimmering orb rose from her palm and floated overhead to cast its light down a stone staircase spiraling away into the earth.

Sonoe shivered and pulled her light wrap close about her shoulders. The temperature in these subterranean vaults never climbed much above the chill of an early spring night, even in the heat of summer. With the magelight bobbing along in front of her to illuminate the way, Sonoe descended. After exactly fifty three steps, she reached a landing. Stretching before her, a rough-cut corridor curved away into the gloom.

The flame-haired sorceress paused and breathed in the musty air, tasting the residue of past magic.

You tried to erase your trail Taya, but I know your signature too well!

Taya Onjara had despised her ever since their days at the Kan Onji School, when Sonoe had been an impoverished student, obliged to spread her legs to all comers in order to earn enough for tuition, and Taya had reigned as the wife of the king's brother.

They soon became rivals. Both possessed Talent to a very high degree and the arrogance to flaunt it—Taya, by virtue of her exalted rank, and Sonoe, because of her burning ambition. It was inevitable that they should one day vie against each other for supremacy.

That day came when the school's regents announced a contest of magic, open to all the senior students, to be held on the first day of the new year. The winner would receive free tuition for the upcoming term—important to be sure—but Sonoe really craved the respect and prestige a victory would bring. She felt sick and tired of noble-borns like Taya skewering her with their snobbery.

Sonoe bested Taya, but just barely; nonetheless, her triumph had been sweet. She indulged in a smug little smile as she savored the memory.

Soon thereafter, she came to the attention of Keizo, newly installed on his throne and searching for a suitable woman with whom he could enter into a contract. Sonoe's common-born status made her ineligible for a royal marriage, but if she accepted his proposal, she would have certain legal rights as his official Companion, including the expectation of life-long support, even though the king must one day put her aside to marry. Keizo's choice to take a Companion instead of a wife had confused many in the court, but Sonoe didn't question his reasons. She had a chance to rise higher than she'd ever hoped, and she had accepted with no regrets.

Several months after her attainment of full membership in the Kan Onji, the head of the Kirian Society, Master Shen Shineza approached her and invited her to join. She didn't learn until much later that Taya had tried to block her nomination. When Master Shen died and left the Society without a leader, Sonoe lobbied for the post, but as future queen of Alasiri, and by right of precedence, the helm of the Society fell into Taya's hands.

That loss had been a bitter blow. Sonoe had raged for months. The office should have been hers by right of superior magical skill. For the sake of the Society, she did her best to keep her anger cloaked in a mantle of amiability and cooperation, but occasionally, it broke through. She and Taya had nearly come to violence a few times, but had always managed to step back from the brink.

Controlling her feelings had been easier when there had been more active members in the Society, but, in the space of only a few years, their numbers had dwindled due to retirement, death, and the lack of suitable recruits. Sonoe found this good in a perverse way, for it made her plan so much easier to execute.

Everything depended on the Key, that all-important piece of magic harbored within Keizo's daughter.

If only she could somehow study the Key's unique energy signature before the Sundering! She had thought to try breaching the shields put up around it by Taya, but without the help of another mage, she risked killing Jelena prematurely. She had decided to abandon that course because she didn't want to bring in an outsider.

Now that I've found what I need...

Sonoe planned to seize the Key for herself once it was released from Jelena's dying body. First, she would summon the Nameless One, calling upon him to claim his prize. When he appeared—and all depended on her quickness—she would use the one weapon against him for which he had no defense. After using his true name to bind the Nameless One to her will, she would then turn his power against her fellow Kirians, destroying them. Rid of the only ones capable of stopping her, she would put the rest of her plan into motion by using the Key to unlock the source of the limitless magical energy that would give her power enough to fulfill her destiny.

Despite the magelight, shadows crowded around her, and her own shadow—a crazy, elongated thing—stalked her along the rough-hewn walls of the corridor. She followed the passage to its end at a simple wooden door. She tested the iron handle and found that it turned easily. She pushed the door inward and sent the orb floating ahead to illuminate a small, round room.

Carved into the hard-packed earth, a magical symbol marked the exact center of the circular chamber. Sonoe breathed a sigh of relief as she recognized the glyph for travel.

As soon as she crossed the threshold, she could feel the thrum of powerful arcane energies coursing through her veins like strong wine, setting her teeth abuzz and her skin to tingling. She walked over to stand on the symbol.

Sonoe reached into the front of her tunic and withdrew the black stone that served as her link to the Nameless One. She closed her eyes and let her mind relax and open. She felt for the strand of energy that connected the stone to its source and sent her consciousness winging along it.

When she pierced the icy black curtain that shrouded the astral space where the Nameless One existed, she called out to him.

I have found the portal, Master!

The Nameless One's anger surged along the link and smote Sonoe's mind. *Your incompetence has kept me waiting! Your screams of agony will be sweet when I punish you!*

Flames erupted all around Sonoe, engulfing her in smoke and the stench of burning flesh. Horrified, she watched as her skin blackened and withered against her bones. She opened her mouth to scream, but never got the chance as she felt herself sucked into darkness.

* * *

She landed hard on her side, skin scraping against stone. The bone-chilling cold dealt her shrinking body yet another blow, and for a few precarious moments, she could do nothing but lie on the brutal stone and gasp for breath.

Total darkness engulfed her, but even though denied the use of her eyes, she had her other senses, and they all screamed warnings of eminent mortal danger.

Some*thing* waited, crouched in the dark—something ancient and unspeakably evil—and Sonoe knew without a doubt that it could see her perfectly well.

Slowly, she rolled over and levered herself onto her knees. A quick mental assessment of her body revealed no serious injuries.

So. The flames were an illusion.

Fighting the shivers that wracked her body, she conjured a magelight and looked around her.

Sonoe found herself on the floor of what appeared to be a natural cave. She sent the magelight shooting up to illuminate the many teeth of rock that hung from the high ceiling, then brought it swooping down in lazy circles to cast light into nooks and crannies too numerous to count. All the while, she remained acutely aware of the entity that lurked just beyond her sight, watching.

Climbing to her feet, Sonoe pushed her tangled mass of hair out of her face and waited, the magelight hovering at her right shoulder. The foul presence of the Nameless One seemed to exist everywhere at once, and yet Sonoe could sense a distinct vortex of particular intensity in the shadows to her left. She turned to face that direction and watched as the shadows coalesced into something more solid.

As a trained sorceress and Kirian Society member, Sonoe knew better than to relax her shields in the stronghold of her master. Though the attack that had brought her here had taken her by surprise, she would not make the same mistake again.

The Nameless One lashed out, his polluted energy pummeling her from all sides. She withstood its corrosive force, but just barely.

Will I have the strength to do this? He's so much more powerful than I'd thought!

Breath harsh with strain, she cried out, "Master, please stop!"

Give me one good reason why I should not burn you to ash where you stand, whore!

"Because then I cannot deliver to you that which I promised!"

She could feel herself weakening.

I can't take much more of this!

"The plan is set," she gasped. "The Kirians will gather in three weeks time to perform the Sundering! I...I..." No longer able to talk and resist the Nameless One at the same time, Sonoe threw up her hands and frantically traced a sigil in the air before her in a last, desperate attempt to stop the onslaught.

Abruptly, the attack ceased. Sonoe stumbled backward, slipped on a loose stone and went down, turning her ankle as she fell. Pain, sharp and hot, surged up her leg, wringing a soft moan from deep within her chest. The sound of grinding metal filled the air around her. A bitter curse dropped from her lips.

"You enjoy my pain!" she hissed, breathing hard. A quick mental probe of her ankle confirmed that she had only sprained it.

Thank the Goddess!

The deeper darkness that was the material manifestation of the Nameless One floated closer until it hung over Sonoe like a storm cloud, the two baleful red stars that served as eyes staring down at her.

Of course I enjoy your pain, slut. I enjoy pain in all of its many forms, but yours is especially sweet. I shall have you writhing in a moment, but before my pleasure comes business. Tell me of the plan...

Sonoe told him everything...except the part about her counter-plan, which she kept hidden within the special vault of her mind that no one, not even the Nameless One, could penetrate. Gritting her teeth, she then steeled herself to endure the spirit's vile assault on her body for the last time. When he had finished and had flung her, bruised and bloody, back through the portal, she lay for a long time on the cold dirt floor, unmoving.

The storm is coming!

She climbed to her feet and stood for a few heartbeats, staring at nothing, listening to the voice in her head whispering, whispering...

The storm is coming!

The voice of her inner self.

You must be ready!

"I will ride the whirlwind," Sonoe murmured aloud, then threw back her head and laughed in triumph.

38

A Reason To Live

*J*elena, Ashinji cried, or would have if he'd had a voice to cry with. She did not, could not, hear him.

A man—young, dark-haired and dressed in the worn leathers of a veteran soldier—stood beside her. His lips moved but Ashinji couldn't make out what he said. Jelena moved closer and he gathered her into an embrace that bespoke of emotions much stronger than friendship. She lifted her face and their lips touched in a brief kiss. The man smiled and, taking Jelena by the hand, led her away. A thick, gray curtain of fog coalesced around the two of them as they receded into the distance.

Jelena, I love you! Please...wait for me!

Despair, like a wild thing, tore through Ashinji, leaving in its wake the realization that his wife—his best friend and the love of his life—had moved on without him.

Ashiiiinjii!

Was that his name he heard, or simply the keening of the wind?

Ashinji, come baaaack!

The sound kindled a spark of recognition in his sluggish consciousness. He knew that voice and he knew he should heed its command, but along that way lay pain, terrible pain. So much easier just to drift...

Ashiiinjii! Pleeese, come baaack, nooow!

Ashinji shivered with annoyance, or would have if he'd had a body to shiver with.

Leave me alone...I don't want to go back! Why should I? There's nothing left for me now. Better to stay in this soothing grayness...

The fog dissolved and Jelena once again stood before him, dressed in a long gown of red silk, holding a baby in her arms. She lifted the child over her head, laughing.

The vision struck at Ashinji's frozen emotions, releasing them in a dizzying rush.

This baby Jelena cradled in her arms must be the child he had to leave behind a lifetime ago. What terrible sorrow Jelena must have suffered, giving birth to their child, all the while believing him dead! Should not the child they had made together have both of its parents to raise it?

Ashiiinjii!

He turned and moved toward the sound of his name.

* * *

Awareness returned slowly, and the unintelligible noises buzzing in his ears resolved into muted voices, discussing his condition.

"Look at his eyes. They're moving."

"Yes...I believe you're right. Gran! Come quickly! I think he's waking up!"

Ashi, can you hear me?

Mindspeech.

He recognized the voice that had called to him, imploring him to return and not lose himself forever in the gray fog between the worlds.

With tremendous effort, he opened his eyes.

"Ashi, praise the One! You're awake."

Ashinji struggled to focus eyes that had seen no use in several days. Gran's face floated above him, looking pale and haggard, but clearly relieved.

Confusion washed over him. "Wha...what...h...h...happened?" he croaked. He attempted to sit up, but a combination of pain and weakness thwarted him.

"You don't remember, Ashi?" Gran stroked his cheek. "You've been hurt. Stabbed. You've been unconscious for days; you very nearly died."

Stabbed! When?

The last thing he clearly remembered was walking into the weapons shed. After that, things got hazy.

"I...don't...can't..." It took a big effort to speak. His tongue felt clumsy and thick, like a chunk of wood in his mouth.

"What's he saying, Gran?"

That voice belonged to Seijon.

"He's speaking in Siri-dar, and you would understand if you'd ever made an effort to learn!" Gran's voice was sharp. "I don't think he remembers what has happened."

Ashinji struggled to pull together the fragments of memory that spun like dark motes before his minds' eye.

I went to the weapons shed to put away some practice equipment... Something...no, someone attacked me there!

Images of a violent confrontation flashed to the surface, then with the abruptness of a dam giving way, all the memories of those terrible few moments, all the rage, the fear, and most of all, the sensation of the knife as it bit deep into his flesh, returned in a rush.

"Ai, Goddess!" he groaned. "L...Leal...st...stabbed me!"

"You do remember," Gran said. "Ashi, let the memory go for now. Put it out of your mind. There'll be plenty of time to deal with it later. You need to rest. Sleep, now."

Sleep...that sounds wonderful. I'll sleep, yes.

He closed his eyes.

* * *

When next he woke, the golden light of late afternoon filled the infirmary. He blinked rapidly to clear his vision and saw Seijon, perched on the foot of the bed, arms wrapped around knees drawn up under his chin, eyes closed. He looked like he was asleep.

"Seijon," Ashinji whispered. The boy's eyes flew open and widened with excitement.

"Ashi!" he cried, scrambling to the head of the bed where he flung his arms around Ashinji in a joyful embrace. Ashinji grunted in pain but slowly raised his arms to draw the boy closer.

"I've been so scared you'd die and leave me, Ashi," Seijon mumbled against his neck.

For a few heartbeats, Ashinji felt too overcome to speak. Not until this moment had he realized his depth of feeling for this boy. This was the love between brothers that he had been denied with his own treacherous sibling.

"Don't worry. I'm not going anywhere without you," he whispered.

"Get off, monkey! You're hurting him!"

Gran materialized at Ashinji's bedside, arms sweeping the air before her as if she were attempting to shoo off an especially persistent pest. She glared at Seijon, but Ashinji could see the veiled amusement in her pale eyes.

"No, Gran, he's not hurting me," Ashinji lied. Gran cocked her head, disbelief writ plain on her face, but she refrained from comment.

Instead, she poked Seijon in the ribs and pointed to the foot of the bed. Reluctantly, the boy loosed his hold and retreated to his former position where he flopped down, cross-legged, chin in hand.

"How are you feeling, Ashi?" Gran inquired, speaking Siri-dar as she always did when there were no humans present.

"Tired...very tired, and sore. Leal obviously did a lot of damage." Ashinji paused, reluctant to ask the question uppermost in his mind, but he needed to know. "Leal...is he...?"

"Leal is dead," Gran stated flatly. "And no, you didn't kill him." Her lips pressed together in a thin line. "I don't know the whole truth of the matter, but I believe the mistress had him executed."

"Shit!" Ashinji muttered.

"In case you're feeling some sort of misguided guilt, young man, remember that Leal was a sadistic killer who hated our kind and preyed on those too weak to defend themselves." She glanced pointedly at Seijon.

"I'm not sorry he's dead, Gran," Ashinji countered. "I'm just sorry it happened the way it did."

Gran spent a few moments fussing with his blankets. He lay back and let her, knowing she did it more for her comfort than his. He felt as weak and helpless as a newborn—a sensation he thoroughly disliked.

"Gran, when I was unconscious, I think I dreamed you were calling to me, pleading with me to return. I also dreamed I saw Jelena."

"Those were not dreams, Ashi. I did call to you. As for you seeing your wife, I'm not surprised. It's very common for those wandering the plane of spirit to seek out loved ones, especially if there has been a separation on the material plane."

"I saw her twice. The first time, she was with another man. I could see they had feelings for each other."

"I'm so sorry," Gran murmured.

"No, I understand, Gran. Jelena has accepted my death and has moved on with her life. I would want her to do just that. She's too young to spend the rest of her life alone. It hurt, though..."

He fell silent for a time, eyes closed, meditating on the perversity of his fortunes. "I saw her again," he continued. "She held a baby—our baby—in her arms." He smiled. "Seeing my child for the first time...that's what made me want to come back, Gran."

As Gran opened her mouth to reply, the infirmary door swung open to admit Magnes. Jelena's cousin crossed the room in five long strides, a broad grin on his face.

"Ashi, you're awake! When did this happen?"

"Just a short time ago," Gran answered. "What brings you back to the yard so soon? It seems like you've only just left."

"I came back to tend Mistress de Guera—she's down with one of her headaches." He pulled a chair around to the side of the bed and straddled it. "I've got some news," he said, looking at Gran and lowering his voice. "I've set the plan into motion. Your mistress has agreed to finance the mobile clinic for the Eskleipans. Construction will begin within the week. I estimate it'll take about two weeks total for the entire project, including provisioning."

"This is very good," Gran said, nodding enthusiastically, but her expression soon darkened. "Two weeks. Not a lot of time, yet too much, considering the stakes,"

"What are you two talking about?" Ashinji looked puzzled.

"Escape, Ashi," Gran said. "We've been working on a plan while you've been sleeping." Briefly, Magnes related the details.

"I'll just have to be ready," Ashinji declared. He paused. "What about Aruk-cho?" He rolled his head to the side, directing the question to Gran. He did not worry the yardmaster would betray them at the last moment; rather, he feared the akuta would extend his assistance to the point where his position at the yard would be jeopardized. The very last thing Ashinji wanted was to see Aruk-cho ruined.

"Aruk-cho will be ready. All he needs is a few hours' warning," Gran replied. "If you're concerned about him getting into any trouble, don't be. I promised to shield him and I can."

"Are we really leaving here and going to Alasiri?" Tense with excitement, Seijon's voice piped a little too loud in the afternoon stillness of the infirmary.

"Hush, child!" Gran scolded. "You can't speak about any of this! All our lives depend on secrecy. If the mistress were to find out..."

"She won't from me," Seijon promised solemnly.

"Gran, I trust Seijon completely," Ashinji said. He smiled at the hikui boy and received a grin in return.

"Two weeks, then," Magnes repeated. "Now, let me check your wounds, Ashi."

With Gran's assistance, Ashinji rolled onto his side and lay as still as he could while Magnes unbound and examined his wounds. Even though Magnes probed as gently as he could, Ashinji found it impossible not to flinch. After Magnes had declared himself satisfied, he re-bound Ashinji's torso with clean bandages.

"Are you hungry?" Gran asked. "I can send Seijon to the kitchen for some soup, that is, if you think you can handle it."

Ashinji shook his head. The mere thought of food caused his stomach to roil in rebellion. "No, not just yet," he whispered. "I think I need to sleep for awhile longer."

"Have some tea, then, at least," Gran insisted. "You need the moisture." Ashinji nodded in assent and Seijon scampered off to fetch the tea.

The sounds of late afternoon drifted in through the open windows. Voices raised in animated conversation, the bleat of a goat, the dull *clack, clack* of wooden practice blades striking against each other—all served as a reminder to Ashinji that life in the de Guera yard went on essentially unchanged, and it mattered not a whit whether he lived or died.

He felt grateful to be alive.

Seijon returned shortly, carrying a tray laden with a teapot and four cups. Gran stood up, took the tray from his hands, and set it on a small table beside Ashinji's bed.

"I'll stay with you, Ashi, while you sleep. I'll be right here the whole time," Seijon declared, flopping down in the chair recently vacated by Gran.

"I feel much better, knowing that you'll be watching over me, Little Brother." Ashinji's heart once again swelled with affection for the boy.

"The patient is in good hands, it seems," Magnes said, winking at Gran, who tried her best to look disapproving, but failed dismally.

"Child, you've been sitting by Ashi's bed for three days straight!" she exclaimed. "When was the last time you ate anything, eh? When was the last time I ate anything for that matter?" she muttered as she poured the tea.

"I'm not hungry," Seijon responded, "an' I'm not leaving." His voice rang with youthful defiance.

"Huh! Suit yourself, monkey!" Gran's eyes flashed, then softened. "I'll go to the kitchen later and bring you a little something anyway. You can eat it or not; I don't care." Even in his bleary state, Ashinji could tell Gran cared very much.

With Gran's assistance, Ashinji drank almost a full cup of the lightly sweetened herb tea, then lay his head back on the lumpy, moss-stuffed pillow. The room grew soft and fuzzy around its edges.

Just before he slipped into sleep, an image of Jelena appeared before his mind's eye. She looked up sharply, as if startled, and her lips shaped his name.

He tried to answer, but he hadn't the strength.

39

Bid For Freedom

"Hee hee! It's grand, Tilo, just grand!"

Brother Wambo made no attempt to contain his glee. He performed an impromptu jig, his skinny arms and legs flailing like a manic scarecrow come to sudden, comical life.

Laughing, Magnes exclaimed, "Brother Wambo, if I had known you could dance like that, I would have suggested the temple put on recitals as fund raisers!"

The new Eskleipan mobile infirmary had been delivered that morning from the wagon makers' yard, and all the inhabitants of the temple had gathered in the rear courtyard to admire the order's latest project for serving the poor.

"Brother Tilo, we have you to thank for this marvelous thing," Father Ndoma wheezed, his rheumy eyes squinting against the midday sun. In the harsh light, the old man's skin looked like ancient leather stretched taut over a frame of sticks. The head of the Eskleipan Order had been unwell for several months, and it had lately become obvious that he would not last out the summer.

"I appreciate your kind words, Father, but the person we ought to be thanking is Armina de Guera. It was her gold that paid for this wagon," Magnes replied.

Father Ndoma nodded. "Yes, yes, of course. We shall send a formal letter to the good lady expressing our gratitude." A fit of coughing wracked his frail body and sent him sagging into the arms of Jouma the chirugeon and Ayeesha the midwife. Wambo shot Magnes a worried look.

"Perhaps you'd better go inside out of the sun, Father," Magnes suggested. The rainy season had not quite ended, but already the days waxed warmer as spring took firm hold of the land.

"Ayeesha and I will escort you, Father," Jouma said, gently taking the old man's elbow. Together, he and the midwife steered their leader back toward the cool interior of the temple.

After the three had disappeared inside, Magnes turned to Wambo and said, "He grows weaker by the day."

"Ndoma and I came to Darguinia together," Wambo replied, voice heavy with sorrow. "So many years have gone by since, so many people have passed through our doors.... Some we could heal, others we could not. For those whom our skills were not enough, at the very least, we helped to ease their passage to the other side. Now, the time draws near when I will ease my old friend's passage and take up his mantle of leadership."

"Everyone here has complete faith in you, Brother," Magnes responded with heartfelt sincerity. He recalled the day when he had first arrived at the temple of Eskleipas, his spirit withering beneath the crushing weight of depression born out of guilt. Wambo and his people had offered him a haven, a place where he could, in time, come to terms with what he'd done and perhaps find absolution through helping others. During his time as an Eskleipan Brother, Magnes had managed to ease his tormented soul, and if he did not feel entirely at peace, he felt as near to it as possible.

"I can have the infirmary stocked and ready to roll in two days, three at the most," he said. "Fadili and I have had time to make plans, so we know exactly what we'll need. I bought a map of the local area in a shop near the palace, so I think it's fairly accurate...I've marked the outlying villages we'll stop at. I estimate we'll be able to stay out two to three weeks at a time."

Wambo nodded as Magnes spoke, thoughtfully tapping his strong white teeth with the tip of a forefinger.

"Hmm, yes. Excellent. You and Fadili will both be missed, of course, but this is important work! Jouma will have to resume the contract work with the yards. Hmm, we'll be spread a little thin.... Perhaps it's time for a recruitment drive!" He slapped Magnes on the shoulder and grinned.

Magnes sighed. He felt torn between his desire to admit to Wambo the other use to which he would put the infirmary and his instinct to protect everyone at the temple. He hated the fact that he had to deceive his friend, but in the end, it was far safer that no one else in the temple besides Fadili should know the truth.

He glanced up at the hazy sky. "Speaking of the yards, it's time I was getting over to de Guera's. They've got at least five matches today, so I'm expecting a lot of injuries."

The rest of the temple folk had returned to their duties, leaving Magnes and Wambo alone in the sunny courtyard. Magnes started toward the temple pharmacy where he kept his supply bag. Wambo fell in beside him.

"How is your friend the elf doing?" the old man asked.

"He is much better," Magnes replied. "The elves are a tough race. I don't know if a human could've survived the kind of wound Ashinji did. He is healing remarkably fast."

"That is good to hear." Wambo paused for a moment before continuing. "Tilo, when you first came to us, I sensed you were a young man in trouble. I have never asked you to reveal anything about yourself or your past, nor am I asking now." He halted, and fixed Magnes with a discerning eye. "Whatever the circumstances that brought you to us, I am glad. I am glad that you became our brother."

Magnes' breath caught in his throat.

It sounds like Wambo is saying goodbye, as if he somehow knows I intend to leave and won't be back. But...how could he know?

Until this very moment, in fact, Magnes himself had no idea he wanted to leave Darguinia for good, but now he realized that it had been his intention all along. He shifted nervously from foot to foot. Overhead, doves cooed and rustled in the eaves. A cloud drifted over the face of the sun, plunging the world into cool shadow. The wind began to gust and the smell of rain infused the air.

"I'd better get going," Magnes said. Wambo nodded and turned to head back the way they'd come. Magnes watched him go, a deceptively fragile old man with a core made of the strongest steel. He would miss Wambo, and all the others at the temple who had come to mean so much to him, but something had changed. It took Wambo's uncanny perception to bring it to the fore so Magnes would acknowledge it.

The time had come for him to return home to Amsara and face what he'd done. Thessalina deserved to know what had really happened, and Duke Teodorus' spirit deserved the peace that the telling of the true story of his death would provide.

"Tilo, there you are!" Fadili called out, hurrying over to the pharmacy door where Magnes stood, thinking. "It's getting late. We should go over to the de Guera yard now. The first matches are nearly over."

"I was just getting my things," Magnes replied. Hinges squealed as he pushed open the weathered wood door and stepped inside to retrieve his bag. Re-emerging, he smiled at the younger man and said, "Let's go."

* * *

"Everything's ready, my friend," Magnes said in a low voice.

"I'm ready as well," Ashinji replied. Fighters, not so injured that they couldn't walk but requiring Magnes' services anyway, were trickling into the infirmary. "Let's go outside," Ashinji suggested.

Magnes nodded and called to Fadili. The young Eskleipan, who squatted over a female slave's leg examining a nasty gash, looked up, eyebrows raised. "I'm going outside for a bit. Can you handle things?" Fadili flipped his hand dismissively, as if to say the question need not have been asked.

Magnes chuckled. "Fadili is turning out to be a fine healer. He really doesn't need my supervision anymore."

"I can see that," Ashinji replied.

The two men stepped out of the infirmary into the cool of the blustery afternoon. The wind ruffled Magnes' brown curls and sent loose tendrils of Ashinji's blond hair whipping about his angular face.

Ashinji grew stronger with each passing day, but he was still far from total recovery. He tired easily and his wounds continued to give him a great deal of pain. The flight from Darguinia would be very hard on him and Magnes worried the effort might prove too much. Still, what choice did they have?

"Let's walk over to the women's barracks. Gran's waiting," Ashinji said, his voice catching a little as he spoke. He grimaced and rubbed his side.

"Ashi, we can wait another week if you need to," Magnes suggested, keenly aware of the pain his friend tried to conceal.

"No, we can't," Ashinji replied, shaking his head. "If we wait much longer, it will be too late. Gran tells me she can feel the power of the Nameless One growing swiftly, even this far south. No, we must go now."

They reached the shelter of the women's barracks just as the first fat raindrops speckled the sand beneath their feet. Ashinji called out in Siri-dar, and a few moments later, Gran emerged from the dim interior of the long, low building. A frown deepened the creases at the corners of her mouth.

"Something has happened," she announced. "I felt an unusual surge of energy from the north. It feels as though the Nameless One has broken free somehow, and yet, I still feel the main core of his energy remains below the Black Tower. I don't understand this and it frightens me."

"The mobile infirmary will be ready to go in two days. We can leave then," Magnes said. He looked first at Gran, then Ashinji.

"Would that it could be today..." Gran shook her head in dismay, then sighed. "Very well. Day after tomorrow, then. I'll inform Aruk-cho."

"I'll tell Seijon," Ashinji said.

"No. Best to keep the boy in the dark until the last possible moment," Gran advised. "His self-control is not the best."

"Fadili and I will come with the wagon late in the day to show it to Mistress de Guera," Magnes said. "We'll stretch things out until it's time for the evening meal. Since we sometimes stay and eat, no one should get suspicious. The most dangerous part is getting you," he looked at Ashinji, "and Seijon into the secret compartment below the storage bins. If anyone sees you..."

"No need to finish those words," Ashinji replied grimly.

"Once you two are in, Fadili and I will simply drive out of the yard."

"What will you do, Gran?" Ashinji asked.

"Don't worry about me," Gran answered. Her impassive face gave away none of the secrets Magnes knew lay behind her pale eyes. "I can come and go as I please. No one will challenge me." The rain fell steadily now, though not in torrents like it had earlier in the season; even so, the yard soon became a watery expanse across which people and the occasional goat stoically sloshed.

Magnes studied the two elves. Both stared out into the rain, their angular faces pensive. He knew the two of them shared a terrible burden—a task they must perform once they made it back to Alasiri, something neither one wanted to do, but had to, just the same. Gran had only hinted at its nature; what little she had revealed, Magnes had not fully understood, but that did not really matter. He was determined to see them safely to the border so they could return in time to accomplish what they must.

Once that's done, I'll go home and face Thessalina.

"I'd better get back to work," he said. "Day after tomorrow, then."

"Day after tomorrow," Gran repeated.

Ashinji held out his hand and Magnes clasped it.

"Thank you, my friend," Ashinji said. "Thank you for everything."

"You don't need to thank me, Ashi. We are family, after all," Magnes replied.

Ashinji smiled. "Yes...we are."

* * *

Two days later, Magnes stood with Fadili beside the infirmary wagon while Mistress de Guera admired what her funds had made possible.

"Why, this is wonderful!" she exclaimed. "You'll be able to do so much good work with this infirmary." She made another circuit of the wagon, nodding in approval. Corvin and Aruk-cho stood close by, both with crossed arms and neutral faces. A crowd of curious yard dwellers had gathered around at a respectful distance, whispering and pointing.

"It is gratifying to know my money is being put to such good use. When you first came to me with your proposal, Brother Tilo, I'll admit I was a little reluctant, but now that I see the infirmary..."

"You'll agree to fund it for the foreseeable future, I hope," Magnes interjected, his voice dripping with charm. From the corner of his eye, he could see Corvin frowning. Mistress de Guera opened her mouth to respond, but Magnes forged boldly ahead. "We've estimated that it will take a mere ten to fifteen imperials a month to keep it fully stocked. Surely, such a small sum will hardly be missed from your coffers, Mistress, and you will get the satisfaction of knowing that so many people will be helped by your generosity."

"You missed your calling, Brother. You should have sought employment at the palace. You'd have made a fine courtier," the mistress commented wryly, one carefully tweezed eyebrow raised high. "Very well. I'll agree to fund your infirmary...for the foreseeable future." Magnes bowed his head in thanks.

I hope she doesn't withdraw her patronage when she learns I won't be coming back, he thought. *Well, I've done my best. The future of the project lies in Fadili's hands now.*

"I know you have much work to do, so I'll let you get to it," the mistress stated. She motioned to Corvin with a terse flick of her finger, and the two headed back in the direction of her residence. The onlookers began to disperse. Magnes stood watching until he felt Aruk-cho's massive presence loom at his back. He turned to face the yardmaster.

"Gran has told me about tonight," Aruk-cho rumbled softly. "I will be ready." Magnes nodded, his eyes shying away from the akuta's craggy face. He did not want Aruk-cho to see his fear.

Despite how carefully we've planned this, something might still go wrong!

He stared at the yardmaster's draft-horse sized hooves and imagined how easily they could crush a man's skull.

He felt very glad Aruk-cho could be counted as an ally.

* * *

He had never been especially devout, but on this night, Magnes found himself offering prayers to any god who would listen. His entreaties must have been heard, for the night sky clouded over and hid the face of the moon, shrouding the earth below in almost total darkness.

As planned, Magnes and Fadili took their supper with Gran, Ashinji, and Seijon in the fighters' mess, along with many of the other slaves. A cheerful mood prevailed, for tomorrow the entire yard would enjoy a day of rest. Generous rations of beer and wine helped the humor to flow, ribald and lusty.

Magnes kept a watchful eye on Ashinji, aware that his friend's wounds still hurt him much more than he would admit. Even so, Ashinji gamely joined in the banter, knowing the five of them must all be seen behaving normally tonight. When the female slave named Leeta sidled up and sat next to him, pressing close and whispering in his ear, Ashinji made no effort to evade her.

Gran appeared interested only in her dinner, but Magnes could tell she, too, kept a careful watch, mainly on Seijon. The boy struggled to remain calm, but anyone who took the time to look would see his agitation.

Magnes leaned close to Fadili. "I'm worried about the boy," he said in a low voice.

Fadili glanced casually at Seijon, then back to Magnes. He nodded almost imperceptibly. "Shall I take him outside now?" he whispered.

"I think that'd be best."

Fadili made a show of finishing his meal, then stood up and approached Seijon, who sat to Ashinji's left.

"Come, boy. I'll look at that rash of yours now," he said, loud enough that several others sitting close by overheard. Leeta snickered and someone else guffawed.

Seijon looked up in surprise. "I don't..." he began, but Ashinji quickly interrupted.

"It's nothing to be ashamed of, Little Brother. Go with Fadili." He flashed the boy a reassuring smile. Seijon opened his mouth again as if to protest, but Magnes could see comprehension dawning in his golden eyes. Fadili beckoned with a tilt of his head, and wordlessly, Seijon got up and followed him out of the mess hall, the hoots and catcalls of the others ushering him away.

Ashinji's eyes briefly locked with Magnes' before he returned to his dinner and the seductive attentions of the gorgeous, red-haired Leeta. Drink had made her bolder, and Ashinji had a tough time keeping her at bay. Brazenly, her hand advanced along Ashinji's thigh until he seized it in his to halt its upward progress. Magnes sighed and shook his head. Leeta exuded sexual energy like an intoxicating perfume. Magnes marveled at Ashinji's self-control, but his friend had far more important things on his mind this night.

Magnes finished the last of his food, then stood.

"It's time I was getting back to the temple," he announced. "Gran, Ashinji, I'll not be back for awhile. Fadili and I are taking the infirmary wagon out of the city for a couple of weeks."

"We'll miss you, Tilo," Gran said.

"If the One is merciful, I'll be here when you get back," Ashinji added.

"Take care of yourselves." Magnes waved and exited the mess. Quickly, he strode to where the infirmary wagon stood parked near the weapons shed, all but invisible in the darkness. As he approached, a deeper patch of shadow detached itself from the gloom and glided toward him.

"Everything's ready," Fadili whispered. "The boy is already inside."

"Gran and Ashinji should be along very soon," Magnes replied, his lips close to Fadili's ear. "Have you seen Aruk-cho?"

"No," Fadili said, then added, "Are you sure we can trust him?"

"Gran and Ashinji do, and I trust their judgment." The two men moved into position beside the wagon, Fadili crouching down by the front wheels, Magnes standing at the rear. Anxiously, Magnes peered into the darkness, straining to catch any movement. Snippets of sound drifted past his ears—discordant voices raised in song, the trill of a nightingale, the restless sigh of the wind. Magnes forced himself to take deep, slow breaths, but his heart insisted on pounding against his breastbone until he thought it might tear itself free.

Where're Ashi and Gran? What's keeping them?

The wind picked up, gusting through the yard, laden with the smell of rain.

This is good, Magnes thought. Rain would discourage lazy sentries from too much diligence and keep the drunks ensconced in the taverns, thus reducing traffic on the streets.

"Someone's coming!" Fadili hissed. Magnes pressed against the smooth wood of the wagon and held himself still.

Gran materialized out of the darkness like a wraith, gripping Magnes' arm with startling strength. He stifled a yelp, then whispered, "Where is Ashi?" in a voice edgy with apprehension.

"He's coming. He had to take care of someone first," Gran breathed in reply. Magnes didn't need to be told the name of that someone. "I should have taken care of her myself, but Ashi wouldn't let me!" The old elf woman made no attempt to hide her irritation.

"I'll go get the horse," Fadili whispered. He disappeared into the dark. Magnes let out a ragged sigh.

Gran squeezed his arm reassuringly. "Don't fret, Ti...I mean, Magnes. Aruk-cho has taken care of his end of things, as have I. When the mistress sits at her desk tomorrow morning to go over the accounts, she will find a small pouch with two hundred gold imperials inside. She won't understand at first where the money came from, but when she discovers that we are all gone, it will make sense to her. Aruk-cho has promised he will try to talk her out of sending the slave catchers after us...or rather, after Ashi, for it's his loss that will sting the most."

"Do you really believe Mistress de Guera is in love with Ashi?" Magnes asked.

"It isn't as far-fetched as it seems," Gran replied. "Ashi is beautiful, even by elven standards, but perhaps love is too strong a word. I know she desires him and is powerfully intrigued by him. Maybe she does love him...Ai, here he comes!"

A figure approached, slipping furtively through the shadows. Magnes breathed a sigh of relief.

"Ashi!" Gran hissed. "We must hurry. Aruk-cho is waiting by the gate!"

"I'm sorry," Ashinji whispered. "I couldn't get away from Leeta. I had to go with her to...to her bed."

"Ashi you didn't...?" Magnes began, then stopped himself.

He owes me no explanations. He did whatever he had to.

The soft thud of hooves on sand signaled the arrival of Fadili with the horse.

"Let's go!" Magnes bent down to reach under the wagon bed, his fingers questing for a tiny knob protruding from the undercarriage. He found what he sought and pressed. A panel popped loose and swung down, revealing a square opening cut into the wagon bottom.

"Is that you, Ashi?" a small voice whispered from inside.

Before he could answer, Gran gasped. "Someone is coming!" she exclaimed.

A light, bobbing and swinging, approached the wagon.

"Quick, Ashi! Get in now!" Magnes hissed, but Ashinji had already hoisted himself into the secret space. He reached down and pulled the panel shut with a snap.

"Magnes, act as if nothing is amiss. You have a reason for being out here," Gran reminded him, her voice almost inaudible. "I will meet you at the gate." She melted into the darkness as completely as if she, herself, were made of shadows.

Magnes walked to the front of the wagon to help Fadili harness the horse. The two of them worked in silence, each knowing the next few moments would prove decisive.

"Stop what you're doing, healer and step away from the wagon!"

Magnes recognized the voice snapping orders from the dark. He and Fadili turned around as five figures moved with quick, purposeful strides to surround them.

His heart sank in dismay as he faced Corvin, Armina de Guera's majordomo, and four armed men.

40
The Chains Are Broken

Magnes stood his ground.

"Good evening, Corvin," he said.

Corvin swung the lantern up and caught Magnes in its glow. "I thought you and your assistant had left already."

Magnes could not see the other man's face, but he heard something in the majordomo's voice that set off alarm bells in his mind.

"We were about to." Magnes raised his hand to block the glare of the lantern. "Do you mind?" Corvin lowered the lantern, but his face remained hidden. Fadili shifted nervously at Magnes' side.

Two of the burly guards flanking Corvin inched forward.

"Have you seen anyone out here?" the majordomo asked.

"Just you," Magnes replied. "Why do you ask?"

"Don't lie to me, healer!" Corvin spat. "I saw the tink slave come out here, and I saw him run toward this wagon!" He jabbed his finger in Magnes' face.

"I don't know what you're talking about," Magnes replied coolly. "My assistant and I haven't seen or spoken to Ashinji since we left the fighters' mess."

The guards surged forward, swords drawn. Fadili cried out in alarm.

"It's all right, Fadili!" Magnes shouted. "What the hell are you doing?" he yelled at Corvin.

"Shut up!" Corvin growled. "Move a muscle and I'll have you both gutted like fish." He motioned to the remaining guards. "Search the wagon," he ordered. One man scrambled aboard the infirmary through the front while another threw open the rear doors and climbed in the back.

"You won't find anything," Magnes said softly.

Corvin stepped in close enough for Magnes to smell the aroma of garlic and wine on his breath.

"Do you know the penalty for aiding an escaped slave, healer?" the majordomo asked. Magnes remained silent. "I'll tell you, though I'm sure you know already. You lose both your hands. Now, what good's a healer with no hands, eh?"

Magnes shrugged. "That's not anything I need worry about," he replied. He shot a sideways glance at Fadili. The younger man's eyes shone white with fear in the light cast by Corvin's lamp.

"If I find the tink hiding in your wagon, you'll know for sure what it's like, and so will your boy, here." He tilted his head toward the terrified Fadili. Magnes took a step backward and fetched up against the side of the wagon. Through the wood, he could feel the vibrations made by the two guards as they tossed the inside of the infirmary, and abruptly, his fear turned into anger. It took all his will to hold his fury to a simmer, for to allow it to boil over now would only invite disaster.

Magnes and Corvin stared at each other across a chasm of suspicion and anger. Intellectually, Magnus understood—sympathized even—with the other man. Corvin was sworn to the service of his mistress, obligated to obey and protect her from all things detrimental to her, including the theft of her property. Magnes respected the majordomo for his loyalty, but he would not let that stop him from doing what he needed to do.

Several tense moments passed, and then one of the guards poked his head out of the back of the wagon and reported, "Naught in 'ere, sir."

The other guard emerged from the front and dropped to the ground with a grunt. "Empty," he confirmed.

"You see?" Magnes said. "It's as I've said. We've not seen your lady's pet since we left him in the fighters' mess. Why don't you go and look in the bed of that tall redhead—Leeta, I think her name is? When we left, she was practically riding him there at the table."

Corvin lowered his head and spat on the sand. "Tell me now where the tink is and I won't report you to the authorities," he said quietly. Magnes thought he heard a note of desperation in the majordomo's voice, causing him to wonder if the man feared some reprisal should he let Armina de Guera's most prized slave escape.

"How many times must I say it? We don't know where he is. Now, let us leave in peace." Magnes took a deep breath and waited. For a single heartbeat, everyone stood perfectly still.

"Get them," Corvin muttered and the guards pounced.

Fadili screamed. Instinctively, Magnes tried to shield the younger man with his own body, but without a weapon, against armed men in close quarters, he was helpless. A guardsman rapidly overwhelmed him, then crushed him to the ground, holding him down with the brutal pressure of boots upon neck and back.

"Don't hurt my assistant!" Magnes gasped, struggling for air.

"*Tell me right now where the tink is or the boy dies!*" Corvin screamed. Fadili's terrified sobbing filled Magnes with sick dread.

If he dies because of me...

"Enough, Corvin! I'm here!"

Ashi, no! Magnes cried, but only in his mind, for sand filled his mouth and he could not speak.

"Let the healers go, Corvin," Magnes heard Ashinji say. "They're telling the truth. They had no idea I was here."

"You're a liar, tink," Corvin sneered. "I saw you talking to them just before you disappeared. You'll pay for this little escapade, I assure you, and don't think the mistress'll go easy on you just because she fancies you. Oh, no... that'd set a very bad precedent!"

"Let the healers go," Ashinji repeated. Corvin laughed harshly in reply.

What transpired next Magnes felt, rather than saw. An explosion detonated close enough to pop his ears, yet he heard nothing. The pressure on his body lifted, and he scrambled to his feet, staring in astonishment. Corvin and all four guards lay sprawled, unmoving, on the ground. Beside the rear of the wagon, arms upraised like an avenging angel, stood Gran. Blue flames sputtered from her fingertips, then flickered out. Slowly, as if emerging from a trance, she let her arms fall to her sides.

How is it that Fadili and I are not unconscious? Magnes wondered as he reached down to help the trembling apprentice to his feet.

"Are you hurt?" he whispered, but Fadili could only shake his head, still too overcome with fear to speak. Magnes glanced at the fallen men, then looked at Gran.

"Are they dead?" he asked uneasily.

"Shouldn't be, but we don't have time to worry about them!" Gran snapped. "Someone inside's bound to have felt the explosion and will be out to investigate. We've got to leave now!"

Quickly, they all climbed aboard the wagon. Fadili and Magnes positioned themselves on the front seat while Gran wedged herself in among the shambles at the rear of the wagon's interior. Magnes waited until he heard the secret panel in the wagon's underside slam shut before he picked up the reins. He shook them, and the horse leaned into the harness. The infirmary rolled forward, and Magnes turned the animal's head toward the gate. He tried not to think of Corvin and his men lying on the sand, or of the consequences they would suffer because of tonight's escape.

"Aruk-cho has opened the gate," Gran called out. "Drive straight through without stopping," she ordered. The wagon's wheels glided easily over the sand. The black maw of the gate loomed ahead, and from behind, Magnes could hear voices raised in alarm.

Despite Gran's order and his own fear, Magnes had no intention of leaving without a final word to Aruk-cho. He reined in the horse just inside the gate.

"Go! Go!" hissed Gran, but Magnes ignored her.

"Aruk-cho!" he called out softly.

The akuta stepped from the shadows, his massive body a darker shape against the black of the night.

"You must leave now, healer, or else all will be lost." The akuta's voice, like gravel swathed in velvet, sounded calm.

"I couldn't leave without saying farewell to you, Yardmaster. I hope that someday, we will have the good fortune to meet again." Magnes looked down as he heard the soft *snick* of the secret panel opening beneath the wagon.

"As do I." Ashinji's voice floated out of the dark below and Magnes could just make out his form standing by the front driver's side wheel. "I am in your debt, Brother," he added, "and if the One decrees it, then I shall some day have the chance to repay you."

"You owe me nothing, Little Brother," Aruk-cho replied. "*Na'a chitatle ko.*"

"And to you, my friend," Ashinji said.

"Ashi, get up here!" Gran ordered. "We've run out of time, now go, go!"

Magnes slapped the horse's rump with the reins and the wagon lurched forward as Ashinji, with Fadili's help, swung up to the front seat, then scrambled back into the interior of the wagon. The horse broke into a lumbering trot as the wagon bumped and lurched over the uneven paving stones of the alley.

Magnes could not look back to see if Aruk-cho had managed to close the gate in time to avoid discovery, but he had confidence in the yardmaster's ability to take care of himself. Aruk-cho would give them the head start they needed.

Magnes concentrated on steering the wagon through the maze of alleys that laced the environs of the Grand Arena, heading for the main ring road that encircled the entire complex. Once he had gotten clear of the arena district, he planned to take the most direct route out of the city.

He halted the infirmary on a side street just south of the main entrance to the Grand Arena to allow Ashinji to rejoin Seijon in the secret compartment. The clouds above spat fat droplets of water onto the land below. The wagon rolled through the rain-slick streets, passing shuttered shops, houses with windows aglow, and taverns with half-opened doors through which raucous laughter and snatches of song spilled out into the night.

Occasionally, a person on foot would emerge from the darkness ahead and hurry past to vanish into the mist behind. Otherwise, the streets were deserted. Magnes strained his ears for sounds of pursuit, but he heard none, and Gran, with her superior hearing and magical senses, had warned of nothing so far.

As they approached the outermost districts of the city, Magnes had to fight the urge to whip the horse into a gallop, knowing a wagon barreling through the streets late at night would almost certainly attract the attention of the constabulary. So far, they had passed several guard posts, unchallenged. The wet weather kept the city guards indoors, as Magnes had hoped.

No one had spoken since leaving the de Guera yard. Each of them remained wrapped in a cocoon of darkness and quiet, alone with his or her own thoughts. Magnes' heart ached at the memory of cheerful, gentle Fadili screaming in terror as a guard had pressed a sword to his throat. He felt saddened by the possibility that the young apprentice healer might be forever changed by the trauma he had suffered at the hands of Armina de Guera's guardsmen.

The hours passed and gradually, the slums of the outer districts gave way to suburban estates and then to open countryside. The rain slacked off, and overhead, the pale face of a three-quarter moon appeared amid shredded, racing clouds.

Gran finally broke the silence.

"Pull over to the side," she said. Magnes did as instructed, pulling steadily on the reins until the wagon slowed to a stop. He set the hand brake, then turned to face Gran. She pushed past him and before he could ask if she needed any help, she had swung down off the wagon to the road.

Not for the first time, Magnes found himself surprised by the old elf woman's vigor. She moved a few paces down the road and stood perfectly still, staring toward the city. In the moon's cold light, her hair shimmered like silver-washed bone. It had come loose during the altercation at the yard and now hung down her back past her waist. Her slim body and flowing hair transformed her figure into the semblance of a young girl, yet an aura of immense power crackled about her like a mantle of lightning.

She turned in a slow circle, as if scanning the four directions, then walked quickly back to the wagon.

"I sense no pursuit, but there's a large group of people just ahead," she said. "I can't tell who or what they are. They could be soldiers or a caravan of traders."

Fadili fidgeted beside Magnes and for the first time in many hours, he spoke. "Perhaps we should wait here until sunrise."

"Perhaps we should," Magnes agreed. He climbed down and ducked underneath the wagon to rap on the undercarriage. The secret panel slid open and Seijon's head popped out.

"What's happening?" he asked breathlessly.

"We've decided to wait here until morning," Magnes explained. "There's a big group of people on the road just ahead and we don't want to risk an encounter."

Seijon slithered out of the hole to the muddy road. Ashinji emerged a few moments later, moving slowly, his hand pressed to his lower back.

"If we're careful, we should be able to stay behind them," Gran said. She laid a hand on Ashinji's arm and spoke a few soft words in Siri-dar. Ashinji nodded and allowed Gran to take his head between her hands. She closed her eyes and a few moments later, Ashinji's eyes fluttered closed as well. They remained thus for the space of several heartbeats, then Gran's eyes opened and her hands fell away.

Ashinji sighed deeply. "Shiha," he whispered, which Magnes recognized as the Siri-dar word for "thanks." It seemed to him that his friend's pain had been eased.

Ashinji turned to face Magnes. "We need to take the shortest route north—preferably northwest—but there's the problem of the Soldaran Army blocking our way."

"Yes, and traveling by the main roads is risky, even though it is faster," Magnes replied. "I think our only choice is to head northeast, toward Amsara. I know a less traveled route and there is a small road—a path really—that veers off the main road just south of the Amsara border and heads west. It bypasses the castle by a few leagues and ends up at the southern edge of the Eanon Swamp. You'll have to skirt the swamp, unless you know a way through..."

"There are those of our people who do know ways through what we call the Shihkat Fens, but I'm not one of them," Ashinji said. "No, we'll have to go around." He sounded weary and resigned.

"Eventually, we must try to get horses," Gran said. "Fadili will have to leave us soon, and then we'll be on foot. Without horses, this journey will take too long. We wouldn't make it to Sendai in time."

"I still have some money which I'll gladly give to you," Magnes offered. "It's not a lot, but we should be able to bargain with a farmer or two for some nags." He looked up at the moon's position. "We have a few hours before the sun comes up. You all try to get some sleep; I'll keep watch."

Magnes settled on the front bench of the wagon to await the sunrise, while the others found what space they could in the back. Soon, the chirp of crickets and the slow sounds of people sunk in slumber were all that disturbed the quiet of the night. Magnes felt tired, the kind of tired that comes from an emotional as well as a physical place. Tonight had been harrowing, and yet, they had managed to win free with the help of an ally and a huge amount of luck.

Just how much longer our luck will hold...that doesn't bear thinking on right now.

His thoughts turned to Jelena.

My little cousin...a princess!

He tried to imagine her joy when she and Ashinji were reunited.

Gods, how I wish I could be there to see that...to see you, dear cousin, and hold you in my arms once again, but I know it's not possible, at least not for a very long time. I swear on my life, though, I'll do everything I can to see that your husband gets home safely to you and your child.

He turned his eyes heavenward.

"Please," he begged to any gods who might be listening, "let us all come through this and be together again some day! Is that too much to hope for?"

The gods, if they heard, did not answer.

About the Author

Leslie Ann Moore has been a storyteller since childhood. A native of Los Angeles, she received a doctorate in Veterinary Medicine from the University of California. She lives and works in Los Angeles and, in her spare time, she practices the art of belly dancing.

Printed in the United States
144549LV00004B/149/P